THE W

Also by Valery Leith in Gollancz

THE WAY OF
THE ROSE

Valery Leith

Map by James Sinclair

First published in Great Britain in 2001 by
Gollancz
An imprint of the Orion Publishing Group
Orion House, 5 Upper St Martin's Lane,
London WC2H 9EA

This edition published in 2003

A CIP catalogue record for this book is
available from the British Library

ISBN 0 575 07303 9

Printed in Great Britain by Clays Ltd, St Ives plc

For my nieces and nephews:
John
Danielle
Lauryn
Cara
Kevin
Nicole
Denis
Eric
You guys are the greatest.

CONTENTS

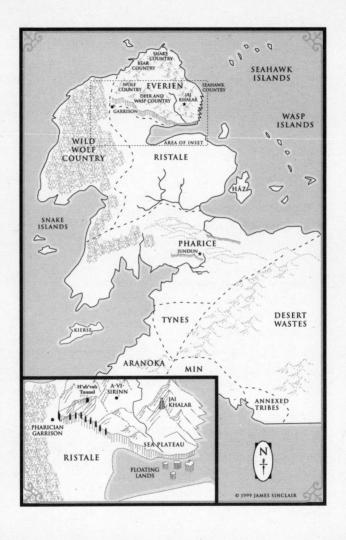

© 1999 JAMES SINCLAIR

TRUTH AND TIMESERPENTS

When a spider spins a web, she doesn't use a ruler or a compass to calculate her angles. She weaves a perfect pattern every time, making corrections and changes at need as she goes along—but no one ever told her how. She doesn't even possess a brain by the standards of people. She will never stand back and appraise her web from a distance—she is too small. But she will eat the prey she catches in it, and she will lay eggs whose inhabitants will weave their own webs.

So who is being clever—the spider or the web? And is consciousness the beginning of knowledge, or its end?

I am Jaya. I have been both the spider and the fly, and I can tell you this: the fly and the spider and the dew that makes the web visible are all part of something larger and more strange. For the spider to be conscious of herself, to know what she is, would mean she would equally know all that she is not, bringing great loneliness. But we all know about that. Because we are human. We nurse both consciousness and loneliness, inventing gods to keep us company while the spiders keep spinning in perfect ignorance. We are severed from the world—that is why we worship animals and use them and keep them close to us. Even as we subjugate them, we miss being like them. They are connected.

The timeserpent has a human face. It was built by human thought. But it was never human, and when its mouth yawns open, its face is seen to be a joke that all but disappears in the folds of its time-devouring and infinite body. It is the actualization of the impossible. The timeserpent's mathematics defy the understanding of a man or woman for whom time is like a wind, with direction and force. The timeserpent is not conscious like we are. It speaks our language with about as much effort as we need to make our hair grow. The timeserpent is no more aware of us than this—maybe less. But we conceived it. We made it.

How do we feel about that, children of Everien?

Well, how does the ocean feel about humans, her progeny? We cannot know. We have grown so far from our mineral origins that the ocean does not understand us, but we, somehow, still cry out for her in our very blood. How does a man feel about the timeserpent, which is his? He created it but does not understand it. The timeserpent is the parasite of the world, conjoining and severing the world from itself, leaving holes and bridges, gateways and windows, lattices of possibility climbing in every direction.

We are a self-propagating accident. We are meaning from meaninglessness and back again. And when we made the timeserpent, we birthed the accident of accidents, the math that breaks our minds. Discovering fire was child's play—it was the big toy by which we built our castles of abstraction. But this time we are being left behind. The nature of timeserpents being what it is (or isn't), there's nothing to say that the perverse creature didn't create us so as to bring itself into being. That the web didn't weave the spider. Look hard and you'll see: there is nothing at all to prove that causality only runs one way.

TIMESERPENTS ARE THE *bane of storytellers. They cut to the ending without reference to its antecedents. They put contradictions side by side, just for laughs. They tunnel connections between things that have none, and cut sensible things in half. They spoil magic tricks. Being a person in the presence of a timeserpent is a little like being a beam of light in the presence of a prism. You really don't have a choice but to be cut up in pretty pieces and bent at an oblique angle.*

So: if you are reading for truth, stop now. You will find more in the dust on your windowsill. Truth and timeserpents are like oil and water.

THE RELATIVE
HARDNESS OF HEADS

"Shit," Istar said into the frozen night. After the wraith of her breath disappeared, she repeated, "Shit shit shit."

She wanted to tear her hair out. But she had cut off her braids when she tried to climb the cliff to escape Eteltar's secret world. Now there was nothing to get a grip on. Instead, she grabbed the bones of her skull and squeezed with gloved fingers. She never ceased to be astonished by the hardness of her own head.

That was why she couldn't believe it was possible to kill a man by crushing his skull like a melon. To do so would require unimaginable strength.

Yet if Taretel was behind this deed, she should not be surprised. Taretel, who in some other world or some other time had the wings of a bird and the mind of a wise man, was known here in Everien as a murderer and madman. He must have killed Birtar. Why, she could not understand. But there was much about Taretel that no one understood.

It had happened in the night, in the snowfall, when the winds came howling from the west, bearing ash and ice and everything in between, for the Li'ah'vah had passed there, changing air to stone and night to day. Last night, while Istar was dozing, Birtar must have come to watch the giant who everyone believed to be a Sekk master—everyone but Istar. There had been a time when Birtar had regularly done this duty, being one of the few men in her borrowed army, besides Pentar, that Istar could trust. But after what had happened yesterday, she had refused to allow Birtar near to the prisoner.

Yesterday. She had thought her situation complicated then—but now yesterday's problems seemed gloriously easy to solve. Yesterday had marked the end of the first week following the passage of the Li'ah'vah through Everien's mountains, a week during which Istar's small army had been making steady progress toward the old camp above Fivesisters Lake, where Jakse had found the Knowledge cave. Yesterday, when Pentar had urgently come to summon Istar to talk strategy, he had brought Birtar to watch the prisoner for a short time. Normally, Birtar adopted a dispassionate attitude toward Taretel; but yesterday his manner had been strange. He had approached the bound and blindfolded Taretel with a swaggering air, one arm extended as if prepared to shove or slap the bigger man; but as he got closer, his reluctance to touch the Sekk became apparent in his posture, and in the end he drew his sword and prodded the prisoner with its tip as if Taretel were a shark or other sea monster that he had caught by luck and now didn't know what to do with. A snarling noise came from the black-clad giant, whose silver braids blended with the snow like the plumage of an arctic bird. At Istar's side, Pentar stiffened.

Nonplussed by Birtar's behavior, Istar said, "Don't provoke it." She was careful not to call Taretel "he." To speak of Taretel as human would only complicate matters. "It cannot walk quickly and it is bound. There is no need to keep it at sword point."

"Nevertheless, I will," Birtar answered somewhat shrilly. "It is my sword, and I will use it as I need."

Istar thought his fear and Pentar's were ludicrously magnified, but she said nothing. She turned to Pentar.

"What's the matter? Tell me what's happened."

Pentar visibly collected himself, trudging some little distance away from Birtar and the Sekk as if unwilling to speak with Istar within their hearing. She kept the Sekk in her peripheral vision. She trusted neither it nor Birtar.

"It's Tash," he replied. "You remember how easily he fell back before us in Tyger Pass?"

"He did not live up to his reputation," she said.

"He is a shrewd commander. I am sure that he knew he was at a disadvantage and decided to draw us into a location where he could have us at his mercy."

"What are you talking about? Where is he now? I don't see how we are at anyone's mercy. We are a small force and no one knows where we are, and with the Li'ah'vah slicing up the landscape it is hard to see how Tash will have anyone at his mercy."

"This is not the time for overconfidence."

"I am not overconfident. You still have not told me what you know. Keep the analysis and give me the facts."

"Very well. I sent a bird to Jakse and it has not returned. We know that he was associated with some of Tash's people at Fivesisters Lake, and we can only assume that Tash knows about the Sekk cave by now. He was going downland from Tyger Pass, but he could have beaten us to the road and overtaken us. He could have gotten to the cave ahead of us."

"Could have, might have . . . what other evidence is there for this story? You sent a bird and it didn't come back. That could mean anything."

"Come with me."

He had stopped at the base of a large pine standing in partial isolation within the canopy. Istar could see that footholds had been sliced in the bark, and there were rope burns on the dead lower branches. Seahawks used lookout trees when they could, and this was a typical specimen. She glanced over her shoulder toward Birtar and the Sekk. The latter was backed against the trunk of a tree, still and subdued, while Birtar, sword still out, paced in restless half circles around him. Istar was uneasy about leaving the two unattended, but Pentar was looking at her in such a way that said she had better climb the tree or he would begin to believe her Enslaved by the Sekk.

She climbed. Pentar soon disappeared below, although she could hear his voice calling up to her through the branches.

"Look west-northwest. Do you see the lake?"

Istar was struggling to get a clear vantage in that direction, since the tree seemed to want to give her a solid foothold only on the south side. At length, climbing a little higher than she really ought to, she fought her way to a position where she could look through the branches and see the horizon to the north. To the far left, where the slopes of the mountains made a steep V, she could just discern the lower end of Fivesisters Lake, frozen solid and covered with snow. The trees that had displayed their brilliant colors the last time she'd been in these parts were now naked, visible as a gray, characterless furze. The evergreens still hid the slopes of the hills, though, dark and secret.

"I see the lake," she called, and then, almost immediately after, "What the hell's that?"

There was smoke coming up from the dark trees on the shores of the lake. A lot of smoke.

"Do you see it?" Pentar's excited voice drifted up.

"I see smoke. What's causing that?"

"A camp. A battle. Hard to say, specifically—but that's where Tash was headed."

Istar shaded her eyes against the snowglare and looked carefully. "That's one hell of a fire. I've never seen a forest fire in winter."

Pentar said something she could not make out, and she ignored him for a moment, still looking intently. From this perspective she could not see the area where Xiriel's cave had been purported to be. She wished that Xiriel had sent a bird or left a message in some other way. No one but he had a clue what to do about the cave, and Istar had been puzzling for some time over how to handle Jakse if she reached him before Xiriel could. Xiriel had left Jakse to guard the cave on behalf of the rebels, but Jakse had later taken up with Dario, a Clanswoman who had thrown her lot in with Tash. A typical Wasp, Dario was obviously hedging her bets as to who would emerge ruler of Everien: Tash or the rebel Clansmen; and as long as Jakse was associated with Dario, Istar could not trust him. She could not very well walk up to the cave and take over under such uncertain circumstances. For that matter, she did not know what the nature of the cave and its artifacts might be. Besides, with the captive Taretel in tow, she was wary of going anywhere near a reputed Sekk lair. Who knew how her prisoner might react if confronted with a Sekk—much less, how he would react if what Xiriel believed were true, and the Lake of Candles was in fact the very wellspring from which the Sekk were born. Istar felt insecure enough hiding out in the woods with only her own loyal followers to answer to, without blundering straight into a possible conjunction of Tash, the Sekk, and Jakse.

But the smoke could not be ignored, and she couldn't hide in the woods forever. If nothing else, their provisions were running out, and in late winter hunting was difficult, and foraging, impossible. The men were spooked at the vision of the Li'ah'vah, and eager to return to some outpost of civilization from which they might hope to get news of their country and families.

Istar stared at the smoke. She didn't know what to do.

She slithered out of the tree and, without looking at Pentar, said, "I agree that it is worrisome."

"What should we do?"

"Well, we must not panic," she said. "Tomorrow we move to the rendezvous and see what the scouts have to say. Maybe they can give us more information."

"So we do nothing?"

"It is only one night," Istar said mildly, and turned to go. She didn't like leaving Taretel out of her sight.

Pentar said, "Wait. Just stay a moment, and talk."

Istar fidgeted, but complied.

"I don't like the way you spend all your time with the Sekk," he said. "When I'm talking to you, sometimes I don't know if I'm talking to you or to him."

"Him? Don't you mean 'it'?"

"You know what I mean. There's something different about this Sekk."

Yes, Istar thought. *There is. You don't know the half of it.*

"I've heard the stories about Taretel, and I've now seen his cave. We recovered some of his writing and we crossed over into that other . . . place . . . where we found you and a lot of birds, and some kind of crazy writing on the cliff face, like an Everien symbol-code."

"What?" Istar was shocked. She knew that Eteltar had been carving something on that cliff, but she had never been able to stand back from it enough to get a good look at it. "How did you see his sculpture?"

"When I came down the rope, of course. And again, when I dragged you back up it—but you wouldn't remember that part. You were unconscious. The writing was singular, Istar. If we had not been in such haste, I would have explored the cave, too. And then what would I have found? The grave of Eteltar? Istar, tell me. It weighs on you, this secrecy. I can see it. Just tell me what happened, and then we can decide what to do."

But Istar wasn't listening to him. What had Eteltar been writing on the cliff, and why? The desert below, he had told her, would not be inhabited for a long time, and only the time-traveling horses of Or ever went there. So who was he writing the message for? And what did it say?

"Now you're off in a fog again!" Pentar grabbed her by both shoulders and shook her. "Istar, we're in a wood in the middle of winter, we've seen a Li'ah'vah loose in Everien, our men are scared, and Tash is nearby. You must get out of your own head and act."

Suddenly she was angry. Pentar didn't know the first thing about it; he had not spent half a year climbing impossible cliffs and jousting verbally with the capricious half-man Eteltar, as Istar had. She had spent all her energy trying to convince Eteltar to trust her, to love her, to help her and her people—only to be ripped away from his remote niche in time when Pentar had "rescued" her. Now she had to confront every day the spectre of the Sekk that Eteltar had left behind like a ghost. Why, if it weren't for Pentar and his do-gooding intervention, she would have woken up that morning to a new beginning with the winged man. Had Eteltar not made love to her? Had he not told her his history and what had happened to divide him so? Therefore, in time he would have showed her what he was sculpting. In time he would have let her pass through the hole in the sky, the interdimensional portal that led to his ice-cave, where she might comprehend the research he had done. In time, maybe, they would have together found a way to make him whole again. And then Istar would have been whole. She would not be a wretched half-man of an Honorary herself, doomed to this stupid existence, deprived of love and children and all the things she had never wanted because she had never been allowed to want them but now she did—damn it. But now all that was left of the one she wanted them *with* was Taretel, the blindfolded Sekk kinslayer who would probably lay Istar's throat open, given half a chance.

Seething, she narrowed her eyes and spat in the snow.

"You never should have come for me, Pentar. I didn't ask you to rescue me. I never asked you to save me, but you keep bloody doing it. Did you ever once think it might be better to leave me to my fate?"

He stared at her, stunned. The cold bitterness in her own voice surprised her, but she found she could not soften it.

"Istar, don't—"

"Leave me alone! You want the men? Take them. They're yours. I'll take my prisoner and go."

"You can't—"

"Watch me."

She turned and, evading his grab, pounded through the snow to where she had left Birtar and the Sekk. Pentar called after her,

"You're fucking suicidal, Istar! That's it! That's the last time I do help you!"

Birtar was sweating and pacing, blowing plumes of air as he circled the Sekk like a nervous guard dog. He was apparently oblivious to the drama that had been developing between Istar and Pentar, because he glanced once over his shoulder when he heard her coming, then returned his attention immediately to the Sekk, saying, "He's vicious. Even without a weapon, I fancy he's dangerous."

"What is going on?" Istar said sharply. The Sekk was standing there all too coolly for her comfort. Birtar was not the type to get worked up over nothing.

"He keeps lunging at me and trying to head-butt me," Birtar complained, and Istar noted that the snow was a ruin of disturbed pine needles and clods of torn earth where some violence had occurred. "I'm going to have to cut him in a minute. Why don't you bind his legs?"

"It was quiet until just a minute ago," Istar said, alarmed at Birtar's use of the personal pronoun—Sekk were invariably referred to as "it" or "they" to make it easier to kill them. "Have you done something to provoke it?"

"No!" Birtar answered a little too vehemently, and she saw that he was terrified.

"That's all right, Birtar," she said softly, surprised at the composure in her voice so soon after her outburst at Pentar. "I'll take over."

He glanced at her once and shook his head. "It's too late for that. Don't you see what he's doing?"

"*It's* just standing there," Istar said.

"No!" cried Birtar, dancing first to one side and then the other, keeping the Sekk always at sword point. "He's being quiet now you're here, but he was not like this before."

"Then I won't leave it," Istar said simply. "You can go now. It's all right."

He shook his head adamantly, like a stubborn child, she thought. She did not think the Sekk was Enslaving Birtar, despite his bizarre behavior. There had been no singing, for one thing, and no eye contact.

"You didn't touch it, did you?" she asked.

"No! Are you crazy? Istar, get it through your head—this one's

9

a killer. He killed Ranatar, he killed whole villages. He killed my brother. Agh, I could be sick just to look at him."

"The Sekk is a prisoner," Istar reminded him. "We agreed it was my responsibility. Now step away."

"Taretel is mine. For Thietar. He's mine."

Istar was shocked by Birtar's behavior; after all, he had forfeited his right to kill the Sekk in favor of Istar, and he had supported her command of this dubious army wholeheartedly. But there was no time to think about what had changed his mind. Istar drew her sword and edged into a position from which she could intercept Birtar if he attacked the Sekk, or vice versa. "Don't be stupid, Birtar. You won't bring Thietar back by killing Taretel."

He hesitated, lowering his blade fractionally, and she seized her moment, throwing herself bodily against Birtar and knocking him aside, then interposing herself between the unarmed Sekk and the Seahawk, who now sprawled in the snow, furious.

"The Sekk Taretel is my prisoner," she said coldly. "No one may take its life but me. Or is this the faith you show me after your fine, brave words before Atar and the other deserters?"

Birtar got to his feet, brushing snow off himself and shaking his head.

"You're mad," he whispered. "What they said is true. You're as mad as he is."

Things might have gotten ugly then, but Pentar arrived with three young soldiers and told Birtar to clear off.

"Listen to me, Birtar," she heard Pentar say to Birtar. "Do not be provocative. Do not tread so lightly with the Sekk! You know what this one is capable of."

Birtar glowered and said nothing, but they went away together, Pentar returning only long enough to grumble in Istar's general direction that their conversation earlier was forgotten, as far as he was concerned, and he would make preparations to meet with the scouts as she'd wished. Istar had thought that was the end of the episode with Birtar—an emotional outburst brought on by stress, and too much time spent in the wilderness, and fear of the Li'ah'vah. Certainly she was in a frayed and edgy condition herself.

She had fallen asleep thinking not about Birtar, nor Pentar, nor the men she was supposed to be leading, whose attitude toward her was so dubious. She was thinking about Eteltar, and his wings, and his smell. It was an uneasy repose, a soldier's half-sleep. Yet she had not awakened to the sounds of murder. There had been no cries, no sound of a scuffle, no warning. When Istar roused two hours before dawn, she could see her prisoner standing against a nearby oak. Taretel was in his characteristic posture: legs slightly apart, hands bound behind his back, blindfolded and gagged but showing no indication of being cowed or in despair. His head was up. Alert.

He never slept.

She shivered and shook off a sprinkling of snow that had drifted from beneath the branches of the firs to settle on her cloak. She blinked and yawned as sleep tugged at her again; then she gave a little start. There was something on the ground at the prisoner's feet. Istar rose, lit a torch, and went toward Taretel, who made no move. Birtar's body was lying buried beneath an inch and a half of new-fallen snow.

She looked at Taretel. Because of the blindfold, there was no expression in his face to be read, yet she stared at him anyway. She could not comprehend this act. Birtar had defended Taretel to the other Seahawks, even though he believed him Sekk, and even though he had good cause to hate this silent renegade who had brought about the death of his brother, Thietar. Because Istar vouched for Taretel, Birtar had agreed that the prisoner might live.

Now Taretel had murdered him. It did not seem to have been much of a fight. The snow was disturbed, but there was no mark on Taretel. Birtar's head was crushed, and a great deal of blood had come from the soft eyes, the ears, the mouth, and the nose, freezing in the snow where he lay.

She walked around the clearing, wondering what had happened. Birtar had not drawn a weapon or injured Taretel. Istar and her prisoner had camped some distance from Pentar and the soldiers as a safety precaution against just this sort of thing, and even now, with Istar walking around with a lit torch, no one in the main camp took notice. During their daily travels, Istar and Taretel were in the habit of walking well behind the rest, and he was never out of her sight. She was very careful with him, even more cautious than she needed to be, probably to compensate for her personal feelings for the man . . . or *thing* . . . or whatever he was.

But she had not been cautious enough.

Now she felt ill. After yesterday, she should have known some-

11

thing bad was going to happen. Yet she had to sleep. Everyone had to sleep sometime, damn it.

Taretel did not stir while she made her examination of the scene. She found herself observing details: the mud on Birtar's bootprints, the places where snow had dropped in quantity from tree branches above, the fact that Birtar's dagger was missing and was neither on his corpse nor on Eteltar. As she did these things she felt strangely emotionless. It would have been more in character for her to fly raging at Taretel and seek revenge, but she felt no desire to do so. She possessed, in fact, a complete lack of feeling.

"Why?" she said softly.

Taretel did not answer. He never did.

IT WAS ALMOST light. She tied Taretel to a tree and went to tell Pentar what had happened. She did not tie him very tightly. Somehow she was hoping he would take this chance to be gone.

The camp was stirring, already a nervous hive of activity as the men anticipated meeting up with the scouts that had been sent out to assess the effects of the Li'ah'vah. Istar had designated the southern end of Fivesisters Lake as the rendezvous, and they should reach that point today with a bit of luck. There was no guarantee they would be able to get there, of course; already they had encountered one barrier in the forest that they could not pass through: a distortion in the air and in the earth, accompanied by a sheer, thin noise like very dry wood burning. They had avoided this area; they had no choice. Whenever they tried to get close enough to see what was wrong with the landscape, their thoughts became disordered and they wandered in useless circles until they were obliged to return.

"It is some malignant effect of the Li'ah'vah," Pentar said. "It makes everyone queasy and fearful. Let us stick to the solid ground we know."

Under different circumstances, Istar might have been tempted to press an exploration; but with Taretel attached to her, Istar's priorities were different. She only wanted to find out what had happened to Everien; where the timeserpent was now; and who else had survived its eruption. Today, she had hoped to have that satisfaction, by the shores of Fivesisters Lake. She tried to cheer herself up by reminding herself that in a few days, the scouts might even reach the Knowledge cave that Xiriel had discovered. Maybe he would even be there—she had been hoping for it. Now she needed a piece of good luck more than ever.

She found Pentar talking to a couple of the youngest men, instructing them on how far ahead to scout and what to do if they encountered another region affected by the timeserpent. When he saw the look on her face, he sent the boys off and went with her apart from the others. Quietly, she told him what had happened, and together they walked back to Istar's separate camp. Pentar looked at Birtar's body and swallowed hard. She watched his face crumple, aging by years in a matter of seconds, and she wondered what she herself must look like. Birtar had been a devoted suitor to her sister. What would she tell the twins, if she ever saw them again?

Pentar stalked around the perimeter of the clearing just as she had done, observing everything with the same dark intensity. Occasionally he stooped to examine the snow more closely. When he returned to her, they stood silently for a few minutes.

"It is plain that they fought," Pentar said at last, looking at the snow.

"I disagree. There is no blood."

"They may have wrestled. Look at the way the pine needles have been dug up from under the snow and tossed around. That doesn't happen by normal traffic."

"That happened yesterday, when Birtar was teasing the Sekk. Taretel never attacked any of us before."

"That doesn't make him any less dangerous. But I'm not sure it was Taretel who started the fight."

Istar snorted. "I agree that Birtar was acting strangely yesterday, but if he wanted Taretel dead, why didn't he just come up behind him and cut his throat?"

With that, Pentar produced a slender knife. Istar recognized it as Birtar's hunting knife.

"It was lying in the snow, five yards behind Taretel. It could have been knocked aside in the scuffle."

Istar swung her head in frustration. "What the hell is going on, Pentar? Birtar was talking like a lunatic yesterday. You don't think he was Enslaved, do you?"

The dark-eyed Seahawk took a deep breath and cleared his throat. He said, "Birtar came and spoke to me yesterday. He said something I did not understand. He said that he knew for certain that Taretel is not a Sekk."

"*Not* a Sekk?" Istar snapped. "Then what quarrel could he have had? You see, Pentar? Birtar did not assault Taretel, and Taretel did not kill Birtar. He couldn't have—he was bound and weaponless. It must have been some other creature; who knows what monster might stalk these forests. . . ." She knew she sounded absurd, and she let her voice trail off. This was her fault, and she couldn't bear it.

"We found no tracks of creatures or monsters. Listen, Istar, and I will tell you a pretty riddle. After what happened yesterday, I kept an eye on Birtar. I followed him into the forest, where I found him weeping. He did not wish to speak with me, but I pressed him, and in the end he told me that Taretel is not a Sekk, that he did not sing, that he bled but then healed too quickly—and you have seen how he recovered from a hamstringing that would have lamed other men for life. Birtar also said that back in Tyger Pass, Taretel had spared Thietar for some reason."

"These things may be true," Istar said. "But what caused Birtar to say them to you, and never to me? He watched Taretel like . . . well, like a hawk. He was fascinated by him. He helped me to mind him, and he defended Taretel against the others. But yesterday, he was vicious and unreasonable. What happened?"

"If you had killed someone you loved, and then it turned out you had done it for no reason, or had made a mistake, how would you feel?"

Istar stared at him. She had forgotten he was talking about Birtar and thought for a second he was talking about her. Her heart skipped. A coldness flooded through her stomach. She couldn't answer. She was thinking about the seahawk she had killed in Jai Pendu, whose death she had felt more than all the human deaths her sword had counted, combined.

Pentar looked at her face closely, but he misunderstood her emotion. He nodded slowly. "Ah, you see it now! Birtar slew his brother thinking him Enslaved. But Thietar was not Enslaved. Scared, maybe. Entranced in some other way by Taretel, but not Enslaved, not possessed of a mad violence. Birtar did not have to kill him. He could have picked him up and carried him home. If he had done so, maybe Taretel would have attacked; or maybe he would not have attacked. It is too late now. But Birtar knew he had brought his little brother into Tyger Pass to hunt on Birtar's behalf, and now Thietar was dead by Birtar's hand. And he blamed Taretel. Not for *being* a Sekk, but for *not* being a Sekk. Taretel had changed Birtar from a hero to a murderer."

Istar reeled. She could dimly see the sense in it, and now she looked back on Birtar's actions and words since she and Taretel had come from the cave in Tyger Pass, and she wondered what inner torment he had gone through as he worked out all of these things in his mind.

"You think he attacked Taretel and Taretel killed him."

"I am almost certain of it."

"Why didn't you tell me what Birtar said to you? Why didn't you warn me?"

Pentar rubbed his scalp with both hands, tugging the skin around his eyes taut. This made him look like a great, thoughtful cat. Sadly, he said, "It was only last night he said these words to me. And he did not appear angry so much as defeated. He was upset, but not on the verge of violence. Or, I didn't think he was."

"I don't believe this," Istar said.

"The others," Pentar said, "will not take this news well. They already see your Taretel as a curse on all of us. They even think Tash fled because of him."

"Tash fleeing is hardly a curse on us!"

"Still. They are afraid."

"Birtar was right. Taretel is not Sekk," Istar said. "He is a man divided, and you see only one aspect of a complex nature."

"I know that," Pentar said. "I have read as many of the texts from his cave as I could understand. I realize he was once very wise. Istar! I know that those bones you carry mean something to you. Eteltar's loss is a tragedy, to you, to our Clan, to Everien. But it would be a greater tragedy to let this demon with Eteltar's face carry on doing harm. Remember Ranatar! Remember the Hawk Girls. Thietar. And now Birtar."

Suddenly it was too much for her. She did feel guilty about Birtar—and thus she went on the attack, resuming yesterday's rant. "It's your fault, Pentar! Why couldn't you have left me on the cliff where you found me? We were doing well enough without your help. What right had you to forcibly bring me back here?"

"You saved me from the Sekk once," Pentar answered quietly. "I was no happier to be recalled from its service than you. And you have commitments. Here. In Everien."

Istar swore, spat, and kicked at the snow violently, possessed by inexpressible outrage.

"You don't know anything," she said finally in a tight voice. "I wish you would stop saving me."

"It is too late for that," Pentar said, meeting her eye and refusing to back down. "We will make a cairn for Birtar, and then we will go. You should speak to the men."

Speak to the men . . . were they even *her* men, anymore? Had they ever been? Grietar had given them to her for some reason of his own, probably a foul one. They had no special loyalty to her, and they had seen some of their own number leave already, driven away by fear and hatred of Taretel, the "Sekk demon" as they called him. And since Tyger Pass, she had had her hands too full of the prisoner to act out her command convincingly. The men were mostly given their orders by Pentar. It was not a good situation to be in as a commander, and she knew she had made a muck of it. She did not relish the idea of addressing them.

"Tonight," she said. "I will talk to them tonight. We will lose most of our daylight burying Birtar, and there must be some pause to say rites over him. We will postpone our journey to Fivesisters until tomorrow. I will take Taretel down to the stream and see if we can get any fish under the ice. While the rest of you build the cairn."

It was a coward's choice, and she knew it; but there was no use pretending she could trust anyone to watch Taretel but herself, and it would be an act of unusual stupidity to leave him within sight of the men once they had learned what had happened to Birtar. Pentar nodded soberly.

"Tonight, then," he said.

SHE PASSED THE day quietly. The prisoner's behavior had not changed. She wanted to remove the gag and question him, but she didn't dare. It was all very well for everyone to agree that he was not a typical Sekk, but the fact that Birtar believed Taretel not to be Sekk and Taretel managed to kill him anyway—apparently with no more effort than that needed to swat a fly—unnerved her. Pentar thought her bewitched, but she was not unwary around Taretel. She hadn't forgotten the stories she had heard about the

16

murder of her kinfolk, and she hadn't forgotten the strange behavior of the Hawk Girls. She hadn't forgotten the way Eteltar, hiding on his arid cliff, had tried to disown the actions of the Seahawk warrior who now stood before her, silent but listening, she felt. Always listening.

At dusk she brought him back to the camp and sat with Pentar to eat. She was gathering her courage to address the others, who set themselves apart from her and Pentar and the Sekk. Pentar, she knew, was in a difficult position as well. He had to act as a bridge between Istar and the men who served her. It was a tricky task. As they ate, she tried to explain her thinking to him, hoping to win him to her cause.

"I don't know what is meant by evil anymore," she said. "I used to think it was the Sekk, plain and simple. They were evil. They hunted us for no purpose other than to cause us pain. But after a while I began to see they were just doing what they do. A Sekk massacres humans like a wolf massacres sheep. A wolf will hunt a deer and kill and eat it, but when it encounters sheep it will tear their throats out and leave them dead by the dozens. Is the wolf evil? Or is it something about the sheep, something passive, something spiritless, that also kills the spirit of the wolf and makes him disrespect them? I watched the Sekk and I watched people and after a while I thought, Maybe it's like the wolf and the sheep. Maybe we are allowing ourselves to be taken. Maybe, like the sheep, we are no longer wild. And so, the stronger the Knowledge of Everien, the greater its power over us, the weaker we are against the Sekk." She paused, thinking about what she wanted to say, and Pentar filled the silence somewhat nervously.

"An interesting theory. It explains why you saved my life and then treated me like a pariah."

"Partly. I'm not finished, Pentar. I thought for a while that the wolf and the sheep might explain the Sekk, but that did not help me understand evil. I still felt its presence. It wasn't—isn't—definite, it's like a cloud. I feel it almost all the time. Except—" She had started to say, "Except when I was with the winged man," but didn't. She hurried on. "You warned me, Pentar. When I slew that Sekk child, you warned me to be careful. And later in A-Tar-Ness, the Hawk Girls tried to warn me. I didn't listen. I didn't understand my danger."

Pentar turned his head toward the black-clad man. He said

nothing. He was waiting.

"I don't know how to say this," Istar said.

"Is it about—" Pentar jerked his head toward the captive warrior, reluctant as ever to call him Taretel.

"No. Not really. Maybe. Oh . . ." She squeezed her eyes shut and shook her head rapidly back and forth, struggling to articulate herself. "He has done terrible things. He has murdered without provocation. He has . . . he has done terrible things." She was repeating herself. She had to say it, had to make herself form the words, but it was as though she ran up against a wall inside herself. Why couldn't Pentar read her mind? Why couldn't he guess what she was going to say? "How can I judge him?" She compromised, sliding off track for a moment. "He opened the White Road. He was himself broken. And I . . ." She had to say it. "I think . . . I have killed him. There, it's true. I have killed him, or I will kill him."

"He doesn't look dead to me."

"He's worse than dead!" Tears leaped into her eyes.

"Istar." Pentar looked on her pityingly. His great, sad eyes and his drooping jowls fixed on her, so that for a moment he appeared almost maternal. His tone was the sort one uses with a troubled child. "How is it that you are supposed to have killed him?"

"In Jai Pendu," she whispered. "I killed the seahawk. And in Taretel's cave, there was a notch in the breast of the seahawk statue. It was cut in the exact shape of my sword. It was how I opened the trapdoor and found him. And now. Now. Somehow it's already too late."

She checked herself. The flames had lowered suddenly, and the shadows of her hands gesturing jumped and bent on the blue-gray snow. She was too animated. The tension in Pentar's body could be seen in the set of his waist and the way his hands gripped the knees of his crossed legs.

"I am being used," she said. "There is evil in Everien. I don't mean the Pharicians. They are no friends of mine, but that is not what I mean. It is something else. Something invisible and strange. It holds us all captive. Look at him!"

She pointed dramatically to Taretel. "That is no man to be kept in chains! That is no madman! What have we come to?"

There. She'd crossed the line. She caught a whiff of Pentar's fear, rancid and sudden as if he had actually spat his fear over her across the embers, the way some snakes spit their venom.

"Istar, you don't know what you're saying. Your judgment is impaired."

"Everyone's judgment is impaired. Something is wrong here."

"That's because of the Li'ah'vah. It would not do well to run from the danger of the timeserpent only to be caught in the net of the Sekk."

"It is time to speak to him. This evil, we do not know its nature, or its purpose. Taretel among all of us is the one most likely to understand the deeper meaning of these strange events. As long as we keep him blind, we are also blind."

"Istar! I warn you, if you carry on this way, I will have to act against you. Birtar lies dead, by the very hand of this . . . whatever it is. I have only just persuaded the men not to mob and cut your prisoner to pieces in vengeance for the many deaths that weigh on its head. And now you want to honor it as a man and speak to it? This is a grave insult to the spirit of Eteltar."

This brought her to her feet like a cat. "You know nothing of the spirit of Eteltar! I will do it."

Pentar's breath was flying out in silvery rags as he followed suit. He eyed her a little sideways, like a bullfighter.

"Give me your sword, Istar."

The hauteur in his voice offended her as much as the implication of the words. She was not mad. She was not incompetent. She was right! In a flash she imagined giving it to him, straight in the heart, the rhythm of his life pulsing up the length of her ice-cold blade. Just as she had killed the seahawk: on impulse, perfectly, without hesitation.

She checked herself, but he had seen her intention cross her face like stormclouds race across a sky. He slipped to his right and came at her around the fire, shouting for help.

Taretel stepped to block him.

This will end badly, Istar thought. *One way or another, I will lose here tonight.* She drew her knife and in two quick strokes cut the bonds from Taretel's hands. Her sword flew into her other hand and she began to back away. She saw Taretel reach up and tug the blindfold from his eyes, the gag from his mouth. He did not appear agitated.

"Run, Taretel!" she screamed, and to her amazement, he did. She had half expected him to stand and fight: even unarmed as he

19

was, he had already showed himself capable of inflicting devastating force. But he didn't fight—he whirled suddenly and shot off, fleet as a deer in contrast to his size, and the snowy darkness swallowed up his white cloak in seconds. Istar blocked Pentar when he tried to follow, matching him move for move as he tried to get past her and her sword.

"Catch the Sekk, you fools!" Pentar ordered the men. "It is loose in the wood!"

At the same time Istar cried out, "Let him go! He'll kill you if you go near him!"

Some of them hesitated. They had seen what had happened to Birtar. The others plowed into the snowy forest anyway, beating at ice-covered branches with their swords and shouting at each other in an effort to rouse their fighting ardor.

"Istar, our friendship is over," Pentar said. He used the Seahawk dialect to drive his point home. "You have tested me one time too many. I withdraw my allegiance to you."

He tried to get around her again, hell-bent on catching Taretel. She cut him then, a diagonal slash from shoulder to rib that sliced through his leather hauberk before he managed to parry; and then she ran off into the trees.

She deliberately didn't follow the big man at first, hoping to divert Pentar's attention away from the pursuit of Taretel. No one followed her, and soon there was nothing but the rasp of her breath and the crunch of her boots in the snowcrust. Her fingers were icy, but inside her furs sweat was pouring down. She stopped.

Far away to her left she could hear them calling to each other. She couldn't make out any words, but by the tone of the cries, she gathered that they hadn't found him yet.

She lowered her sword, shaking all over. Above, an owl cried, giving voice to the uncertainty and loneliness she felt bearing down on her, as deathly as the cold itself.

"By the ghosts of my ancestors, what have I done now?" she said to the night.

IMAGINE A LILY

𝔓entar's hauberk was neatly sliced across his heart and the padding beneath it was torn; but he was not hurt except in a symbolic sort of way. Truly he felt heartsore, and by the time he led Istar's men—no, they were *his* men, now, he reminded himself—down to the shore of Fivesisters Lake, he was badly in need of some kind of good news. It was still light; they had made excellent time. Pentar's frustration at being unable to stop Istar's foolish behavior had likely spurred him on during the day's march; and he knew for sure that the desire to be out of the vicinity of Eteltar had spurred on the others. Still, they were a day late, and he didn't know what to expect. They were to meet with four scouts, each sent on a different path but all instructed to return to this point, at this time or as close to it as possible. Pentar felt starved for news. The weeks he had spent up in the mountains felt like years, and now he had returned to a world that was profoundly different from the one he had always known.

He found signs carved on the lake. The wind had swept the snow away, and someone had cut a crude message in the surface of the ice. Pentar let out a whoop, and the others came from all around.

The message was written in the symbols of ancestral Seahawk, known in Pentar's clan from the time before his people had sailed to Everien from the barren outer islands. It said, "Jakse sunrise here," and nothing else. *Jakse?* Pentar wondered. How had Jakse gotten into the picture all of a sudden? The scouts must have carved the message—Fivesisters Lake was two dozen miles long and over a mile wide at the southern end, and only the four men Istar had sent out knew where the Seahawk group would be seeking such a sign. Yet the last Pentar had heard of Jakse, he was dealing with Dario's people near the cave Xiriel had asked him to guard. Dario was known to Pentar. Like Istar, she was a daughter of Chyko—and maybe it was some sororal jealousy that had made Istar suspicious of Dario without ever having met the woman. Pentar had argued to Istar that Dario was an ally of theirs, a rebel in disguise functioning within Tash's army; but Istar had argued back that Dario was a Wasp, and never to be trusted. Now that Istar was not here and he was not preoccupied with arguing with her, Pentar found that Istar's warnings were echoing in his mind, making him cautious about both Dario and Jakse. He didn't like the fact that his men had apparently linked up with the older Snake warrior.

"Let's hope it's not a trap," Pentar said to the men, and had them disperse in the trees. "We are due for some good luck."

Philosophically, Pentar decided that he would not have gotten much sleep that night anyway, thinking about Istar and her Seahawk killer on the loose in the wilderness. Thinking about Birtar and feeling he had failed somehow, he settled down beneath the low-hanging branches of a young stand of pines that had sprung up where a great one had fallen some years before. Their branches provided both shelter and cover, and he dozed on and off through the darkest hours. He was awake well before dawn, and he went alone to the point where the writing had been left and hid amongst the trees. He expected Jakse to approach from the forest, and had instructed the men to hide themselves and remain alert. Dawn came and there was no movement in the wood at all. Animals knew that Pentar and his men were there, and they did not show themselves. The sun began to come up over the mountains. Pentar looked around him in the light, belatedly worrying that the message might be several days old and that Jakse might have come and gone long ago. Then, gazing over the glare of morning light off the lake, he saw a single, slim figure coming across the ice.

The man was backlit by the clear light, so he was a stone's throw away before Pentar was certain he was Clan: he wore a Pharician cloak, but his head was pale and shaven, and he carried a cutwire casually from his right hand, swinging it from side to side. In his left hand he was holding a pair of white ducks by their feet. When he drew near to Pentar, he tossed them on the ice, and said, "We have had good hunting, waiting for you here. I will show your men where to get more. Do you remember me? I'm Jakse."

Pentar greeted the Snake cautiously, going out to meet him on the ice.

"Are you alone? I understood you were mixed up with Dario and that she was working for Tash."

"Dario is not with us anymore. We were separated." Jakse looked him up and down. "Have you met Tash? He was headed to meet you in Tyger Pass."

"We chased him off. But I would not like to meet him again."

Jakse laughed. "Seahawk, your caution is understandable, but if you think I have forgotten our alliance from the autumn at the cave, you underestimate me. Come, I am alone, as you see me. Let us trust one another. There is a Li'ah'vah on the loose, and the Pharicians still crawl all over our homeland."

Pentar relented and called his men out of the forest; but he did not apologize for doubting the other rebel. Jakse warned him not to bring the Seahawks on the ice. "We are too visible from the air, here," he said, "and the Pharicians are fond of using bird scouts, even as fond as you Seahawks. Come, I will take you along the shoreline to our camp, and then we can really talk. Where is Istar?"

Pentar had to tell him the story of Istar while they walked, and it did not make a pleasant tale. Jakse listened carefully and said very little, and when at midday they got to his camp, where Pentar's scouts had already been collected and were sheepishly relaxing, he laid a hand on Pentar's arm, and said, "It is not your fault, my friend. And I know it is a hard blow, but you must take heart. Come, share a meal with us, and I will tell you what news I have gathered."

By the time they reached Jakse's camp, Pentar had warmed to Jakse, and he was elated to see that the camp was well dug-in and provisioned. There was plenty of firewood, and before long he had stripped off and washed, and beaten the worst of the soil from his clothes and armor. Jakse had liquor, "liberated from an abandoned village last week," and he pressed it on Pentar and the other Seahawks. Before the day was over, Pentar was feeling, if not happy, then at least temporarily relieved of his burdens. Then the food started to come off the fires, and whatever moral problems had been plaguing him seemed to fade into the background. Jakse's people were not good cooks, but they were competent

enough to satisfy men who have had little of fresh food in weeks—
mainly squirrel and the odd scrawny rabbit, at that. There was fish
caught through holes in the ice, duck, venison, hare, and even—
again, thanks to the abandonment of a nearby village—potatoes.
Pentar observed his men's reactions. The younger ones almost
swooned; then they began to jostle and bicker for the best portions.
Some things never changed.

The two leaders sat apart. Now it was Jakse's turn to speak.

"It is a simple thing," the Snake began, passing Pentar a dripping
joint of venison. Pentar looked at the meat with delighted indecision:
where to begin eating such a long-denied feast? He took in Jakse's
next words rather slowly, and by the time he made sense of them, a
silence had fallen so that only the crackle and snap of the fire seemed
to react to Jakse's extraordinary statement. "It is simpler than we
could ever have guessed. The Sekk are destroyed."

When the silence lengthened, Pentar trapped between desire to
bite into the food and shock at the meaning of what Jakse had just
said, the Snake ventured to explain his meaning.

"The Lake of Candles was their source. It was a kind of membrane between Everien and the Liminal, and when Tash
approached, Dario and I decided to destroy the lights. We put out
every single one of them. There are no more Sekk."

Pentar bit into the meat and chewed rapturously. It was tough,
but he didn't care. It was the best meal he had had since leaving
A-Tar-Ness. At length he asked, "How can you be so sure? Maybe
there are other lakes. Other 'membranes,' if you will."

"Yet all accounts reaching me from far and wide say that the
Sekk have vanished. In a village in Bear Country, a Sekk disappeared into thin air at the same moment that Dario shot the lamps
in the lake. Do you know what Xiriel used to say?"

Pentar took another good-sized bite, fueling himself. He knew
what Xiriel's ideas could be like and his brain felt tired already.

"Xiriel thinks that the reason the Sekk don't bleed or leave
behind bodies when we slay them is because they simply return to
their lights in the cave underground. Imagine a lily that dies back,
but its bulb remains through the winter, and in spring it blooms
again. The Sekk were immortal, seemingly limitless in number,
and indestructible. Until we found their source. Now they are, to
use Ysse's term, 'exterminated.'"

"I don't believe it."

24

Jakse shrugged. "You don't have to believe it. But I'll warrant we have no more trouble from the Sekk. And if it took Tash's invasion to drive us to such extremes, then it was worth it in the long term."

"Jai Khalar?"

"Swallowed by the Li'ah'vah. The Fire Houses are all but destroyed. And you'll be glad to know, with the Eye Tower gone, we have no more need of Seers. There is the matter of Hezene, of course. His daughter Ukili was in Jai Khalar when it vanished. When word reaches him, he will not be happy, for a large force was also garrisoned at Jai Khalar and a good many of them went with the castle. But none of this . . ." Jakse waved the bone dismissively. "None of this is the half of it. The Li'ah'vah has carved up the countryside, and out of the holes it's left behind, strange things are beginning to emerge."

"I thought you said the Sekk were vanquished."

"I'm not speaking of the Sekk. I'm speaking of monsters. Creatures so fearsome you would not wish to look on them, much less fight."

Pentar said, "I've seen a few of those. In the Floating Lands, for example."

"I don't think you've seen anything like this."

Pentar was getting full and, consequently, sleepy. "Let's not speak of monsters, or timeserpents," he said. "Tell me what's become of Tash. And what about the Fire Houses?"

"No one can get near the Fire Houses," Jakse answered. "It seems the closer you get to the region enclosed by Jai Khalar and the Fire Houses, the stranger things become. Time slows, and it even seems—I'm not saying this is true, but it seems as if time runs backward. You remember things that haven't happened yet."

"That could be useful," Pentar remarked, spearing a piece of flatbread on a stick and holding it out over the flames to roast.

"Not really. Think of the confusion! Anyway, I don't know about any of that and at this point I can't say I care."

Pentar smiled. "I know what you mean. I am sorely tempted to turn round and go right back to Seahawk. I cannot see any point in becoming embroiled in the affairs of Everien proper. Seahawk can function independently, or nearly so. And my men are no longer what you could call patriots. Many of them were used by Night. They are weary of this life. They want to be with their families."

"I don't even know where my family is," Jakse said. "The time-serpent has cut a line between me and them, and I can't get through the time distortion in the forest no matter what I do."

"Is that what it is, when the air flickers?"

"Yes, I think. Birds can pass over these distortions, provided they fly high enough, but on the ground they cannot be crossed."

"What about underground?" Pentar said suddenly.

"Underground?" Jakse asked with his mouth full.

"Well, a timeserpent tunnels, doesn't it? Could you walk down its tunnel?"

Jakse's eyes lit up. "I don't know," he said, swallowing hurriedly. "By my Snake forefathers, you are right! Why didn't I think of this? And I call myself a viper!"

"We would have to find the end of one of its tunnels," Pentar said. "We saw the thing from the ridge above the lake, going in and out of the earth like a needle sewing cloth. It's a question of finding one of those places where it definitely went in or out."

"It originated in the Fire Houses," Jakse said. "We don't know where, or when, it is now." His face sagged and he let out a sigh. "What if the areas we can't pass *are* actually signs of its tunnel? Maybe it doesn't dig in the ground literally."

"Maybe," said Pentar. "I didn't say it would be easy. I didn't even say I wanted to do it. I was only thinking out loud."

Around them, the older men were singing and playing dice games on trampled snow, while the younger ones fell asleep almost with their noses in their drink bowls. Pentar smiled. "It will be good to see them out of danger. To be honest, if you had told me that all was well in Jai Khalar and that we were being summoned thence to build the central army, I think I might not have had the energy to go. These events with Istar and Eteltar have drained me of energy, and I am tired of witnessing deaths I don't understand. I am not meant to be a commander, Jakse. My heart is not in it."

Jakse let a brief silence fall, and Pentar listened a little sleepily to a lyre well-played by one of Jakse's men. As if he were reluctant to bring up the subject, Jakse cleared his throat a little and shifted in place before speaking again.

"Of course, there is Tash to be considered," he said.

Pentar jerked into alertness. "Where is Dario?" he asked suddenly. "You said she shot out the lights with you. Where is she?"

"She broke from us when the Li'ah'vah came. There was a . . .

26

a disturbance, I guess it was a Li'ah'vah passing as we talked about, running in a line down the hillside near the cave and out into the lake. We were on one side of it, and Dario was on the other. After the Li'ah'vah passed, I couldn't see her anymore."

"Was she alone?"

"No. Some of her people were on the other side of the line, too. Remember, when I met her she was working for Tash. But I think I had convinced her to join us."

"What you're saying is that she could have been reunited with Tash, on the other side of that . . . seam, if that's what it is."

"It's possible. I thought you said *you* were chasing Tash."

"We were. I did not think he had gotten as far as the cave before the Li'ah'vah came. But I cannot be sure."

"I don't believe that she would join again with him," Jakse said. "Not out here in the wild. She had no reason to do so. Her purpose was to defeat the Sekk, and she achieved that. I hope, I pray, that she made it out of that cave alive. But I have not been able to get across the seam to find out." He paused, and the pitch of his voice dropped. "Pentar."

Pentar stirred. He knew what was coming.

"Will you come with us? To the cave, or nearby at any rate. Maybe we can get across this barrier."

"I understand that you might feel compelled to find Dario," Pentar replied carefully. "But there are larger issues at stake."

"I know that!" Jakse cut in before Pentar could reiterate his desire to go home. "Believe me, I am aware that the Li'ah'vah is no friend of ours, even if it has routed the Pharicians—and I am not at all sure of that. But don't you see? If we don't figure out a way to get past these discontinuities in our land, we cannot touch the other parts of Everien. Have we fought all this while only to stand by and watch our country be ripped apart?"

Pentar held out his cup to be refilled. As he leaned forward, the leather of his hauberk parted where Istar had cut him. He had lost Istar, who had been his guidestar since the Sekk had held him in Slavery. The Sekk were gone now. What was his purpose to be?

Jakse filled Pentar's cup in silence, waiting respectfully for his answer. Pentar drank.

"I don't know," he said honestly. "I don't know whether I have it in me. But I will come with you for a short way, and we will see what is to be."

CONSIDERING TASH

When a Pharician flier marked as a high imperial bird came sweeping into camp just on the cusp of evening, Tash leaped up and called it to him with great excitement.

"It is from Illyra, or maybe even my father!" Tash cried. "They must have realized that the Carry Eye has failed me, so they sent me direct tidings. It took bloody long enough. . . ."

Everyone watched while Tash unrolled the message, calling for someone to feed the flier at once. Shiror stood by his shoulder and overheard Tash muttering as he began to read, occasionally quoting from the scroll.

The message was from Arkkao, brother of Ixo. It had taken him many weeks, he said, to find a bird capable of flying to an individual man and not simply to a place. He hoped that other regions of Everien were better off than the part of Wasp where his Clan lived. Thanks to the creation of the Li'ah'vah in the Fire Houses, Jai Khalar was gone and the Fire Houses were in ruin. Tash's soldiers would bring the Clansmen no news of Tash, and Illyra was unfriendly. Arkkao was appealing to Tash personally because his sister had said that Tash was not as evil as would be expected of a Pharician. And he had heard that Pharician men hoarded their women like jewels—was he not obligated to provide for his concubine and the mother of his son?

"His high-handedness is offensive," Tash said in a deep voice. "How dare this Clan bumpkin speak to me as an equal?" He read on silently. When he was finished, Tash threw the message at Shiror, but it caught the wind and rolled haphazardly across the crusted snow. Tash was boiling with dissatisfaction.

"Where is my castle? Where is my wife? The emperor will—" He censored himself. No one spoke. Shiror possessed the practiced ability to stand perfectly still without appearing frozen or tense, and he was employing it now. Tash looked ready to explode. It was almost a minute before he mastered himself enough to speak again.

"It is spring there," he said. "They rejoice that the Sekk are vanquished. Some even saw Sekk disappear before their eyes, and no one has been troubled by them. The Deer have abandoned their cities and are dispersed among the fields to plant crops. The Bears are rounding up their livestock. Whole areas of Wasp are impenetrable because of the timeserpent. Wolf Country is divided. Seahawk sends ships to the Floating Lands and marches goods along the sea plateau because they cannot reach Jai Khalar by the passes. For that matter, *Jai Khalar is not there!*"

He guffawed. "Monsters plague them from out of the seams sewn by the timeserpent. The Fire Houses are in ruin. They are using the last of the big weapons against the monsters. Soon they will run out and they cannot build more. When am I coming back?"

Shiror let out a dry cough of a laugh and Tash cast burning eyes on him.

"You laugh?"

" 'When are you coming back?' " Shiror quoted back at him, holding Tash's eyes. "My lord, it is a far cry from 'Go home, you Pharician interloper,' is it not?"

Tash snorted and tried to shrug the remark off, retreating into the sulks for which he was famous; but Shiror stooped and retrieved the scroll.

"If you had stayed in Jai Khalar, we would now be inside the timeserpent."

Tash spun on his heel, his cloak whipping around with him and snapping Shiror on the leg. He did not seem to have heard the words. He stalked away a few paces, surveying the torn landscape of Snake Country.

"Timeserpent," he whispered so that even Shiror could barely hear him. "What a weapon!"

He stormed around the camp randomly, looking for someone or something to take out his frustration on and settling eventually for the youngest of his officers, who was making the mistake of whistling as he picked ice from the hoof of his mount. Tash cuffed him mightily across the head and sent him sprawling, and as the boy lay there in the snow looking startled and uncomprehending, the prince suddenly offered him a hand and dragged him to his feet.

"Ah, it is not your fault, Lumula," he said, and turned away, punching his own gloved fist and kicking the snow. "I am failing! I am failing and I do not like it!"

Shiror did not know what to do. Tash subsided eventually, but he gave every indication of being about to go into a blue funk, which occurrence Shiror urgently wished to prevent. It was one thing to sit and brood darkly while in a safe castle, and quite another to do it when men and horses are under your command and snow surrounds you everywhere—and a timeserpent is on the loose.

Shiror considered it to be a great piece of luck that another bird came to them a few hours later, one of the birds Shiror had sent scouting to look for the Knowledge cave. It returned, exhausted, with singed tailfeathers. Shiror was attending to it and puzzling over the fact that it had found no people (if it had, it would have pestered them until they gave it a message or token) but yet had found fire, when Tash called for him to demand to know the tidings.

"There is only one explanation," Shiror said to Tash. "The bird has found our enemies at the cave. Otherwise, it would have not come back without a message."

"Enemies?" Tash perked up at once.

"At the Knowledge cave, or between here and there," Shiror said.

Tash was over his mood. "Let's go," he said. "Tell the bird to guide us and be quick about it."

While they were riding through the wood, Shiror tried talking to Tash about the value of Arkkao's summons. He was personally convinced that Pharice had much to learn from the fighting and hunting methods of the Clans, which seemed admirably suited to their extreme environment. Shiror had been party to a number of Hezene's colonial efforts, and it had often been his job to go in after the sword and bow and siege work had been done, and actually bring the people into line with Hezene's policies. You could not tax the starving or trade with the destitute. Shiror knew much about making Pharician ways palatable while still improving the prosperity of the conquered lands, which benefits would be felt by the emperor. He liked it that Tash, whether he knew it or not, had managed to endear himself to at least one of the big Clan families. For even during his brief stay in Jai Khalar, Shiror had listened more than he talked. He knew who Ixo was, perhaps better than Tash did, for to Tash she was only a sex partner.

"Ixo is a fine woman. She has borne your child, and you are still the son of Hezene, no matter what has happened to his daughter. He has acknowledged you before witnesses."

"Witnesses? I don't even have his little Speaker, what's her name? Chee."

"The emperor cannot blame you directly for Ukili's fate," Shiror plowed on. "Someone has to take command of the Clans, and Illyra lacks diplomacy. And it sounds as if the Clans will welcome you with open arms if you accept Ixo as your wife and her son as your own."

"Son?" Tash said sharply. "She was not even showing a belly when last I saw her. It has not been that many weeks since we left Jai Khalar."

"Time no longer runs the same in all places, my lord."

"Son . . ." Tash considered. He was obviously pleased by the idea, but his brow soon furrowed with other worries. Hezene had done him a great honor by giving him Ukili, and Tash did not like it that she had come to harm under his protection. To acknowledge a Clan son so soon after losing Ukili . . . it could not be wise.

"Let us see what comes of this Knowledge cave," Tash said. "And while you're at it, have your birds look out for that Dario and his men. I wish Kivi was here! He knew all about this cave."

BY THE NEXT morning, smoke was pouring into the air over the forest in the direction they were going. It looked as though a strip of land just above the lake was ablaze. Later that day, as the Pharicians traversed the road along the south side of Fivesisters Lake, the same scout bird returned with a scrap of woolen cloak.

"Does this mean the birds have found Dario?" Tash asked.

"Possibly," Shiror said. "This is the sort of material used as standard in Jai Khalar. But I think Dario would have written us some form of message. The cloak more likely belongs to a rebel."

"I am ill accustomed to working in such enclosed spaces," Tash complained, as his horse tossed its head and rattled the bit nervously. He gazed up the winding road. It made only a narrow cut in the forest, which itself grew on steep and tortuous slopes between jagged stones. The hills seemed to close in, and the only open space was out on the ice. "I wish we could ride out across the lake. It is more like the terrain I know."

"On the contrary," Shiror said. "If we hope to ambush the rebels, or at any rate to find out who they are before they've spotted us, we must dismount at once and get into the trees."

Tash's lip curled. "I hate this sneaking around. I am beginning to wish I had returned to the south. How can blood run freely here? It freezes as soon as it is let. Ah, come on, then! Single file— and damn these trees."

Under different circumstances Shiror would have strongly urged leaving the horses behind, but he judged that Tash knew quite well the disadvantages of riding in such an environment and had already made up his mind to carry on anyway. Shiror hoped Tash would change his mind when they got closer to the fire.

Tree to tree, the bird led them through the dense woodland. After two hours of slow progress, they came across the tracks of a small band of men, horseless.

"Well, they are not much, for better or worse," Shiror remarked. Tash sniffed the air.

"Something's burning," he said. "Come on."

The tracks led them uphill and out of the trees, to an exposed hillside strewn with rocks that looked small from a distance but proved themselves to be the size of imperial oarships up close. There were six Seahawk men climbing around among the boulders, not very stealthily, as though they were looking for something. While the Pharicians watched, the men moved in uneven circles, doubling back on themselves to no particular purpose.

"They look like a bunch of drunken chickens," Tash remarked. "What are they doing?"

The party began to make its way back down the hill, observing the same irregular, senseless pattern of movement. The scout bird erupted in a series of chattering communications, as if it, too, were impatient with the display of pointless incompetence.

"I can't watch this," Tash said after a few minutes. "Come on. Follow me."

He dismounted and left the horses with one of his men, then took the rest through the trees to a point where they could intercept the Seahawks on their way down the hill toward the lake. There was smoke coming from within the forest.

"What is all that fucking smoke?" Tash asked no one in particular; then, watching the deranged behavior of the Seahawks, he muttered to them, "Come and get it, you stupid Clansmen! No wonder Everien is in such a muck if this is how people behave—"

He sprang back, startled. The Seahawks had been taking turns charging across the hill and then falling down as if striking an invisible barrier. They looked like substandard court jesters. Then, all six moving as one, they all charged forward and when they reached the point where each had fallen, a fire sprang up directly out of the snow.

The Seahawks did not fail to fall down, but this time they scurried away from the flames, which rose three manlengths in height before subsiding as suddenly as they had come. At the same time, there was a crackling sound within the forest, and somewhere downhill a tree crashed to the earth. More smoke rose, somewhere close to the lake.

Tash signaled to his men and pelted from the trees. He had misjudged the steepness of the hill, and by the time he reached the Seahawks fifty yards above the tree line, they had had time to recover and draw their weapons. But they were outnumbered, and Tash was full of fury. He went in swinging his curved cavalry sword and cut down the first of the men before the others had time to scatter—which they did. They took shelter behind rocks, and one, a barefaced youth of about fifteen, threw his weapon to the ground and offered up his hands in surrender.

Tash was a little disappointed. He scuffed at the body of the dead Seahawk with his booted toe, nodding to his men to round up the others, relieving them of their weapons and binding them. He personally took care of the boy who had surrendered. All of them were dragged under cover into the trees.

"Where are your commanders? Where is the rest of your army?" He placed the point of the knife against the soft part of the boy's belly, between his navel and his groin. "Come, no games, scrawny Clansman! I recognize you from Tyger Pass. I know your troop's numbers and that you are led by the giant with the white braids."

The young man stammered incoherently. Spittle flew from his lips.

"H-h-how—"

"Never mind. I never forget a face. Did you think you were clever, that I retreated? I was only ever watching you."

Had the Seahawk been more than an untried boy, he might have recognized the bluff and bravado for what they were. He might have thought quickly enough to deduce that if Tash had to *ask* him where his commanders were, then the Pharician could not have been following them. But the reference to Taretel had disturbed him on some primitive, nameless level. And the point of the knife was persuasive, while the Pharician's heavily accented Clan speech was backed up with physical bulk and black, snapping eyes.

"They . . . we are going to the barrier. To try to cross. Where the timeserpent . . ."

"Are you saying you know how to cross over the places where the timeserpent has been? Is that what you're telling me, little scratch?"

"M-m-maybe," said the young soldier, making a visible effort to be obliging. "I mean, I d-d-don't know, myself."

"I didn't think so," Tash sneered. "I saw you, falling on your faces."

"I only know Jakse said we must try."

"Jakse, eh? The maggot. What about Dario? Have you seen my commander, Dario?"

A vehement shake of the head. "No, I swear it! We only just came from Tyger Pass, as you know."

"Address me with respect, you hollow-boned piece of nothing. I am your prince—or didn't you know that? On your knees. Now!"

The soldier went down readily enough, but there was a reaction among the others. The reaction wasn't verbal, and it wasn't obvious, but anyone sensitive to the ways of the Seahawk Clan would recognize it instantly as the beginning of an insurrection, quickly checked, but not appeased. The Seahawks knelt to no man.

"Shiror, what do you think?" Tash said. "I think I should kill them. I suppose you will tell me they could be useful."

Shiror was still supervising the binding of the prisoners, his philosophy being, Always bind captives before taking action. If you were going to kill them, it was easier to do so after you'd made certain they couldn't run away. He kicked and punched a number of the Seahawk prisoners in order to get them to keep their sharp blue eyes off his. He checked their supplies.

"They have had support of some kind in recent days," he said. "There is fresh food here. We should seek out the nearest town."

Tash shook his head. "Forget it. I have no time for that. Where is the cloak?"

Someone produced the scrap brought by bird messenger, and Tash thrust it in the face of the soldier he was interrogating. "Whose cloak is this? Do you recognize it?"

"It could be anyone's," the Seahawk said. "From Jai Khalar, that's all I could say. I . . . I suppose it could be Dario's. Didn't she come from Jai Khalar?"

"*She?*" Tash sneered. "I am speaking of Commander Dario. Who are you speaking of?"

The boy lowered his eyes in confusion. His face was flushed dark pink, shading almost toward lavender in the extreme cold. "I must have been speaking of someone else."

"Indeed, you must have!" Tash guffawed. "*She*, indeed! Well, then, it is hard to see what possible use you will be to me. I think we'd better kill them, Shiror."

"Very well," said Shiror, and tugged at the first of the men, who were roped together, to draw them apart from the Pharicians. "Does it matter to you how they are killed, Prince Tash?"

Tash shrugged. "Whatever," he said in Pharician. "Do as you please."

Roughly Shiror hauled the men through the trees, remarking to the soft young one who had surrendered first, "It is a waste of your life, boy. The Sekk are gone. We know this from Arkkao in Wasp. Your battle is won."

One of the more seasoned soldiers said, "Our battle will not be won as long as our land lies in enemy hands." But the boy said nothing.

Shiror smiled and said to the man, "Then you are a fool. Better to prosper under Tash than return to your Clan feuding. And without the Sekk, what will hold your people together?"

"We will fight Pharice," said the defiant one. His eye was turning purple where Shiror had had to subdue him.

"You will lose," Shiror said. "Accept our rule and grow. Your families are starving. Your villages are burned. Pharice can bring aid, we can offer you what your people need in trade for the Everien Knowledge. Tash is a fair man—you should consider carefully before you throw your lives away."

"We have pledged to Xiriel to guard the Knowledge cave. We would not be forsworn."

"Xiriel is the very one who brought this timeserpent down on all of us!" Shiror said. "The Eyes don't work. The Li'ah'vah has torn up this land. And the birds say that the Fire Houses are destroyed."

"What do you offer, then?" cried the Seahawk, red-faced, tears welling in his eyes. "To help you mop up what is left of my people and offer the legacy of the Knowledge to the emperor? Are you not happy? The Li'ah'vah has done your work. You have abused the Fire Houses just as Kivi said you would. You have let loose this terror, and now you want the cooperation of the Seahawks? I can only guess what would have happened had we not destroyed the lights in the cave. You would be marching around as Slaves, I am sure, for the Sekk would have had you, one and all. No. I will take death."

"Ah," said Shiror. "Then you know where the cave is."

"Of course! But we cannot get to it. The timeserpent has . . . *changed* things. Somehow."

"Is that the cause of the fire?"

As if he realized he'd already said too much, the Seahawk shut up.

Shiror said, "It was not Tash nor any Pharician who brought the Li'ah'vah. The Fire Houses lie in the keep of your Clans, rebel Seahawk. We tried to stop them, but we could not."

The blood drained from the faces of all the Seahawks. There was a long silence. Even the boy looked desperate and defiant. He scuffed at the snow.

"I don't believe you."

"I am not a liar. But come. You wish to be executed? It is well. We will soon come to a place where you can die and be eaten by your animal cousins."

Shiror made to lead the prisoners into the forest, calling to the men in Pharician that they were about to perform a formal execution. All five of the Seahawks were summarily tied to trees.

"Don't use arrows," Shiror said to his men. "We need all the arrows we can get. Use blades. Cut their throats. That is the best way."

"Please," sobbed the boy. "Let us die honorably."

"Honorably? You were quick to throw down your blade, hatchlet! My master will not let you live as long as your friends go free and plunder the Knowledge cave that is part of the kingdom of Tash. Where are they, you little shit? *Where is the rest of your army?*"

"They went to the lake!" the boy cried, and the others groaned but could not stop him talking. "They think they can cross the barrier if they go out on the ice. The fire has already burned away a big section of the wood, but we cannot cross over to the side where the cave is."

Tash came up behind Shiror. "Well done, Shiror," he said. "Now kill them, and let's go. Down to the lake."

BROKEN GLASS

$Snow$ was the first thing to greet me when I emerged from the cave and into what I later learned was Snake Country. An abundance of it, sculpted bone-smooth, obscured the hillside and the frozen lake below, blowing in sheets from the jagged peaks and making lacy forms in the air. I had never even seen snow. Now I observed the deep, blurry footprints of the hunters who had shot at me, and I felt the wind strike me with a ringing sound, and in the whiteness and emptiness of that wild world under its deep blue sky I knew I had found everything I had ever sought. Implicit in the mountains with their cracks and crevasses, their icefalls and the sky that invisibly scoured their sides with a howling sound, was a potential for adventure such as I'd always yearned for. I didn't need to pretend or wish anymore. I didn't need anyone else to fight my battles. Every challenge I could hope for was here before me.

I sneezed. I was still clad in my ordinary dress and sandals, and my velvet cloak yielded before the wind as if it were made of no more than the thinnest tissue. My feet were turning pink and blue in the needle-sharp snow.

I didn't want to go back into the cave, but it was warm and safe there, and I knew I wouldn't last long on the exposed slopes. I picked my way into the darkness, shuddering all the while. I had been too long in darkness and solitude to have any desire to return to either; but I had nowhere else to go. I crept through the cave, hoping for some light, any illumination at all, when I got to the big cave with the lake; but there was none. The echoes of Tarquin's shouts still shivered in my memory, together with the boy and the wind and Chyko and the horse exploding into being all around us. That was over. Whatever it had been, whatever pulled inside me

38

when I thought of Tarquin or Midnight Blue, or Chyko whom I'd allowed to violate me in compensation for the far worse crimes I'd perpetrated on him, all of that was over. I couldn't afford to dwell on it—not now.

There was no sign of my ghostly pursuers, no echo of music. I had to feel my way around the cave. Floating on the surface of the lake were shards of glass. I picked one up and handled it gently lest I cut myself. I know now what glass is. It is the boundary between abstraction and concrete reality. Through the Water of Glass I had been able to see and act from my safe position outside Everien. And within the Glasses were encoded the powers of the world: energy, vision, and life. The Fire of Glass is energy. It was found in the Way of the Sun and it awakened the Artifacts from their long sleep in the hills of Everien. The Water of Glass is vision, and it connected parts of the Knowledge to each other. It was stolen from the Way of the Eye, and I was its keeper, though I did not know it then. My blindness and confusion were all symptoms of what had happened when Quintar and his Company ripped the Glass from its abstract state in the coding of Jai Pendu and made it real. I should have been destroyed as my father must have been destroyed when Ysse took the Fire—but instead I made the Company of Glass and bound myself to Everien both through the Water and through the Company.

You can touch glass. Light shines through it but it is also solid. And written invisibly within it, written in sound, are the patterns that can make the abstract come into being, that are also the patterns that the living imprint upon cold abstraction. I am supposed to be one of those patterns. The Sekk were patterns like me—impressions if you will—but they are gone. The Clanspeople broke them when they shot out these globes. Maybe those tiny lights were the last of my people, the last Everiens. Maybe they could have told me the meaning of this—or maybe they were already ruined. Attacked by fell things, like me. Ripped limb from limb, like my mother. Lost. Like my father.

Jihan said my father had hidden the Knowledge like pieces of the jigsaw in time. But why? Who was he hiding them from, and who did he wish to find them? I assumed it was me. Why else would he leave me so many clues? But if they were hidden, they must have somehow been dangerous, and until I found out the source of my father's Knowledge, I would be foolish to continue my search.

I didn't even know what the pieces would make. I didn't know what part I'd played, until now—only that I'd been a strange hybrid of power mingled with blind instinct, as Night; and helplessness mixed with self-awareness, as Jaya. Here in Everien at last I had retrieved the self-awareness, and I even remembered who and what I had become during my existence as Night. But I was still helpless. I needed power, and I needed purpose. For I was gripped with a great sense of urgency. If only I knew where to look for these things. If only I didn't feel so fucking lost.

One at a time I picked up the shards, and they sang to me, just as the white-faced dead-eyed ones sang to me through the windows of my father's house. Through my fingertips I could feel them thrumming, and in my head I could hear the music. They were telling me their stories.

I took as many as I could carry out into the mouth of the cave, where there was shelter from the wind but also light to see by, for the darkness pressed me in a disturbing, all-too-familiar way. Then, picking up each piece of broken glass in turn, I listened.

"I am Balthasar, Knowledge Guardian, and my province is the chemical derivatives of plants and animals. I am the amalgam of a thousand men and women, and I was made to guard and protect their Knowledge outside the spiral of time. Prove your immortality, and I will offer up all my Knowledge. Oppose my will, and I shall grant you madness, the opposite of wisdom."

I reeled. There was such strength in the proclamation. I wondered at the power of will that could produce such a statement, and then I considered that these were the voices of a thousand people united as one and distilled into this pattern of sound. Incredible!

The others were greatly similar. They spoke of different provinces of the Knowledge.

"I am Derenyi, Knowledge Guardian, and my province is the ordering and function of stars . . ."

"I am Ono, Knowledge Guardian . . . the history of philosophy and the downfall of art . . ."

"Seel . . . magnetism, the movement of bodies, the final spirallene laws, ultra series calculus . . ."

"Rustar . . . sexual ethics, the harmony of animal species, reproductive coding, and ecology . . ."

They went on and on, splashes and spray from a tantalizing ocean of information.

Then, at length, I realized that I held a shard that was silent. Utterly silent. What was wrong with this one? There was blood on it. I brought it close to my face and touched it with my lips. Very faintly, I could hear my own voice.

"I am Jaya, the Innocent Eye, the Invisible Flower. I am the Guardian of the Ineffable. My function is to See and Know and so become Wise. I am not an amalgam. I am one person, and I have been created for this purpose. If you find me, help me. My way is the conversation between Sun and Eye, the playing-out of life and decay, the flowering of the Rose."

I let out a cry and dropped the shard. It landed in the snow and lay there like a living thing. *I have been created for this purpose?* What did that mean?

I summoned my courage and picked up the shard again, but now it did not speak to me. It did not even whisper. *It is just as well,* I thought. *Maybe there are some things about myself I don't want to know, after all.*

I gathered up the broken glass and bundled it in my cloak. I left the cave as though pursued, although in truth for maybe the first day in my life, I was not. Now I was really cold, and the glass was heavy and sharp. All the legacy of Everien's Knowledge was here, and I hadn't the faintest idea what to do.

I was in trouble. I had only one link to other people, only one hope of rescue, and it lay in the tracks of those who had shot their arrows at the floating glasses in the underground lake. I felt crazy for pursuing them, but what choice did I have? I couldn't hope to survive without help. I had never experienced cold of this kind and it would be beyond me to describe its effects. My whole body ached and burned; I found myself rushing down the hillside, eyes half-shut against the wind, cringing and shaking. The snow cut my feet and soon I was inhaling air that stabbed my lungs like a multiplicity of sharp knives, but I could not seem to slow down. My muscles lunged and jumped of their own accord, as if Midnight Blue had possessed my very skeleton and I was now compelled to behave like a nervous animal. I could not master myself. As I stumbled along the trail of the hunters, tense and gasping, I observed that my mind was no longer what it had been before. The exhilaration of freedom was still there—indeed, it was probably the only thing

41

that saved me from freezing—but hard on its heels came the understanding that I was not qualified to survive in such a world as this fierce wintry outland. I had no understanding of such extremes, and there was no one to help me. I had to grit my chattering teeth and hope I would soon catch up with the archer, or reach some kind of shelter.

I had set off downhill, encouraged by the prospect of getting out of the wind and also by the advantage of downhill momentum. But it was not a mere matter of traversing a smooth slope. There were ridges and dips and swerves in the land, and I found myself climbing as much as descending, sometimes using my hands to balance and draw myself up. Twice I floundered in deep snow and recovered my footing only after a terrific struggle that left my heart drained and my muscles toneless. I could no longer feel anything in my fingers or feet, and though I wrapped my hair around my throat and crudely tied it to protect my neck and chest, I was wheezing as my lungs closed on the frigid air. I topped a small ridge and squatted briefly in the lee of a large stone, wiping my nose with the back of my wrist.

I could see lines of burning on the land where the timeserpent had sewn its thread. Some were black scars. Some were walls of fire; others, walls of water. They divided the high country into uneven patches. Some of these patches lay in shadow, some in light. Some flickered. Some were white with winter, and some were green with summer.

Some were gray, and not natural at all, as though the land had been removed and replaced by a mechanical part.

"So the Knowledge is a jigsaw puzzle?" I said to myself. "Never mind that! The *world* has become one."

I felt sick. Probably it was the poison from the arrow that had grazed me. *Better me than Ice,* I thought, and for the second time I made the error of allowing myself to spend a moment thinking of Tarquin and his horse who was so opposite to Midnight Blue as to seem identical, and I let fly a small wish that they had found a way to something like safety.

Not that I believe in safety. When you have seen your mother's safe world destroyed with a few notes of song, when everything you have been taught was true is suddenly stood on its head, then the very idea of safety seems to carry danger within it like a lurking malignancy. As bad as my situation was, courting death on the exposed hillside, I did not wish I was home. But I did wish . . . I wished something for Tarquin, something other than that crazed geometry of house and garden and forest, and a horse built around nothingness so that impossibility lies in his guts instead of food.

Wishes are dangerous, especially in the bitter cold of mountains that give no hope of granting them. Suddenly I felt even smaller. I gathered what there was of myself and made myself follow the trail of the archer. So far, she had run down the hill more or less parallel with a group of others; her tracks had crossed theirs, swung wide, and then rejoined the rest. I assumed that she had followed after them, since I was fairly sure I would have spotted a large contingent of men moving down the hill, where I might have missed one single person. I could not trace the single set of prints more than a few yards ahead of where I was, but I could see evidence of other tracks where temporary paths had been cut in the snow. All of them disappeared eventually into the thick forest of firs that covered the foothills above the lake. And above this forest, there was a haze of old smoke that had drifted on the wind.

I did not want to go into the forest. *If I am to die,* I thought, *rather I should die out in the open than in a wood—any wood.* Or I would have escaped for nothing. I pressed on, driven by the wind and by the need to move and keep myself alive, but I was in a black mood, for I felt myself being forced into a kind of trap. Then I saw a plume of smoke rising from among the trees, and deep among them, a glimpse of orange flame. Heat! Now I knew I would not be able to resist entering the wood. I hit an icy patch and slid a hundred yards on my backside, and when I was able to get to my feet again I found myself running, careering down the mountain and toward the tracks of the hunters with every bit of spirit that remained in me.

Once among the trees and out of the wind, I felt less distressed, and it seemed to me warmer here, an impression reinforced by the fact that the snow was softer and frequently fell from the branches above in great clods, as if it had melted and then slipped. I could not walk so quickly, for I was wading often up to my knees and sometimes to my hips. After a little while, the snow lessened and then, through the trees ahead, I saw a great dark patch like a stain. I continued on and the snow suddenly disappeared, leaving behind a rush of water and a large, muddy expanse of ground on which

43

there grew no trees at all, only a few blackened stumps where the fire had passed. I smelled ash and the remnants of smoke, and I halted, perplexed. The tracks I had been pursuing were vanished. What had happened here?

Whatever had come here and caused this burning had done so well before I came out of the cave. The area was still cooling, but the fire must have stopped some time ago.

Time. I wondered about time, for it was impossible not to consider that this fire might have been caused by the Li'ah'vah. But when? From what I had learned in my father's house, and also from what I had so recently witnessed, Li'ah'vah played strange games with time. If I had been drawn through the Liminal between my father's house and the Lake of Candles owing to the efforts of the timeserpent, then I should have emerged from the cave in plenty of time to see the Li'ah'vah pass through this forest and wreak its havoc. But this was not the case. Did that mean that the fire had preceded me? Or did it mean, as I feared it might, that the fire had not yet happened?

I was nervous. I began to walk along the black, muddy edges of the burn scar, following it downhill in the direction of the frozen lake. Up in the sky, daylight was wheeling quickly toward darkness, reinforcing my fear that time was not behaving as it should. I was afraid of encountering the fire, but I was equally drawn to it, knowing that I would soon die of exposure otherwise.

I picked up tracks again after a little while. There were several sets of booted prints skirting the edge of the blaze; I followed them eagerly. I began to think of what I would say when I met the people who had shot at me, forming phrases of explanation and excuse that did not convince even me. Chyko had spoken of me with such hatred that I had to assume the archer had not been shooting accidentally when she aimed at me.

Maybe I would not approach them directly, after all. Maybe I could wait by their camp and steal a bit of food and a fur or two. A warm wind was blowing up from the lake, carrying with it ash and smoke, and I retreated among the trees, now as muddy and wet as I had formerly been frozen.

The tracks of the archer had long since been mixed in with those of her companions whom I had not seen, and now these tracks also vanished into the burned area only to reemerge pointing farther downhill, toward the lake itself. One by one the sets of prints ran up against the bases of trees and vanished, so that looking up into the pines, I was obliged to conclude that the people had actually climbed the trees so as to avoid leaving a trail.

This was very strange. For one thing, conifers are difficult to climb. I know this from long experience, as I often tried to secrete myself from Jihan's watchful eye by hiding in trees. Secondly, I could not understand why they had done it. Who or what was pursuing them? You could not escape a Li'ah'vah in this way. And if they were afraid of the fire, surely the last thing they wanted to do was climb a tree.

I was disappointed and confused, and I shed a few bitter tears, for I had been hoping to find a lodge or shelter of some kind, and now I was little better off than I had been up on the mountainside. But after a little while, curiosity succeeded frustration, and I decided to follow these strange people if I could. I picked a tree that looked as if it had already been climbed by someone with rather heavy boots. The bark was scored and scraped, and as I got up the first few dead branches I could see where the brown twigs had been broken and sap oozed from the trunk. Pine trees really are no joy to climb, and I had lost all feeling in my feet, but I made quick enough progress. I was about halfway up the tree's height when I saw that the snow had been disturbed from a good, strong branch just on my eye level. It appeared that someone had walked out on that branch and then disappeared. I looked down. Snow from the branches had toppled in heaps and lay within the carpet already lining the forest floor, but there was no sign of a body falling into the snow.

I hauled myself up and edged out on the branch as far as I dared. I saw that of the adjoining trees, one had a damaged branch just below the level I was on. It was possible—crazy, but possible—that somebody had leaped across from this branch, caught that one, and in doing so caused a partial break. They would have then had to scramble closer to the trunk and find a safer branch. Startled by the thought that someone had made a leap as bold as a flying squirrel's, I hesitated for a minute. Who were these people? Was this their native wood? If so, why were there no paths or blazes?

And how dared they shoot at me and then run, leaving me here to freeze with no explanation for their deeds?

"Cowards," I muttered, and returned to the safety of the trunk. Even on a good day, I didn't think I'd attempt such a jump, and this was not a good day. Besides, what was the point of leaping from tree to tree when you could walk?

"Avoiding pursuit," I answered myself, needing to hear someone speak. And then I clapped my own hand over my mouth. I had heard a voice other than my own.

It came from far away, a sort of shout or call. The sound was deep and long, like a human voice, only slow and distorted. My insides jumped and I clutched tremblingly at the tree. Accompanying the voice came a heavy booming sound, beating a rhythm like a big drum. The sound multiplied, so that instead of one drum beating, there were many. It was a sound like thunder, drawing closer. More voices rose up, deep and strange, speaking a language I did not know, and speaking it so slowly that their mouths must have been as big as dragons'.

Who were they? Did I want them to find me?

I raised myself by one more branch so that I could get around the other side of the tree. I heard deep, metallic clanging. The rhythmic rumbling continued. Then I saw horses! There were men riding down the other edge of the burn scar toward the lake. But they were traveling with an unreal slowness. I guessed their number to be about twenty, but it took a long time for the whole group to come into view. There were eighteen men and nineteen horses. The extra horse was not a pack pony, but a tall warmblood laden with excess baggage. Their every movement seemed to hang in the air as if the air were thick.

Then I saw a small bird fly up from the brush on my side of the burn, fly wobblingly across the blackened area, and on reaching the other side, suddenly slow, so that each wingbeat was fully articulated for my viewing.

I clutched my stomach. I shivered violently.

I keep blaming the poison, but maybe it was not that. I had a bad, guilty, strange feeling in my stomach. I wanted to disappear but I couldn't. I looked at the riders and I remembered Chyko and all he had said about me. *Night* he had called me, and I knew now that it was true. I felt sure that I was connected to some form of evil, and as much as I did not want to look into this part of my memory, I wanted to do something to make it better. But I didn't know what I possibly *could* do. I was in physical distress myself, and when I thought of all their arms and shields and the hooves of their horses and their muscles and their voices hoarse from shouting, and then I thought of myself, I could see no way forward. Chyko had captured and raped me. He had brought me into total submission. What was I going to do to defend myself against an entire company of men in the dead of winter—much less right whatever wrongs had been done to this world with its fire-scars and broken lamps? Damn it, I didn't even have shoes on my feet!

But I had to do something.

But I could do nothing.

I could feel myself getting stuck on the contradiction, paralyzed.

"Jaya Paradox!" I know it was only my imagination, but the thought was so vivid that I could almost hear Jihan's voice tickling my ear. *"Your nature is to perform the impossible. Don't hesitate!"*

The leader of the riders had stopped. He was wearing a red cloak rimmed with fur, a shirt of fine chain mail, well-worn brown leather leggings, and fur-trimmed boots. His skin was dark and his teeth were very white, and even when moving so incredibly slowly, he bore with him a potency that wasn't confined to one part of his body but seemed to seep through everything about him, every move he made. He was much, much bigger than Chyko, more overtly threatening, and I could tell from the faces of his men that they were in awe of him.

He was trying to drive his horse forward, into the burned area. It was no longer hot, and I could not see why the animal refused him; nevertheless it did. Eventually the leader dismounted. Words were exchanged, low-pitched, drawn-out, strange to the ear.

"It is between us and the cave. We must shut our eyes and go through."

I saw the men behind him put their hands to their heads as though in pain, but the leader relentlessly walked forward. His foot was about to set down on the singed needles, when he dropped the reins and brought his arms up to cover his face as though struck by a terrible blow.

"F . . . i . . . r . . . e . . ." I heard him cry, and he stumbled backward. The horse reared, slowly. Another man came forward and took the leader's arm. Together they turned downhill and continued along the edge of the burn scar.

I could not think what to do. Once upon a time, I could have showed myself, stretched out my hand, and with a few notes of song made every one of those great warriors my own, blood and soul. Now I cowered among the branches, shivering. This scene, however it might unfold, had already happened. It would happen despite anything I could do. I had made it happen. The twists and turns of chance and fate were invisible to me now, for I was in the world; but there had been a time when I had woven the beginnings of what was now before me, and now I must watch it play out with myself cast in the role of helpless witness.

A surge of anger went through me. *It's not my fault*, I thought.

I am not excusing myself, nor denying my actions in bringing the Company through the Liminal at Jai Pendu against their will. But it is the truth that I had been left with a great machine of sorts by my father, who had not troubled himself to also leave me an instruction book or a caution of any kind. Is it any wonder that, in my trial-and-error process of learning what his books and symbols and powers were and how they worked, I committed gross errors?

Then I knew that I had always been seeking my father; that he was the only one who could possibly explain his impossible house to me, much less the deck of cards, the book, the cloak, and the lamp. I knew neither his name, nor what he looked like, nor where or when he was. I had to keep the faith that my mother had kept— that he was trying to return to us but was somehow delayed or prevented—or else I would lose heart, and that I could not afford. Somewhere lay an answer to the riddle that I myself had become.

The riders had all passed me by, and still I could not summon the courage to make myself plain to them. I was cold and it was dark. I slipped from the tree and trailed them down the hill. They were making for the lake, and as I watched they rode out onto the ice.

A premonition shivered in my veins. Where was the Li'ah'vah? Where was the fire? Why were they so foolishly going onto the lake? I knew it was bad. I came down from the tree, and I walked out into the burned area, but nothing happened to me.

"Stop," said a woman's voice. "Come out of the fire. Who are you? Turn around."

Fire? I was in a burned patch, not a fire. I turned, but I couldn't see anyone. I took a couple of steps, went into the clean, unburned snow, looked up. Through the branches of a large fir tree, I could just make out the white half circle of a face. Then, from behind a tree a little farther down the hill, a man stepped out. "Are you hurt?" he called. I fell to my knees in relief.

"It's just a girl," said the man, starting toward me. "Dario, are you coming down?"

I watched a slender woman come out of the tree directly above me, not exactly gracefully but economically. She had a bow in her hand and she was peering at me intently in the gloom.

"Thank you," I whispered, extending my hand pleadingly. "Thank you for saving me."

She sprang back as if I were a viper. A terrible hardness came across her features.

"Sekk!" she whispered hatefully. Already she was reaching for an arrow.

I threw myself at her, determined to get inside the radius of her bow before she could shoot me again. We went down in the snow. She was much stronger, and she was wearing leather and fur and metal. I stood no chance against her unless I could convince her to listen to reason.

"I'm not Sekk," I gasped. "Don't kill me without letting me speak!"

"Dario, what are you doing?" called the man. I couldn't see where he was because Dario was all over me.

"Sekk!" Dario hissed, panting as she tried to hold me down. "The last . . . fucking . . . one!"

We wrestled. Hanji had taught me some things, so I was not without skill; but the archer was functioning with the strength of her own terror. I found myself laid out on my belly, snow up my nose, too weak to fight back. Her dagger came out.

I couldn't cry out. I heard myself gasping, found that I was thinking several irrelevant thoughts at once. I saw booted feet and realized that someone was trying to drag the woman off me.

"Wait, Dario! Just calm down—"

She let me have an inch and it was all I needed. I threw myself backward, squirming free and crabwalking away from her, kicking out at her to keep her away from me—but she was *burning*!

We were in the middle of the blackened area. I could see the man's boots where he stood helplessly in the snow. He looked terrified. Dario was screaming. We rolled over and over; I beat at the flames on her, my own clothes and hair too wet to catch fire. We were across the divide.

Suddenly Dario seemed to realize she was all right. She pressed me to the ground and again the dagger appeared. I felt it hard against my ribs.

"I have to do this," she said through clenched teeth. "Don't try to charm me. I must . . . *stop struggling!* . . . I must finish the job."

She hadn't killed me yet. I still had a chance.

"Please," I gasped. "I can . . . h-h-help you." My voice sounded guttural and the pain in me was rising on an excruciating note. If I made a sound, if I let out the scream I so badly wanted to, the knife would go into my guts. I lay still, panting in tiny breaths.

"Hoy!" A man's voice again. Pharician this time. "Hoy! What's this? Catfight? Gently now, girls . . . put the dagger down, little peach, or you won't get a kiss."

I don't think my assailant understood enough Pharician to appreciate how insulting the newcomer was being, or she probably would have transferred her animosity from me to him.

"Get back!" she shouted in Pharician with a thick Wasp accent. "It's a Sekk! Don't look in its eyes! Don't listen to it!"

From my position facedown in the pine loam, I couldn't see this man, but it was easy to guess that he was one of the troop that I had watched go past. I heard him walking toward us with slow, measured steps.

"*Eeeasy,*" he said now, as though soothing a frightened horse. "Let me take over here, little Clan girl. This is a job for men."

The woman spat. "Don't be stupid," she snapped. "The Sekk are dangerous!"

"Don't make me shoot you," the Pharician said. "Take the knife away so I can see you aren't going to hurt her. That's it."

"You fool!" said the woman. "I told you, it's a Sekk! Call for more men, in case I am Enslaved."

I had been concentrating all my effort on getting enough air without impaling myself on the woman's knife. I felt so much relief when she moved the knife away that I was content to do nothing for a while. Before long, more Pharicians came, in answer to a piercing whistle from the first. A pair of boots appeared within my peripheral vision. Dario, still holding tight, dragged me a little away from them. I could smell her fear and distress.

"I am Shiror," a man said. "Who are you?"

"Shiror, I am Dario, commander of Prince Tash's forces in these parts."

"Dario? *You* are the famous Dario?"

"Yes," said my assailant tartly. "And this thing I hold is a Sekk, so might we talk after—"

He did not let her finish; in fact, he spoke over her. "And where have you lot been? Consorting with the rebels, I hear. Jakse is still allied to Lerien and Kassien, and I hear you have allied yourselves to him. But Tash is Prince of Everien and Pharice rules here, not Lerien."

"I know that, Shiror," said Dario.

"What fools the Clans, to put a woman in charge of a command. We assumed Dario was a man. Kivi should have known it is in a woman's nature to be deceitful."

Dario said, "It is in a Wasp's nature to be deceitful. I went with Jakse so that he would show us the location of the cave the rebels were so interested in. The cave of the Lake of Candles."

"I have heard all about your precious cave from Jakse's boys. It is a big dark hole with warm water in it. Surely even the rebels can do better than this?"

"It was not so before we destroyed the lights," Dario said. "That cave was the source of the Sekk. We killed them all, and then the Li'ah'vah came. This girl was the last of the Sekk. I shot her, but she did not die. She came out into the forest. That is why I must kill her. She, I mean it, is a Sekk master. Give it an opportunity, and it will make Slaves of you all."

"Wait a moment," Shiror said. "If you were caught on the other side of the barrier, then how did you get here?"

"*It* brought me over," Dario said. "We knew we had to cross to get back to the valley and meet the rest of our group, but we couldn't pass the fire. I was just about to try soaking myself in water and racing through, when this Sekk turned up. My clothes burned, but the fire didn't catch me badly. My men will now be assuming me dead."

"How many men?"

"Twenty-six. One was killed by the fire when we tried to go through. Shiror, I don't know if I can make you understand. That girl is a Sekk, the last of the Sekk. In the cave, I tried to shoot her, but I only had one arrow and somehow it must have gone astray."

"If she can cross the timeserpent barriers, then it's a good thing you didn't kill her."

"But Shiror, she's dangerous—"

"So are we. Lumula!" The young soldier behind Shiror stepped forward, standing to attention. "Pick up the girl and bring her along. Come, Dario. We'll go down to the shore and you can tell your story to Tash."

*

51

I WAS A captive again. I didn't mind; Lumula took off his cloak and threw it over my shoulders, then picked me up. I felt very tired, and I wished I was somewhere else.

I had crossed the timeserpent border, and nothing happened to me. I did not slow down or speed up. For some reason, this did not completely surprise me. I understood many things now, but I could not explain how I came to know them. Not entirely. I now knew that I had visited Everien before, in shadow-form, as Night. This I had recalled as soon as the arrow bit me and I crossed into the warm lake underground. I had remembered it the way one remembers a dream that is suddenly triggered in the middle of the day: whole, clear, and certain—but completely unconnected to the rest of life. I remembered how Quintar had attacked me when I touched his men in Jai Pendu. He had dragged me through the boundaries of the Liminal and into Everien. I, as Jaya-the-girl, had not been aware of this exchange, or maybe Jihan had succeeded in hiding it from her. Either way, Jai Pendu had sailed away, leaving a part of me behind in the Floating Lands. While I, Jaya, was trapped in the dark forest endlessly riding, another aspect of me had remained on the Everien side of the Liminal. This was the nature of my prison in the forest: I could not escape because my other aspect—Night—was severed from me. As Night, I had passed through the Floating Lands and emerged in the hills between Snake and Wolf Country, where there were filaments and remnants of the timeserpent tunnel among the H'ah'vah holes that the Wolves use.

My misadventures had developed rapidly. In the form of Night I had been compelled to use others to achieve my ends, for I had no material power myself. In this divided state, I had been weak and half-blind. I had nothing but the loyalty of Quintar's Company for their leader, crystallized in the form of the Company of Glass. That was when I had called men to me, striving in vain to reach Jai Pendu and get home.

I don't think I can explain. After all, if you have always had fingertips, then you have never realized the meaning of what it is to touch. You touch without awareness.

If you have never had fingertips, you obsess and philosophize endlessly about what touching would be like, without ever slightly understanding this sense.

Only if your touch is taken from you and then returned, only if you have shifted back and forth between one frame of being and another, do you begin to encircle the meaning of touch. Just like a Li'ah'vah encircles time, that abstraction we guess at without understanding.

I had let the Li'ah'vah loose—or, at any rate, I had participated in its release.

I knew better than to think it could be controlled.

DARKNESS HAD FALLEN. The vastness of the mountain-ringed sky had closed down like a glass over a flame. The frozen lake lay white and still except where the figures of the horses walked out in a wavering line across it. After extensive discussion with the one called Shiror, and a cursory look at me, Tash had made his plans. He wanted Jakse's men, and he knew they were somewhere on that ice. He intended to surround and capture them tonight, before they could escape into the trees around the perimeter of the lake.

I bit my lip. I sat on the shore beneath Lumula's cloak, hands bound behind my back. Dario had begged them to gag me, but Tash's chauvinism prevented him from taking the advice of a female leader. Lumula wasn't paying very much attention to me, and I didn't blame him. Everyone was transfixed by the vision of the riders as they ventured across the ice.

I knew it was going to happen. It had to. Yet there was no visible warning. One instant, the night was still and pristine. The next, the lake was bisected with a sheet of fire, burning by virtue of what fuel I could not see. The air wavered like water and the fire itself made a thin, keening noise that rubbed my nerves the wrong way. I saw the leader motioning for the riders to stay back, and I knew he had to be thinking of the danger that the heat presented to the stability of the ice; but there were no cracks that I could see, and the lake remained solid. They had ridden right out into the middle of the ice and now the horses turned anxiously upon their own hindquarters, seeking escape; through the snow their hooves met slick ice and lost purchase, driving them to ever-greater fear. Then, like a curtain, the fire parted and its denizens spewed forth as molten earth from a volcano.

I stood up. Lumula gave a cry and ran along the shoreline in zigzags, as if he couldn't make up his mind whether to help his comrades, or to flee. Much more slowly, only half-aware of myself, I, too, began to move across the ice, stepping in the tracks of the Pharician horses. I no longer felt cold. My blood raced.

The creatures within were made all of flame. They possessed no shadows nor declivities: everything about them was radiant and expansive. Instead of shadows, they trailed black, terrible smoke. The dark-skinned warlord fell back before them, hastily motioning his men into a rough perimeter, trying to contain the monstrosities that confronted them. It was as if someone had taken all the pages of my father's transparent book and laid them on top of one another, so that one kind of creature was mixed with the next. There was a creature that looked like a lion, until it moved and revealed itself to be spineless, a kind of slime-mold with the ability to mimic things but possessing no spine or brain of its own; there were giant centipedes with hands protruding from each body segment, wielding obscure tools. There was a fish that turned inside out, and birds that seemed to be made all of razor blades that hunted it. And there were crawling, embryonic, eyeless things, half-formed and mute. And then I saw the face of the timeserpent, a mockery of humanity that leered from among its fellows.

I watched the surface of the lake carefully, but these weird abominations did not seem to touch it. Nothing melted or gave way beneath them, though by all logic they should have liquefied the ice and floundered in the deep water. Yet they seemed to be giving off heat somehow, for the riders who had come from shore to meet them all threw up their hands and arms around their faces as if to shield them from the fire, and the horses shied away as though stung.

I began to run. I was possessed with the idea that I must act. It was a dangerous situation. These aberrations were burning with the energy of another realm. Their fire was real, but it did not belong here in Everien. Who could say what would happen if they ventured any distance from the terrible rift that the Li'ah'vah had made? And if they could come through the Liminal into this world, could someone ride from Everien into the wall of fire and enter theirs?

Even as this thought crossed my mind, I saw Tash swing gracefully from his horse and stride toward the conflagration. He was headed straight for the fire with a purposeful stride. His followers all shouted at him to stop; the fiery creatures rushed at him as if to frighten him away; and he ignored all of them. I put on a burst of speed. My heart roared.

There was a momentary stillness among all of the players on the ice. I was sprinting flat out, slipping and skidding, but none of them saw me. Their attention was on the denizens of the fire, and on the one man who defied them. The red-cloaked leader had thrown back his furs, and sweat could be seen shining on his dark face. He was shouting to the flame creatures, and they were snarling and jeering back at him.

"Come out!" he screamed. "Come out and fight, you pussies!"

You fool, I thought. *You don't know whom you challenge!*

With the last of my aching breath, I let out a piercing scream. The monsters looked toward me. The timeserpent recognized me, and I felt my mouth go dry and my heart shudder like a rabbit's.

The timeserpent's mouth remained closed, but the dark marking that resembled a human mouth on the head of the timeserpent moved, and instead of hissing or tapping, a thin human voice issued forth. *"You have set us free, Jaya. You have set free the worst nightmares of your makers, and you have no Sekk to help you."*

I was still far away over the ice. I fingered the glass shards through the flimsy material of my cloak. The timeserpent's voice was right in my ear, and I knew I would not have to shout to make myself heard.

The voice said, *"Do not interfere between us and these Pharicians. They may not pass. We rule the Liminal now."*

I hesitated. The timeserpent was a terrible creature, and I now recognized the other creatures that crowded around it. They were the things that had looked over the wall of my garden. Now they were all afire.

"We have the Fire of Glass! We have the Water of Glass! We even have the Company of Glass, scurrying down the halls of time like the lost souls they are. You can do nothing to us, Jaya Paradox!"

I whispered, "Go back. This is not the Liminal. Do not show yourselves here."

"No one may cross this border. We guard the Liminal now—we guard it, Jaya, not the ancestral animals of the precious Clans! They are no longer protected by their special place in time. All times are ours, now."

The Pharicians had backed off, and some of them were turning to look at me. The packhorse had broken free and was racing across the ice toward me. I only had to catch it. Catch the horse, get on its back, and I would be away with provisions and protection from the cold. And then if the fire creatures destroyed the Pharicians, it would not be my problem.

"It will always be your problem," hissed the timeserpent as if it had read my thoughts. *"Truly you have lived up to your name, Jaya Paradox. For your makers knew that if you were to prove their art and graduate from being a mere code to being a living human being, then you would perform that very act of human stupidity that will be the downfall of all your kind. Ah, they were damned no matter what happened, for if you remained a mere abstraction, then they could not live on. And if you gained your own humanity, then you would bring them down worse than if they never were. You are the definition of cursedness, Jaya Paradox!"*

"I am not cursed!" I screamed. "Go away, you evil conniving timeserpent!"

The timeserpent laughed gustily. *"Do not deny it. I know. We know. You have sought out the Knowledge and tried to use it. You blundering child! Your makers would not know whether to rejoice or despair. You have proved their godhood, their genius. And you have made your own downfall and theirs. For I conceived myself in an impossible place where the laws that govern time do handsprings. Trapped there forever with the other monsters and horrors—trapped by your human conscience, or so I was meant to be. So the Everiens ensured protection for themselves from the monsters, but they did not understand me, the timebreaker that they had wrought with their engines of abstraction. But in his search for you, Tarquin the Free has released all us Made ones. And now we will destroy you. We will destroy the possibilities for our own making. This is what your species has done! We are your creations! We know nothing but futility, for our existence has no place in this world or any other. And we feel nothing but hate, for you and for ourselves. We will crush your world."*

"You will not crush me," I said. "If what you say is true, I am as powerful as you. Wait 'til I find my father!"

My words were empty, but I was so angry, I had to say something. How I wished then for a sword and the power to use it such as I knew that Tarquin possessed, and Chyko, and all the Company. How I wished for power. But I had none. The fire roared higher. Suddenly, along the very edge of the flames, a band of men appeared—twenty or thirty, running like mad toward the safety of the shore; but Tash was between them and the land. They looked like small bits of char, silhouetted against the extraordinary light. Their swords and bows made a series of X's in the air, but they were running as if they fled, not as if they attacked. Jakse's band had been literally smoked out of their hiding.

Some of them broke past Tash's guard, cutting so close to the fire that I saw tentacles reach out for them, snaggle-toothed jaws snap and miss. Some were charging straight, toward me, their hair and cloaks afire as if they had tried to enter and been turned back.

I had to run, but I couldn't. I was suddenly too tired. The ice was shifting under my feet. I saw the fire flare, then abruptly die, and a gust of hot wind reached me, together with the groan of breaking ice coming late across the lake like the aftershock of an earthquake.

There was a shout, and the red-cloaked Pharician leader charged the newcomers. I was about to be caught in the pincers of the two groups. I was beyond tired. I wanted just to stand there and let it all go, but I found myself stumbling, running for the shore. The Pharician riders intercepted the newcomers; I heard screams and the sound of metal striking metal. I looked over my shoulder and saw the ice break beneath a horse, the animal unseating its rider as it scrambled frantically to regain its footing on the ice, failed, and finally crashed into the shallows and bolted into the woods. I saw bodies fall—no swordplay, just sudden, devastating blows, and then everyone running at once as the ice caved in. I slipped and sprawled on the ice, bruised and spent, and when the first of the riders picked me up by my cloak on the point of his spear, I went limp as a doll.

ENEMIES OF THE FIRE

There was a whirl of fire around Pentar, and he was slipping as he fought. He was profoundly frustrated to find himself in the middle of this battle, in which horses fell, fire-monsters seethed and taunted, and Jakse's men threw themselves into the flames headlong, like maniacs. Pentar managed to parry the spear thrusts of a Pharician rider, who wheeled his steed and tried to chase him into the flames. Pentar dodged and slipped, unwittingly helping himself, and his opponent's horse came up against the heat, reared, and wheeled away from the fire. After that, his rider was too busy controlling the animal to pursue Pentar, who took the reprieve as an opportunity to get away from the swiftly cracking ice.

Jakse had headed what Pentar considered a suicidal charge; but emotions were running high following the sudden execution of the Seahawk prisoners. Pentar blamed himself; he should have challenged Tash then and there, instead of hiding in the forest hoping for more information, or contact with Dario, as Jakse had alluded might be possible. Then his men were dead, and Jakse's scouts said they had seen Dario taken prisoner by the Pharicians, as well. Determined that Dario, too, should not die, Jakse had waited until the riders were out on the ice and then charged. It was a stupid mistake, but Jakse had been deaf to Pentar's warnings.

Now Jakse was a hundred yards away, fighting Tash hand to hand. Pentar knew they could not win this battle. Jakse's men were hurling themselves at the fire. He couldn't understand why. He heard one of them scream, "I am coming, Master of Snakes! Wait for me!" and charge in; at that point, he assumed that everyone but himself must be presumed insane until they proved themselves otherwise. He called for his men to rally round, intending to cut his way through the Pharicians and get to the shore.

Two of his youngest soldiers were badly burned. One ran up to him, crying, "Pentar, I tried to stop them entering the fire, but they wouldn't listen!"

"Come on," Pentar said, gesturing with his sword. The Pharicians were preoccupied dealing with the fire apparitions, and he knew that if he led his men away quickly, they had a chance to escape. He didn't know how he rounded them up, for his voice could scarcely be heard above the fire, the screams of horses, and the ominous cracking and groaning of the ice.

"Run for shore!" Pentar cried. "Forget the Pharicians! Save yourselves!"

He could not gather all of them, but the men loyal to him disengaged themselves from their enemies and fled. The Pharicians on their horses jeered and followed. Pentar glanced back.

"Help me!" Jakse was crying. "Pentar, in the name of Ysse, do not desert me now!"

Tash had cut him and he was down on one knee, holding his side. The red-cloaked Pharician stood over him, firelight painting his face red and gold. Pentar hesitated. Tash would show no mercy; of this he was certain.

"Pentar!" Jakse shouted again. "Don't leave me!"

The Pharician horses were closing in; soon they would make a ring around Pentar's men. Pentar looked back at the fire. The ice was breaking up; he saw a horse flounder, then begin to swim. One of Jakse's men, consumed by fire, ran from the flames and attacked the Pharician horses mindlessly. Pentar turned away and ran.

Shiror, on his gray charger, had outflanked him.

"Come, Seahawk!" he shouted, spinning his horse and redirecting his spear at Pentar. "You cannot elude me forever! Surrender, or be driven into the flames."

"Come and fight me on your own two feet, horse-coward!" Pentar screamed. His hands were blackened and the pain of his burned skin was making him irrational. Shiror laughed.

"Thank you, I think I shall retain my advantage."

Just then, a piercing scream cut the air. Tash came racing toward the shore, juggling Jakse's bald head as he rode. More Pharicians had gathered around him and were coming to support Shiror.

Shiror said, "Seahawk, listen well. We are both enemies of the fire. Will you lose your head like Jakse, or will you accept defeat? It is death or captivity."

Pentar glanced around. He and his men were completely surrounded, and the ice behind them was breaking up. Paradoxically, the fire was still advancing.

For the first time in his life, Pentar threw down his weapon.

Afterward, he would come to wish he had accepted death instead.

A SERVANT OF
THE WORMS

On the night before the Down festival, the Pharician city of Jundun was preternaturally still. Inhabitants who could afford to leave were already gone, taken on wagons or boats to the coast, carrying their household documents, best silks, and small trinkets—anything of value that was light enough for the byrdmen to spirit away to Byrdland when they invaded the landsmen's homes. The very wealthy might hire guards to stay behind and watch over their possessions, but most of those who could be hired as guards came dearly on Down Day. They would rather be out of Jundun themselves, and had to be bribed heavily to stay during the ritual invasion of the byrdmen. For the less fortunate, the night before Down Day was spent in tense anticipation of the nightmare that was to come. Although the night was a holiday of sorts, there was no drinking and little use of drugs, for these could spoil one's alertness during the all-important Down Day. Anyone who managed to get hold of a Courage or Fortitude potion was wise if he saved it all year to imbibe on this most stressful of nights.

Jundun, which ran according to precision clocks and long-ingrained patterns of behavior, stopped dead at sundown the day before Down Day. The byrdmen capered in their roosts, calling to each other, singing, and scrambling from place to place long after the usual hour of silence. They defecated out of schedule. For one night, the rules meant nothing. At sunrise, they would be at liberty to descend from Byrdland and run freely among the houses and streets and shops of Jundun. It was one day of chaos for the strictly controlled lives of the Pharicians in Jundun—and like everything else, it was just one part of the emperor Hezene's grand plan for life. For, by giving chaos boundaries, the emperor hoped to control even chaos itself.

From the beginning, Hezene had established a tradition of holding a vigil that night, inviting those aristocrats and officers unfortunate enough to find themselves stuck in Jundun to join him. An all-night soiree was held at the palace, the only refuge in Jundun forbidden to the byrdmen on Down Day. The highborn flocked there from sundown, locking themselves in behind tall windows and thick walls. Stimulants from jungle chocolate to Everien sita were drunk copiously. Dainties were nibbled with the air of the last morsels before the onset of doom. Board games and dice were played for no stakes. Palace whores danced, but only up to a point: sex was the last thing on men's minds that night. Nervous talk circulated. Hezene in his gold robes sat apart, usually in a high semicircular room that looked out over the palace gates. From there he could see the spires and struts of Byrdland that blotted the sky, and watch the stars fade and their black backdrop decay to warm color. He would watch the chala grow bright and translucent where the dawn finally struck it like a long, slow gong of highly polished gold. Hezene had sat there every year of his reign, sometimes all night, watching the stars crawl across the sky as the sands in the big hourglass ran down. Mad silhouettes jumped and capered in the chala. Lights burned all night in the houses beneath as scared townspeople tried to warn the byrdmen not to enter. And Hezene watched the carefully calculated order that was his kingdom snap like a dry reed.

No one interrupted Hezene during his vigil. That, too, was tradition. But there was another tradition, known only to a few. Each year on the night before Down Day, deep within the inner chambers of the palace, the privacy of the infamous secret society called the Circle was lifted. The members, all of them, though they must come from far and wide, convened and conversed—not through cryptic messages but in the flesh.

Their disguises had been removed, which had the perverse effect of making the Circle's participants unrecognizable to one another. Almost every member of the Circle was obliged to go about for every other day of the year under heavy disguise so as to appear perfectly human, so that members of the Circle sometimes encountered one another during the course of the year, all unknowing, each convinced by the disguise of the other. But on the night before Down Day, they came all but naked to the palace. Byrd arranged secret passage for them underground, through the emperor's bolt-hole that he kept functional in case of revolt. Men removed cloaks and hoods and beards to reveal scaled and feathered faces beneath. Other men appeared perfectly ordinary, but they came with cats who assumed regal poses beside the fire. The human handlers sat with heads bowed, awaiting telepathic instructions; in a reversal of roles, they would be no more than Speakers on behalf of the animals, just as Byrd was a Speaker for the emperor.

It was Byrd himself, of course, who presided. He might not be the most powerful member of the group, but he was their host, and this night was his favorite of all the year. Deep in the secret chamber of the palace, he perched on the grillwork that surrounded a small fountain, his talons interrupting the ornate and perfect patterning where he gripped the iron. A pool of gold light illuminated him, and around the perimeter of the room, statues of animals and men cavorted and fought in frozen stillness, the fire throwing their shadows against the thick draperies that covered the walls. All the doors were barred. None would hear this conference, and none would observe it, except for the legitimate members of the Circle—and, on this occasion, one other.

For at the last minute, two men came in leading a prisoner. One of the men had a patch over one eye and a sailor's hook where his hand should be; when he entered, he removed the hook to reveal a withered claw. He slid the patch away and the second eye was bright red, like sunlit blood. He bowed to the assembled, and said, "This is the prisoner you asked for, Byrd. He has been kept hooded since we landed."

Now he pulled the hood off the man's head, revealing a red-haired Seahawk. The man looked pale and confused, and there was a residue of spittle and possibly vomit around the corners of his mouth.

Byrd nodded and the man was compelled to sit. His other handler took off his cloak and gloves and sat beside him, for the two were shackled together. From beneath the cloak of the second handler, a tiny monkey crawled out and perched on the man's shoulder. He ruffled the handler's hair, and the handler said, "This meeting does not come a moment too soon."

Byrd didn't reply to the handler's statement; instead, he flapped his wings for attention and began to speak. He wanted to open the meeting with a general statement, outlining the agenda for the meeting before letting anyone else speak, to gain control. He said, "So far our objectives are progressing favorably. The Clan political structures have been totally disrupted and they are at our mercy economically. We have determined the function and purpose of the Fire Houses and we have seen them, if not destroyed, then at least put out of order."

A female voice cut him off. "What about Se? Where is he?"

The voice was throaty and sharp-edged. The captive man stirred and turned his hooded head toward the speaker, who sat in the second ring of couches, well away from the fire and the light. Byrd's reluctance to answer was obvious; but he hesitated only momentarily. There was a distinct feeling in the air that when this woman asked a question, one answered.

"Se has not reported. He may be trapped in one of the isolated time regions. Or he may be dead. But that is irrelevant. At the moment, he is not needed."

"Maybe it's time to talk about our final goal."

"Not now. The situation is unfolding rapidly, and we must—"

"If not now, then when?" asked the woman coolly.

"Zene, we are all brethren. We must hold to some common purpose."

"Common purpose? We are of divided nature even within ourselves. How can we have a common purpose?" Now the scorn in Zene's voice, hitherto veiled at least thinly, was fully exposed. A collective shiver passed through the members of the Circle.

Carefully, Byrd answered. "I am for the downfall of all Knowledge. It will only lead to horror. We all know that."

"The Knowledge is not passive," said Zene's feminine tone; but her figure remained hidden in the shadows and smoke. "The Knowledge is too pernicious simply to be erased or destroyed, and it would seem it cannot now be contained. Consider the timeserpent!"

"All the more reason to be sure the Knowledge is not used," said the monkey's handler. The monkey was sitting on the man's head, gesturing and cheeping to illustrate his point.

"Or to use it ourselves," Zene added smoothly. "Friends, this moral high tone does not become us. The Knowledge is our legacy, it belongs to us as payment for what was done to us. To let it languish in the hands of foolish Clans—"

"—is safer than taking control ourselves," Byrd interjected in an effort to control the meeting. "Hezene will not tolerate us so

64

well if we step out from behind the Clans."

"The Clans and their Animal Magic," remarked a man with a lizard's face from behind a cloud of fragrant green smoke. "Bunkum galore, O fellow Round Ones."

"They are primitives, one step from animals," Zene agreed.

The Seahawk prisoner stirred. He had been taking all this in with a dazed air, unable to reconcile what he had always believed about the Circle with what he was now seeing. Naively, he had expected the Circle to consist of a group of whitebeards who dressed in velvet and gold and sat amongst books discussing spiritual matters. Or something. But not this.

"No offense, Grietar," added Zene gravely.

The Seahawk laughed. "Me, offended?" He looked around at the menagerie. "You must be joking."

Zene rose to her feet liquidly—she moved like a skilled whore, Grietar thought. She came out from the shadows and seated herself a small distance from Grietar, who began to wish he was not feeling so ill.

"I miss Mavese," Zene said, and now her voice was closer to a whisper. There was something about her tone, both soothing and disturbing, that captivated Grietar. As Zene spoke, he had the feeling that she was trying to seduce him; that she might even be describing *him*, and not Mavese, weaving a spell with her silky words. "He was cunning without books, charismatic and inconspicuous at the same time. He was strong and flexible, and he was like to us even though he was not Made. These men of intellect that Hezene puts his trust in, they do nothing for me. Give me a self-reliant individual, and I am satisfied. I should have given Mavese to the worms. He would have been an excellent servant; but I respected him too much for that, and I fear he has walked into his own demise. This is always how it is. They need our guidance, even though they beg us for their freedom."

Byrd made a dismissive noise. "Remember, our chief purpose in using Mavese was to avail ourselves of his timeslipping ability; but that rather depends on where and when he turns up. There is no point in being disconcerted by his absence. He has consumed the dead offspring of a barren species; now he is part timeserpent."

"But what good has he done? So many secrets divulged to him, and where is he? This meeting is *mandatory*!" Zene looked around at the assembled, and there were stirrings and scent-releases of agreement and partial agreement, but no one spoke.

Patiently, Byrd replied, "Thanks to him we were able to penetrate the Floating Lands and to explore the relationship between
timeserpent language and the old Snake that Wakhe and Yanse
spoke. Also, we have a lead on this Seer Xiriel—a link to him. This
could be a good contact for us."

"*If* we knew where Se was," Zene muttered half to herself.

"Do we have a report from Wakhe?" someone asked, breaking
a tense silence.

"No," said Byrd. "Remember, Wakhe has to communicate by
tapping, and none of the messenger birds are skilled enough to
repeat complex beats. He has managed to notify us only that he is
alive. He says Se is dead. I don't know if that's true."

"There is a story there," Zene commented, tilting her head back
and looking at Byrd through gleaming slits of eyes. "Byrd, why did
you tell none of us why you were sending Wakhe? You made it
seem you were only using Wakhe as a foil for Se."

"I needed them both there. Wakhe was my cover, to take attention away from Se. I did not foresee the events at the Fire Houses,
although it had crossed my mind that Wakhe's gift for codes could
be useful. I expected it to be Se who provided the critical help. I
needed someone to go in and get the skeleton from Tyger Pass for
me and infiltrate Tash's power structure. In that respect, Se failed
utterly."

He turned his beak in profile to Grietar, studying him with one
glassy eye.

"I have not cheated you," Grietar mumbled in a voice made
weak and scratchy from lack of sleep. He had suffered badly on the
sea voyage to Jundun, having alternately puked and complained
for three days solid along the coast of Ristale before retreating stu-
pefied into the hold, drugged by the second mate in the straits of
Haz. By the time he sailed up the river to Jundun, he was wishing
he was dead. He was supposed to be a Seahawk; now he'd been
shamed into a submissive posture, sunk among cushions, and
lulled by the warm, perfumed air of the palace.

"For those among us who were not privy to my first contacts
with Grietar Seahawk," Byrd said, "a summary perhaps is in order.
Grietar, tell my associates what you found in Tyger Pass."

Grietar made an effort to pull himself together. Maybe these
other members of the Circle could be won over to his point of view.

Maybe some of them would be sympathetic. He put on the most pleasant expression he could muster, although the flesh of his face felt as though it were being dragged down by weights.

"During the run-up to Jai Pendu's last visitation," he began, "when Seahawk lands were drained of men and arms, all having been sacrificed to Ajiko's army, I alone of the old families held true to Seahawk tradition and kept my fighters to myself. For this I was blacklisted by Lerien, my own kinfolk would not trade with me, and more and more I found myself relying on distant contacts to make my living. That is how I came to the attention of the Circle; and I was instructed always to seek Everien Artifacts, whether or not their use was apparent to me.

"Byrd will tell you that occasionally I came by a Seahawk heirloom that could be traced to Everien origin, and always I mobilized my personal financial resources to acquire it; and when that did not work, I used force. I believe we have always had a good relationship, you members of the Circle and myself, for all that we have never met before today."

"Yes, get on with it," said Byrd. Grietar licked his lips and continued.

"I would not have made much of the skeleton, I confess; in fact, I would probably never have found it had it not been for the unaccountable behavior of those two orphan girls from the miller's town at Seals Fjord. I was in the mountains with my men, hunting as we do, when these two wild things began pelting me with stones. They drove me into the fold in the hills above Tyger Pass, where I saw a cave that looked most intriguing. I could see that handholds had been carved in the stone to make it more accessible; a food store, I thought. I decided to explore it. They pursued, and attacked me with ice and stones and anything else they could throw, and I could not retaliate, for they are only poor, wild creatures. As I entered the cave, I saw the bodies of other men, frozen with their weapons out. I glimpsed other things, too: boxes, and I thought I saw the glint of jewels. The Hawk Girls were in the entrance to the cave, and they continued attacking me. I thought this must be their lair. Then I tripped over the skeleton, and I picked up one of its bones to threaten them with, and they vanished. Just like that—they were gone. The bone was large enough to use as a club, but when I hefted it in my hand, it was incredibly light. So I began to examine the rest of the skeleton, which was laid out formally. It was not some ordinary set of bones."

He paused. It seemed absurd, but he could feel his insides turning to jelly at the very thought of what had happened after that.

"Grietar?" Byrd prompted.

"I gathered up the bones and took them outside to see them better, in the light." The words came out in a series of stilted gasps.

"And?"

"*He* came. From out of the back of the cave. There were no tracks, no sign anyone had been there, but he came."

"Who?"

All attention was on Grietar now. The room seemed to close in. The various smells of these creatures began to encroach on him. He felt himself on the verge of panicking.

"The Sekk," he whispered. "A tall man he was, with white hair and a sword. . . . His eyes were very fell. I knew he was a Sekk, because he was not real. I could not look at him."

"So you ran."

"I ran, yes. I held tight to the skeleton and fled from him. I wished to explore more of the cave, but I panicked."

"And do you mean to tell me," said Byrd sternly, "that this giant Sekk simply let you go? Is that how it happened?"

"What does it matter now?" wailed Grietar. "This all happened a year ago or more, depending on your reckoning."

"Well, this is the first you have told us about this 'Sekk,' " Byrd replied. "You said only that you had discovered a winged skeleton. Do you mean to say that the Sekk did not pursue you?"

"N-n-no. I don't think so."

"You went straight home with the skeleton," Byrd prompted, fixing a steady, cool eye on the Seahawk.

"I went to Ranatar. I thought she could tell me something about the skeleton."

"You did not come to us first?" Byrd hissed.

"I . . . I thought . . . I didn't know what it really was. I asked Ranatar, and she said it was a winged man. I . . . I offered it to her in exchange for the hand of one of her wards, a girl I wished to court. But she told me I must put it back where I'd found it. I said that I would, but I had already decided to call upon my contacts in Pharice. Then, afterward, there was a Sekk attack and Ranatar was murdered."

"And we sent traders to take the skeleton from you to Snake

Country. You were well paid, were you not, Grietar?"

"Yes, yes, of course I was. But how could I know that the traders would be attacked?"

"You knew that some sort of guardian attended the bones. You knew that Ranatar had been killed. Had anyone or anything threatened you in that time?"

"No," said Grietar staunchly. "Except, well, it's not really a threat, but the Hawk Girls seemed to follow me everywhere. I kept seeing them, and feeling afraid."

"And when you learned the caravan had been attacked in Tyger Pass?"

"Well, I made arrangements to bring the skeleton to Snake Country safely. As you know, Byrd, by that time you were constantly asking after your goods. As soon as I saw an opportunity, I sent a retrieval party after the caravan."

"Grietar, you were to go and get the skeleton *yourself.* Personally."

"But there was a Sekk guarding it!" Grietar protested. "It had already taken all the guards I sent with the caravan. Then it took Thietar, and his brothers were lucky to escape with their lives. And Istar was right there at my fingertips! The best Sekk huntress in Seahawk, maybe in Everien."

"You should have gone with her."

"I sent fifty men! I sent you word of where they would be, when, and how to intercept them. Surely this information was of considerable value."

"It is true that Se should have been able to get there in time to meet Istar when she emerged from Tyger Pass," Zene said. "That much is not Grietar's fault, though I can see little else in his account to excuse him from blame. But that we should lose this skeleton is a sore blow. We could have used those bones in the Fire Houses. We could have created fliers such as the world has never known. Men have always dreamed of wings." She broke off, staring silent into the darkness. The Seahawk reclined, rubbing his eyes and yawning and wondering if they would give him a woman for his bed that night. Zene continued in a snappish tone, "You, Grietar, should have made sure we did not lose this thing."

"I took it from the cave! My courage cannot be disputed. It is not my fault if the Sekk captured it. Tyger Pass is a wild place. You might have taken it by ship."

"Not in winter, you fool. You should have gone with Istar, let her deal with the Sekk, and then you could have killed her and taken the skeleton. Do not avoid the truth! You sat on your backside in A-Tar-Ness acting like a king. It takes more than one favor for the Circle to become king."

Grietar felt sick and ugly, and weary. He wondered whether he was really exuding chemical smells that Zene and the others could read, but not Grietar.

"Istar would not have accepted my presence. She hates me."

"Are you afraid of a woman? A young woman with no mate, no status—"

"No status? She owns half the Clan, thanks to the murder of Ranatar. Hundreds of Seahawk men owe her their lives. She stood up to Night."

"Night!" Zene scoffed. "How can one small phantom cause so much trouble?"

"You would not jest if you had seen Night."

"It doesn't matter," Byrd cut in. "You are a coward, Grietar, and now it appears you are also a fool. You have wasted your opportunity for greatness and have caused us considerable inconvenience."

Grietar tried to sit up. "I was only trying to . . . I don't understand. . . ."

"You don't understand? Listen to me, Grietar. I am Byrd, Speaker to the emperor. Nothing better than a glorified toerag. Oh, when Lor convinced me to become tame, he thought he honored me. But I only did it for revenge. What kind of life can I have? I am alone. I am smarter than many of you men, but I have no purpose. What does a bird need with abstract thought? Philosophy? Neurosis? It makes me want to fall out of the sky. And what good is this brain without an outlet? Performing conjuring tricks and impressing foreign statesmen, that is my function in the world! I have been twisted from within. Your world made you what you are. The mountains and the sea and the forests are your parents. *Whim* made me what I am. Whim, and the music of a people who fled from their own creation. There is no world for me. For any of us here in this room, excepting yourself."

Grietar looked as though he were struggling to understand. He extended one hand, palm up, in a gesture of empathy, reconciliation. Byrd let out a false laugh, an imitation of a human sound.

"There. Does that seem a plausible reason for my hatred of you, of the Knowledge that made me—of other animals? I even hate the others in this room, and they hate me." Noises of assent. Faint smells came even to Grietar, and he wondered what they meant to each other, these cunning half-beasts with their scent-talks and tapping languages and slithery behavior. Byrd squawked, "Are you satisfied? Are you satisfied that you understand my nature?"

Grietar wanted to laugh. He knew he shouldn't, and the only thing that checked him was the fact that there was no one in the room to laugh with him. There was no one else to exchange glances with, to catch and pass back and forth the ridiculousness of being scolded by a small bird with a big head and his bizarre scaly, furry, and winged compatriots, each of whom was more absurd than the last. When Grietar didn't reply, Byrd actually hopped up and down on his perch, fluffing his feathers.

"The arrogance of your attitude astounds me," he said. "As if you had any hope of understanding me, my purposes, my point of view. I could feed you a thousand lies, and you are too stupid to see through them. What makes you think you can perceive my reasons for doing what I do?"

Grietar was catching on now. Byrd was trying to be sarcastic . . . or something.

"Then . . . you don't mean what you said? The reason you hate us?"

Byrd opened and shut his beak a few times as if struggling for words. Farther back in the shadows, a couple of rats tumbled over another in mirth. "I don't need a reason to dominate, to destroy, to ruin your little happiness. It is begging to be done. It is pleasure. Grietar, you are a particularly stupid and gullible example of your kind. You beg to be exploited."

"I don't really see what power you have," Grietar said, sniffing. "The emperor is like a god. He has never even mentioned you. What can you do? Whisper in his ear when he is sleeping?"

"That is not the worst way to get things done. But if you don't believe my power, I will be happy to prove it to you."

"No!" said Zene. "We cannot afford a display of any kind, and it would be wasted on this one, anyway."

"What do you suggest, then? He's too stupid to make him an agent."

"I wouldn't dream of making him an agent. We could kill him

71

cold, but it would be a waste of all our investment in him so far. I have a better idea, Grietar, for what to do with you."

Suddenly the sweat on Grietar's brow turned cold.

"I'm sure I take your word for it," he said. "I mean, about your power. Uh, what are you doing? There's no need—"

Zene threw back her cloak, and he saw that she had striped pigmentation on her face that made her almost unidentifiable. She parted her dress and between her breasts was tattooed a butterfly. She approached him, hips swaying, and the butterfly moved. It was a weeping wound; in fact, there was a needle's-eye hole in her breastbone. Something golden was gleaming inside.

"I possess certain adaptations," she said. "They have been the bane of my life, like my mother's before me, and her mother's and grandmother's. I have insect talents. No one can cure me." She put her finger on the butterfly's body and it came away dripping with a thick gold. "These adaptations," she added, "can be extremely useful at times." She waved the finger at him. It looked like honey, he thought. He was disgusted and fascinated. Within the hole in her breastbone, something was moving around. Did she have *parasites* in there?

"I don't need to know this. . . ." he tried to say, but she put her other forefinger on his lips. She slid the golden finger into her mouth and sucked it. Sexy, he thought in spite of himself. Then she blew in his face.

Grietar squalled like a baby.

Grietar's vision went blurry, and terrible pain seized his eyes. There was a piercing feeling like a needle passing straight into his pupil, and everything went unbearably bright. The pain eased off, but he still couldn't see. There was a feeling of movement within his eye, and he realized suddenly that there was a worm moving around behind each eyeball. He screamed again and struggled with a frenzy, clawing at his face, writhing and bucking but unable to escape the restraints of the creatures who held him to the couch. He shut his eyes and tears poured from them, and blood. A horrid smell filled his nostrils and he realized some sort of pus was oozing from beneath his eyelids.

"Good," Zene cooed. "That's very good, indeed, Grietar. For the first time in your life, you may be worth something."

He cried out and panted quickly like a scared dog, but there was nothing he could do. She stroked his head as the worms settled into his eyes. Snot poured from his nose and his belly ached with the force of his sobs.

"Shh," Zene said. "They are my children. They live in you, now. They will give me your eyes. They connect you to me. You are mine now, a servant of the worms."

BIGGER. BETTER. MORE.

After the others had left, Byrd remained by the open window that led into the secret passage. Grietar, supine on the couch, radiated various evil and unnatural smells. He could be heard moaning softly as the worms penetrated his mind. Byrd ignored him. He was waiting. Outside, the first shrieks of Down Day had begun. *Controlled chaos, the genius of Hezene,* Byrd thought. He puffed out his feathers, suddenly cold, and shifted from one foot to the other, thinking of his seed cake. The emperor would soon send for him. He wished Zene would hurry.

She did not keep him waiting for long. She materialized out of the mist of the small hours, seeming no more substantial than the chiffon skirts and veils she wore in many layers. Now they dragged in the damp gutters; Down Day, for the first time in many years, was to be graced with rain—a bizarre and unfathomable omen in this arid country. It was a rain that descended from the chala in a series of poles and gutters and pipes, and rushed through channels in the street. It was a rain that made a noise of a hundred drummers. The rain made Byrd feel suddenly and inexplicably weary, as if the events of the evening had taken a physical toll on him even though he had done nothing but speak, and listen.

Zene slid down the passage and into the room she had only recently left. She was holding a silk bundle close to her chest, as if it were a baby.

"I have never spoken of this to anyone," she said. "It has been passed down through my family, generation after generation, going back to the time when we took over the castle and grounds of Baron Horas near the borders of the Wolf forests. The story has it that a stranger, a half-naked archer with a wicked eye and outsize testicles, brought it to Horas's house and put it up as collateral in a card game. Horas won and the traveler departed, but it bore a curse that led to Horas's downfall. The forest came and grew around Horas's manor house, and then other beasts came, sometimes falcons, but sometimes nameless creeping things that lived unseen in the forest, until Horas was obliged to flee. It is said that after he left, ghosts took the place over and the rooms switched places. Then, even they abandoned it, until only a little old woman with the eyes of a wolf remained, and she was the caretaker of the house when my family came to it, and she fled into the forest to be with the animals rather than live under the same roof with us. As you know, my family were . . ."

"Wormslaves," Byrd filled in.

"We prefer to call ourselves Servants of the Golden Ones," Zene said without malice. Byrd nodded his acceptance of the correction.

"What is this thing you speak of, and why do you bring it out now?"

She beckoned him to sit on her shoulder, and then she let the coverings fall away. Byrd saw a beautiful book, bound in leather; but the pages were all transparent, as if made of very thin and flexible glass. Wedged between the pages was a large card of the type favored by fortune-tellers and professional gamblers. On the face of the card was a winged man.

"Ever since I set eyes on that Seahawk"—and she nodded in Grietar's direction—"the Golden Ones have been clamoring within me. They urge me to place this book in his hands. It may be that they will have the opportunity to wield it, through him."

"But don't you understand what it is? What it does? Have you researched it? Have the Scholars examined it?"

"Never!" she snapped. "It is secret. It is sublime. It is full of death."

"Giving it to this weakling seems . . . rash," Byrd said, as mildly as he could because his heart was racing with apprehension. Zene had always been unpredictable and self-contradicting; he'd assumed it must have something to do with the multiplicity of the beings who lived within her, a mad crowd that sometimes swayed one way, sometimes another. Now, though, her actions bordered on the insane. He smelled the danger coming from her and knew that if he gainsaid her, she just might be berserk enough to grab him by the throat and throttle him right there in the emperor's

75

palace. This was not the sort of death he envisaged for himself—not over a measly book.

"It is time," Zene answered in a high and medial voice. "Mysteries are now coming to their most exquisite point of contradiction, the very zenith of paradox. I act as I am given to act, and so must you, Byrd. Help Grietar to get to Everien. Surely it cannot be difficult to slip him among Hezene's scouts or soldiers. You have done it before, for Se and Wakhe."

"To disastrous effect, some might say," Byrd muttered to himself under his breath.

"What was that?"

"Nothing." Byrd knew she had taken his power from him this night. Forever after he might remain Speaker to the emperor, but the Circle was no longer circular, if indeed it had ever been. In truth it had always been an ellipse folded over on itself, and now its crux was upon Zene. Byrd was somewhere on the periphery.

He was cold and hungry, and he could hear the shrieks of byrd-folk wailing in the streets outside. He missed Chee. He missed having chicks in the nest, and Chee's songs and her endless preening. Somewhere along the line, he had lost his stomach for this twisted life.

"I will do what I can for Grietar Seahawk," Byrd said. "You may leave him with me. I will concoct the necessary stories."

"Good," Zene purred, and for a moment two gilt butterfly wings appeared within her irises. She stroked Byrd's ruffled feathers. "I will place this book in his hands, and the Golden Ones will know what to do, when the proper time comes."

GRIETAR LAY IN torment. The pain was worse than anything his most ardent detractors might have deemed justifiable, and considering that some of them had recommended the pulling-out of his fingernails one by one, this is not a truth to be taken lightly. He was deserving of suffering by anyone's standards, to be sure. He had talked himself into wealth and power, using cunning where other men used strength; using his own moral weakness as a weapon by which to bring his victims down. Cheating, bribery, and extortion were his preferred means of operation, but he was also possessed of a lucky streak that seemed often to place him in exactly the right place at exactly the right time to best ply his advantages. Nobody in Seahawk liked Grietar with real affection, but a lot of people owed him, and most seemed to consider him a necessary evil. Some said he would get what was coming to him; but most of these people had gone strangely quiet in recent times, and one or two had fallen under Grietar's yoke. Since the timeserpent's birth, Grietar had moved unchecked in his home country.

In short, Grietar had come to think of himself as someone with special powers. It was only in Jundun, deep in a hidden part of the palace unknown to Hezene the emperor, that Grietar began to find out what special powers are really like.

The pain lasted for nearly three days. During that time he was kept bound hand and foot to prevent him from clawing at his eyes or running around wildly in an effort to escape the agony as the worms writhed through his eye tissues and into his brain. To keep him from injuring himself through the force of his spinal convulsions, they wrapped him tightly in a linen sheet. Two attendants made sure he didn't swallow his own tongue or choke on his own vomit, and they wiped his eyes and nose, which oozed pus and black humors that Zene said were the parts of his brain the worms could not use.

He lost weight rapidly, and in the first days of their journey from Jundun he had to be given fluids by injection beneath his skin.

Sometime during those first days, Grietar died but did not know it. The pain had erased him, crushed his identity, regressed him to childhood and then infanthood, all the way back to when he had been just an embryo—and then it stopped.

The worms were in control now.

They let him sleep at first. He would be no use to them if his body were damaged. They let his heart beat and his metabolism recover. They let consciousness return as the pain subsided.

He was being carried on something horizontal that rocked and swayed. His blurry eyes focused and refocused as his body was pitched up and down. He heard the attendant's voice speaking to him, telling him to lie back down, not to strain himself. He couldn't move properly, he was restrained, and he felt weak and light-headed. But his head no longer hurt, and his eyes were working. Five days out from Jundun, Grietar lifted his head. Then the worms opened his eyes, and he saw *everything*.

*

RISTALE WAS AN ocean. There were ships on it, and floating buildings, barges of dimensions he could not comprehend. To the west, where the Wolf forests were supposed to cover the hills that bounded Ristale, there was only more water. A string of tree-clad islands trailed across the sea, nothing more. The ancestral home of the wolves was flooded along with everything else.

Grietar blinked and saw the plain, the blooming rapeseed shoulder high to the horses, the flights of birds tracking across the sky. All around him were horses moving at a clip, Pharician soldiers riding in formation. He smelled rape and horses, and the uniform yellow of the flowers washed his eyes like a tonic, so that for an instant he forgot anything had been different.

But only an instant. For, superimposed on this vision came the other vision, just as clear, just as real: the sea. They both seemed equally real; but how could he be on the sea? He had only just landed in Jundun, was it a few days ago?

"Lie down, lie down," said a woman's voice, and he realized she was speaking Pharician. Grietar's Pharician had only ever been passable, but with the help of the worms, he could understand her. He came away from the ocean vision and found himself firmly planted in a bed on a litter. A middle-aged woman with a tired, worried face was in the litter beside him. She was slight and cheaply clad in dyed linens that did not smell very clean. Her face reminded him of a wrinkled apple, but her hands pressing him back down into the blankets were strong. The litter swayed on the shoulders of its bearers. Grietar lay in astonishment, hardly noticing as she rubbed salve into the sores where he had chafed his limbs against the cloth restraints. She hummed to herself, and taking a wet cloth into her hands, she leaned toward his face. Then she looked in his eyes, and he into hers.

She screamed.

Grietar seized her wrists. Feeble as he was, he held her. "Shut up!" he ordered. "Stop screaming."

She looked away. She would not look at his face.

"Why do you scream? Woman, answer me!" He was speaking fluent Pharician.

"Your eyes," she sobbed. "They move. They are silver, and they move, inside. And . . . and . . ."

"And what?"

"Worms. They crawl out of the pupils and look at me."

78

He let her go and she stumbled out of the litter. He saw her rush across the grass, dodge the path of a horse, and vomit. The litter kept moving.

He put his hands to his eyes but did not touch them. It was so good to be free of the pain, he really didn't care if there were worms in his eyes.

The plain became a sea again, and he was lying on the deck of a boat without sails that glided silently over the deep. He looked down at his body and it was not his body. It was a pile of silvery creatures that writhed and conjoined and separated. He slithered piecemeal across the deck until he came to rest at the feet of the beautiful insect-woman. What had her name been? Zene.

"Where am I? What is this?"

"So, you are awake," she said.

"I thought I was dreaming." He gazed in horror at his body-that-wasn't.

"Don't be upset," Zene said. "Maybe the new vision is too much for you. Don't look so deep. See? Your body is perfectly all right."

As she spoke, his own body returned—a little thinner, and dressed in Pharician clothes, but unmistakably his own. The ship, however, disappeared. He was back in the train of horses and armed men, jogging across Ristale into the sun. The woman who had attended him was running alongside a second woman who rode on horseback, conferring with her and gesturing excitedly. Grietar's head hurt. A bee was noisily flying around his head. He swatted at it, and in a tiny voice Zene said, "Stop it! I'm trying to help you. If you won't see with your eyes, then at least listen with your ears."

"I don't understand," he said weakly. "Where am I, really? And where are you?"

"We are both in a place that belongs to the worms, and that is all you need to know about it."

The Liminal. Grietar shivered.

"It is not the Liminal," Zene said. "The Liminal falls under the dominion of the Everiens. Where you and I are is a place of free possibilities."

"Is there really an ocean in Ristale?"

She laughed. "There will be, someday, if our road reaches its end."

Grietar slitted his eyes and saw the water again, the ship, the faint outline of the insect-woman. This time, when Zene parted her robes, she had six breasts instead of two. Butterflies came out from between them in a cloud.

"Now, listen carefully. You are among an invasion force on its way to Wolf Country. Hezene is sending four thousand troops to the H'ah'vah tunnel. His commander, Tia, has requested them. Tia says that he can take the entire valley in a year given this number."

"But Everien is carved in pieces," Grietar protested.

"I know. Despite conflicting reports from other parts of Everien, and even darker rumors about the disappearance of Jai Khalar and the rise of terrible monsters, Hezene chooses to believe Tia. A straight military plan makes more sense to the emperor than a lot of mumbo jumbo about timeserpents." Zene smiled.

"What is my function?" Grietar asked eagerly, glad that she was no longer angry with him, and shrinking from the memory of the pain of the worms. Perhaps she had punished him enough. She must be giving him another chance to prove himself.

"You will come to command all those troops," Zene said. "But not yet. You will bide your time and wait for guidance from within."

"You mean . . . ?"

"I mean the worms." A large blue butterfly landed on Zene's left palm. She stroked its wings delicately, crooning to it. "You will not see me again, Grietar, once you have crossed the tunnel. The Liminal of Everien is beyond my scope to penetrate. Trust in the worms, let them guide you in all things, and all will be well." She smiled at him and stretched her hand toward him. The butterfly slowly beat its wings, which were gilded at the edges, ragged and beautiful.

"But . . ."

Zene threw the butterfly at Grietar. It soared through the air, getting larger and larger the closer it came to him. He saw its bright underparts, the velvet rounded contours of its worm body, and the deep-sky majesty of its wing colors.

Then he was back in Ristale, and the whole world was lemon yellow and suffused with the smell of rape.

GRIETAR WAS CARRIED passively day after day. He took to wearing a hood to shade his eyes, and the second woman took over from the first attendant, who was now demoted to assistant cook for the regiment. The new woman was harsh and brusque, but she did not look him in the eyes and she did not scream. The pain came and went, and so did the visions. With practice, Grietar found he could see things that weren't there, whenever he wanted to. It was some time before this inference had established itself in his mind. At first there were only impressions of places and people that did not exist. There were layers of vision in the world, sometimes laid over one another like the paper roofs of chala he had witnessed in Jundun, other times taking turns like patterns in a patchwork quilt.

Under normal circumstances the amount of information presenting itself to his senses would have driven him mad and unconscious, in that order; but there was something more to him now. Another level. A place where a feeling lived, not quite a voice, but a presence nevertheless; and it was a wise presence. It had many aspects all knitted together. He felt sure that this presence was more than he, Grietar, could ever be; yet by his attachment to it, he transcended himself and became part of it, and this was a satisfaction unlike any he had ever known. This place, this level, this presence, told him not to fear what his senses offered to him. When he was overwhelmed, it would speak for him. It would direct and guide him. He would be able to let go, like a child, before its (their?) superior wisdom. Or so it seemed to him as the army crossed Ristale.

He felt bigger. He felt better. He felt more.

He didn't want to go back to being only Grietar, that weak and pathetic husk, so dependent on food and drink and sleep and self-indulgence. Now he was something better. He was purer. He served and was served. This was his happiness.

And he needed happiness. Because sometimes, behind the veil that guarded his world, he saw monsters, and they frightened him; but more often, he saw machines, and they terrified him beyond his understanding.

Bigger. Better. More.

Grietar was as small as a worm within himself, and the worms of Zene filled in all the unfilled spaces that had once belonged to him. The machines snickered at the worms, and the worms moved expectantly within Grietar. They were getting ready for something.

*

AN OASIS IN THE RIPPING

King Pallo's favorite hobby was collecting Pharicians, and the more of them he had, the more Pharice-like his country became; but although this sometimes made him nervous, it didn't make him stop. Maybe it was the Pharician in him, or maybe it was some inherent Wasp caprice, but King Pallo enjoyed his secret game. And what could he do? The Pharicians just kept presenting themselves. He could scarcely turn them away.

Pallo himself had arrived in this particularly remote section of Wolf Country entirely by accident: he had been catapulted through a sewer in A-vo-Manik and turned up in a similar water pipe in A-vel-Jasse. He hadn't known where he was but, terrified of timeserpents and being underground, and darkness in general, had climbed up an access ladder and into a corner of Everien that found itself cut off from everyone else.

He later came to believe that it was this passage through time and space that had *changed* him, made him different from the others. But it would be many years before the implications of that difference would come to light.

Most of the land that was to eventually become Pallo's kingdom belonged to the Wolves, but it contained a little corner of Wasp as well. There was a monitor tower that the Wolves had never deigned to use, and now its Eye was dead. Pallo used to spend a lot of time up in the monitor tower looking out across Everien. There with a simple spyglass, he saw out across the Ripping and down into Everien.

On the day he caught his first Pharicians, there had been a blackness where most of Bear Country should be, as if the whole land lay under a particularly dark cloud, but even as Pallo looked on, the land brightened from east to west, lit by some invisible sun that raced across the sky and then fell again, so that an entire day passed in the space of a few minutes. Pallo looked hard with his spyglass, but he could not see enough detail from this distance to tell whether the people in Bear Country were moving around at a similarly accelerated rate—or, indeed, whether people were moving around at all. He wondered whether the Bears knew that they were moving through time much too fast. It did not occur to him to ask himself whether his time was right or wrong—he merely assumed that, because the timeserpent had not come here, this land was operating on the "old time," the time before the Li'ah'vah.

As for the rest of Wolf Country, today it flickered unevenly as if day and night were succeeding one another so rapidly that neither one could take hold in the eye. Pallo couldn't see past the mountains into Snake Country or Seahawk Country, but down in the central valley, where the Li'ah'vah had done the worst damage, the land had been sliced into curving sections, each of which appeared to obey a different set of time-laws. Sometimes it was difficult to peer through the rest of Wolf Country to see the lowlands—for although today Wolf Country was "flickering," two weeks before it had brooded under the same slow darkness that now gripped the corner of Wasp and Deer Country just below A-vi-Sirinn—the darkness of a seemingly endless night. Sometimes Pallo could see the smoke over A-vi-Khalar in the far distance, a smudge on the blue sky. What a burning they must have there, he thought, if he could see it all the way up here with no Eye to aid him.

Even years later, Pallo could remember how he had wrapped his cloak tight and paced the monitor tower, letting his glance fall to the activities of his own people as they trudged through last night's fresh snow. No one in Wolf Country knew of Pallo's role in the creation of the timeserpent or the massacre of the Deer at A-vi-Sirinn, and he had been too ashamed to speak of it. The Clansmen who lived in this part of the world counted themselves lucky that the timeserpent hadn't eaten them, and were kind to any survivors they met who had somehow made it across the Ripping. Pallo had been befriended by a Wolf chieftain called Ravel, who accepted his guidance on matters concerning the Ripping, the Knowledge, and the monsters, and who in turn sent men to test some of Pallo's theories about his new country. He had been willing to talk for long hours about timeserpents and the

83

difference between H'ah'vah and Li'ah'vah, and monsters, and Jai Pendu, and he had not laughed at Pallo's "magic" book of maps, which he took with him everywhere.

On that fateful morning, Ravel had been leading a party of men out to hunt. Ravel himself carried a flamethrower captured from one of Illyra's men in the attack on Xeel's village at the end of the old year. Pallo had been glad not to be going with them, and he didn't care if anyone called him a coward. The salamanders that had been creeping upcountry from the wreckage of the valley were proving difficult foes even for the courageous Wolf warriors. Pallo knew they wished for the aid of a few Wasps. How many times had he heard Ravel complaining to his men that a good Wasp was worth ten of them? The axmen had hung their heads. To be compared to a Wasp was almost as bad as being compared to a Bear, and the only thing worse than that was to be called a Deer. The latter was a cause for either a duel or suicide, depending upon the disposition and courage of the insultee. But Ravel was right. Men who got close enough to the salamanders to cut with their axes were grabbed and eaten on the spot, and even an axe-throw could not be made without entering within the range of the salamander spittle, which corroded metal in minutes and flesh in seconds.

Pallo shuddered. Well, the Wolves had only encountered the salamanders because they had been curious enough to go downcountry to see what had happened to everybody else, and they had found the source of the Ripping where the Li'ah'vah had slid through the earth and erupted into the forest. The hole it left, they said, made a H'ah'vah tunnel look like a rabbit hole, and the darkness inside made the darkest night seem like daylight. Pallo thought that the latter observation was illogical—how could there be a darkness darker than darkness itself?—but he was not about to challenge the accuracy of this description by having a look for himself. He would rather be called a Deer than face the monsters crawling out of what had once been Everien.

Pallo took a last, sighing look around the semicircular windows. He had lived to see the end of the world, but the Powers that rule time had not bothered to mop up the detritus, and there was nothing to do but sit back and wait for the last flickers of life to die out. He turned his attention to the H'ah'vah tunnel that led to Ristale, wondering whether he would ever persuade Ravel or anyone else to get the courage up to try crossing into Ristale. Pallo privately doubted that he would. The tunnel was never used, being dark and treacherous and cursed, and most of all long. Very long. It went all the way under the mountains to Ristale, and it was cursed because Night had once used it to steal Wolves and attack the Pharician forest garrison.

Then he saw it, hovering in the entrance to the tunnel. A bird. Not flying, but hanging in the air, motionless, as though frozen and unable to fall. It was pale gray, not very large, but the sunlight hit its wings strikingly.

Pallo dropped his spyglass and practically fell out of the tower.

"Ravel," he screamed, so loudly that the Wolf heard him half a mile below. "The H'ah'vah tunnel! Quick! Something's happening!"

When they got to the edge of the tunnel, the bird was flitting about in the pine trees. It was a Pharician flier, and it was plainly upset and out of sorts. Pallo thought it looked weak and ill, and made Ravel feed it; Ravel looked at him as though he were insane. The bird looked at Ravel, screamed, and stole a tuft of fur from his cloak. Then it shot back into the tunnel and disappeared.

"They're coming," Pallo said nervously. "The Pharicians. That bird was sent to gather information."

Ravel had not wanted to station a guard there, but he did so. For three weeks, nothing happened. Ravel came to Pallo and told him if he wanted to know what was happening in the H'ah'vah tunnel, he had better go and look himself; but no Wolf would enter that cursed place. Pallo begged him for one more week.

"One more *day*," Ravel had growled. And that night, a lone Pharician had oozed through the entrance of the tunnel in slow motion, collapsing exhausted in the snow.

"You were right!" Ravel told Pallo, clearly impressed. "Now what do we do?"

"Leave it to me," said Pallo. And so his indirect conquest of Pharice began; for he never had to lift a weapon, and of the soldiers who took his commands, none lost blood nor drew it. It was to be a singular war.

"IT IS NOBLE TO build a better mousetrap," Pallo had confided to Dheri once, years after Ravel had died and while slightly drunk. "Men have thrown their lives away for less. Let us work on the portcullis design tomorrow."

Dheri was a builder, and his greatest life's work was King Pallo's castle. The fortress had been built according to the Pharician style, out of square stone blocks mined near the Ripping, where, for some reason, the earth seemed to part more readily before the tools of the stonecutters. Maybe, in the adjacent time frame, the stone was *already* cut, or melted by the faster pace of that time frame—for Dheri the builder had heard the Scholars say that the faster a thing moved, the hotter it became. In any case, the first Pharician workers had had no trouble in removing the stone from the Everien range, where Wolf Country bordered Wasp. Though they were soldiers, they knew how to build, and King Pallo was lucky in that Dheri was among the first wave to arrive through the H'ah'vah tunnel to Ristale.

He had been called simply "Dher" in those days, for he had not yet acquired the Deer suffix that Pallo was to award him. Dher and his troop had made cities for Hezene all over his empire, even as far away as Aranoka where the jungles made even walking a hardship, let alone large-scale construction.

Dher was considered a gifted engineer, but he was not the leader of the seven hundred men that Hezene sent into Everien after the catastrophe at the Fire Houses. A colonel called Beule had that duty, for he was the commander of the Ristale garrison adjacent to the H'ah'vah tunnel that the emperor planned to use to penetrate Everien undetected. It was the very same tunnel that Night had used to attack the Ristale garrison with Slave forces, so in those fevered days and weeks after the eruption of the timeserpent and the loss of all contact with Jai Khalar, Hezene had been pleased as rum to turn the tables and send his men *into* Everien.

Beule was a man of few words. As was typical in Pharician battle squads, Beule had very little to do with directly commanding the men, but used his most immediate subordinate to do all of his dirty work. Beule was, in essence, a little emperor, while his second—in this case, an enthusiastic young lieutenant colonel called Tia—was the acting tyrant. As they prepared to enter the tunnel, Tia had been flushed with excitement, Dher remembered—for as it turned out, every other means of accessing Everien soil from without had failed due to the vagaries of time and location within that tortured, divided country. Beule, Tia, and the seven hundred, including Dher, were the emperor's best hope of getting into Everien.

Beule had timed their passage through the tunnel so that they would emerge in Everien at night, thereby buying themselves time to secure a good position while still under cover of darkness. The Scholar Rokas had reminded Tia that, because time in Everien was severely disrupted by the timeserpent, he could not count on knowing what time of day or even year it would be on the other end of the tunnel; but Tia did not seem able to take account of this, and shooed the Scholar away. Dher could see that the commander was overexcited. No one really expected to find any Clansmen directly on the other side of the tunnel, anyway; the region was too remote to boast a settlement of any real size.

The men had suffered in good spirits the slippery floors of the H'ah'vah tunnel, its near imperviousness to light of any kind, and the eerie way that it seemed to swallow their voices rather than magnify them as any other tunnel would have done. They knew that such anomalies had to be accepted in Everien. Even so, in reaching the far end, they had met with an unpleasant surprise.

The tunnel rose to the surface in what at first appeared to be a vertical wall of still water. Beyond this point, everything looked and sounded slow and thick, and the winds that flowed through the H'ah'vah tunnel sometimes seemed to strike this barrier and blow back harder, and at other times to accelerate and be sucked into the wavering slowness at the surface. Bassy, sepulchral noises came from without, and the light there was sticky and weak.

Tia beckoned to Dher. His skin, normally golden brown, looked saffron in this light, and his eyes were totally black. Dher felt his nerves tightening, and his breath came a little faster. Tia said, "Have you ever seen anything like this in Aranoka?"

Dher shook his head, realizing that such a question only revealed the unexpected depths of Tia's ignorance about Everien. Tia now turned reluctantly to Rokas the Scholar, who, without being prompted, offered, "It may be a shock wave resulting from the disaster at the Fire Houses."

"And how are we to penetrate it?"

The Scholar thought for a moment. Dher wondered if there really was anything in the old Everien texts pertaining to such phenomena, for the Scholar's eyes shifted when he answered, and he scratched his nose for no reason, just as if he were making up a story.

"It is best to use a head-on assault," the Scholar said.

Tia grunted. Dher knew that Tia was no different than most

soldiers: ill disposed to the privileged Scholars with their soft bodies and, one suspected, their softer heads. Tia would not trust this man with anyone's life. "Very well," Tia said. "You go first."

The Scholar blanched. "However," he added hastily, "I suggest we send a bird to collect samples of whatever it finds on the other side. To reassure us that we will be safe."

"Is that wise?" Dher put in, unable to resist playing with the Scholar. "What if it gives us away to whoever or whatever is out there?"

"True," Beule said, stroking his beard and nodding. "But it is better than charging headlong into the unknown."

"Yes, yes, exactly!" Rokas agreed. "Let us first determine if this barrier can be crossed by living things. For mine is only a theory, and—"

"Shut up," Tia said. He glanced at Beule, who nodded. "Give me an unmarked bird. A smart one."

The byrdboy was summoned and instructed to select a plain bird without imperial markings, yet intelligent enough to bring back good clues about the world on the other end of the tunnel. The byrdboy whispered to his charge and released it. It flew into the light as if entering a hurricane, bobbing and beating hard against the air resistance at the end of the tunnel. Then it gave a cry, and was gone.

They waited. The troop was told to stand down, and food and water were broken out to refresh them after their long, dark journey. The men spoke in whispers or not at all. So did the deep earth affect people, Dher had learned from experience in the mines of Aranoka. For himself, he shut his eyes and tried to conserve his strength, but Tia kept asking him questions and pacing up and down. At last, the bird returned.

The troop let out a cheer, and Tia smiled for the first time, patting the byrdboy on the head as he held his charge aloft for Beule to inspect. The bird was unharmed. It carried a small pinecone and a scrap of burned pine in its claws, and a tuft of Wolf fur in its beak. The byrdboy praised it melodiously in his own tongue, then touched its feathers with surprise. He began to examine the bird carefully, at last appealing to Tia, who permitted him to speak because he was well-disposed toward the boy and his bird at the moment.

"He older. Six maybe seven year. Older. Gonna die maybe soon."
"What?"

"Look, see feather? See claw, see beak? See eye? He same bird, but much old."

Tia shuddered. "Take it away," he said angrily. He turned to the Scholar. "Well?"

"I don't know! I have never heard of such a thing. The boy must be mistaken."

Beule had turned away and was smoking his pipe while a boy servant offered him scented oils for his nerves. Tia had the reins in his hands.

"We will do a second test," Tia said to Rokas. "Now it is your turn."

He looked at Dher, and Dher looked at the Scholar. He drew his short sword. Rokas preceded him down the tunnel, quivering but not protesting. Like a sacrificial animal going drugged to the fire, Dher thought. He also thought Tia was being unnecessarily cruel and that the young commander's ambition far exceeded his experience; but these same qualities made Tia a dangerous man to cross. If Dher showed anything less than total cooperation with Tia, it would be his head on the block. Tia was not secure enough in his leadership to listen to anyone's advice, even an older, more experienced campaigner like Major Dher.

So Dher had pushed the Scholar along the tunnel. When the end drew near, Dher halted. The air throbbed. Ahead, the walls of the tunnel seemed to deliquesce, and he had the strange and hypnotic feeling that the light from outside was beating against his face in irregular pulses. He felt sleepy.

"Go on, you white-livered book-mutt!" called Tia to the Scholar. "Dher, if he doesn't go, put a bolt in his back."

Dher sheathed his sword and slipped his crossbow from his back, fitting a bolt with a distracted air. He wasn't at all sure it would fly straight, but he followed Tia's command and aimed it at the hesitating Scholar.

"I'm going, I'm going!" Rokas cried, waving his arms.

"What do you see?" Dher called softly, hoping Tia could not hear him over the noises made by the barrier. "Are there men out there?"

"No men," the Scholar said. "Only trees and sky. There are shining things moving, like fires, and the sky—"

"Go on, you fat pig!" Tia shouted.

Dher could dimly see what the Scholar meant. He began to edge forward along the tunnel, prodding the red-robed man on. As if through a blown veil he could see the horizon between land and sky, and he could see the shadows moving along the ground as the sun passed quickly overhead.

"That's strange," he muttered.

"Push him on!" Tia urged.

The Scholar tottered forward, hands outstretched.

"Angelic beings!" he cried. "Servants of our emperor, men who fly, beings woven of light, not flesh . . ."

Dher did not like it when men waxed poetic in times of stress. It usually meant a nasty death was to follow.

"Go, then, or end up a pincushion," he exhorted through clenched teeth. The Scholar glanced back at him once, then raced into the blurry world outside. And disappeared.

The troop made the darkness rustle behind Dher's back.

"Well?" demanded Tia.

"I can't see him."

He heard Tia coming up the tunnel toward him. Dher blinked and yawned, confused by the sight glimpsed in the gel-like barrier that formed the end of the tunnel. The slurred images were beginning to resolve into a picture of a world, and there were indeed bright things moving . . . but *winged beings*? Not quite. More like fast, blurred trails left by things too quick for the eye.

Then, abruptly, a bird flew out of the light. It was as plain and ordinary, and as incongruous, as an old shoe left in an imperial jewel box. It passed Dher and Tia, calling, and swerved to meet the byrdboy.

"It has a message!" Dher exclaimed.

"Give it here." Tia snatched the scroll from the astonished byrdboy. While he was reading it, Dher turned his dazed attention to the bird. It seemed very much like the first one they had sent. In fact, the two were grooming one another and chattering like old friends.

"I no understand," said the byrdboy. "This never I see. How Jundun bird come to Everien?"

Tia wasn't paying attention. He was too busy chuckling and flapping the message.

"Good! Our people are already there."

Dher wanted to see the message himself, but he waited deferentially for his commander's orders.

"They have established control but urgently require reinforcements. We are come just in time!"

Tia raced to share the news with Colonel Beule, leaving Dher to wonder why a man hadn't been sent to deliver this message, rather than a mere bird. Unless the H'ah'vah tunnel *was* dangerous, in which case . . .

"We will move forward immediately," Tia said, returning from a hasty conference. "Dher, you go ahead. I appoint you my sub. I would not ask you to walk before the men were this a battle, but they will need you to give them confidence or they may shrink from the obstacle before them."

Dher nodded his acceptance. Tia could not be expected to lead from the front, although if Beule had any sense, he would force his second to do just that—Tia was starting to think of himself as the commander, not Beule. Officers almost never went to the front of the troop, unless they were either crazy bastards like Tash, or else virtually assured of victory without risk to themselves, in which case they could be seen in the van, shouting and waving their weapons. Dher didn't relish the thought of being Tia's sub, but of such was a man's career made in the Pharician army. If he succeeded, he could expect promotion while in the field, maybe even his own command once they were established in Everien. And why shouldn't he succeed? On the other side of the tunnel waited friends. All that was left for him to do was to walk forward in the Scholar's footsteps. If that dry little turd could do it, so could he.

Tia was ordering the men into ranks behind Dher. Suddenly, Dher's chest swelled with pride, and he drew his sword.

"In the name of Hezene!" he cried through a tight throat. "Onward!"

Breathing short, white breaths in the cold air of the tunnel, he moved forward at a run. As he progressed, the swirl of images outside grew more confused. The air seemed to press and pull on him almost at the same time, and his body felt alternately light and heavy. He tried to assess whether he had reached the point where the Scholar had disappeared, and could not. He tried to speak, and could not. He felt he was swimming, then drowning; and finally, eyes open but seeing only a kaleidoscope of bright and senseless things, he felt he was floating.

HE JERKED AWAKE in a snowbank. There was a spear pointed at his chest and when he convulsively began sitting up, his breastplate clanged against it. Dher shrank back.

The spear was Pharician, its tip polished to an exquisite point, its barbs gleaming wickedly; but the man who plied it was Clan. Of his face Dher could see very little: a thick black beard obscured the features. He wore fur leggings, a chain-mail tunic, and a tattered Pharician-style infantry cloak that had seen many better days. Nothing on him showed Pharician rank, but he wore the Wolf paint on his forehead. It was just visible beneath his helmet, which sported a single, curving horn like a rhinoceros snout. The tip was black with old blood.

Dher looked around quickly, taking in his surroundings despite the shock. He had been dragged some fifty paces from the exit of the H'ah'vah tunnel, probably by the other men who were ranged around him, their weapons drawn, their eyes brought to bear on him as one. Some were Bear, some Wolf, and one, to his surprise, was a blond-haired, rather youthful-looking Wasp who addressed him in perfect Pharician.

"I am King Pallo," he said. "Welcome to the Oasis in the Ripping. You cannot leave, unless you return to the tunnel from which you came, as your bird returned some years ago in order to lure you here. See? Your men are just beginning to follow you now."

Dher was now allowed to sit up, and he saw the first rank of soldiers as they materialized from the tunnel. They looked like statues at first, moving incrementally in tiny jerks on the other side of the watery barrier, but as they broke through into Everien, they suddenly speeded up. By then it was too late. They had been trussed up in nets by King Pallo's men, who dumped them in the snow and bound them, and returned to capture the next rank as they slowly oozed through the gap.

"So may a handful of men capture a whole army of Pharicians in their prime," said King Pallo. "Welcome to my country. You lot are what I have been waiting for all these years, and we will do great things together!"

TIME ON HIS SIDE

$\mathcal{I}$t took over a month for the whole army to pass into Everien, with those who were already captive powerless to warn the others about what awaited them on the other side of the barrier. When Pallo learned that the real commander was Beule and that he would be among the last to arrive, he ordered Beule executed the moment he emerged, "for cowardice," he said, adding, "And I want no revolts among my new soldiers. Come, Dher, drink mead with me and let us talk. We have many plans to make."

At first their conversations were conducted in the cave dwellings that the Clans had been obliged to retreat to upon finding themselves hemmed in by the timeserpent within the Oasis, as Pallo called it. In these early days, it was not altogether clear to Dher what lay beyond the Oasis, in the Ripping—only that monsters came through the seams sometimes, and sometimes "other portents," though no one would say exactly what those were. Contact with the rest of Everien was nonexistent, with the small population of the Oasis dependent entirely upon their own efforts for survival.

Pallo, it emerged, wasn't a "real" king with an army and acknowledged landholdings; he was a self-declared savior of the people who had decided to take matters into his own hands. He had a few loyal followers—one of them an old Wolf called Ravel—and a very active imagination.

"One thing I've learned in my travels," said the fresh-faced boy to Dher, who was easily ten years his senior, "is that things ain't always what they seem. And that power is there for the taking. Just because a man looks authoritative, it doesn't mean that he is."

Dher found this philosophy baffling, especially coming from a half-breed Pharician like Pallo, and said so. Pallo only laughed.

"Everien is a crazy place, my friend. Nothing goes quite to plan, so you have to be an opportunist here. Tell him about the tunnels, Ravel."

The skinny old man with a bald head and only one eye let out a wheezing laugh that turned into a coughing fit. "The tunnels, ah, the tunnels. We could use an engineer to explain the tunnels to us, although I think a witch would be more effective."

"What tunnels?" Dher asked.

"The H'ah'vah tunnels, like the one you came through. This part of Everien, from A-vo-Manik in Wasp to A-vel-Jasse in Wolf, is riddled with H'ah'vah tunnels. Or rather, we think—"

"You think," interrupted Pallo.

"I think, rather they are Li'ah'vah tunnels. Or some of them."

"Li'ah'vah . . . isn't that just another word for the timeserpent that has been made in the Fire House?"

"Indeed," Ravel said. "It is a creature of legend. Some say a Li'ah'vah and a H'ah'vah are the same thing. Some say the Li'ah'vah was older. But others believe that the Li'ah'vah could tunnel through time as well as stone."

"I've been in a Li'ah'vah tunnel once, in my youth," Pallo remarked. "But it didn't travel through time. It was just a big tunnel."

Ravel said, "That's exactly the reason most people think the Li'ah'vah are creatures of legend. Because the time-changing properties of their tunnels don't seem to exist anymore, and, well, what works in one time should work in another. Isn't that the whole point of a time-tunnel? *But*"—and here he held up a finger to indicate a caveat—"ever since what happened at the Fire Houses, I personally believe that anything is possible. Maybe these tunnels have been reawakened somehow, recently. Take that sewer that the two of you washed up in. It was a natural tunnel, and it existed long before the city was built. Who's to say that it had nothing to do with the timeserpent?"

From the expressions on the men's faces, Dher gathered that they were reciting an old discussion, partly for his benefit, but mostly for theirs.

Pallo said, "We will know the answer to that question only when Wakhe returns." He turned to Dher. "Wakhe, you may recall, was the Pharician Scholar who caused the timeserpent to be created in the Fire House in the first place. He and I were sent here together as a result of the initial shock wave. We found ourselves in an old sewer in A-vo-Manik, on the opposite side of my kingdom from here. Wakhe proved difficult to manage. He returned through the tunnel and was never seen again. I stayed. Ravel and I and some others made a systematic inspection of all H'ah'vah tunnels within the boundaries created by the Ripping. We watched and guarded them, to see which might be safe as bolt-holes when the denizens of the Ripping attacked, and which were potential sources of invasion from without."

Ravel interjected, "That is how we happened to have men stationed at the entrance of the tunnel to intercept Rokas when he came through. Then we interrogated him about the makeup of the force he brought with him."

With time on his side, Ravel went on to explain, the would-be king Pallo found it all too easy to lie in wait, seizing each of the Pharicians as he emerged until he had the entire army penned up in Wolf caves, guarded by real wolves, and frightened out of their wits. By the time Dher arrived, Pallo already knew who he was and what his abilities were concerning the construction of buildings and roads and the organizing of men; and without any apparent reservations, he took Dher into his confidence almost immediately. For his own part, Dher saw how badly Pallo needed someone like him. It was almost as if they were fated to meet.

"I am going to bring this country into the future . . . whatever future may await it. I am going to address the dangers of the Ripping. If I were to return to the Fire Houses like Wakhe, I would age there as ordinary men. Here, I have extra time. I have good maps. And most of all, I have plans for our defense. Now that I have so many captives, so much free labor, I am going to become king in both word and deed. And you, Dher, are going to help me."

So it was that Dher came to design first the Ripping Wall and, when that gave Pallo the status he needed to be confirmed in his authority, subsequently King Pallo's castle. Of course, there were times when he, like all of his compatriots, thought of escaping back to Ristale through the H'ah'vah tunnel; but then he would think of the bird, and change his mind. The thought of returning home only to find that he had aged years in a matter of minutes was too depressing. And, in truth, he enjoyed the responsibility and relative autonomy of the project.

Nor was Pallo in any hurry. Some men might be alarmed at finding their lives slipping away at high speed while, in an adjacent land, time moved more slowly. Not Pallo. Maybe it was because he had the unique advantage of never seeming to age; he once confessed to Dher that he believed he was still living as if he remained in the Fire Houses, as though a piece of *that* time had come with him across the Ripping and stayed around him like a cloak to protect him from the swiftly moving wind of *this* time. Pallo did not explain how, if this was true, he could see and hear and speak to the people of *this* time, and Dher didn't think the king really knew, himself. But Pallo made it clear that he saw in his situation a unique opportunity to build up a strong nation, independent of outside intervention. No one could invade: the Ripping was impenetrable by men, and as far as the H'ah'vah tunnel was concerned, Pallo merely stationed a constant watch on it. Nothing passed through at a rate faster than about an inch per minute, so there would always be ample warning of Hezene's successive attempts at penetration. Over the years, the fighting talent that Hezene had supplied gradually integrated with the locals. They settled down, mated with the indigenes, and built up a strong army. They hauled matériel for the castle. They bent their backs, they hunted, they worked. And Pallo's use of the occasional messenger bird with a carefully worded phrase or two ensured that this supply was regular and seemingly endless.

Dher tried to imagine how it must look from Hezene's point of view: men passing into Everien, sending no word at first, and then sending birds back through the tunnel asking for more help, which promptly disappeared as soon as it was sent. Sooner or later, the emperor would tire of such games, but as only a month or so passed for every few years in the Oasis, Dher probably would not live to see that day.

To speak of living and life spans, Dher found Pallo himself becoming an increasing enigma. From the day he stood over Dher and offered him friendship to the day his castle was finally complete, he changed not one whit. Dher himself acquired gray hairs in that building, and within ten years of the castle's completion, his hair began to fall out. The king's hair stayed blond. His skin stayed smooth, and his body remained lithe except for the small bulge of an incipient potbelly that was hardly surprising considering the king's penchant for honey cakes. Dher suspected that, though Pallo could scarcely be termed a natural authority figure, he put down his far more intimidating rivals simply by outlasting them. Other men tired; Pallo retained the exuberance of youth. Whatever explanation Pallo might have tried to offer about being caught in the Li'ah'vah's eruption, it was disconcerting to see him stay the same year after year.

Other eminent Clansmen campaigned against Pallo's castle, saying it was a waste of time and effort, especially when the abandoned Everien towns still stood, pristine as when they were built, unworn by time. Pallo opposed their use vehemently.

"We cannot inhabit the old Everien towns!" he declared to his followers. "Forget the mineral baths and the glass windows! We are better off in caves and tents."

"Caves and tents?" scoffed the other leaders, Wasp, Wolf, and Deer alike. "What good will they do us against the beasts of the Ripping? And what of the rest of Everien? Sooner or later, Tash will break through and come calling. Are we to defend ourselves from our huts?"

"That's why I am building a castle," Pallo would say, and everyone would groan at his delusions of grandeur, and the whole argument would begin all over again. Dher never learned the source of Pallo's distrust of Everien buildings, but he heard enough to guess that it had something to do with his memories of Jai Khalar, and probably also the traumatic experience of being in the Fire House when the timeserpent came, and subsequently getting timespewed halfway across Everien. And, maybe, it had something to do with the book of maps that Pallo carried. He had schemata for many Everien structures, and some said that in the Fire Houses he had brushed too close to the Knowledge to ever trust anything Everien-made again.

Faithfully, Dher constructed the fortress, and by the time it was done he had risen in status and had been renamed Dheri as a member of the Deer Clan. During the building of the castle, his friendship with Pallo had grown, and they had stood side by side on the walls during the winter of the castle's first year of completion, when a thundering herd of what looked like sharks with six legs came pouring out of the Ripping and attacked the Oasis. The castle walls held true, the Wasp archers successfully poisoned and killed most of the attackers, and the avalanche caused by their stampede left the castle high and dry: Dher had taken such possibilities into account when he selected the site. Suddenly, Pallo's self-declared kingship was no longer the brunt of jokes. He had more soldiers than anyone else, and because they observed Pharician discipline, they made less trouble for him than the end-less quantities of squabbling younger sons made for the Clan chief-tains who relied on their own loins to build their power. With his castle complete, Pallo the Young really was a king.

And by the time the work was finished, old Ravel the Wolf was dead, and Dher became Pallo's closest advisor. The years flew by. Dheri successfully introduced some of the ways of the Deer people of Ristale into this small corner of Everien. Without access to downland agriculture, the Deer were forced into herding. Dheri taught the young people, including his own six children, how to ride the horned deer and how to use falcons to defend the herd from wolves. For their part, the Wolf Clan were much impressed with the sight of the deer-mounted men with their falcons perched on crossbars set on spearheads, racing through the snow and driv-ing away entire packs of wolves at a time. The Wolf men, steel-bladed though they were while the Deer continued to use sticks in hand-to-hand combat, did not look quite so far down their noses at the Deer anymore. In fact, considering that the explosive weapons that Tash had introduced were unpredictably dangerous during avalanche season, the Wolves had to admit there was something to be said for the effectiveness of the silent, winged hunters.

No, Dheri did not miss Pharice. But Tia did, as did a number of the newer officers who found their way through the tunnel and were absorbed into Clan society. From the seven hundred troops that Dher had marched with, there were now two thousand men of fighting age, counting fathers and sons; and an additional five hundred had been poached recently and were beginning to settle in and breed. The Pharicians were a minority, but a growing one, and their impact was felt on the country that already boasted a mélange of cultures. Tia and his ilk did everything they could to create a "Little Pharice" and never stopped thinking of themselves as the civilizing force among savages. Yet the extremities of land-scape and climate, not to mention the vagaries of Ripping monster activity, meant that order and rigid rule simply could not work here. Everien was a scruffy place, all the more so now that the old structures had been abandoned and the sparkling Artifacts of the Knowledge were fallen into disuse.

"Just you wait," Tia would sometimes say, late at night when the Clansmen were all gone from the castle common room and the

Pharicians were deep in their cups. "One day Hezene will figure out how to penetrate to us. Maybe not in our lifetime, but in our sons' or grandsons'. Remember, time moves slower there. The seasons spin too fast for us, and we will not live to see the outcome. That doesn't matter. Hezene will come one day, and our people will be vindicated."

In truth, Dheri did not believe him. Even Tia was now called Tiavel. Their days as the heralds of the Pharician Empire were over.

WHEN HEZENE DID finally send more soldiers, Dheri was with Pallo in the king's planning room, which overlooked the bridge leading to the castle as well as the Ripping Wall. His eyes, though not so sharp for reading, were as good as ever for distance, and he spotted the train of returning deer-riders as soon as they appeared on the snowy road. The bird-messenger detached itself from the party and began to fly in dips and swoops toward the tower. Dheri touched Pallo's arm and the king looked up from the charts they'd been studying for a new forgery near the river. Pallo reached for a spyglass and strode to the window in two long, economical paces. Dheri followed more slowly, joints stiff with arthritis and the endless cold.

"You are a charmed man, my King," he said as his ropy hands gripped the stone sill for balance. "You move like a youth."

"Ha!" said Pallo. "Another load of Pharicians! Hezene just keeps feeding me men! If only he knew."

The bird-messenger swooped through the open window and offered up its message. Pallo read it with increasing delight.

"Ah, it's so much fun, Dheri! I've been wanting to tell you about this for years, but I wasn't sure if it was going to work."

"If what was going to work?"

"Remember your old commander Beule the coward? Well, before we killed him I made him write a message to Hezene. I have been waiting to see what Hezene would do, whether he would take the bait. And it seems that he has. Instead of the small scouting parties he has sent up until now, including your group, he now has dispatched an army of four thousand men into the H'ah'vah tunnel. Their first men have just reached us and are being questioned. This could be our biggest capture yet!"

Dheri listened thoughtfully. He was now sixty years old. He had eleven children by three women, and five had sons of their own. Pallo looked younger than all of Dheri's children. He was excited, thrilled with his trickery (typical Wasp, Dheri thought), and keen at the prospect of a large coup.

"You will have no labor shortage this summer, my friend," Pallo said. "But there is more. There is a man among this force who is Clan. He is a Seahawk-born trader called Grietar, and it is said he wields a book of Knowledge."

Dheri still didn't speak. To him the Knowledge meant nothing but trouble.

"Four thousand men?" he muttered. "The prison will be full."

"Aye . . . but they need not be prisoners for long! We will have a strong army. Let the emperor send ten thousand! Nothing would please me more. Come, Dheri. You may as well talk to them. Help them to get settled. Explain to them that they will be here for a long, long time."

BEFORE THIS ALL STARTED

It was as if Ice had gained some special vitality by finally avoiding the arrow that should have killed him; or else, maybe, Tarquin had simply forgotten what it was like to be mounted on such a steed. Ice was not a heavy horse; he was nowhere near the size of the plow horses that the Deer and Bear Clans used, and the warhorses that the heavily armored Pharicians rode would tower over this silver stallion. But Ice's quickness could not be denied, and what he lacked in musculature, he more than made up for with fiery aggression of a kind that many horse-trainers would call perverse. The animal was hale, and every lineament of him worked smoothly. Even his coat seemed to sparkle in the new moonlight, and though he moved at blinding speed, so that Tarquin had to work hard to keep himself glued to Ice's rhythm, the horse did not try to unseat his rider.

As final proof that he was in full command of himself, now Ice carried Tarquin along a White Road that was more coherent than any of its predecessors. It was as if some tiny cog had slipped into place at last, and the strange machinery of the Liminal was now revealed as something better designed than a collection of monstrous parts—it was *almost*, Tarquin dared to think, as if the Liminal had acquired the order of waking thought. It was no longer the mash of dreams he had come to know, and dread.

For now, anyway, the White Road was just a road.

The way was chalk bordered by a white stone curb about two feet in height. It passed through grassland that had been grazed short by what Tarquin guessed must be wild herds, for he could see no sign of fences or shelters. The road flirted with a winding stream, now crossing it, now running alongside, now diverging, only to bend and return to the river again. On either side rose pine-clad hills bristling with sharp spires of white stone, veiled by mist and darkness. Slowly the road climbed, until it was hugging the right-hand side of the valley. The ground fell away to the left, dropping sheer to the pale rush of water that was the river, its noise fading gradually as the path climbed. Now there was no curb on the right side, and Ice dropped his stride to a smooth trot. They were traveling at a more earthly pace than Ice's usual blur of speed, but all the same Tarquin saw pebbles go flying from his sparking hooves and disappear over the brink. Still they climbed.

He wondered where in Everien they were. He could see no lights, no signs of human habitation anywhere; but the road was well kept.

"Ice," he managed to say. "Could we stop for a minute? How my back aches."

Ice's ears flicked back at the sound of Tarquin's voice, but he did not alter his pace, and Tarquin's efforts to persuade him to stop by shifting his weight only made the horse speed up.

In a matter of a few minutes they had climbed to a dizzying height, and now the road turned in to the mountain, which was bare of all but the most tenacious and wizened trees that eked out a precarious existence in the cracks of white stone. Tarquin hazarded a glimpse over his shoulder and he could see that behind him was no longer a valley or another set of mountains, but a vast plain bordered on the south by a glint of sea.

Ristale? He might have said so, and guessed that he could be riding up into the southern mountain range of Everien, possibly on a road very like the switchback path that climbed to the sea plateau. But this was impossible, for the road had mounted into the hills and was climbing between the peaks, which could not be done from Ristale because of the thousand-foot-high cliffs where Everien had been wrenched away from the rest of the world.

This could not be the border of Everien.

But it looked like Everien. Tarquin shivered and leaned forward, holding on to the heat of Ice with a feeling of childish need. He was beginning to wish he had not asked to go back. This was not a world he knew.

The moon disappeared behind the mountain. They were no longer ascending, but had passed into a deep cutting only a few cart-widths across. Tarquin automatically thought of ambush, and found himself uneasily studying the rocks overhead to either side. This was the kind of place he would have positioned his men if he wanted to intercept a Sekk Slaving party, or bring down a rampaging monster. He felt vulnerable and wished for the cleft to open soon.

But it did not. The road plunged into the mountainside itself, and everything went dark. He could just make out the milky path of the road ahead of him, and he could see Ice's mane and the tips of his ears as if they were starlit; but they were not. It was merely that the faintest of lights filtered into the tunnel from an unknown source, for he could also see tiny flickers of mica in the rock walls where they caught hold of light that would otherwise have been imperceptible. Ice's unshod hooves rang out assertively, but above them also rose a ghostly howling where the wind eddied and rushed in the hidden chimneys and caverns of this dark place.

He tried not to listen to the sound of the wind. He told himself it was only wind; it was not music; it was not singing; it had no other meaning.

The dark journey lasted too long for his peace of mind. To protect himself from the unyielding blackness, Tarquin closed his eyes from time to time, retreating within his own thoughts. Ice did not run steadily. Sometimes he walked; sometimes he broke into a wild run; sometimes he cantered smoothly as if to show off his conditioning. But little by little, the horse's progress took them down deeper and deeper, until Tarquin wondered if they were going to travel right through the earth itself and into whatever void lay beyond.

How Ice could see where he was going was a mystery to Tarquin. When Tarquin's eyes were shut he had the impression of light passing across his eyelids: whirling brightness and sharply cut shadows; but when he opened his eyes to catch a glimpse of these things, there was only darkness again. It was as well. If all the most glorious vistas of the White Road were spread out before him in a display of fantastic beauty, still he would have shut his eyes. He was thinking of Jaya.

He knew she wouldn't stay so vividly in his memory for very long. It is the cruel way of the mind, to make the past fade and change but never altogether leave. No matter how hard he tried to fix the details of her being—the shape of her wrists, the fall of her hair, the catch in her voice, the startling smallness of her body when briefly he held her—no matter if he committed them all to

103

memory with the greatest of care, still he would forget her. His memories would take on their own life and the truth of her would soon be lost.

But all through that ride, she lived in his mind. Again and again he relived her words, her movement, her touch. She was real to him now, and far from trying to forget his past, he wanted nothing more than to evoke it. For a long time he had been running away from the sorrow and unquenched anger and guilt of his mistakes at Jai Pendu, guided by a blend of high principle and futile despair and, maybe, stupidity. As long as his Company had been compromised, he had known he would have no hope of rest, of any kind of salvation. He could hope for his pain to lessen and to fade as he ran from it, but he had nothing to run toward. Nothing to replace what he had lost. His life had ended twenty years ago at Jai Pendu, and Tarquin was the sort of man who is freed by this. There was nothing more to lose—that had been the attitude of Tarquin the Free.

Now, when he looked at his actions and his motivations, everything seemed different. Unexpectedly, out of the middle of disaster and discord, his purpose and passion somehow congealed in the form of this girl (woman?) whom he barely knew but was bound to with a kind of inexorable heat.

It was a strange, unfathomable feeling. He hardly knew her. Maybe if he knew her, he wouldn't even like her. Yet in no time at all she had come to mean the glue that held together the fragments of a shattered life, repairing them to a fragile, re-formed shape— his life had not been what he thought. It might in fact become something totally new and unforeseen.

Jaya's face formed in his mind, eyes half-closed, lips parted. He felt lust; protectiveness; curiosity; and finally a possessive recognition that identified her as his and his alone. *Why had she let go his hand?*

It was dangerous, intemperate, and probably stupid, this feeling. He was no hot-blooded youth of twenty. He ought to know better. But this was not merely some ill-advised romance. To Tarquin, Jaya represented more than just a woman—a lover, a companion, a mate. She was the sense to everything that had happened in the past twenty years. If he could find her, fix this mess they were in, then something good would have come out of what up until now he had only considered a tragedy and a mess.

Suddenly, darkness gave way. Ice's muscles bunched; his head dropped, and for a second Tarquin thought the horse was about to buck him off. Then his eyes adjusted to the barrage of light, and he realized that they were descending the last few yards from the cave that Ice had taken him through. They were disgorged into a flat whiteness that seemed to go on forever without landmarks. Everything was buried in snow and ice, yet there was a fog in the air, and even the sky had a sheen of whiteness.

Tarquin shut his eyes and threw his arm over his face. A cold, hard wind began to blow, a wind fraught with freezing knives of sleet that sought out every gap in Tarquin's clothing and bit his skin like terrible insects. His heart was pounding like a kettledrum and his breathing roared loud in his throat as his chest tightened, shrinking against the frigid invasion of the wind. Ice's mane was rising and falling like a torn wave, brittle strands of frozen hair snapping off with the force of his passage. Everywhere was white, but now faint shadings began to appear: ragged edges of cloud; the bluish tones of algae-laden snow that reminded Tarquin of his Seahawk home and told him they must be near the ocean; and a pallid orb over their heads that could only be the high and distant sun.

Ahead, roiling mist obscured his view of what was otherwise a featureless plain. To the left there was nothing but cloud rising straight from the snow, and to the right he could just make out the shapes of mountains that offered suggestions of shapes against the white sky. Even as his mind added up the information and compared it to his catalog of Everien memories, Ice was pulling up his stride; and not a moment too soon. For Tarquin had just come to the realization that they were running along the top of the sea plateau and that the mist must be rising from the plain of Ristale, one thousand feet below at the bottom of the sharp precipice that Ice must now be approaching, although Tarquin could see nothing of it. His fingers, already blue and losing feeling, tightened on Ice's rough mane, and his legs worked to maintain balance as the horse slowed with an abruptness that would have unseated an unprepared rider.

Tarquin was thrown against Ice's neck and he lay there, soaking up the animal's heat and thanking his stars that they had not run over the edge. But then, he knew by now that he could trust Ice. He patted the horse's neck in wordless appreciation and peered ahead into the mist. Ice was still walking forward. A foul-smelling but slightly warmer wind was blowing toward them from what looked to be a vent in the ground, and Tarquin saw a break in the snow where rocks protruded, slick and dark. A few tendrils of steam escaped.

"I don't remember this," he muttered, dismounting. He strode closer to the source of the warmth, which was irresistible after the freezing wind. The ground was broken and it dipped into a sudden declivity. Stinking air hit him. Sulfur. He had a flash of recollection of his encounter with Chyko within the red crystal, where they had squatted by a river of fire while nearby, obscured by snow, terrible creations of metal and fire had belched and rumbled, tearing up the landscape. Then it was gone, and he was with Ice on the sea plateau.

He looked across the divide created by the vent. The mist had parted and he could see the land beyond. There was no cliff. He was not even on a plateau. He was on a plain that went on and on, stretching far south beyond the reach of Everien's mountains. The dark mass of a herd took up a good portion of it. He blinked and shook his head.

"Ice, where is the cliff? We are supposed to be *above* Ristale. There is a cliff just ahead there. I would know it anywhere."

He jumped from rock to rock, covering his face with his cloak to escape the worst of the stench, and crossed to the other side of the steam vent. The land was crisscrossed by steam vents, but it was level, indistinguishable from the bland emptiness of Ristale. Just on the border of his vision before the fog closed in, he could see a herd of reindeer moving slowly toward the sea. He guessed there must be thousands upon thousands of them. He turned. Ice was walking with his nose down as if looking for grass but finding none.

"Ice!" Tarquin cried, excited as the realization hit him. "Is this Jaya's time? The time of the Everiens? The Scholars always said that the cliff must have been torn upward at the time of the downfall of Everien, same as when the Floating Lands were cracked apart and the Everiens fled in Jai Pendu. Is it true?"

As if in answer, the horse's head came up and he let out a long, trumpeting whinny. It sounded like a challenge to other stallions; but there was no one else there.

"We had better go to the gates of Everien," Tarquin said. "I for one can't take much of this cold. Let us find this ancient civilization quickly! If we are going to do what has never been done, then let us at least do it before we freeze and crack to smithereens."

He crossed back over the vent and dragged himself up to mount Ice once again. The wound in his side was hurting badly, and the cold exacerbated the pain. He supposed that if Chyko's knife blade had struck a killing blow, he would be dead by now or at least incapacitated; still, he was surprised that he had made it this far after taking an internal wound. When he examined the flesh of his rib cage, he saw that the penetration wound had stopped bleeding and was already partially healed. Maybe the displacement by the time-serpent had affected his body in some way.

He gritted his teeth and decided not to think about it. He felt that fate owed him something, and he wasn't going to question his good luck. Besides, the injury still hurt him enough to be an inconvenience and a drain on his energy. He might have been lucky, but he was a long way from becoming victorious.

Ice moved off at a good clip. On any other horse, the journey to the mountain passage guarded by the invisible city Jai Khalar would have taken a couple of days. On Ice, it took less than an hour—which was just as well, for Tarquin was wearing next to nothing. He had not slept one night since leaving the forest where Night held Jaya, and before that he had been in the warm underground lair of the Snakes. This transition to archaic, frigid Everien was, to say the least, a shock.

He must have been insane in the wake of losing Jaya. For back amid the cracking and rending of Everien by the timeserpent, his romantic words had been not only rash, but stupid: "Take me back to before this all started." It was a noble thought, but now here he was with no clothing, no provisions, no assistance; no grass, even, for his fiery mount to eat. When Kere had offered to help him go into the past of Everien, he had expected to find himself among the splendor of the ancients, *inside* Everien with its protecting mountains, its great cities, its Knowledge. Instead, Ice had brought him to a cruel winter. He needed help soon, or he would die.

Just inland of the sea plateau, there was a gap in the ring of mountains that encircled Everien like a wall. To the right, set in a sharp ridge of mountaintop, the Eye Tower of Jai Khalar had kept watch invisibly on Everien's borders as well as her interior year after year. Tarquin had never known whether to pride himself on the fact that he could see what others could not, but at this moment, as Ice carried him toward the natural gates, he kept his eye fixed on the place where Jai Khalar should be, willing himself to see the ancient city. In the bitter cold, his concentration had narrowed and fixed on the idea of riding through those gates and up the road to the Citadel, where he would beg for assistance from anyone who might give it. The ancient Everiens were said to have as great a genius for medicine as for everything else, and he knew that, at the very least, they could offer him protection from the elements and grain for his horse. Maybe he would not find Jaya right away, but he would find others like her. Wise people who could help him.

But he couldn't see the Eye Tower. True, sleet was blowing in his eyes, and the mountains were winking in and out of view according to the clouds' caprice; but he began to fear that something was not right. The shape of the mountains was similar to what he knew, but it was not the same. And the "gates" did not look right at all. There seemed to be a slight gap in the mountains, but it was not the same shape as Tarquin remembered. And as they drew closer, he saw that beyond the gateway, instead of an open valley, there was a wall of ice several stories high.

All of Everien was buried beneath a glacier.

A FACE IN THE EYE

Tarquin experienced some bad moments as they approached the impregnable white wall. Ice was plowing diligently through the snow like an icebreaker, his head bobbing up and down and his muscles working without faltering. The closer they got to the edge of the glacier, the bigger it became, until they halted in its very shadow. Overhead, a large falcon cruised slowly back and forth, watching them. Tarquin covered his face with his hands.

"Ice," he said, "this can't be true. This can't be the right time. You have come back too far."

The horse had been standing with his weight spread over four splayed legs, breathing hard. He did not possess the thick coat needed for this climate, and his sweat was freezing on his sleek sides. Now Ice shifted beneath Tarquin in such a way as to remind his passenger that all of this was being done strictly as a favor: he was not tamed.

"But we'll die here," Tarquin protested. "This is suicidal. There are no people here. There can be no civilization in such a place. Jai Khalar is not there. The monitor towers are not there. Everien cannot have been born yet."

Even as he said the words, they unsettled him. How far back in time had they come, if Everien civilization had not yet even *begun*? And if there were no Everiens, maybe there were no people at all.

"Please," he said, holding fast to Ice's neck like a child, and shivering. "We have come back too far. We'll die. Take us to a time when there are monitor towers, at least. And at least take us to summer!"

He held his breath for a moment, thinking that perhaps he was taking the horse's powers for granted; that for his insolence Ice might very well dump him there and leave him. He clung for all he was worth with his legs and arms while Ice rose up on his hind legs, pawed the air, and let out another shrill cry. Then the horse was running along the bottom of the mountains, and the snow was whipping away beneath his hooves. It yielded to stones and mud and then to grass, and the sun came out like a yellow flag, bringing the heat and smells of green things growing. Ice shrugged Tarquin off his back, and while Tarquin was still rolling across the soft ground and trying to get upright, the horse fell to grazing as if he had a mind for nothing else.

"I'm sorry if I doubted you," Tarquin called to the horse, spitting dirt and rising. "I suppose when you travel thousands of years in a few heartbeats, it's easy to get it a little bit wrong. . . ." But his apology trailed off. He had righted himself and, shading his eyes against the glare of the sun, looked back toward Everien. The sea plain was bare of snow, but the glacier was still there.

He pressed his hand against his aching flank where the knife injury throbbed. He was hungry and his head hurt, and the sudden change in temperature soon set him sneezing. He cursed expressively; Ice grazed, unperturbed.

"Ice," he said carefully, "I think we had better go to the time when there is no glacier. The time when there were cliffs making the sea plain a plateau. But when the Everiens were here, too. Those times."

The horse blew a long snort and kept tearing the grass. Tarquin didn't much want to mount again, but he had little choice. He had the impression as Ice moved off beneath him that the horse was tired, too.

For it was a great span of time that Ice covered. He moved off toward the sea gates again, and this time the glacier yielded before him, receding before Tarquin's eyes so that by the time Ice raced into the valley, Everien was green, not white. He was watching time ooze across the land like a shadow. Tarquin entered the cold geometry of the valley, and the clouds rushed across the sky; the sun was a shining ribbon; the moon leaped about the heavens like a bouncing ball and winter's snow came and went from the lowlands in a breath. The shapes of the earth changed. Landslides; erosion; forests rising and falling; rivers cutting and wind depositing dirt softened Everien.

But there were no people.

Ice slowed to a trot, and then a walk. A herd of tiny deer fled before him. He stopped and began grazing.

Tarquin slid off his back. The horse must be tired. Soon there would be some sign of the ancient Everiens, he was sure. Maybe they had begun as a simple forest people, like the Wolf Clan; or maybe they would arrive on ships, like the Seahawk Clan. Except the Everien ships would have to be powered by the Knowledge, and full of a magic only they knew how to decipher. And then Tarquin could ask them for their help.

Light-headed, he wandered across the greensward where Ice had deposited him. He turned his head to keep the horse within his peripheral vision, and to his shock, he saw a monitor tower rising above the pine trees.

Suddenly, he wasn't tired anymore. He plunged through the forest until he had reached its base. The tower was in perfect condition. It bore no moss or vines, nor even the stain of dirt deposited by wind or rain. Tarquin climbed inside.

Throughout his life, the monitor towers had been mysterious structures. The glasslike globes they contained had not functioned until after Tarquin had brought the Water of Glass back from Jai Pendu, and Mhani had connected all the monitor towers to the Eye Tower in Jai Khalar so she could look out across Everien and watch the Sekk. But all of that had happened after Tarquin left Everien to begin his self-imposed exile, and what little experience of the Eyes that he possessed was an experience of Eyes tainted by the invasion of Night. So he climbed the tower and approached its resident Eye with a mixture of eagerness and fear.

The Monitor Eye was an imperfect sphere, slightly elliptical like an egg, about the size of a large orange from Jundun. It was sitting in a simple metal bracket, the fittings of which glowed slightly. He looked inside.

There was a crackling and singing in his ears. Lights wavered and shifted in the glass.

"Eteltar! You fool, don't you see the mess you've made? Look at the cliffs you have raised! Look at the devastation! You must return before there's more damage! Eteltar! Can't you hear us?"

He wasn't sure he could "hear" the voices, exactly. There seemed to be many of them, but he couldn't remember the specific words, only the sense and feeling of what they said. He felt disoriented. He closed his eyes.

"He's the wrong one," the voices said to each other. "Who are you? Explain yourself!"

Tarquin opened his eyes. There was a face in the Eye. It was a face he had seen once before, in a vision. Its skin was white, its hair was silver, and its eyes were blue-violet. It was a Sekk.

Tarquin let out a strangled cry and tore his gaze away. He vividly remembered the dreamlike experience of seeing this *thing* before; but during that vision, he had been looking in a mirror. Now his eyes were shut, but he could still feel the Sekk looking at him. He was still subject to the song that was ringing inside his head, without benefit of his ears.

"Who are you?" it sang. "Who are you?"

He struck out at the Monitor Eye with his fist and it rolled from its pedestal. Tarquin backed away, nearly falling through the trapdoor that had brought him here; then, with a monkeylike agility that came from fear, not skill, he got out of there as fast as he could.

SEVEN SYMBOLS

$\mathcal{I}$ don't want to see any more of ancient Everien," Tarquin averred, clinging to Ice's back once again. "They are Sekk! The Everiens are Sekk, and Jaya is Night, and that story that says I lost my mind in Jai Pendu? Well, it's a lie. I couldn't have lost my mind then, Ice, because I'm losing it now."

Ice took him out of Everien. He took Tarquin down the switchback trail that was now carved in the sides of the cliff that lifted Everien from the plains. The cliff was raw and new, and the trail was rough. The incident that had raised Everien and its sea plain a thousand feet could not have happened long ago. They began moving across the great emptiness of flat Ristale.

Eteltar?

Look at the cliffs you have raised?

What was going on? Eteltar had lived a generation before Tarquin's time. He had been Ysse's champion and advisor.

The sky began to change colors as Ice moved across Ristale faster than the sun. Tarquin shut his eyes. He didn't want to see the White Road again, not so soon. He reasoned with himself that soon Ice would have to stop and rest for a longer time, and then maybe Kere would make his way out of the horse and Tarquin could get some answers. For now, he just had to trust the horse.

He began to doze on Ice's back, and he lost his sense of time. The next thing he knew, he could feel that Ice was walking on sand. Wind gusted from ahead. Tarquin opened his eyes to the light of gloaming reflected off a seamless, clear sky; a light that did not reach the dark blue sand where night was sleeping. They were passing through a desertscape where the earth looked solid, and the sky, incandescent. Behind them were stark mountains of dark stone that was beginning to show up red in the gathering light. Ice slowed and stopped. For a long time, they were still. The shadow of the horse and man formed weakly and stretched before them on the sand. The stars were melting into dawn.

Tarquin was cold and hungry but also empty and light, as if his body would not be much needed here. To his left rose a series of jagged rock formations in dark red sandstone, culminating in a sheer cliff. It was this cliff that was blocking the light from reaching the sand.

He dismounted and felt Ice sigh. He patted the horse's neck affectionately, and the stallion turned his head to look at Tarquin out of one eye. Ice bared his teeth slightly and blew a cloud of hot breath. Then he moved off, disappearing in a patch of shadow beneath the rocks. Tarquin could just make out a faint gray blur and he saw that the horse had lowered his head to drink, probably out of a pool where water trickled down from above.

For a little while, Tarquin just stood there, listening to the soft wind and feeling the ground beneath his feet again. Waking up.

He turned in a slow circle and took in the fact that there were more cliffs behind him, high and magisterial. He followed Ice's tracks back to the place where the cave entrance had been. There was now no aperture. He touched the rock. It was warm, gritty, and unyielding. He turned and put his back to the cliff. Ahead was a stretch of desert and then more mountains. As their shapes began to resolve in the new light, he recognized this place. Those were the Khynahi Mountains.

Or.

Ice's birthplace.

But why?

Maybe this was just some kind of way station. Or seemed awfully far from Everien—but Ice had come here once before, when he was distressed. A stab of worry raced through Tarquin. Ice *seemed* all right. Maybe a little tired, which was unusual; but even a transcendent being had to rest sometime, didn't he?

Tarquin thought he had better check. He followed the horse into the shadows of the rocks. The sun had reached the distant mountains, and it turned the sands of the distant desert to pale gold, but it had not yet reached the foot of the cliffs, and in the culverts between the red clay rocks, the light was still dim and chill. As he drew closer to the lumps of stone, Tarquin realized that what he had taken for boulders at a distance were much larger up close than he'd thought. Their arrangement into irregular cliffs, caves, twists, and curves was complex, almost a maze. It was the sort of place lions would love. He drew his sword.

Ice was no longer by the pool. Tarquin stopped and called, listened, then looked for tracks. He could see hoofprints near the water, but none leading away. He stooped and tasted it: sweet, cold, laced with minerals but none of them foul-smelling. He drank deeply.

"Ice!" he called again, more urgently. A piercing whistle answered him from above. A familiar head appeared, crowned with spiky white hair.

"So that's where you've got to, Kere," Tarquin said, craning his neck to see the boy perched on the rocks. "Why are we stopping here? Is he tired? Is he hungry?"

"We are both hungry and a little tired," Kere said. "But we have stopped because this is as far as we take you, in your present state."

"What do you mean? Where are we going, ultimately? You told me you could help me."

Tarquin could not see the boy's expression clearly, but from the tone of his voice, Kere was not overly troubled at having failed to deliver on his promise.

"This is as far as we can go. Before this, there were no horses of Or. No Ice, no ancestors, no timeslipping. This is the beginning place, if a circle can have a beginning."

"This?" Tarquin looked around again, wondering what he'd missed. The landscape was sterile and desolate except for the odd bit of scrub wedged between the rocks and the birds that were rousing now and whirring up and down the cliff face. He knew that deserts could support more creatures than sometimes appeared possible, but this place was so remote that he failed to see what Ice, or Kere, thought he could do here, and said so.

"I don't understand what that glacier was about, Kere. How could there be a glacier on the land and monitor towers at the same time? How long ago did Everien exist? Did the Everiens live before the ice came? Is that how they were destroyed? Were the Everiens overrun by ice?"

Kere gave a squeak of laughter, then covered his mouth, chortling.

"What's so fucking funny?" Tarquin snapped.

"You have made a funny joke, Tarquin. Overrun by Ice. Very funny!"

Tarquin rolled his eyes in exasperation. "You haven't answered my questions. As usual!"

With characteristic stubbornness, Kere repeated, "This is the beginning." He got up and began to monkey-climb in the rocks.

Tarquin yawned. He wasn't sure what predators might be around, or even whether they were somewhere near to the byways of the tribesmen of Or. Maybe a caravan would come here, pass by this watering hole. Maybe they would find a wisewoman like the one who had healed Ice before.

But when he looked out over the emptiness, it seemed impossible to him that anyone would ever come here on purpose. He walked out across the sand for a while, looking for some sign of a road or other feature that might explain why Ice had come to this particular place, of all the emptiness of Or. The sand was heavy beneath his feet, but the sun on his back felt good. He walked a quarter of a mile and turned.

The sun had cleared a ridge slightly to the south and its rays spilled diagonally across the cliff face, showing its surface in sharp relief. The rocks did not climb very high before melding together to form a solid cliff that rose vertically for hundreds of feet. This was not a sheer, squared-off, uncompromising rock face, but one with numerous cracks and holds. The stone had a rounded, feminine appearance, unlike the jagged cliffs that separated Everien from Ristale, for example. Tarquin could see caves and ledges and places where trees had even managed to cling, breaking the stone. There were birds up there, too, black motes circling against the pocked red surface of the sandstone. He saw Kere, limbs splayed across the rock about forty feet above the rocks, and wondered if the boy had gone egg-hunting.

Then his eyes strayed again to the surface of the cliff, and he saw that the red stone was not pockmarked randomly, by nature. There was a pattern of some kind, carved in the stone. A pattern made to be read from a distance, or from the air.

Symbols.

Seven symbols. Everien symbols.

He recognized six of them. The seventh was unknown to him.

"Kere!" he screamed, and the boy let go with one hand, dangling free for a second before he recovered his grip on the cliff. Tarquin began to run across the sand. With every stride he watched the boy struggling to regain his hold; when Kere had achieved a more stable position, he turned his head and waved at Tarquin. Tarquin slowed to a walk, his right side aching, and waved back. He walked the rest of the way back, letting his alarm subside as he watched Kere slither up the remainder of the cliff with more athletic ability than he would have credited to the boy.

By the time Tarquin reached the base of the stones, Kere had gained a ledge not far below the carvings in the cliff; or at least this is what he said, leaning over the edge so that only his white head was visible, while Tarquin scrambled up the boulders in an effort to get within earshot. He could not see the symbols from here; the shape of the rock would not permit it. Nor did he imagine he could climb up by the route Kere had taken. He managed to get up the first series of large boulders, but once the cliff straightened to a vertical line, he halted, daunted.

"I've got to get to a position where I can read that writing."

"Wait a minute!" Kere called. "Let me see if I can find you a rope."

He disappeared.

"A rope?" Tarquin shouted. "Where the hell are you going to get a rope?"

The boy didn't answer, but a few moments later he reappeared with a huge coil of rope. He tossed an end down to Tarquin, who caught it and then began coughing. The rope was desiccated and brittle. Tarquin doubted that it would hold.

"My last experience with you and ropes, Kere, did not give me much reason to trust you again. If this breaks, I will be either killed or injured so badly I would be better off dead. I think I will stay where I am."

"Very well," said Kere equably. "I will explore and describe what I find. This is a very big ledge, and it has been added to by judicious carving of the cliffs. There are a number of handholds—ladders, almost—cut in the rock. Someone has climbed it with spikes and rope, as well. There are the remains of some sort of shed outside, and there is a cave with various pottery vessels and woven baskets that are falling apart."

"There is writing on the cliff," Tarquin reminded him. "Can you see it? Can you tell how it was made? And is there an easier way up? Through the cave, perhaps?"

Kere went away and did not come back for a long time. Tarquin studied the cliff face. He wanted badly to get up there and see for himself, but he was not at all sure of his climbing ability. He tugged on the rope and it seemed firm. He waited some more and when Kere didn't return, he started raising hell.

"Kere? Kere!" His voice broke and he coughed, then emitted a series of curses remembered from distant youth. He broke into Seahawk dialect. "Always I am shouting after this little bugger and never by the salts of the north channel is he answering me! Damn it!"

In the end he had to trust the rope. It was not quite as bad as he'd first thought. There were handholds, but they had been worn in by someone bigger than he. Now he began worrying about the prospect of this giant inhabitant coming back. He didn't feel game for a contest of strength—not until he'd had a meal, anyway.

"I haven't eaten for hundreds of years," he muttered to himself as he dragged his body up the stone. "Maybe thousands."

At last he drew himself over the edge, panting, sweating in the high sun, and very thirsty. It was immediately clear that whoever lived here had not returned for a long time. The ledge was liberally daubed with bird shit, and there were small animal bones scattered about where some predator, probably a falcon, had let them fall. What Kere had described as a shed was just the ruined remains of a cloth-and-wood tent of a very primitive kind, and it was splintered and in tatters. The fact that it had not rotted was remarkable, Tarquin thought, and wondered whether rain ever fell here.

The ledge curved to fit the contours of the rock, some of it tapering off to the right where the tent had once been, and the rest disappearing around a corner. Above, the cliff was subtly concave, making it impossible to see the entire symbols carved in the rock, although by craning his head all the way back and squinting, he could see that the surface had been worked in some fashion. In fact, it looked as though the seven symbols he had seen from a distance were each comprised of thousands of tiny markings, too delicate and faint to be deciphered.

"Kere!" he shouted again, and to his relief received a faint reply from around the bend in the ledge. He wiped his brow. At least Kere had not vanished. He could not have said why, but he would not care to be by himself there. It was too eerie. This was the loneliest place he had ever been—and Tarquin was a man whose life had long been defined by solitude.

Tarquin found Kere standing at the mouth of a small cave. He was standing very still, something of a feat for Kere considering that the collection of bones, sinew, white hair, and rags that comprised the adolescent's figure was so awkwardly compiled that he usually had to keep moving to maintain equilibrium.

"What's wrong?" Tarquin said. "Is there danger inside?"

Without turning, Kere shook his head slowly from side to side. Tarquin came up behind him, but he couldn't see properly in the gloom. He heard nothing, smelled no animal musk, so he stepped past Kere and entered.

Inside the cave, everything had been swept clean. There was a depression in the floor in the shape of a man with outstretched wings. Ranged around it were a number of small statues in the shape of animals. They were carved in stone, but they looked so lifelike that Tarquin wouldn't have been surprised if one of them had stirred and begun to prowl around, hunting the others.

"They look just like the Animal Guardians, remember, Kere? But they're so small. . . ."

Once Tarquin had entered the cave before him, Kere had recovered from his paralysis and followed the older man with an approximation of his usual restless energy. Now, before Tarquin could caution him, he stooped and picked up one of the animals. It was a horse statue.

Tarquin remembered what the blind woman had said. *The horse outran them and could not be caught.* She said that was why there was no horse statue among the giant guardians in the desert of Or.

"What do you think this means?" Tarquin said.

"I don't know. But I'll just keep this." And Kere tucked the statue beneath his arm.

"Should you do that?" Tarquin asked sharply, but the boy shot out of the cave with the speed of a trained thief. Tarquin was about to go after him when something caught his eye.

There was something lying in the depression, right about where the heart would have been in the winged man's body. It was a teardrop-shaped glass ampule, and there were symbols set in it.

Tarquin knelt and carefully moved the lion statue and the boar statue out of the way. When he touched them, they were warm,

119

and his fingers sang as if he'd touched the vibrating wood of a violin. He quickly put them down. He had the feeling that they might spring to life and attack him. *They must be called Guardians for a reason,* he thought.

He leaned across the depression, noticing that the shape of the extraordinary body might have been artfully carved into the packed clay, or it might have been formed by a real body lying there over a long period of time. There were dark stains where the bones should have rested, the arms folded across the chest, the underlying structure of the wings revealed. He shivered. Had a real man lain there, consumed slowly by maggots?

Then where were the bones?

Or was this only another sculpture, another abstract rendering of an episode from an unknown story?

He picked up the ampule. It had the same six symbols as the stoppered Pharician bottle that Kere had filled with timeserpent venom. Tarquin had tried to give that vessel to Eteltar among the ruins of A-vi-Khalar, but Eteltar had already discovered it. But this container also had a seventh symbol, the same one he had read on the cliff. All of the symbols were Everien in origin.

"Kere!" Tarquin shouted. "What does this mean? Come, you must have some explanation. Why did Ice bring us here?"

He ran outside and halted on the ledge. After the cool darkness of the cave, light and heat battered him as the desert sands began to radiate the sun's increasing warmth. Feeling suddenly dizzy, he blinked and shaded his eyes. Kere was standing at the far end of the ledge, paying no heed to the fact that he was trampling the remains of some kind of structure beneath his feet as he shifted them. He was looking up at the cliff, craning his neck and stretching on tiptoe to get a better view of the patterns inscribed there. He did not seem to hear Tarquin.

"It's like quicksand," Kere said cryptically.

"What is?" Tarquin tucked the ampule into his jerkin pocket and glanced nervously at the desert, thinking of the sandstorm he had experienced among the Animal Guardians the last time Ice brought him here. It would be all too easy to be swallowed up in those merciless sands, sucked down into a vortex and never seen again. But Kere had to be talking about something else. "What's like quicksand?"

"Writing backwards into time. Changing what was so that you

can change what is, and what will be. Oh, it's a very clever trick, but infinitely dangerous."

Now Kere was weaving back and forth, struggling in vain to get a better view of the cliff.

"What the hell are you *doing*, boy?" Tarquin demanded. He didn't really expect an answer; not when Kere was in one of these moods. But the boy suddenly turned and looked at him full on, and Tarquin saw that the fixated expression on his face was only barely supported by physical strength. His eyes were bloodshot, his lips dry and cracked, his skin color faintly greenish beneath its dark brown shading. He drew a weak breath, his eyes fluttered, and he began to sway.

Tarquin lunged forward and caught him just as he was about to fall.

"I'm sorry," Kere murmured, flopping weakly in Tarquin's grip. "I lost my concentration for a moment there. We'd better get off this cliff, in case Ice comes."

"For once, I wish Ice wouldn't come!" Tarquin groaned. "I can't bloody talk to Ice."

"Help me, Tarquin. I don't think I can get down by myself."

"Shh. Stay here." Tarquin had lowered the boy to the ground, and now he propped him up in the shade of the cliff. "I'll fetch some water. You rest."

"But Ice . . ."

"Ice will have to stay back for now. I can't carry you down the cliff without a rope, and anyway, we need to talk. Now be quiet. I'll be right back."

He went into the cave and found a pottery jar and some twine. He quickly wove a makeshift sling for the bowl so that he could bring it up and down the cliff without using his hands, and then descended to the water hole. While he was filling the jar, he squinted past the rocks to the sand beyond. He felt uneasy, and after a moment he realized it was because he could hear some kind of rumbling from across the sand. He put his ear to the ground.

Hoofbeats? Maybe.

Tarquin wasted no time in getting the water to Kere. The boy had fallen asleep, and when he roused he could manage only a few sips of water at first.

"I think," Kere said at length, "someone is using that cliff up there. It is the code for timeserpent, cured of its barrenness."

"Are we sure we want that?" said Tarquin nervously, thinking that one timeserpent was more than enough, thank you very much.

Kere went on. "But if he only had the code, how did he get the potion that the code makes? He had no such equipment here. Someone else made it for him. In the Fire Houses. Who? And when, and how? I have the feeling that by answering one of those questions, we will answer all of them."

"What about Jaya? Do you know where she is?"

"I don't know where Jaya is. Do you remember the other side of the White Road? The black horse, the creature Night? Do you remember how I explained that they could be close and yet far away?"

"I remember." Tarquin shuddered. Here in the desolation, beneath the inexorable sun, the fear he had felt of Night stumbling after him down the White Road came back to him with a startling power.

"There is another side to the White Road. Just as the black horse walked on the other side of the White Road and threatened Ice, so does something shine through that cliff, if only we could see it."

"What shines?"

"I think . . . the actualization of that writing, the solid form of that abstract code. On *that* side of the White Road, someone is calling."

Kere shut his eyes and Tarquin put the jar to his lips again, urging the boy to drink.

"This is too much for you, Kere."

"I don't know who it is," Kere said without being asked. "It isn't Jaya, because Jaya was with me beside the fountain when we called the timeserpent. It's someone else. It's someone who actually *understands* the Knowledge."

Tarquin realized he was shaking. He drank some water himself, but it didn't help.

"Only the Everiens understood the Knowledge."

"Yes."

"And they are gone."

But even as he said it, the words caught in his throat. Ice had taken them back to the time when Everien was buried deep beneath a glacier, before even the volcanic cones had risen, before the cataclysm that had raised the sea plateau a thousand feet above Ristale. And there had been no one in Everien. No people, no monitor towers, no roads. *Nothing.*

Tarquin rubbed his temples.

"I just don't get it," he said. "I thought . . . I thought the time-serpents were wrapped up in the matter of Jaya. I thought if I helped them, I would help her. Are you telling me the timeserpents sold me a lie?"

"A timeserpent, by instinct, will say or do anything to preserve its own existence."

"Then all that about eggs . . . ?"

"Was a trick. A timeserpent doesn't need eggs to reproduce. It's infinite. It doesn't even have fixed genders. In fact, in that cave there was only one timeserpent, not two."

"How could it be in the same time and place as itself? Surely even a timeserpent has limitations."

"It had become trapped there, called to itself—that was why it needed help. Normally a timeserpent will exist in at least two times—that's how it's able to move, by resonating from one time and location to another. The thing had become trapped beside itself and all it could do was flicker back and forth from one location to another, or appear at two locations at the same time."

"You never said how it came to be trapped."

"I don't know. Possibly someone or something had put it there, shoved it to a remote corner of time and place and hoped it would stay there. But it built a cult around itself and enlisted the Circle to help it escape. And it enlisted us."

"Us." Tarquin thought back. He had taken the vial and brought it across time and space to Eteltar. He had told Eteltar what to do. And Jaya . . . together, Jaya and Kere had somehow called the timeserpent through the membrane of that fountain, called it to the house where Jaya lived. And Jaya had leaped into the timeser-pent. Jaya's face had been on the maze. "But why, Kere? Why did they use us?"

"The timeserpent used us to bring itself into existence."

"It already existed."

"Not exactly."

"Not exactly? Either it did or it didn't, Kere."

"Here is the critical thing you must understand. Most creatures live on a debit system. They have to be born before they can live,

123

and then their lives are added up. But the timeserpent operates with a kind of cosmic credit. Being able to bend time, to eat time, means it can exist before it's created. It can arrange for its own creation. And that's what it's done. It's tricked you into making it."

"I haven't made anything!" Tarquin argued. "I've seen the timeserpent. It's made of flesh. It has teeth. How could any person make a thing such as that?"

"All it's made of," Kere replied, "is an idea, and the idea is codified in those six symbols, if you know how to read them. Once the White Road was open and people could pass back and forth, then the Knowledge of Jai Pendu was no longer confined to an abstract realm. And with the Artifacts anchored to reality, time was injured and began to bleed in Everien. Well, a timeserpent smells that kind of blood. Information could pass across these wounds. Jaya and Wakhe could communicate, for one. The engines of the Fire Houses called the timeserpent. It arranged its own Becoming."

"It sounds like word games to me," said Tarquin. "Thought games."

"Thought games: exactly. This is what abstraction leads to. It's the mother of Paradox and its womb is glass."

"What about Jaya?" Tarquin said sharply, triggered by the phrase "mother of Paradox."

"The timeserpent devoured her; its human aspect came from Jaya. But she was not human, before. She, too, was only a thought. Now she has passed from abstraction to reality via the timeserpent. Jaya, too, has been born."

"She's alive?" Hope sprang up in him, then anger at Kere for withholding information. "How do you know all of this? What else did the timeserpent say?"

Kere shook his head sadly, as if pitying Tarquin for his stupidity. "Do you have any idea how *big* a timeserpent really is? You can't *talk* to a timeserpent. Not like we're talking. Its language would explode your head. You talking to a timeserpent would be like a worm in your gut talking to you. A barnacle talking to a whale. I have done my best, Tarquin. Through Ice, I am a complex being existing in many dimensions, and the most I could do was exchange gossip with its tail rattle. My understanding of these matters is limited."

"Not as limited as mine," Tarquin said, shaking his head. He was lost in thought; but Kere had revived and began to show signs of his usual nervous agitation.

"I'd better move them to their rightful places," Kere said. He stumbled into the cave again and began gathering the Guardians up into his cloak. Then he climbed from the ledge, despite Tarquin's protests.

"I have to," Kere said. "The *majala* will come, and they must be in their places."

TOO MUCH A PASSENGER

There was no discouraging Kere. Tarquin followed the boy down the cliff face and told him to sit quietly while he brought more water; but when he returned, Kere was gone. Wearily, Tarquin followed his tracks, only to have his worst suspicions confirmed: fifty yards from the red rocks, Kere had turned into Ice and had run across the sand.

Tarquin began to trail after him, dragging his feet. What was Ice up to? And what was the meaning of the carving on the cliff? Or the vial with the symbols he knew? The symbols that had been written on the timeserpent venom he had given to Eteltar, so very long ago . . . actually, to be correct, that event would not happen for many years. Tarquin was now standing in the very morning of time, far from home.

Eteltar's mission had been to repair the timeserpent, to make it whole again. To give it the power to reproduce.

He began to feel that he was missing something very important. Ice had a reason for bringing him here. Kere might not be able to explain to Tarquin's satisfaction, but in his gut, Tarquin trusted the wild horse. Ice had returned to the desert before, when he was sick and needed help. He had taken Tarquin to the Animal Guardians, and Tarquin had learned from the blind healer that the horses of Or had never been captured by the Everiens. They had never become Guardians. Yet Tarquin had seen them run among the grave and imposing statues as though they were attracted to them.

We are before that time, he thought with an effort. *The horses are free because Kere has taken the Guardian for Ice to hold.*

Ice is the Guardian of the horses.

And he can run across time.

How is it that Ice can run across time, anyway?

Tarquin drew out the ampule and examined it once again. He opened it with great care. The fluid inside was dry, but there was a residual crystalline powder lying like dust at the bottom of the container. It did not *look* like timeserpent venom. It was cherry red. Poison? He wondered. Had this winged man imbibed it, and died? But how had it passed from Eteltar, in the future, to the winged man, now?

And what was it for?

He brought the ampule cautiously to his nose.

It smelled of roses.

BY THE TIME he'd caught up with Ice, he had taken to occupying himself with fantasies of the meals he would consume if ever he returned to the world of people and campfires and beds. As it was, he was far from that world. He was not even surprised to find that, when Ice's tracks had changed once again to Kere's tracks, there were statues of animals set at intervals across the sands. Kere had been busy. The animals were spread far and wide, and where the statues were, the sand was darkening as if a black stain spread across it from within. Already they had grown. The boy had scooped up all of the animals in both hands; but now some of them were as high as Tarquin's knees.

"*You* put the Guardians in their places?" Tarquin said incredulously when he finally found Kere, deep in meditation before a motionless, curled snake statue.

Kere shrugged. "Someone had to do it."

"Had to? Why?"

"To protect the animals, of course. So long as the line remains unbroken and the codes are kept in an uneaten time and place, the animals are safe."

"What line?"

"The line of inheritance. The Animal Magic is continuity," Kere said. "Continuity with the past. These animals cannot be rewritten in the Liminal. They have been fixed with their own identity. If only Eteltar had been able to save more!"

"Eteltar? Has he been here?"

"He has been here. He is gone now. See the Seahawk Guardian? It is flawed."

Tarquin turned. The statue of the seahawk moved, beating its wings awkwardly as though trying to burst out of the stone that was its own composition.

"Eteltar had to violate it, to expose his own animal essence. He drew in the skyfalcon, too. The seahawk will always be confused."

Tarquin glanced at Kere, wondering if he was being teased as the boy added, "Perhaps that is the source of its irrational violence."

But if Kere was playing with him, Tarquin couldn't be bothered to rise to the bait. He stared at the seahawk statue, mouth open. It writhed and twisted, throwing its head back and opening its beak. Its throat rippled with a soundless cry. Then, as he watched, the statue burst open and a great bird, larger than Ice, broke free. It rose in a spiral over the other Guardians, then spun on its own tail and flew toward the cave and the ledge. In the red light of sunset, Tarquin saw it rise to the ledge and perch there for a moment, its head turning from side to side. Then it spread its wings, sprang into the air, and disappeared piecemeal as if swallowed by the sky. He heard himself gasp as its tailfeathers vanished through some invisible aperture.

"The skyfalcon goes free. The seahawk remains, damaged."

Tarquin turned his attention back to the seahawk statue. It seemed to shrink and then slowly grow still. Everything about it was fierce and cold. He shuddered. This bird was supposed to represent *him* and the magic of his Clan.

"It is a curious Guardian," Kere said. "Alone of the Guardians, it exists in this time and place, as well as in another. It guards the gates of time."

Tarquin looked away from the seahawk. He did not wish to be reminded of the inheritance he had renounced, nor of all the responsibilities he had left behind. If he began to think of Istar and his family, he would only feel guilty over things he could do nothing about.

Yet it was time to be doing *something*.

"Kere, I feel I am too much a passenger. I must get myself together. I must come up with a plan."

"You are too much a passenger," Kere agreed, rubbing his back as though his kidneys were sore. "I suggest you find the source of the seventh symbol. Oh! There is something I've been meaning to give you."

He reached into his tunic and felt around. Tarquin watched him expectantly. Ever since the eruption of the timeserpent near the Fire Houses, Tarquin had been indexing Kere's rather dramatic change in behavior with growing amazement. The boy seemed to have come into his own at some point when Tarquin wasn't looking, and Tarquin felt himself caught off-balance. Now came the coup de grâce. Kere drew out the very flask of timeserpent venom that Tarquin had brought into Jaya's house and offered to Eteltar.

Tarquin stammered, "But . . . I lost that. In Jaya's house. I meant to give it to Eteltar, but he already had it. . . ."

"And now it has found its way back," said Kere with a smile. "Take it."

Tarquin took the container delicately, half-expecting it to bite or burn or shock him.

"But don't drink it!" Kere warned.

"I wasn't going to."

"At least not until Eteltar has turned it into the River." He pronounced the last word to rhyme with "diver."

"The *what?*"

"I have important business," Kere said, and turned away with a sniff and a series of nervous twitches.

SPLINTERS OF ICE

Tarquin passed the heat of the day under the wolf statue, where it was cool and shady. He debated the advice of Kere with himself. He could not make sense of half of what Kere had said, and as for drinking the stuff he had found up on the ledge . . . it was about the stupidest idea he'd ever heard. This potion was probably what had killed the winged man.

But would Kere advise him to drink poison? Not after all they had been through together, Tarquin thought. He lay down on the black sand. The sky was so deep, he felt numb just to look at it. There was a sadness at the bottom of him, and it stretched upward into his throat like the string of a bowed instrument or the taut skin of a drum. The sadness resonated with the dark and sparkling sky.

I am not enough. I have failed.

In Jaya he had found something he could believe in, someone he could care about, a way of looking at the world that, for those moments they were together, anyway, made everything fall into place. As she had become more real to him, more tangible and even *attainable*, he had grown stronger and stronger. He had become capable of acts he never would have dreamed of setting out to do, in his old life under Ysse or in his years of traveling.

But she had been torn from him, and he knew he would not find her again so easily. She had let go his hand. She had gone somewhere he couldn't follow. Just like the Company.

I need to be something more. I am not enough to do what I have to do.

He stayed under the statue until the heat was gone from the sand, and longer still. The sun fell and was gone. Tarquin could think of no reason to move. He was in true despair. It came over him inexorably, like a shadow. He could not muster one thought to fight it. He lay there shivering as the desert cold came on, no longer caring what happened to him—or pretending not to. For he knew he did care; that he would not lie down to die; not now. He knew he would do what he had to in order to survive. But that was no consolation. So he lay on the sand and pretended it was all over.

The wind picked up. Sand blew over him, scouring his skin and beginning to cover him. He lay under its punishment feeling deeply sorry for himself.

I would do anything, he thought. *Anything, anything, to solve this. To find her. To make it better.*

The Animal Guardians grew bigger and bigger. The black sand swirled.

He sat up. Beyond the ring of the nearest Guardians, the sand had lifted and was forming a moving curtain, black and sparkling. He heard hoofbeats. Ice came trotting up to him through the storm, settling just out of Tarquin's reach. He snorted and dipped his head as though trying to communicate. Tarquin looked into the wild eye of the horse and felt himself shiver.

Ice stood there uneasily. Tarquin continued to be dazzled by the stallion—no matter how many times he saw Ice, or rode him, it was always just like the first. Ice was a welcome storm, a wild whirlwind you had no choice but to surrender to. Yet now, for only the second time in all his experience of the horse, he could see Ice as an animal who felt himself to be vulnerable. The horse began roving from point to point, head down, looking for grass. Tarquin noticed with dismay that the stallion's ribs showed.

One by one, out of the wall of black windblown sand, people began to appear, walking across the sand toward Ice. Each carried something bundled close to his chest. Most of them were men, dark-skinned, robed in the simple garments of Or; but some were female, and one or two were fair and tall as if they could even have come all the way from Everien in the north. Their numbers grew and grew until they had become a throng. The nearest came within a few yards of Ice, and stopped. A semicircle formed around the horse, who danced from side to side, trying to stare at each one of them head-on.

Then Kere came forward, pushing others out of his way. He, too, carried a bundle.

"Kere," said Tarquin. "What are you doing?"

But Kere didn't heed him. He approached Ice and held the bundle up to the horse's head, and Tarquin saw that it contained a tiny baby! Ice was sniffing the child and lashing his tail, more like a cat than a horse.

"Kere!" Tarquin called again. He had gone cold. Were these people really feeding Ice their babies? But Kere had *been* fed. He couldn't stand side by side with Ice—the two were never in the same place at the same time—and besides, he was just a boy. He didn't have any children to offer.

Kere looked at Tarquin calmly, and said, "We are outside time, now. Now you can see what you couldn't see, before. Now you can go where you couldn't go."

"Who are all these people?"

"All of them have lived within Ice. He is very old, you know!"

Tarquin shook his head in astonishment. "Well, what are you all doing?"

Another voice answered him, a woman's low and scratchy tone from the perimeter of watching people. "I remember you, Tarquin the Free. You took my advice, and saved us all." He turned and recognized the old healer from the caravan of Or, the blind woman with diamonds where her eyes had been. She had diagnosed Ice's ailment and set them on the road to eluding Chyko's deadly arrow. Tarquin's mouth fell open to see her here now.

"You're part of Ice?" he asked in astonishment.

"How else would I know his troubles?" she said gently. "Now I am in a position to help you. For you are a divided being, though you do not know it."

And she handed him the scabbard he had given her in recompense for her healing of Kere. He took it with a shudder. He felt afraid to touch it.

"Divided?"

Her next words shocked him, and with every phrase, his emotions intensified until he was boiling over. She said, "Divided. It is how you were able to resist Night. Why you could not be captured in the Glass. How you displaced yourself all the way to Snake Country to come to Ice in the nick of time. How you saw Jaya."

"*How do you know those things?*" Tarquin was nearly shouting. Her words sank into him like stones flung into deep water. He was unable to moderate his tone.

"I was with Ice then," she said simply.

"*You* were with Ice? Then when we met you in Or . . . ?" He turned to Kere in confusion. "How is it possible that you were alive, there?"

"I slipped us in time," Kere admitted, not looking directly at Tarquin. "To when she was still alive. Or rather, Ice did. We were desperate. The arrow, it was awful. . . ."

"So this old woman, she's dead, then!" Tarquin pointed accusingly at the blind woman. "She *is* dead, isn't she?"

"She lives in Ice," Kere said evasively.

"Eteltar called us," the old woman said softly. "He summoned us to carry Ysse to Jai Pendu. We made the road, but Ysse did not ride Ice. She used the road like an ordinary road, and took her own horse, and her sword. She was not able to see Ice, not the way you have come to see us."

"I . . . I only knew about Kere," Tarquin stammered.

"All of us in Ice," said the witch doctor gently, "were always in Ice, and always will be. Rarely will more than one of us appear. But we are always present."

"What's that got to do with me?" Tarquin said nervously.

"You are one of us," Kere blurted.

Tarquin began to back away, crossing and uncrossing his forearms, palms down, in a canceling gesture.

"N-no. With all due respect, I was never fed to a horse at birth."

"It is better for the chosen if they never knew their lives as humans. There is less conflict that way—although, for some, like little Kere the baby here, the conflict is innate. For others, like me, the Eating took place much later in life, and was a gift from Ice. It is our vitality that sustains Ice, you see, and an old lady like me cannot offer much of that. But I know a thing or two, and when Ice took me, the best part of my physical life was long gone."

"When he *took* you?" Tarquin pursued, thinking the phrasing sounded obscene.

"When he killed me," she said levelly.

Tarquin found himself gasping for breath. Ice was dancing back and forth, his ribs showing, his nostrils flaring. The carnivorous horse was hungry.

"It is the only way to be truly free. To master time."

Hastily Tarquin said, "I don't need to master time."

"No?" asked the witch doctor. "Then we are all of us here mistaken. Because it looked to us like you asked us to take you to Jaya.

133

And that you will not accomplish as a passenger. Already we are weary of carrying you, and your journey has just begun."

Kere added, "The places you want to go are almost unreachable. We cannot help you there. Not unless you also help us. A sacrifice works both ways."

Tarquin began taking deep, slow breaths. *Try to think of nothing,* he told himself. *Try to think of nothing. Try to th—*

"Anything," Kere said in deft mimicry of Tarquin's own voice. "Anything, to solve this."

"Bloody hell!" Tarquin exclaimed. "How did you hear me say that?"

"We are already together," Kere answered softly. "It has already happened. You simply can't see it. Yet."

While Tarquin was trying to compose himself, Kere again began to walk toward Ice.

"Kere, stop it," Tarquin said in an authoritative tone. "Just stand still for one fucking second, and let me think!"

"I no longer wish to be human. I will stay with Ice now."

"What do you mean?" Tarquin cried. "Won't I see you anymore?"

Kere shook his white head, smiling. "I'm afraid not. Aren't you relieved? Aren't you glad? You always said I was a pain in your ass."

"Y-y-you are . . . but . . . Kere, why are you going so suddenly? I mean, will you really vanish? Forever?"

"I will vanish," Kere affirmed. "Forever. I will join the legions within Ice, and he will be free to use my lifetime."

"Don't do it!" Tarquin protested, but Kere made a silencing gesture.

"Now Ice is free," he said. "For you, my friend and teacher, you will have to make your own way, too. Can't you see I'm trying to help you? The only way for you to go farther is to become a part of the White Road." He paused, gazed at Tarquin with what seemed inordinately adult eyes, and added. "Anything? Would you truly do *anything,* Tarquin?"

Then, before Tarquin could react, Kere tossed the baby toward the stallion, who reached his head up toward the flying body. Tarquin looked away. He couldn't watch.

When he looked back, Kere was gone, and Ice was up on his toes, prancing and trumpeting. Tarquin found he had tears in his eyes and a tightness in his throat.

"But Kere," he whispered. "You were the closest thing to a son I ever had. . . ."

The people began to back away. Ice trumpeted again, whirled, and looked at Tarquin.

"Oh, no, you don't!" Tarquin said, backing away and putting his hand on his sword. "We're friends, Ice, remember?"

But either Ice did not remember, or he had never seen it that way at all. Tarquin turned and fled among the Guardians, with the horse charging after him. Sand flew everywhere, and out of the corner of his eye Tarquin could see the madness that was Ice following him like a breaking wave.

Kere's voice was whispering inside his head. The hurricane of Ice's hooves, the airborne sand, the darkness and the *majala*, the weight of the horse hurtling toward him, all of these wild stimulations were offset by the boy's soft voice heard in his mind.

Find it, stupid. Find Eteltar's potion. Administer the cure.

Ice passed him on the right, snorting, playing with him. The horse spun, reared, and came at him. Tarquin saw his black belly and flashing hooves as the sky disappeared.

Then the world was all Ice.

Ice, teeth bared, nostrils red as hot coals, hooves slashing. Ice, merciless, angular. Tarquin put his hands up over his head and Ice descended on him. Sharp teeth raked his head, bit into his throat, and he felt them close over his spinal column even as the rest of the horse struck him with full weight, breaking bones and sending him flying like a rag doll. He had no more sense of feeling in his body, but with a kind of detached awareness he understood that his throat was being ripped out. He knew that the hooves were trampling what was left of his lower body.

And then, with those predator's teeth, the horse began to chew.

Tarquin was no longer able to think. It was all over. There would be no escape. He was dying.

A VERY LARGE BONE

Istar ran for some time before she dared pull up and listen. The wood was silent. They were not following her, and as for Taretel: he could be anywhere.

It never occurred to her to let Taretel go, and make her own way. Not once.

She waited for the appearance of fragile daylight and then crept as close as she dared to the spot where she'd last seen him, hoping to pick up his trail. From this vantage she was able to observe Pentar and his men moving out to make the rendezvous with the scouts. A warm feeling for Pentar rose inside her. He could have hunted them both down, Istar and her prisoner; but he didn't. Once she would have called him a sentimental fool for his loyalty, but now that they had parted, she knew she would miss having him at her back.

Damned ghost-creature Taretel, bloody white-cloaked big whatever-he-was. She set out after him with a whole mix of emotions roiling in her guts. Guilt for Birtar's death at his hand; anger that she could not control him; nostalgia for the elusive spirit of Eteltar, with his wings and his cliff-carving; curiosity.

Maybe curiosity was too mild a word. Rather, call it fascination. The feeling she held toward Taretel was one she had previously associated only with Chyko, her lost father. It was an obsession bordering on worship. Even in childhood, she had tried to assume Chyko's fierceness, to embody his bold ardor. She felt she had to become Chyko, to keep his reputation alive in her. She had tried hard to do this, often at the price of friendship and maybe even love. It was almost as if she had tried to become the tiger she'd heard of in legend. But now, encountering the silent apparition of

Taretel, she had chanced upon a real tiger. Now she realized that she knew nothing of fierceness or strength.

All her efforts meant nothing. She remained small and weak by comparison to the great warrior. A tiger, she had realized when she looked at Taretel, didn't have to *try* to be a tiger. Where that left Istar in the scheme of things, she didn't care to speculate.

And now, pursuing Taretel, she might as well be hunting a tiger, for all her chances of success. Not to mention that she didn't know what she would do if she caught him.

The sun came up in a wan mist, making the forest slightly less murky than before. She found his tracks easily enough, and by the length of his stride she assessed that he had moved off at a loping run across the hillside. She followed in a huffing trot, conserving her strength. After half an hour at this pace she came to a break in the wood where a fault line ran down the mountainside. She stopped to massage calves that protested at working in heavy snow. Through the parting in the trees she had a view of an Everien laid out in shades of gray. The tall mountains looked flat in this light, and the wooded foothills were silent in the snow but for the mocking cries of crows in the treetops. Taretel's tracks went straight up the crack.

Istar took a few deep breaths, adjusted her pack to stop the straps digging into her trapezius, and resumed the pursuit; but after a few steps up the snow-covered fissure, she halted again.

She had the feeling of too much silence. As though someone were watching her.

She turned and looked down the fissure. It was partially covered by snow, a ragged gash in the mountainside that she had at first taken for an old streambed or earthquake line. But now she noticed that trees had fallen on its edges, still bearing green needles. This crack had been made recently.

"Timeserpent," she said aloud, and her voice came back to her with a funny echo. She could hear the metallic whisper of her own sibilants skating back to her up and down the fault line. If the Li'ah'vah had come here, what had it changed in its wake? Istar had heard legends about Li'ah'vah, the gigantic ancient cousin of the H'ah'vah. It was said that the H'ah'vah could pass through rock by slipping side-on to time, and that this same quality had been shared by the Li'ah'vah of old; but no one had seen a Li'ah'vah for hundreds of years, allegedly. Until Istar and her prisoner had huddled on a ridge and watched one devouring whole sections of Everien, below.

Departing from Taretel's vertical line of prints, she turned and began to move toward the far side of the crack, where the earth was torn and trees had been uprooted. A scant two yards beyond the line of Taretel's tracks she bumped into something. It was like a wall, but she couldn't see it—not even the flicker of a reflection that would be visible if it were glass. She leaned on it. It was not hard. It had a slightly yielding, pliant quality, but she could not push her way through it. She beat on it but could not break it. While she stood there fussing, the land on the other side of the fissure fell under a shadow. And then, gripped in amazement, Istar watched evening descend two feet from where she stood, while on her side of the barrier the sun was steadily climbing.

She looked around, chuckling nervously and wishing she had someone to witness this with her—someone to convince her she wasn't crazy. Taretel's footprints led on up, and now she hurried after him, more determined than ever to catch up. One thing was certain: Taretel hadn't crossed over, at least not here. It was some comfort to her to know that whatever powers he might possess, the power to slide effortlessly across a Li'ah'vah wake was not one of them.

IT WAS TWO days before she reached him. In that time, she had reached the top of the Li'ah'vah crack at a rocky ridge. Taretel's tracks led down into the next valley and then across the side of the slope, bearing west-southwest. Istar knew the lines of the mountains well enough to realize that they were not far now from one of the main passes between Snake Country and the Everien lowlands where Jai Khalar lay. She began to think that Taretel was going in this direction quite deliberately, and she wondered why. After all, his territory had always been in Tyger Pass and the surrounding mountains and fjords.

She was running low on food; however, she ascertained that if she kept on in this direction, she would soon emerge from the mountains in a more settled area. Taretel led a good trail; but he never ventured far from the invisible wall where the timeserpent had been. Istar came to feel its presence on her right-hand side as she walked. Sometimes she even thought she heard a low, soft humming coming from that way.

Then came the morning when, pausing to shake a stone from her boot, Istar again had the feeling of being watched. She froze, looked. The figure of Taretel stood fifty yards uphill at the edge of a copse of pine trees.

She got the stone out and replaced her boot without taking her eyes off Taretel. Pentar's words came back to her. *Birtar said he was not a Sekk . . . he bled but healed too quickly, and he did not sing. He spared Thietar for some reason.*

But he had also killed Ranatar, had massacred a whole village, by the sound of it. Eteltar had spoken of "unnatural urges" after he returned up the White Road many years ago—murderous urges must have been what he meant. And she was pursuing him, in the middle of nowhere. He still had his sword; it was twice the size of her own.

She started walking toward him. He didn't move. There was nothing aggressive in his posture. She felt like a mouse going for a piece of cheese.

For his part, Taretel stood stock-still. As she drew near, she saw that the gag and the blindfold hung loose about his neck, and the ropes binding his hands were gone. He stood and watched her like a statue. The great sword was strapped to his back. The fact that he made no move for it did not comfort her. After all, he had crushed Birtar's skull with one hand.

She halted about three paces away from him, her drawn sword pointed at his chest. For a long moment he did nothing; then, just as she was about to speak, he held out both hands, wrists together and turned upward, and nodded at her.

"Why don't you speak?" she said, and her own disused voice sounded gravelly. His eyes remained steady on her face and in spite of herself, she met their gaze. They were the same eyes as Eteltar's. Exactly the same. She shivered and something inside her went soft.

"Ah, fish-heads," she muttered irrelevantly in Seahawk. "What am I doing?"

Before she could think twice, she had sheathed her sword, reached back into her pack and drew out some rope, and then cut a suitable length with which to bind his hands. She tried to approach him with the same matter-of-fact air she had always used, but something was different now that he was free and his eyes were uncovered. She hastily bound his wrists, a little too tightly because she was afraid; then she slipped the blindfold up over his eyes again. All this while, he was looking at her, until she put the blindfold on, at which point he closed his eyes and dipped his head so she could reach. He smelled like a combination of Eteltar and snow-lion fur and leather. She tightened the blindfold, then abruptly changed her mind, whipping it off with one stroke and shoving it into her belt. She backed away, trembling.

"Now what?" she said, looking up at him. "Carry on the way we were going? Toward Snake Pass?"

His eyes had changed. They were no longer Eteltar's, but they looked at Istar with alien curiosity. She felt she was exchanging glances with another species, just as intelligent as she was, but different somehow. A small shudder went through her, and she broke her gaze away, turning to slide her pack off her shoulders. It was flaccid and half-empty.

"We're running low on supplies," she said in as normal a tone as she could. "Actually, we're out of almost everything. We can get fresh meat, but that takes time. I think we'd better head down-country as fast as we can. We must be getting close to Snake Pass, just beyond that ridgeline. There are people there. Or there were."

Her voice sounded flat in the dead air. She felt that as long as she insisted on talking, she kept the situation on her terms. If she were to succumb to Taretel's brooding silence, she would be somehow under his power. So she simply shouldered the pack once again, resisting the urge to take some food out of it because what little she had must be made to last, especially considering that Taretel carried no food at all. She wondered what he had been subsisting on these past days.

Then she set off, and he went with her, perfectly docile. She let him walk ahead of her, out of curiosity for what direction he would choose, and so that she could watch him. He continued on toward the ridge she had indicated, sometimes curving his path to accommodate, she assumed, the Li'ah'vah disturbance. The crevasse it had dug had vanished and the earth here was undisturbed. Perhaps it had not come this way, or perhaps it had passed deep underground. Yet, although she couldn't be certain, she thought she could hear a faint, almost-subliminal hum coming from over her right shoulder as before. She became certain that Taretel knew where the Li'ah'vah had passed, and he was following that line.

The day passed quickly and when night fell, she was very

weary. Taretel took huge strides, and Istar, full of nervous energy, burned up a lot of it keeping pace with him. They camped at the bottom of the ridge that separated them from Snake Pass. Istar lit a celebratory fire and offered Taretel some of her food. For a second, his eyes took on the expression of Eteltar's again, and she felt a surge of hope that maybe he would even speak; but then he shook his head and looked away from the food, and the animalian gaze returned.

Istar arranged her pack as a pillow and curled up in her cloak to sleep. Taretel was still standing. She had yet to see him sleep in all the time since she'd captured him in Eteltar's cave. It was possible that he did lie down, deep in the night when she couldn't watch him, but she had never caught him at it. More than anything, it was his sleeplessness that made her think he really was only a ghost or spirit.

In the morning, he was gone.

Istar couldn't believe it at first, and even after she was sure he was really gone, she couldn't understand why. He had done nothing to harm her and had not taken food or water but only his sword—so what had been the point of offering himself as a captive in the first place? He had gained nothing, other than unnerving her. She was at a loss to explain his actions.

He had left a perfectly clear trail. Maybe he'd just intended for her to follow and couldn't be bothered to wait for her. But why?

She picked up her pack and set off in a puzzled huff.

Her pack rattled. She stopped. The bones of Eteltar, which she had so carefully bound together in a tight bundle, were now loose. She took the pack off and rummaged through it. She had not managed to recover every single bone in the skeleton of the winged man, but she knew that she had had both femurs. Now only one remained.

"Trickster!" she shouted, and jammed the remaining bones in tight. A right fool she was, thinking he was surrendering to her, or that he needed her help, when all he wanted was to humiliate her and hurt her. He must have lifted the pack from beneath her in her very sleep, and she hadn't even woken. But why had he stolen one of Eteltar's bones? What earthly reason could there be for that? It only proved he was cruel and horrible, she thought.

"Right," she said through clenched teeth. "Let's find out what you're up to, you miserable giant."

Most of the morning was gone before she had reached the crest of the ridge. Taretel's prints were there, perfectly clear. Now and then she could see where he had put a hand down to steady himself, and she realized that she'd been a fool to rely on ropes to bind him. No matter how tightly she tied him up, he was managing to get loose.

Just over the top of the hill, where she expected to be hit by a gust of wind and a view of Snake Pass below, the air went still. Her face prickled, and she could hear-feel the soft humming, now directly ahead of her. Taretel's prints went forward, turned left along the top of the ridgeline, then crossed over again on top of themselves where he had paced back and forth in a rough circle. At this point there lay a great white lump like a boulder, about shoulder high and a horse length across. Rising out of the boulder came a gently arching branch of the same alabaster material. It stretched up and out from the ridgeline as if leading into the sky; then it disappeared. It looked like an unfinished bridge to the clouds. The end was cut off abruptly, leaving a sharp edge.

Istar walked all around it and under it. When she passed under it, at the point directly beneath the disappearing-place of the white structure, she ran into the invisible wall again. The Li'ah'vah had been here, too; it simply hadn't disturbed the earth visibly. She looked up and studied the point where the white thing collided with the seam, and it occurred to her that maybe it was not cut off at all, but rather that she could not see the air that it passed into, because that would be across the seam. Standing underneath the white arch, she reached overhead and touched the slightly porous material of the "bridge." It was slightly warm, and it was vibrating like the wood of a stringed instrument.

She took her hand away.

The material of this structure was not stone. It was too smooth. Also, it was slightly flexible; but it was not wood, either. She looked at the end that was planted in the ground. It was not one round ball, but two rounded ends branching off the main stem. Then she knew.

It looked like a very large version of the bone Taretel had stolen.

ANIMAL MAGIC

Istar considered what she should do. If it was that same bone, and it continued into the timeserpent seam, then if she walked out on it she would see what was on the other side. It was a lucky thing for her; back in the area near the base of Tyger Pass with Pentar and her men, she had been unable to get near the places where the timeserpent had passed. No one could even think straight, or walk in a direct line, when confronted with that section of the seam. Now it seemed that Taretel, with his impudent theft of the bone, had paved a way for her to get back to the main part of Everien. If she could cross this seam and get into Snake Pass, she would be on her way to Jai Khalar, and help.

So she tried to goad herself ahead. She told herself that Taretel had a head start on her, and every moment she wasted thinking about it was another moment he was on the other side of the Li'ah'vah seam.

Of course, Istar, she reminded herself, *that is all assuming that this bridge crosses the seam and does not terminate somewhere in the cursed Liminal.*

With that thought, she even began to hope that the bridge would lead her back to Eteltar's cliff. If only she could return there, she would never try to escape again, or save Everien, or do anything but live in the sun with the winged man and forget all other cares.

She climbed onto the slippery joint end of the bone and felt it vibrating beneath her feet. It was a soft, tickling hum that throbbed an irregular beat. She felt it all the way through her skeleton, even to her teeth and the roots of her hair. She began to walk. As she approached the seam, the air in front of her wavered and parted. The mountain scene melted away. She could see the bone continuing on in a long, curving ascent against a backdrop all of blue, with stars.

Istar walked, entranced.

"Animal Magic," she said to the air and the bridge that carried her away from her world. "Eteltar, is this your doing? Is this how you made the White Road? Out of your own bones?"

She did not expect an answer but she was struck by the vast echo that her voice carried with it, and she looked from side to side, wondering about the size and shape of this void. She could see the bone rise and then slowly descend again, but its other side was hidden in shadow. She stopped. Overhead was a gleaming firmament. There was no wind. The air was warm enough that she could stand still and not shiver. When she breathed she smelled no plants, no smoke, no decay, only air so clear it might blow off the snows of the most remote peaks. Under her feet, the bone subtly rocked. She had the fanciful impression that she was inside some giant inscrutable creature, and it was softly breathing, just enough to make the bridge sway ever so slightly. She felt safe. She did not want to leave.

"Eteltar? You're here, aren't you? I can feel it."

She stood there gripped in sentiment for a long moment. Then, looking down into the blue abyss, she began to descry faint shapes.

She could see things, not with color or depth; but in the way that an afterimage burns itself into the eye, she could make out moving outlines of objects and shapes. They formed and dissolved constantly, and their lines were so subtle as to be almost imperceptible in the floating blue. Mostly she saw shapes as if they were hidden behind a screen or under a sheet, their surface details disguised by the all-encompassing blueness. It was hard to put a name to the shapes. Sometimes she thought she saw a fin or a paw; sometimes an oval eye, staring back at her; sometimes the branches of trees, or were they blood vessels? Sometimes she saw creatures running, creatures that changed shapes from lions to jackals to deer to rabbits to dolphins to geese to camels, changing as they ran. Then she saw swords and tools and intersecting boxes; floating pyramids and cylinders; collections of globules and flashes of implied light. Then she saw symbols, half words, half pictures, not dissimilar to Eteltar's cliff writing. Not dissimilar to the Everien language that Xiriel had told her was like music.

And with the thought, *music,* Istar imagined a woman's voice

144

singing very softly, far up at the top of her head. The voice wasn't her own, and yet its sound seemed to come from inside her, as if the inside of her skull were an echoey box. Istar began to lose track of the feeling of her own body.

Then there was a snarl and a monstrous shape formed in the void.

IT CAME TOO fast for Istar to comprehend, and it was so horrific and complex that she didn't know where to look. Unlike the other objects she had imagined seeing from the side of the bridge, this thing was colored, three-dimensional, and breathing noxious fumes from its many scattered nostrils. It came at her, misshapen and unnameable, resembling first a sea monster tangled in its own coils; then a crumpled suit of armor with swirling cerulean and umber flesh oozing from between the plates; then a set of bagpipes.

Eyestalks on stiff necks came bristling out of a flexible body covered by occasional patches of shell, between which were randomly placed steaming orifices. When the creature clenched itself, terrible gases came out of those holes. They drifted toward her with a foul smell and the premonition of poison. The thing's body was rooted in the blue sky, so that it resembled a complicated and disgusting tumor on the verge of detaching itself from a deep blue skin, but still drawing vitality from that vast source, and so desecrating the air and the light with its aberrant presence. From amongst the eyestalks, the flaccid body clenched, and a long, sinuous neck unrolled, shooting out at her with lightning speed. It cut her head so fast and so sharp, she hardly noticed, until the blood came.

With a kind of desperate optimism, Istar had her sword out. Yet it resembled a hatpin by comparison to the scale of this creature, which now wove itself under the bridge, stretching the blue membrane to distortion and surrounding Istar with a thicket of woody eyestalks that tried to bar her passage. She planted her legs and cut at them like a woodsman. In her head, the woman's voice was still singing, but the song had become a soft, intense chant punctuated by insect noises and odd, purring breaks.

Istar knocked an eyestalk aside with her shoulder and ran forward. She was almost to the top of the bridge, and she cursed herself for pausing, because if she had carried on directly without stopping to stare, she would already be nearly at the other side.

She managed a few good strides, but she could not stop herself looking over her shoulder to see what it would do next. Looking was a mistake. The hideous creature boasted such life as she had never seen. It was so alive, she felt sick watching it seethe and blossom before her. By comparison to its constantly changing, multiplying parts, she felt like a collection of dead twigs.

She hauled her bones and fat across the bridge, dragging the sword. Her head was on fire from the razor-slice, and blood poured down her face and dripped from her eyebrows. The void-creature sent a long, flexible stalk shooting at her: it wavered in front of her face as though seeking a target, then slapped against the cut in her forehead. It had a suction cup at its end, and this attached to the wound and began to pull. Already light-headed, Istar swatted at the stalk with her sword and, by pure luck, cut the stalk off. She grabbed the attached end, jerking it off her head with an agonizing effort, and threw it. She saw it writhing on the bridge beside her as she ran. It slurped at the air, its suction cup still adorned with her blood. More of the same trickled from its severed end.

She was almost across the bridge. She could see the edge of this place and the beginning of the next. At this end, the bone appeared cut off just as it had been from the other side. She couldn't see what was beyond: the end of the bone seemed to vanish into nothingness. The monster behind her was puffing and releasing what looked like vicious seed pods: they landed on the bridge, sprouted multiple legs, and began to scurry toward her. In a blind, primeval panic, Istar ran off the end of the bridge.

SHE TUMBLED THROUGH the mud and came upright amongst pine trees in slushy snow.

The ridge was above her, but now she was on the other side of it, halfway down the slope of Snake Pass. It was just as if she had gone nowhere: except the sky here was dark, and the air was softer, bearing traces of rain. She could smell the beginnings of growth in the wood. Spring was under way.

The bone was still there, incongruous in this familiar scene. Her ears were still ringing with an imagined echo of the singing, and she blinked a few times, trying to reconcile the stars and the monster with this ordinary world. She slapped the blindfold she had saved against the cut on her head and held it there to stop the bleeding. She threw her cloak back and sheathed her sword, which was not even fouled, although she suspected the woody stalks had blunted it. Then she started looking around for Taretel's markings.

SHAKEN, SHE CONCENTRATED on tracking him so as to bring her mind back to the solid world and dispel the terror of the things she had seen on the bridge. Taretel's trail led her across the side of Snake Pass, above the road that represented one of the major trade routes between Jai Khalar and Snake Country. Snake Pass was a narrow valley whose river waters would eventually feed the Everien River that passed A-vi-Khalar on its way to the sea gates.

Istar knew this valley well; she had been sent here as an officer trainee under Ajiko, under orders to prowl the slopes for any Sekk that had made their way out of the wild to threaten the settled lands of central Everien. She and her cohorts had come to know every boulder and stream, every shadow on the green hillsides. Sheep had grazed here in summer, and Istar had spent many a sunny afternoon lying on her back under the blue sky, just breathing, while she was supposed to be on patrol. And on one rainy and awful morning, she had seen her first Sekk. It had taken a shepherd, who came stumbling up to Istar and her partner, Garen. Istar remembered how the shepherd had cradled his broken arm.

"I have fallen," he said over and over again. "I have fallen. I am broken. Help me. I have fallen."

Overeager at the time, Istar and Garen had let the man get too close before they realized something was not quite right about him. By then, he had produced a sickle and charged at them, his strength and speed unreal, his broken limb dangling, forgotten, as his good hand hacked at them as though they were weeds that offended him.

Every moment of the exchange was etched in Istar's memory, and now, as she recollected it, her heart hammered and she found herself breathing in quick gasps, her stomach tight and her hands clenched. Istar had been the first to cross blades with the Slave, but she had underestimated its strength and fury, and she was knocked off her feet before she could strike blood. She remembered getting up in a white fury. Garen had knocked the shepherd down

147

and the sickle had gone flying. Their commander, a wily Wasp called Iriko, had been a quarter mile behind them, but Istar saw him and the rest of the group pelting across the meadow toward them.

"Kill it!" she hissed at Garen, but he hesitated. The Slave looked helpless, and his broken arm was twisted beneath him on the ground. "Hurry!" she urged. "Kill it quickly, before it strikes again."

She started to move toward the fallen machete, concerned that the Slave could still get to it. Garen could not bring himself to do it.

"Can't we just tie him up?" he said.

"You know we can't! Ah, out of the way, damn you!" And Istar had brought her blade down on the Slave's neck, severing the head against the green clover and sheep droppings.

She had gotten congratulations from Iriko for that, but not before she had turned and spotted the Sekk itself, standing in the high grass on the hillside above her. The Sekk had turned black eyes on her. She remembered how the sun struck its shaven head and seeped into the vivid purple and dark brown of its clothing. She had felt those eyes like rays burning her face, and she'd point-ed her sword at the enemy and charged up the hill after it. Iriko had shot at the Sekk master before she could get to it, and it had fled, perceiving itself overpowered. Istar had wanted to hunt it down and kill it herself, but Iriko would not permit it. Not on that day. She had been bitterly disappointed at that.

It had been a long time before she realized that what she object-ed to was the invasion of those eyes. It had been a longer time still before she admitted that she had felt no revulsion at killing the Enslaved shepherd—only relief, that she had escaped his fate. Garen had looked at her in a different way after that, and she had learned that the way to earn the respect of men was to do things they didn't dare do. So had begun her campaign to outdo every man she met. And her hatred of the Sekk, inculcated into her since early childhood, had matured to a frenzied, personal antipathy.

Not many people could kill a Slave, much less a Sekk master. Istar could, and she had made a career of it.

Now she saw the same valley again, asleep under snow, with the tracks of Taretel leading her onward. It seemed different to her now. She thought: *For years I have accepted the necessity of killing anyone who is strange, anyone whose eyes are not right. All because I have been taught to be afraid of the Slaving. Because no one can stand up to the Sekk.*

She remembered those invading black eyes of that very first Sekk, and how they had angered her. She had been afraid of the Sekk. She had wanted to kill it out of fear, to keep it from possessing her.

But what if she had stood up to it?

What if the Sekk couldn't Enslave everyone?

What if she was stronger than the rest?

She snorted. "Istar, you idiot," she informed herself. "Do you remember the *size* of Taretel? Do yourself a favor and stay well back from him."

So she tracked him like a hunter. For days that turned to weeks, she hunted him. They both lived on the meat they separately killed. Istar was low on journeybread and dried fruit, and she began to weaken from the diet of pure protein. Yet her quarry trekked on and on, following the river downcountry, toward the safe valley where Clan boundaries had been weakened in the name of Ysse. He descended to an abandoned village, where he stole potatoes and cheese from a locked cellar. Istar followed and copied his actions.

During this time, she studied him at a distance she hoped was safe. His behavior was slow and deliberate. True, he could cover a lot of ground without seeming to hurry, but Istar thought it was strange that he had none of Eteltar's nervous energy. He was big and brooding, totally unlike Eteltar with his gaunt physique, his great silvery wings, and the sparkle in the air around him—not to mention a fondness for the sound of his own voice. In Istar's memory, the winged Eteltar was never still. Nor did he possess a threatening air. He had killed fish and rabbits, and sometimes other birds, but the thought of Eteltar taking on another human being seemed somehow incongruous. He was too elusive and self-absorbed to bother killing anyone. And if all his passion had been directed toward the intricate, abstract carving in the cliff, then at least he had *had* passion. The white-haired Seahawk giant who shared his names had none. When it came to emotion, that man was like an empty box.

Yet Taretel, too, possessed a quality that could be felt rather than seen. It had made her hairs stand up on those occasions when she had been near him. There was a weight and density about him, a mastering of fear so that it became a disciplined weapon; there was a power. And somewhere, under the furs and the black garments and the skin and bulging muscles, somewhere in the skeleton or thrumming veins, there waited the Animal Magic.

Yes, she knew it was there; but this knowledge couldn't protect her from what would happen when the Animal Magic finally came out.

IT WAS MORNING. She had made a feast of stolen potatoes and cheese the night before, and now she was down by a small stream, washing out her socks and vomiting into the dead underbrush. The cheese must have been bad, she thought. She felt light-headed and strange. Watercress was growing, and she tugged it out of the brook, hoping to eat some later when she was feeling better. Then a piercing, feral scream made her jump, first within her own skin, and then to her feet, her head whipping around in a panic to locate the source of the sound. She had dropped the cress. She nearly let her bladder go. The sound was commanding, to say the least.

A shadow blotted out the light, and the largest raptor Istar had ever seen came plummeting from above the treetops, diving straight toward her.

"Oh, shit," Istar whispered. It was bigger than the Seahawk she had killed, bigger than any Seahawk she had ever seen—it had to be the skyfalcon from Tyger Pass. The bird was silver and it smelled of metal and cold. It sucked air away from her as it fell. She found she couldn't move. Her forehead had begun to throb where the bird had torn scratches in her face up in the mountains. She had taken that gesture as some kind of reconciliation between her and the bird, and naively she had believed that that was the last she would see of the creature. Now she had a moment or two in which to feel foolish, and to fumble for her dagger with icy fingers. Then the beast was on her.

Its living weight felt like a storm. She fell, rolling into a protective ball, and found herself driven down the hillside by the force of the attack. The bird sank its talons into her pack and ripped it open. Istar gripped her dagger and writhed, trying to fix a hip to the ground to use it as an axis on which to twist and strike at the skyfalcon. She was just thinking that the pack had so far saved her life by keeping the bird's claws out of her spine, when she felt herself lifted by her pack and dragged downhill. The downdraft of the falcon's wings blew snow in her face as the ground fell away and she was momentarily airborne; then the skyfalcon let go and Istar fell into a brake of gorse. She rolled to her back, wishing she could use her sword, which was lying in its scabbard pinned to the ground by her backside. There was no way she could draw it while lying on the ground. She levered herself onto her shoulders and crabwalked away from the bird, which had turned in the air and was circling for another pass. If only she could make it to the cover of the trees, she would have the advantage, for the bird's wingspan would prevent it from moving easily among the branches. Istar scuttled furiously. Her pack was torn and she left a trail of rope, dried fish, medicines, and bandages as they were forced out of the rip by her movement. She could feel the lumps of Eteltar's skeleton digging into her back.

The bird cruised over her head and seemed to hover above her. She was almost under the trees now. Another few yards and she would be safe.

It landed on her chest and pinned her right hand with the dagger beneath its left claw. Its head bent and it fixed its beak around the strap attaching her pack to her shoulders. It began to tug.

"No!" Istar shrieked, suddenly comprehending what the skyfalcon wanted. "Get away! You can't have Eteltar!"

She resisted with sudden, unexpected fury. Those hollow bones were all she had left of the winged man. They might be dead relics, but they meant everything to Istar. She fought back crazily, arching her back to try to unbalance the bird and slamming her head up into its chest. She got her dagger hand free and slashed away some feathers before the claw closed on her hand and pinched the nerves in her wrists. She was compelled to drop the dagger.

Istar spat and screamed. She flashed a vision of herself, bloody and eviscerated, her guts scattered across the snow: just another kill for the huge predator. At the same time, a new depth of defiance opened in her belly. She had her feet on the ground and was churning up the snow, backpedaling for the forest with the bird still clinging to her. Its wings snagged on branches overhead. Istar backed into a fallen pine log and used it to hoist herself up. The bird was fanning its wings backward, trying to drag her into the air and away from the trees. Istar planted a boot in the middle of its body and pushed it off.

The skyfalcon shrieked. It looked at her sideways through one eye and then, with a lightning movement of its feather-clad legs, it spun her around and ripped the pack away from her back. Istar reached over her shoulder and managed to seize one of the bones, but the rest of the bundle was tightly gripped in the skyfalcon's claws. It pulled. Istar pulled back. For a minute she thought the whole bundle would burst apart; she held on tight, determined not to give up.

"Let it go!" said a familiar deep voice in her ear, and a set of powerful arms came around her, hands closing over hers. "Let it go! Istar, do not fight me!"

The voice was Eteltar's; but the hands were not the hands of the winged man. Startled, she turned and looked into the eyes of Taretel, her erstwhile captive. The skyfalcon let loose another piercing cry, and in almost the same moment, the bone came free of the bundle and she went toppling back into Taretel. He staggered backward and held her as the skyfalcon, too, went careering away still clutching the rest of the bones.

"It's all right," he said, and she was so stunned she could only stare at him. "They are the skyfalcon's bones, too. Together, the two of us made Eteltar."

ARE YOU SUCH A SINGER?

$\mathcal{I}$ shivered myself into consciousness, feeling angry and horrible and betrayed. I was slumped against a tree some little way from a campfire in the forest. Someone had thrown a cloak over me, but it had come open, and falling snow was drifting onto my bare skin. I could hear horses and men milling about nearby, but there was no one in my immediate vicinity other than a single guard. He was not much older than I, and he looked almost as cold. Under a rather scatty fur cloak, his dress was a bastardized version of one of the Pharician cavalry uniforms that I had seen in my father's books: steel-studded leather jerkin, gauntlets, wide cloth breeches with fur boots instead of the armored ones worn in Pharice. He had squeezed the jerkin over the top of a woolen shirt, and he had a wool scarf wrapped around his head instead of a helmet. In different circumstances, I might have thought he looked absurd; but I was afraid. In addition to the Pharician crossbow and curved sword, he carried a large hunting knife, which he was using to carve something into the bark of the tree. He saw me stir and gave a shout for his commander.

"Prince Tash! She wakes!"

Almost immediately on regaining consciousness, I had begun to feel sick, and now it came on me in an uncontrollable wave. I turned in to the tree and retched feebly, bringing up a stream of bile into the clean snow. My ears rang. Everything seemed exaggerated: shouts echoing among the trees; birds clattering their wings; snow falling in whispered sheets from the branches of the pine. Trying to pull myself together, I put some snow in my mouth. My head was spinning and I felt weak all over. I glanced at the graze on my arm where the arrow had slipped past me, and saw that it had closed without swelling, but the line of the scratch was black as ink.

153

Tash came then, appearing like a king in his hall from among the pillars of trees, his red cloak swirling round him in the falling snow, his head coming up to regard me where I huddled. A grand entrance. I could not help but make comparisons with the men I already knew. He was nothing like Jihan and certainly nothing like Tarquin, but he did remind me slightly of Chyko. It is hard to say why, exactly. He was bigger and darker than Chyko and did not move so gracefully, and he had much more of an air of command about him. His face was artistically scarred in a way that made it hard not to look at him, for the scars seemed to lead the eye to his eyes, behind which the mind of this man was seen to be fiercely concentrated. The nostrils flared wide, twin plumes of smoke puffing from his nostrils. Like an animal, he seemed to be smelling me.

He gestured for me to get up. I tried to, but my feet were so frozen they had no feeling, and I could not get my balance. I fell against the tree. My teeth chattered.

"I thought I told you to look after her!" he barked at the soldier, fetching him a clout across the side of the head that sent the boy spinning. "Pick her up and bring her to the fire. Find what's-his-name. The healer."

"Briest is taking care of the injured, my Prince," the soldier said.

"Injured? They are warriors, tough men! This is just a child, Lumula! By my father's eyeballs, do I have to instruct you in every single detail?"

Lumula came lurching toward me, trying to regain his balance but plainly unable to do so. He reeled from tree to tree, then finally came up to me. He smelled of horses. He picked me up and set me on his bony shoulder like a sack. Together we went bumping off through the trees to the campfire, where Tash shouted for everyone to clear out of the way.

"Watch the prisoners!" he barked at almost everyone he saw. "Make sure there are watchers in the trees, too, in case that thing on the lake comes back."

The young soldier set me down on a saddle blanket by the fire. Perversely, I began to shiver more, not less. My nose streamed. I didn't know whether to be grateful or afraid. I couldn't seem to look at anyone square on.

"Get Shiror!" Tash said to the soldier. Then he turned to me, squatting beside me and putting his hand under my chin to make me look at him. There were little icicles on his glove.

"Do you understand my language?" he asked, slowly and rather more loudly than was necessary. He used the Clan common speech.

"Yes, I understand you," I replied in Pharician, and he rocked back on his heels. He had not expected that.

"Who are you? Where do you come from? Where are your people?"

"I am l-l-l-ost," I said through chattering teeth. "I th-think the timeserpent brought me. I have no people. I am lost."

"Did you call the fire fiends? Or did you send them away?"

I shook my head, unable to explain. He was staring at me intently. I deliberately allowed the cold and the fatigue and the fright to take me over. If he didn't perceive me as a threat, then he probably wouldn't harm me, and I took his interested gaze to mean the same thing that Chyko's gaze had meant. I expected to find myself spreading my legs for him soon enough. It was better than dying.

"They tell me I should kill you," he said. "Dario and the Seahawk prisoners. For all that they disagree with each other, they all agree on this. 'Kill the Sekk,' they tell me."

"They don't understand," I said weakly.

He smiled. "You and I are going to have to talk. But not now." A distracted expression flashed across his face; then he barked a man's name over his shoulder. "Shiror!"

A dark man in a thick blue cloak came running. He nodded respectfully to Tash, who said, "Come and do what you do. You were good with Ukili, and you understand women, do you not?"

Shiror started to demur, but Tash said, "She will be in your charge. See she does not die, but be careful what you say around her. She understands Pharician. She is probably a rebel spy."

Now Shiror was looking at me. He said, "The glass shards she had in her cloak? Dario has a whole collection of them that she got from the cave they all speak of."

"Can we get to the cave?"

"Not without crossing the barrier. We all saw the Seahawks bumping into it like a bird hits a windowpane."

"But it was not fire, there, was it?"

"No," Shiror said gravely. "It was not. I have been thinking of that. Jakse's men have admitted they could not penetrate the timeserpent's trail, but there was no fire until last night."

He looked at me. I looked at the snow.

"Jakse is dead by my hand. His men who attacked us on the ice were all burned, and some of them will die. Only Dario is unscathed." I could not help glancing up, and he was still looking at me as if I were a curiosity. "Dario says these are the bodies of the Sekk," he added, showing Tash a piece of broken glass. I saw it flash in the gray light and the falling snow. *I am Anuna*, it said. *I will speak of the conquest of fevers and the distillation of vegetable essences.*

Inexplicably, I began to cry. It was like a voice from the dead, that tiny thread of words that now had no home. The glass that it had come from was irretrievably shattered.

The two men were oblivious to the meaning of the broken glass they possessed. They did not seem to hear it whispering, for they carried on talking, no longer about me, but now about fishing and hunting and numbers of spears and management of prisoners and snow lions and emergency roads through the mountains; but I wasn't paying attention.

Until Everien, I had never known real cold, or real hunger, or even real people—except Chyko. I had known frustration and anger and fear and grief, but those emotional conditions all seemed faded and insignificant in light of the purely physical duress I now faced. I had come into Everien in a position of abject misery and almost total disorientation, and I had no real experience of any of my senses. I felt stunned and strange, and now other people, strangers, were taking actions all around me while I could do nothing but shiver and sneeze.

I felt a fool, a child; duped. Beaten.

"Hey!" said Tash suddenly, and I was recalled to my situation. "Girl! What's your name?"

"Jaya," I said, sniffing.

"Jaya, this wants explaining, all of it. You will be fed and kept warm, and if you cannot walk, we will make arrangements for you to be carried. In return, I expect your service and your loyalty. If these are not forthcoming, we will leave you to freeze in the wilderness. Do you understand?"

I nodded.

"Shiror," Tash said. "You know the drill. She is not Ukili, so no need to get carried away; but keep her alive, at least for a while."

When Shiror brought me food, I ate it like a starving dog.

I almost choked at first. The vegetables and the meat were pre-sumably Everien in origin, and not the same as the ones I had known all my life. I probably could have coped with that, but the spices that the Pharicians felt compelled to add made the food burn my mouth, and after eating, my eyes began to water and my nose to run.

"Are you trying to poison me?" I asked Shiror, and he slapped me across the face.

"I doubt you can cook better, little bitch. Is this your idea of gratitude?"

I apologized, feeling very sorry for myself as I huddled over my soup. Shiror continued to watch me. After a minute he sighed as if giving in after an argument, and from among the provisions he pulled out a block of something pale and slick. He chopped off a section the size of my palm and gave it to me.

I examined the frozen lump cautiously.

"Your refined appetite will soon change," Shiror said. "That is pure pig fat. Eat it, or you will sicken in this cold."

I sucked on the fat cautiously, mostly because he looked as though he would strike me if I didn't. It was disgusting, but I couldn't seem to stop myself consuming it, so maybe Shiror was right. I didn't realize until later, when I saw the men lining up meek as lambs to receive their portions of the substance, what an act of generosity this was on his part. I am sure he could have let me die without any blame to himself, but he didn't.

"If I didn't know better," he said, "I would have thought you were some kind of princess from my own country."

I glanced at him. He was watching me curiously.

"What if I were?" I said.

"Then you'd be very unlucky to be here in Everien, with us. Especially now."

I perked up, hoping for news. "What's now?"

He shook his head. "If you want to know anything, you'll have to ask Tash. I consider you a prisoner."

Rebuffed, I fell silent. They were only keeping me alive to use me. I simply didn't know how they intended to do that.

TASH MADE NO secret of the fact that he mistrusted Dario, but I could see no reason to believe her loyalties lay elsewhere than with

Pharice. She had done nothing to protest at the killing of Jakse on the ice, and she showed no love for the prisoners that Tash had taken. The dark-eyed Seahawk called Pentar was kept under double guard. ("I remember you," Tash said to him. "You fought under the white-haired Seahawk who thwarted me in the pass. Now you will lead me through the mountains, home.") Pentar was neither burned nor wounded, but I could not help noticing that the glances he let fall on Dario were full of hate. She did not look at him, not once.

There were enough Pharicians to guard the Clan prisoners, and I noticed that Shiror had set himself as Dario's shadow. Outside of Tash's earshot, she bragged incessantly about having single-handedly destroyed the Sekk (she never admitted to the Pharicians that she had failed to shoot me, but I caught her looking at me and making a Clan sign against evil); while within Tash's earshot, she was subdued. I think she sensed he was looking for an excuse to kill her. He was not a difficult man to read.

The next day, Tash took his men hunting, and I was left under Lumula's supervision. Not as intelligent as Shiror, he was easily drawn into conversation. I learned from him that Tash was fond of young women and used them to discover the secrets of Everien. Out of the mouths of uneducated girls came great Knowledge, said my guard. Usually we went mad in the end, but all in a good cause.

"What kind of secrets?" I wanted to know.

"Weapons," he said. "Now, how did you learn to speak Pharician?"

I had already invented a story about being a Snake Clan refugee, to which I now added something about my mother having a maid who was Pharician. When I tested it out on the guard, he guffawed.

"Don't know about that. Never heard of no Clan woman being rich enough to keep a Pharician ladies' maid. But you'll be a spy, anyway. It's all right." He began to laugh, as if my fate were all a part of a play being put on for his entertainment. "You'll learn not to lie to your betters as saved you in this cursed land. You'll learn. Soon enough he'll get around to you, will Tash. Aye, he'll know what to do with you. What's the matter?"

I had suddenly shuddered for no reason, and I felt dizzy. There was a sharp pain behind my eyeballs.

"Briest!" Lumula called. "Come and look. She's doing it again."

I passed in and out of consciousness while Briest looked me over. Lumula asked him a lot of questions, which Briest didn't answer. He left, and later returned with some yellow powder that he told me to dissolve in hot water and drink. I was not surprised to learn that it tasted foul; then it put me to sleep.

IN THOSE FIRST days in Everien, I was disappointed, first in my circumstances, and second—and worse—in myself. I had thought myself intelligent, resilient, strong-minded, resourceful; but as it turned out, I was only slow-witted, weak, and rather pathetic. There were Clansmen among our group, selected by Tash for their mountain-worthiness; they spoke crudely and were reviled by the Pharicians, yet they were survivors, unperturbed by cold, hunger, fatigue, or the unpredictable events of the road. The Pharicians were not so flexible. At every unplanned-for turning point or unexpected obstacle, the Pharician men reacted with either panic or paralysis, retreating to long discussions about order and procedure amongst the officers—discussions that were usually cut short by Tash stepping in and giving a direct order. Yet even the Pharicians seemed better able to cope with life on the road than I. They were, after all, professional soldiers, I tried to console myself. But there was more to it than that. I was tired all the time. Sometimes I couldn't walk. I slept poorly, and sometimes woke fevered. I ate all the time, but I was losing weight, and Briest said the color of my skin was not good.

I think the Clansmen present would have dumped me by the roadside if they had been allowed. Dario's conviction that I was a Sekk seemed to have spread, and for all that Tash favored me, I felt vulnerable. I lay awake at night, knowing something was very wrong with me; knowing that Briest's medicinal teas could do nothing. I kept thinking of the words of the timeserpent. Like a beast trapped inside me, my helplessness clawed at me from within. In the night, when the camp was quiet, I lay in a delirium of part sickness, part pain, part exhaustion, and part fear, and I began to think. Coldly, calculating, first in small useless circles, and then, gradually, with more presence of mind.

Tash questioned me the day after the hunt, while the meat was being prepared for the fire. I had the impression that he was trying to plan his next move, but the Seahawk Pentar was being only marginally helpful in providing information on the mountainous geography, and the camp was in a general state of chaos that set everyone on edge. Shiror walked around muttering about "contagious Clan chaos . . . never seen anything like this in all the empire" and sometimes it looked as though the prisoners outnumbered the captors, although it only appeared that way because Tash had sent out scouting parties to find a way back to Everien without running afoul of any more timeserpent trails.

"I need to know how you did it," Tash said. "Dario saw you at the cave. You were on the other side of the timeserpent trail. She could not cross the fire. I saw men consumed by it, out on the ice. How"—and the assessing look he gave me reminded me that in my weakened condition, I didn't appear very impressive—"how did *you* cross?"

"I just . . . walked," I said, looking into his eyes so he would know I was telling the truth. "Well, after Dario jumped on me, it was more as if I rolled, but at first I just walked into the burned area and—"

"Burned area?" he said sharply. "What do you mean?"

"Where you couldn't pass. I saw you."

"You *saw* through the timeserpent barrier?"

"Yes. When you came up to the barrier, everything you did was very slow, and you tried to go through, but you couldn't. Then you cried, *Fire!*"

"Because there *was* a fire!" Tash said as though affronted I should contradict him.

"There *had been* a fire," I corrected gently, using formal High Pharician to emphasize the syntactical difference in what we had seen. "It wasn't there anymore."

Tash shuddered.

"If the timeserpent altered the times of the adjacent pieces of land," I said slowly, feeling my way, "then perhaps I was ahead of you. Maybe, for me, the fire had already passed."

"Ah!" He leaped on that. "But I have already interviewed Dario, and she says there was a fire on her side, too. It sprang up as soon as they tried to cross. She said nothing about a 'burned area.' "

I took a deep breath. "Well," I admitted, "then the difference must have something to do with me."

"You are Sekk. Dario could not have killed every one. She failed to kill you." He paused, his eyes probing me. "Is it true, Jaya? I have seen how she looks at you."

"No," I said quickly, but I was flustered at his accuracy. I remembered the glass shards and the Knowledge Guardians they contained. *I am Jaya, the Innocent Eye.* How was I supposed to explain?

"You came out of the cave. We know this. The cave of the Lake of Candles, where Sekk spirits lived in floating globes on the water. Was it so for you as well, Jaya? You lived in a glass ball, before this?"

The questions were so strangely sincere; so full of a mixture of superstition, hostility, and wonder, that I wanted to laugh.

"I guess . . ." I said vaguely. "But these creatures you call Sekk, they have hunted me, too. Not in Everien, somewhere else." I waved my hands to compensate for not being able to explain. "I have heard them singing."

"And you? Are you such a . . . singer . . . as well?"

While I was trying to think what to say, he pressed me: "I know nothing of the Sekk other than what people tell me. Dario says all the Sekk are gone, but if you are a Sekk, why do you not Enslave us?"

I looked at my hands. I couldn't think straight, I was cold, my head hurt. I could feel tears welling behind my eyes.

"I think," I said carefully, "that everything has gone mad. Here, in Everien, and in my home, too. The Sekk aren't supposed to be Slavemasters—not masters of humans, anyway. I'm not supposed to be here. And those monsters we saw in the fire . . ."

"What about them?" Tash said eagerly. "Can you fight them? Can you *control* them?"

"No!" I gasped. "Why would I want to do that?"

He sat back and looked at me, long and low under heavy eyelids.

"You will want to do *something*," he said wryly. "To earn your keep. You told me, earlier, when you were more frightened and not so canny as now, you told me that you could help me. Dario is afraid of you. You faced the monsters in the fire. I think you will want to do as I ask. I think you will want very much to help me." He paused, and I felt myself being studied, but I didn't know what I was revealing. *I* was accustomed to doing the observing and studying. "Do you think so, Jaya?"

I licked my lips. When I tried to speak, my voice cracked and gave out. I coughed. Tried again. This time my voice came out a whisper. "What is it you want?"

"I want many things. But to begin with, I want a way through any timeserpent trails we encounter on our way to Jai Khalar."

I had no reason to believe I could bring a whole army through such a barrier, but I didn't say so. I kept my head bowed.

"And, the next time any of those monsters come around—or, for that matter, the timeserpent itself—then I want you to deal with it."

Deal with it?

"I think you know what I mean," he added.

AFTER THAT, WHENEVER there was time, either at night when we were camped, or while we were actually on the move, slogging through snow and mud to follow the directions of the scouts, Tash came and spoke to me of engines and battles and the military problems he would have to solve.

"The Knowledge is there for the taking," he said. "Someone will put it to use, and that someone might as well be me. The sooner I can tame Everien, the sooner I can return to my home country in glory. I miss my horses."

I knew the kinds of machines he meant. And I knew more. My youthful reading had not been in vain. I sketched them from memory, and sometimes from invention. These things came easily to me. Even when I was creating new forms and variations on the forms I knew, it was not as if I were doing so for the first time. I was rediscovering old abilities and awarenesses I had forgotten while in the forest. My education was coming back to me in a rush. It was good to use my mind again, and I did.

But I did not draw or write in Tash's presence. Those activities I undertook alone, in a dreamlike state, and I found myself humming and even singing softly as I did so. Sometimes I sang the musics I heard when I handled the glass shards I had saved. And then it was as if these musics grew and multiplied and became something else in my head, until there was an inner music. If I followed this song that sang itself, I was led to the conclusions I needed to find.

Also, I was feeling ill nearly all the time, and the singing distracted me from feeling sorry for myself. It led me along and got me through the days. I had no one to talk to, and the singing became an indirect way of talking to myself.

Lumula observed me darkly now. I wondered if he was remembering his initial words to me, about how Tash would use me, and now realized that I was different. Unlike Tash's former victims, I willingly let myself be co-opted. And I could explain my meanings. I did not swoon and cry, for all that I felt unwell and seldom raised my voice or moved beyond what was necessary for my bodily needs.

Tash took to riding beside me in the litter, examining my drawings of firethrowers and giving little exclamations of pleasure every so often. I had seen the looks the men exchanged with one another whenever Tash emerged from the curtained litter looking satisfied, and I knew what they thought we were doing. But Tash had not touched me. It came as a relief: Chyko had used me without apology, as if I were no different than a horse to be ridden at his bidding. As if he had been doing me a favor, in fact. At first I had been too shocked to resist, but since then I had had time to think about it, time for resentment and hate to build in me. These feelings were all the stronger to compensate for my anger at myself for not resisting Chyko—for allowing him, even, to think that I didn't mind so as to avoid his explosive temper—so that I was fairly sure I would fight to the death if any man touched me now. The fact that Tash did not touch me made me willing to show him what he wanted to know.

I tried to show him principles; but he was impatient. "I want solutions!" he cried, shaking his fist in the air. "I am not a Scholar. I am a warrior."

"I am not a warrior," I answered. "I have only ever been a student."

He looked at me long and hard. "I can't decide about you," he said. "Whether you are stupid but honest, or cunning but pretending to be a fool."

"I am neither," I said.

Tash said, "I think you come from a place very different from what I have known."

"That," I answered, "is the most insightful thing I have heard you say yet."

He looked pleased at first; then angry as he realized that he was

163

being evaluated by his own prisoner.

"You need to think of a way for us to get past the timeserpent and recover Everien," he said. "We ride alongside the seam and we will look for a flaw in it, a way to cross. You will then take me to the Fire Houses, or what remains of them, and we will put your ideas to the test."

"All right," I said, yawning. "Listen to the singing. Maybe I can sing back to them."

He stared at me. He had no idea what I was talking about. I wanted to say, "This is not my real life, I am not a prisoner in a frozen land," and have it come true. I wanted to snap my fingers and call Jihan to explain things to me. But Jihan was not there, and my house was far away. Somehow, stupidly, when I planned my adventures as a girl, when I imagined myself journeying out in the world and having escapades, I had always believed I would remain, essentially, me. Now it didn't seem so clear-cut. I felt myself dwindling and confused amidst the Pharicians and all their physical power. At the same time, another part of me was growing stronger. There were things I knew that they would never know.

But I didn't know why I knew those things.

At the very root of it, I felt very, very alone.

EVERY SO OFTEN we passed close enough to the barrier for its monsters to spit at me and talk to me. I don't think anyone else saw, or surely they would have panicked. The horses showed no reaction. But to me, the occasional eruptions of timeserpent seam were disconcerting. And whether we were near to its barrier or not, the timeserpent often whispered in my ear. Sometimes, with my arm being wounded, I would fall into a fever at night, and then I would hear it whispering.

"Your father never planned this," the timeserpent said. "It is so silly, really. You, humankind, can grasp small granules of time and you make your plans accordingly. You have no sense of the sweep of the beach. You don't know where the sea is. Your concept of planning is a ruin of mischance."

"Go away," I answered. "You *aren't*. You wish you existed, but you don't."

I knew my words were empty. In truth, the timeserpent could have sucked me into the Unworld that lived in its gullet. It could have rendered me Never. But it didn't, and this puzzled me. Why did everyone want to save me?

I was no longer wholly sure I wanted to be saved.

But the glass shards sang to me, and sang, and sang. I could not stop my ears. There were thousands of people in those voices. Thousands of thoughts and feelings, connections, sensations, habits. And for every datum, every scrap of information, there was loneliness. For this Knowledge had been taken out of its context of life and death, and trapped in these shining, transparent planes of glass.

How sad I felt for them: the Sekk. How well I understood Chyko's anger at what had happened to him.

But what could I do now? What could I do?

I felt too small to make a difference.

HELLO, KILLER

 Tash was in my litter in the late morning of a fine day when we heard a commotion outside. We had been riding along a river valley, headed for the heart of Everien according to the scouts, and making good progress in fair weather. So far, we had managed to skirt the timeserpent boundaries and still make our way, and my abilities had not been put to any concrete test. When the shouting first broke out, I thought that Pentar and his prisoners had tried to escape. There was a noise of weapons and horses neighing. Tash sprang out of the litter, calling for his sword. Shiror was already coming toward us, his eyes wide, his blood up.

"The skyfalcon has returned—" he began, but Tash brushed past him. We were in a cleared cutting running through a pine forest beside a river, at the narrow end of a valley that opened out as it descended toward central Everien before us. To the right, near the river, a huddle of men had gathered around one of their own. I heard gasps and muffled moans. To the left, a tall pine tree was swaying under the weight of an enormous skyfalcon.

It was a beautiful thing. Its wings spread, and as we watched, it glided from the tree, landing on the roof of my litter with a thud. The litter shook and the fabric tore, but the bird kept its wings spread and flapped them slowly as it clung to the litter, balanced so perfectly that the frame did not collapse. I peered out the side fearfully and saw its silver eye watching me. It had a white stick in its curved beak.

Tash, who had raced toward the tree where the bird was, now had to turn and come back toward me. I glimpsed his confused face, and the sword that had been brought to him by a hurried Lumula was now brushed aside.

"Ah, the skyfalcon," said Tash. "It is my father's gift to me, and a mischievous one, as well. A dangerous thing, but much loved by me. He has followed me here, for I am his lord."

Tash walked up to the skyfalcon with the air of a king claiming his own. But as he spoke, the bird had transferred the object in its mouth to its left claw. Tash had to dodge a snakelike strike from its outstretched beak, which snapped shut on the fringe of his fur cloak. Tash was jerked and twisted mid-stride, and he stumbled to his knees before recovering and pulling away, out of the bird's range. The skyfalcon resumed its one-footed roost on the litter.

"The bird won't let anyone near it," Shiror said with a conciliatory air. "It's taken Raz's arm off at the elbow."

Raz let out a nerve-shredding scream.

"Shoot it!" Tash cried, examining his damaged cloak with evident distress.

"No!" I sprang out of the litter with more animation than I felt. I looked up at the great bird that was crushing the struts of the litter between its talons. "Let me try. Please."

"What if it flies away with her?" Tash said to Shiror. "This could be some kind of trick."

I laughed. "I think I am too heavy for anything smaller than a horse to carry! Please, Prince Tash. Let me try."

We looked at each other. He was much softer than Chyko, I realized. Much easier to manipulate.

"Watch yourself!" he said. "You were lying down in your litter all day yesterday with a fever. Don't push it."

I smiled. "I'll be all right."

Tash was grumbling darkly and shifting in agitation as I approached the bird. The skyfalcon had cleverly shifted its balance so that it stood on its right foot, so as to hold the length of white stick in its left.

"Hello, killer," I said. The bird looked at me sideways. It dropped the stick. Before anyone else could react, I stepped forward and picked up the stick from the snow where it had fallen. It was not a stick. It was a bone.

"I think it's a man's rib," I said curiously, examining the bone.

"We're going to shoot the bird," Tash said. "Get out of the way."

But the skyfalcon was too quick for him. It was off the strut with a snapping sound, passing over their heads and then rising with astonishing speed.

"I can see through it!" Shiror cried. "Look, in its wings! I can see a green country!"

I saw it, too: only a glimpse, but an astonishing one, of hills and green grass and blue sky, all in miniature within the cut-out shape of the skyfalcon's wings. Then the bird was too high to shoot, and I relaxed. Tash collected the bone from me. As soon as I let it go, I realized I felt ill and exhausted.

Shiror came and put me back on the litter, and we continued on our way. The seam in the sky ahead was boiling black and red, and the cold air felt heavy, like steel pressing against my cheeks. The Pharicians and their Clan allies were ill at ease. I could see that they had little experience of magic, for all that they spoke of Knowledge and Animal Magic. They were easily frightened by events they couldn't explain; but I have never been able to explain the events of my very existence, and I am not afraid of magic. There in the litter, I knew I was ill and maybe even dying, but I also knew that I had been swept along until now in the grip of a wild illogic that picked me up and set me down and tied itself in knots around me, yet I still had most of my wits. The sight of the skyfalcon had heartened me, and even more so, the brief feeling of that bone in my hands had sent a thrill through me. It was as if the bone, so replete with hidden information that it seemed to sing into my palms, had very nearly spoken to me just as the shattered glass did.

THE NEXT MORNING, I realized I had acquired a shadow. I had not seen much of Dario in the beginning, and I saw nothing of the Seahawk prisoners, who were kept well behind Tash's men and had to camp at a separate fire, under guard day and night. But after the skyfalcon came and brought me the bone, Dario stationed herself beside the litter for the better part of the day, riding beside me and looking at me through the curtains whenever no one else was around to observe her. When Lumula went to fetch my medicine, she parted the curtains and came inside.

"It is the mark of a depraved mind," she said, "that you hide in here pretending to be sick. Do not think you are fooling anyone with your beauty or your grace or your helplessness. I shot out every one of those lights. They were beautiful and I didn't want to do it; but sometimes reason must overcome instinct. I will kill you, too. It is my duty."

I listened, dumbfounded, as this vitriol poured from her. She was staring daggers at me. I wondered why she didn't just do it, and finally I said so. "Why don't you kill me now? If you're so sure?"

Her eyes flickered. Again I could smell fear. She tensed and her hand went to her dagger. "Maybe I will," she said; and again, the depth of her hatred rocked me to the core. Then there was a noise outside: Lumula returning. She flicked the curtain aside and was out of the litter just as Lumula was coming in the other side.

"You look terrible," he said. "I've never in all my life seen such a sickly person."

I wasn't listening. I was thinking about Dario's hate of me.

THE NEXT DAY, we encountered a new obstacle. We were ascending a long hill between steep cliffs, cutting a path straight into the mountains: Snake Pass, I heard Pentar telling Tash. "It is the fastest way back to Jai Khalar."

Ahead, the sky was black, and the land below lay under shadow. I knew right away what this meant, but the others didn't seem to notice anything. I called for Lumula.

"Why is it so dark up ahead?" I asked innocently, as a test.

"Dark?" He looked at me sidelong, then felt my forehead. "Shall I call Briest for more medicine? Can't you see?"

I said, "Please tell Prince Tash that we are coming up on a time-serpent barrier, and he should be wary. It is near the top of this next rise, where the pass narrows. I do not think there is fire, but I can't be sure."

Lumula looked unnerved and scurried away, and then Tash came and fetched me himself. His blood was up, and he was moving around nervously, wasting a lot of energy as men do before a fight. I was made to come out of the litter and walk up front with Tash and Shiror. Tash ordered the procession to stop just shy of the barrier. "I see nothing," he said. "Shoot arrows and let us see what happens to them."

It was still dark on the other side of the barrier, but I could see them go into the darkness, and one or two I could even see landing on the rocky ground beyond. For Tash and his people, every single arrow that was shot into the barrier vanished into thin air.

"Jaya speaks the truth," Tash said. He turned to me. "How do we get through? And do you see monsters?"

The words had no sooner left his mouth than a thing shaped like a snowflake came flying out of the seam. It was all sharp edges glazed with dried blood, but it did not move like an object that has been thrown, it moved like a thing with its own mind and purposes. It spun over our heads, lopping a few off as it progressed. Through a square orifice at the center of the disc blasted an offensive noise. It was laughing.

The Pharicians shot a hail of arrows at the thing, but it was no thicker than a saw blade and seemed to have much of the same function. The arrows bounced off it harmlessly, and it would have gone badly for us if the thing had turned around and repeated its pass. But it slipped into the darkness and was lost from view.

Tash was ordering a retreat, but it had all happened so quickly that his command came too late. Heads were still rolling and bodies gushing blood as his orders echoed from the cliffs surrounding us. Horses neighed and reared, inciting each other to panic. Some of the men were crying, which surprised me, considering the atrocities of war they must have witnessed before this; still, there was something surreal about the inexorable, mindless way the thing had come at us, taken off the heads of three riders, and then vanished. I listened for the timeserpent, but I could not hear its voice. Faint music I could hear, writhing softly, but whether it was in the seam of the timeserpent, or in my own head, I wasn't sure.

We backed off a quarter mile, and guards were stationed to watch for anything that might come out of the barrier. By the accounts of both Pentar and Dario, Tash quickly determined that there was no other way he could get horses and wagons back to Jai Khalar. Snake Pass was the only choice if Tash didn't want to spend six months going all the way back to Seahawk and thence to the sea plateau by boat. I sat in my litter and waited for him to come. I knew what he was going to demand, but I didn't know what I was going to do.

"Jaya, you will get us across," Tash said, perfectly on cue. It was not a request, it was a statement of fact taken for granted. Despite the deaths of three good men, he did not seem very worried. My drawings must have impressed him.

"Prince Tash," I ventured, "I may be able to cross this barrier myself, but that doesn't mean I can help you to do so."

"But you must!" he said. He looked me up and down. "You are not thinking of escaping, are you? The wilderness is no place for you, alone. Remember the condition we found you in? And what about your illness?"

If I didn't know better, I might have thought he was wheedling me. The great and powerful Tash. But he was right. I could not survive on my own. I would have to bide my time, and help him in the meanwhile. But how? I began to cast about for something to say, hoping to distract him and buy myself some more time.

"The skyfalcon," I blurted. "Have you done anything with the bone it gave to me?"

I had chosen my words deliberately, and I saw his eyes flash as he came up against the fact that the skyfalcon had rejected him and offered the bone to me. I didn't care about the bone at this moment, but in the time Tash took to fetch it, maybe something would occur to me.

"Do you need it?" he said eagerly. "Is it an Artifact?"

"It has special properties," I said. Tash shouted for the bone to be brought, and Briest came trotting over with it. Tash nodded at me and Briest placed the rib gently into my hands.

I felt it singing to my own bones. I couldn't understand it, but I felt it go through me like a current. Food did not nourish me, and I slept poorly lately, but this brief contact with the bone made me feel alive again, and strong. I said, "I will need some time, to study this thing, and to prepare."

But Tash was having none of it. "I have no time!" he barked. "Do not get carried away with yourself, Jaya. Come! You have had weeks to prepare. You've done nothing but lie about and think. You must be ready by now."

And he dragged me forward, his left hand on my right hand, his right hand on his curving Pharician longsword. What he thought he was going to do against the flying bladewheel, I couldn't have said. If nothing else, you had to give Tash marks for daring.

I stretched out my arm and put my hand through the barrier. If I paid close attention, I could feel the slightest change in the air current where the times shifted. On the other side, the ground was soft. Moss and grass were growing there, but on this side, everything was dead and gray after the ravages of winter. Just as I had watched Tash approach the barrier in the forest and be repelled, I

171

could look through this timeserpent trail and see the hillside beyond as if nothing were wrong.

But last time, I had seen a burn scar, and smoke, when the fire hadn't come yet. Tash hadn't seen those things. No one but I had seen them.

"Prince Tash," I said, "what do you see, just over there?" I pointed to the place where the barrier was.

"Nothing special," Tash said.

"No sunlight?" I prompted. "Nothing green?"

He stared at me as if I were pulling his leg.

"I see a hillside, with stones, patches of snow, clouds. No people, no animals, just rocks and dead grass. Now what the vexed—"

"Shh!"

He was so startled at being shushed that he quieted down.

"There's a barrier here," I said. "Try and go through."

Tash hesitated. I knew he didn't believe me, and that his first instinct was to tell *me* to go through—but if he made me go first and it turned out I wasn't lying, then I'd be free and he'd be stuck. I could actually *see* him realizing this, and an instant later his hand shot out and he grabbed my arm.

"We go together," he said.

I shrugged. "Come on, then," I said.

I stepped into the barrier with Tash's hand on my arm like a crab's pincer. As I began to cross, the distorted roar of his yell warped the air. I tugged at him, but I was too weak, and my arm felt like a piece of ripe fruit, bruising and crushed in his grip. I could feel the flames around me. They were not hot, but they licked and flickered around me, and the life within them moved, too, winding up around me like plants growing much too fast. I hesitated. If I shook Tash off, I would be free on the other side of the barrier; but in that event, I would be alone in the wilderness with no food or shelter. And I did not know what the next time frame might hold.

While I was trying to make up my mind, my arm was growing hot where Tash was holding me. The flames didn't burn me, but to judge by the strange and backwards screams I could hear coming from his side of the barrier, they were scorching him. His hand was hot. I struggled to loosen his grip, pulling my arm until his hand slid down to my wrist, where it held fast again. I knew he couldn't hold on forever with the flames biting him, and I was prepared to wait him out. But then I felt the rumor of the timeserpent.

It was whispering from inside the flames.

The codes, Jaya, it said. *Yours are public, carved in the machine for all to see. But I am a natural phenomenon. I can sing your codes and send you where I will. But you cannot sing mine. I have not been codified. Do you wish to meet me on such terms?*

The words didn't sink into my mind. I didn't take their meaning. But the voice, that secret timeserpent whisper that seemed by its execution to be only reinforcing a truth I had always known (oh, that is what's so sneaky and devastating about a timeserpent, its ability to give you that feeling of déjà vu, to make meaning where no meaning lies, that is what really worries me), that voice made my skin crawl.

The codes, Jaya. Me in all my inscrutableness, I cannot be broken like you.

"You are a coward," I said with more bravura than wit. "You are always turning up and taunting me, then running away again. Why don't you leave me alone?"

You and I are entwined, chuckled the timeserpent. *It will not be so easy to get rid of me. Unless you intend on getting rid of yourself.*

"It seems to me," I replied in an insinuating tone, "that you have retreated to the Liminal. That you are hiding. You carved up Everien, and then disappeared. And I am here. Perhaps, *my friend*"—and here I affected a confidence that I was far from feeling—"you are afraid to come into this world while I am in it."

Very good, the timeserpent whispered. *But untrue. It is you who are afraid. You don't belong in Everien. You belong here. With me. Do you not wish to see your house again?*

Tash was still dragging on my arm, trying to hold me as the fire attacked him; but he must be in terrible pain. Now, in a flash, the fire was gone. I was standing in the kitchen courtyard of my own house, amongst shards of shattered glass where the window had been broken in the hall upstairs. I was physically present in the house, except for my wrist and hand holding the bone. These appeared to have been cut off as if with a pair of shears; I tried not to look. Strangely, although I couldn't see my hand, I could feel the pressure of Tash tugging on it as if he stood right beside me; only he didn't.

"Tarquin?" I called hopefully. "Tarquin, are you still here?"

In answer, a rock came flying out of the broken window and

narrowly missed my head. I dodged and raised my free arm protectively, squinting into the sunlight. I could hear noises of someone moving inside the house, and after a moment a figure appeared in the doorway of the tower stairs. It was a small and bent old woman.

Not my mother. No. My mother had not lived to such an age. And my mother had not moved with that shuffling, sneaky gait. And my mother would never have greeted me with the words "What the fuck are you doing here?"

"You're a Wolf!" I said with surprise, recognizing her accent from somewhere out of the depths of my mysterious and ill-organized memory. She peered at me with the most penetrating silver eyes I have ever seen, and something changed in her. She recognized me.

"Jaya," said the Wolf woman, her manner softening so abruptly that she seemed to become another person—not a sneaky and hostile stranger, but rather someone who made medicinal teas and held the hands of the sick and told stories meant to distract and soothe. "Jaya, is it you?"

"Do I know you?"

"No, but I know you, my dear." She moved toward me, coming out of the shadow of the house and looking around at the ruin of my home with a little shiver. "I can explain yourself to you, and you must listen, for I am dying. And when I am gone, you must bury me here. My body, removed from the real world and dying in the Liminal, in exchange for you. Now I, Mistel, a simple Wolf Grandmother, know all the tale of Everien, while you, a creature of the Liminal, will live in real flesh. But you must promise me something. You must promise to die under the open sky, and not within a house of men. Give back to the Wolves their due, Jaya."

I stared at her incredulously. "I . . . I cannot make such a promise. I am not . . . trustworthy."

She peered at me keenly. "You don't trust yourself, that much is clear. And I think I understand why. Jaya, you were created to Guard the malformed creatures that were banished to the Liminal, which was a theoretical place. You were given the Knowledge you would need to keep them abstract and harmless. But those creatures of the Liminal were connected by the Animal Magic to the Guarded Animals of the real world, and so they could not be banished utterly. They were beings wrought partially by nature, partially by device. And though they could not find their way through

174

to the solid world of nature in their own time, they evolved the ability to get through by another."

"They evolved?" I said. "How do you mean? I know that things changed; even I could see that. Spice the Lion grew famished and hateful. Other things happened. But I could never see *why*."

"Why is because you began to outgrow yourself. Your Knowledge, your power, the ones you had been designed to keep, all got away from you. The monsters wanted to be free. The time-serpent was plotting its own creation, the White Road was weaving itself through the paradoxes of time. And the monsters desired real form. Whether you or they were the cause is not the point; maybe you caused each other. But none of you stayed within the lines that had been plotted for you by your makers."

"Makers?" The way she said it sent a chill up my spine. She nodded vigorously at my discomfiture, as if encouraging me to accept the worst of my suspicions.

"They used you. You were only a young girl. You were never meant to be more. You were a servant: a powerful servant, but you were not to come to maturity. You were to keep the Knowledge without adding to it, and in return you were to be safe."

She reached over and patted my hand. I could still feel a vague tugging on my arm, like the sea pulling at me; I ignored it. I still could not believe how vivid and real were the sunlight and the walls and the glass. How was I to be sure what was illusion when even now I could not tell the difference between the solid world and the Liminal?

Mistel patted my hand again reassuringly. "But you did not care about safety. Like the very creatures the Everiens tried to make, the creatures that would not hold the form they were given but rebelled and struck out at their makers, you, too, did not obey your designers. You were curious. Too curious. You began to inquire about the monsters. You began to inquire about things that your makers intended to be left alone. And the caprice of your teacher, Jihan, aided you."

"Mistel, why did Jihan aid me? If he was to keep me in my place, why did he offer me so much Knowledge?"

"Because you are born of a contradictory people, Jaya Paradox. They wanted you to have Knowledge, but they couldn't foresee how you might use it. They wanted to create, and at the same time they wanted control. These two things never coexist in nature.

Your makers have never realized this. Not once.

"The Sekk, the Knowledge Guardians, tried to stop you—for it was their job, too, to control nature, which is inherently uncontrollable. They ruined your structure, your house, the things that were supposed to make you what you are; but you survived. You escaped, and your horse saved you in the forest, for he, too, had once been a victim of the time-meddling of the Everiens, and equally, its beneficiary. And then the horse helped you call the timeserpent that the Circle had brought out of the Fire Houses, and you passed beyond the control of the Sekk. You went among humans, and there you are now. While we speak, you are there, in the mud of a torn Everien, and you are dying because there isn't one particle of you that is real. You don't belong in that world. The only thing keeping you going is the Wasp poison that has gone into your veins by the luck of the arrow—and it will finish you, make no mistake. It might take a long time, but it will finish you. That is why you must take the life I give you, whatever days or weeks you have of it, and make the very most."

I sat there listening, for the first time in my life totally humbled. This old woman couldn't ever have been fooled in her life. She had never failed to see into the heart of things—how could she, with those penetrating eyes?

"Why didn't I meet you long ago?" I said. "I have been stumbling around wishing for such wisdom."

She made a dismissive noise. "Wisdom is like shit," she said. "It's just one of those things that piles up over time."

"What am I going to do?" I said, somewhat petulantly, for my arm was aching from the effort of hanging on to the bone, and Tash. "I don't know up from down anymore. The timeserpent mocks me. I had to call it. I had to get out! But now it has come here, too. I have escaped into a world I can't live in because I have brought the timeserpent with me."

Mistel took a long time to answer. "You and the timeserpent are connected somehow. I think that the blossoming of your consciousness is related to its ability to bend time. I think the timeserpent may even be a manifestation of the things Jihan taught you. You cannot unlearn those things!"

"There must be something I can do," I said. "I accept that no one can help me. I accept I must do it on my own, whatever it is. But I do not accept that the timeserpent is my doom, plain and

176

simple, and there is no way I can fight it."

"Good!" said Mistel. "For I believe that someone is helping you, has helped you already, and will help you even more. But you are the fulcrum on which his efforts swing."

"His efforts? Is it Quintar, then?"

"I do not know Quintar. I have never met him. But there is someone else, I have seen him here. He came looking for Chyko, who had your Animal Cards, and when he could not find him, he rode away after him toward Baron Horas's castle."

"Who was he?" I asked eagerly. "Could it be my father? What did he look like?"

Mistel sighed, and her eyes grew distant. "Like Tarquin, he was a Seahawk, once. But he is a dangerous man."

She crossed the hallway and stood at the top of the stairs. "I will leave your house now. There are horrors in that wood, as you well know. But I would sooner fall prey to them and see you live, than while away empty days in a dead house—for it is dead without you, Jaya. Go and live, now, for by the Animal Magic you are fully human now, and your life is bought with mine. And who knows? Maybe you will even find an antidote."

"Are you dying for *me?*" I asked anxiously, reaching for her hand. "Do not die for me, Mistel! I am only a thought! Mistel?"

"Not anymore are you a thought only. Remember your promise," she said over her shoulder. She descended without another word. I saw her cross the withered garden and open the gate. Then she scurried away into the trees. I heard slithering noises and animal calls that I couldn't identify, but they raised my hackles.

"But I didn't promise," I said. "I *can't* promise."

From beyond this world, there was a quick jerk on the bone, and suddenly I was taken right off my feet and the flames curled around me.

You will not bury her. There will be no exchange. Do you think you can buy yourself a human life so easily?

I had no chance to respond to the taunts of the Li'ah'vah, because Tash was pulling me back into his world; but I didn't want to go that way. Angrily, I gave a last, frantic jerk to free myself from Tash's clenched fist. As I crossed the barrier, I felt his fingers slip across mine and lodge on the length of bone I held. It swelled in my hand and burst out of my grip, and then I wasn't holding it anymore. I went tumbling out of the Liminal and into a wet, green Everien.

I landed in thorns and rolled over. I had let go of the bone, and I pictured Tash's startled and angry face when he realized I had escaped. I sat up and looked back in the direction from which I had come. I expected to see Tash on the other side of the barrier, picking himself up and dusting himself off like a mirror image of me. But he was not there. His men were there, and I watched them reacting to Tash's disappearance. They were excited, and they rushed up and down on their side of the barrier. They were moving very rapidly, with little jerks separating their movements as if they were each in the midst of some kind of fit. Their voices twitched and stretched. I noticed that the ones farther from the barrier seemed less distorted.

I was still shaken by Mistel's words, and the contract she had offered me; but Tash's absence from the scene on the outside of the barrier puzzled me. I wondered spitefully whether the timeserpent had gotten him.

Then I noticed three things. One: I could see ghost-images of flames where the timeserpent trail lay. Two: there was a great white lump like a gigantic piece of bone lying on the ground in the exact spot where I had passed through. Three: there was a similar end-of-bone on Tash's side. The two ends of bone did not quite match up, and there was no visible middle where the long part of the bone should be. Tash's men were beginning to prod at their end, to stand on it and lean into the barrier and call. As I watched, one of them walked across this piece of bone and disappeared into the Liminal.

I shook myself off and approached the bone from my end. I could not see its middle, but I now suspected that with my hand on one end, and Tash's on the other, we had somehow stretched it across the barrier, magnified it.

And I realized that the skyfalcon had made us a very deliberate gift.

I walked out onto the bone, into the Liminal for the second time. I saw the span of bone, but it did not cross flames this time. It seemed to be arcing across the entire valley of Everien, so that I could look down on the land from a terrific height. Tash was standing in the middle of the span looking down. I decided to be diplomatic and pretend I had done all this on purpose. I walked across the bridge to meet him.

From this perspective, Everien was an extreme place. The mountains seemed to throw themselves at one another and at the sky with an abandonment at odds with the very blueness, so calm and still, that they sought. I know that Everien is a place punctured and torn; I know that its clouds jerk across the sky, that night and day are chopped and sewn in a patchwork quilt of mismatched times. I was told these things by Tash, and I believed them. But as was true when I first came down from the cave and saw the fire barrier, I noticed now that my perception of Everien was different from everyone else's. They saw a land jigsawed by change, with each separate part juxtaposed surprisingly with some unlikely neighbor. I saw one world.

Everien was green, with snow dazzling its highest peaks, and a froth of gold lining its central valley where the hay was ripening. The sun hung in the south, its angular rays creating spectacular shadowy delineations among the rocks and plants. Enormous herds grazed. The square lumps of houses interrupted the puckered wrinkles and folds of sloping land. The wind was not visible in a cloudless sky, but it was audible, and its force beat against me where I stood. I felt I had come to a place too special to describe, so rarefied and remote was it, so grand its scale, so ambitious its limits.

I could see the herds of the Deer Clan, their ruddy coats contrasting achingly against the rich viridian tones of the pasture. I could hear the cry of gulls, miles from their ocean home, but drawn from the sea plateau to the shelter of Everien. I knew that this place was host to many animals, each of them cunning or strong or resourceful in its own way, and the collection of them interacting in a timeless weave of life and death. The animals were not confused about Everien.

But although I could see Everien intact and unharmed, it would not be true to say that the timeserpent had done no damage, in my eyes. For beneath the surface of this wild perfection lay another image, like another card stacked in the deck beneath this one. And beneath that second image lay a third, and a fourth, ad infinitum or so it seemed to me. I could shuffle the images at will, until the scene before me flickered like a fire.

Everien was also devastated.

It was gray and desolate, the natural shapes of mountains having been regimented and carved into angular blocks. There were stairways and ramps, structures of metal and glass. There were flying objects that were not alive. Strings of liquid light lashed the air, and clicking sounds predominated.

It was rampaged by the monsters I had seen in the fire. They roved, seeking food, fighting each other, ruining the earth. Squads of bright insects settled on bloated corpses. Machines came silently out of holes in the earth to kill the monsters, and sometimes they did. Other times, the monsters dissolved them in acid, or crushed them beneath cruel claws of gigantic proportions.

I watched, transfixed with horror and awe.

Tash seized my arm.

"Hurry up!" he hissed, and the cards reshuffled again. Now I saw what Tash saw: Everien cut in ragged pieces like a grandmother's quilt. The light was different on each part. I saw cart tracks and circles of burning; Clan-made buildings; herds tended by shepherds and their quick dogs. In the distance, over the gap that led to the sea plain, I saw sailsnakes. There was no way to know what time it was.

I felt as if I were walking on someone's skin. The footing beneath was solid enough, the white bridge smooth and flawless, and there were no visible signs that anything was dangerous here. But I knew that on the underside of this bridge lay the Fire, the place where the monsters came from, and that for every bridge we built, there would be a river of fire that oozed these unknown and usually malevolent forms.

And then I glimpsed the timeserpent. It was far away in Deer Country, and I could see it devouring the pastures and ruining continuity there. It had used my presence in the Liminal to enter Everien. I tried to move faster. The bridge was longer than it looked.

Tash was sucking his burned hand and gaping at the visions displayed before him. He was dragging me across the bone, and when I didn't move fast enough, he shook me. For reasons of my own, I was going as fast as I could, but I felt very weak and I thought I might be sick on his boots if he didn't stop it. At last we reached the other side.

"You wizardess!" he cried. "You will teach me everything! Everything you know, I will know, too! Do you understand me? Ah, Jaya, you are better to me than all Kivi's Eyes put together. We are going to do great things."

"We can't get to the Fire Houses yet," I said. "See, there they are, to the left; but they lie in ruins. We still have a long journey ahead of us."

"Can you see the seams?" he asked. "Do you know where we should build our bridges?"

I did not bother to remind him that he had not built this bridge, but rather had accepted the gift of the skyfalcon. Nor did I tell him about the army I could see, marching out of an isolated pocket of Wolf Country and into the central river valley. It was a larger army than any of the Pharician forces I could see deployed elsewhere. But I didn't tell Tash. He was still shaking me as if to impart life to my tired body. He was incredibly tense, but I felt too tired and limp to worry very much. I protested at being shaken and he let go of me. He looked at me, smiling, and then suddenly backed away, staring at my arm.

"Your arm! What's happened to it?"

The black line where the arrow had grazed me was still there, a strange mark more like a tattoo than an injury. Radiating from the single line was a series of small black crosshatches, like the fletchings of an arrow, each about an inch long. It looked like I had a centipede on my arm.

"I don't know," I said wearily. "Maybe it's some kind of Wasp idea of a joke."

Chyko had bragged enough about his Wasp poisons—yet, perversely, Mistel had said it was the only thing keeping me going. It occurred to me that I ought to find out what Dario had put on that arrow.

Tash said, "We have to get everyone across. Otherwise, this is no good to me."

"I'm too tired," I said. The timeserpent whispers had begun again, faintly so that I could hear the whispering without knowing the words that were spoken. "I don't feel well. I need to rest."

No sooner were the words out of my mouth than my knees gave way and I went down on the warm bone. I felt musical rhythms surging through my legs. Tash reached out to support me, but I couldn't even hold my head up anymore. He cursed inventively and at length; then he dragged me to the other side of the bridge and let me go so abruptly that I just toppled and lay there.

I was not playacting. I simply didn't have any energy. The world was spinning and humming at me. Everything had gone as faint as a whisper, and I felt large and empty.

*

I WAS LEFT to lie there until Tash had successfully moved his entire troop, including prisoners, wagons, and horses, across into the adjacent section of Everien. Then Shiror came to take care of me. I was placed in the litter again and bundled up warm. A succession of people tried to feed me, talk to me, rouse me from my stupor. Shiror never left my side, and I took it that Tash had ordered him to watch me constantly. I made no effort to speak with him or even look at him. Physically, I was very weak. Mentally, I was working at a furious rate, trying to make sense of all the information that was boiling over in my head. But I could not seem to calculate or theorize as I knew I should.

Instead, I found myself thinking about Tarquin. I was overcome by a feeling of emotional weight. I thought about his devotion to me, one that seemed without foundation or root. How he had held fast to my hand, *willed* me to stay with him. And yet I had leaped into the timeserpent. Why?

I used to believe things were lighter than they are. Before the creatures came and drove me into the forest, I thought my life was light as air. And then, through the measureless journey in the darkness, I had questioned the very nature and substance of my self. Yet, now it seemed to me that nothing that happened to me in the forest had really touched me. Chyko mating with me like a wild animal had upset me, but the act itself had not penetrated me in a meaningful way.

How can I explain? Every time I thought I knew the size and shape of myself, it turned out I was wrong. Now I was heavy. Now I bled. Now I chewed my food and knew the texture of its paste against my tongue. I was changing all the time. In those days with Tash, I became larger and larger and larger, on the inside. I had mysteries to ponder. I had problems. But again and again, my thoughts returned to Tarquin.

He was a ragged-looking man. By his appearance I would have said that he was someone who should have done a better job of his life, should have made more of himself than he had. His face held that mixture of skepticism and resignation that bespoke his age where lines and wrinkles and gray hair could not. He had an air of lowered expectations.

But. There was a but, and it lay in my feelings. I felt something for him. I felt a pull. His hand on my hand. His certainty. The way he named me. Jaya. As if when he said my name, he made me become myself. *Jaya,* he said, and I felt my heart rise into my throat and beat there like a hummingbird.

I remembered the time he had come to the garden and tried to talk to me. *I'm sorry. It's the wrong time. I made a mistake.* Who was he? He had asked me where the children were. What children? His children? My children? *Our children?*

If only it had been Tarquin waiting at my house instead of Mistel. Was he still looking for me? And how could I look for him, if every time I entered the Liminal, the timeserpent was free to come out?

REVISITING SNOUT

$\mathcal{D}$eath is *a strange dream*, Tarquin thought. He was standing on a familiar beach, at the bottom of a winding staircase carved roughly in gray granite. The sky was a dark blue splotched with yellow where the sun waited just below the horizon, the colors of a midsummer's night. The sea was spinning and curling below. He was in his Seahawk home, a place he had not visited for more than a dozen years.

He was still wearing his spare Snake Clan garments, but his hair had grown into its customary shaggy mane. The wound on his side was completely healed. He had his sword on his belt and Kere's ampule in one hand, and nothing else.

He shivered. If this was a dream, then the wind and the spray were very lifelike. And the house at the top of the stairs had changed not at all. He began to climb. His muscles felt springy and strong. He felt very alive. He breathed deeply of the sea air. There were boats out on the sea, night-fishing, but in A-Tar-Ness there was not a soul stirring out of doors. It must be very late.

He came to the familiar rounded oaken door. It was not latched—it never had been, Tarquin remembered with amusement, on account of an incredibly shaggy dog that always wanted to be either in or out, whichever one he was not at any given time. *Snout*, Tarquin remembered. A stupid name: it had been Ranatar's idea when she was only a little girl. She said it was because all you could see of the beast was his snout, poking through his fur.

Now Tarquin was greeted by a soft bark that changed to a low growl, that changed to a clatter of nails on the stone floor. Soft, long fur hit him with a warm weight. There was a wet tongue and a doggy smell, and a tail that smacked into his face repeatedly as the dog tried to climb over him, paw him, knock him down.

"Shh!" Tarquin hissed. "Sit!"

Disobedient as ever, Snout stood on his hind legs and licked Tarquin's bare arms. Tarquin took in the main room, convinced that he was living inside one of his own memories: nothing had changed. There was his mother's spinning wheel, his sister's dolls, his uncle's lute . . . was Tarquin himself sleeping in one of those closets down the hall?

Someone was certainly snoring.

He hesitated, uncertain what to do. What if this was his last stop before the afterlife? Was there something that was expected of him, some final gesture? Was there something he should have done during this period of his life, something he should have done but hadn't, and this was his last chance?

From the look of Snout, Tarquin would have been about four-teen then.

Tarquin snorted. What could a fourteen-year-old do or not do that would need atoning for? Bloody nothing.

He wandered across the main room and down the stairs into the kitchen. He helped himself to food and mead, a knife, and an old leather satchel that his grandmother had been meaning to mend for about five years—one of its pockets was torn. He strapped it to his belt, slid the ampule into it, and then stuffed in some bread and a hunk of cheese, suppressing his guilt. It was summer. They could make more cheese in time for the cold. He fed some scraps to Snout, who had followed him.

He went back into the main room and paused by the banked fire. He could still feel its ambient heat. Clothes. He would need clothes in the afterlife.

He stole his uncle's blue cloak, the one he had always admired, and a brown-leather tunic that his aunt had left lying on a rocking chair. It was too small for him and stretched across his chest, but it would be warm and sturdy.

He looked down at himself. His boots were falling apart and his trousers were a ripped disgrace. Again he glanced into the corridor where the sleeping closets were, wondering if he dared sneak in and get something better; but just then Snout licked his bare ankles and Tarquin kicked at him, which Snout interpreted as an invitation to play. Inside, his grandmother erupted in a series of loud, gurgling coughs. He heard someone stir, and then the soft music of Ranatar's hushed voice.

He slipped out the front door with Snout squirming after him. Ranatar must not see him, especially if he really was a ghost.

He went down the stairs feeling warm and pleasantly replete. Snout followed him all the way to the beach, where Tarquin hesitated. What if the Seahawk legends about death really were true? Would there be a boat?

Snout whined and Tarquin looked down.

"Go back to the house, my friend," he said, bending to stroke the dog's head. "You do not wish to come with me! You have a long life to lead. Good dog! Go!"

Snout wagged, barked, and dashed off up the steps and into the house. Tarquin stood on the beach wondering what to do now, and scuffed at the sand.

Suddenly, he understood. There were hoofmarks in the sand.

"Ice?" he queried aloud, taking a deep, wondering breath.

The night turned white all around him.

THE VOICE OF THE SKYFALCON

Istar was shaking and nauseous as she collected her scattered belongings. Her hand where the bird had made her release the dagger was bruised and numb, but thankfully it did not bleed.

"What does this mean?" she asked Taretel incredulously. "Why do you speak all of a sudden?"

He stammered a little as he tried to answer, displaying an awkwardness so at odds with his imposing appearance that she didn't know what to make of it. "B-b-because we weren't together then. I-I-I, we . . . I am his voice. The skyfalcon's voice. This body"—and he gestured to himself—"it is like a ghost, but my mind is alive in the bird. He cannot . . ." Taretel let out an odd little laugh. "He cannot speak for himself."

"You are the voice of the skyfalcon," Istar repeated, not sure she was understanding.

"Yes. And he, sometimes he directs me as well. His drives and urges are in me."

Istar remembered Eteltar trying to explain about the "unnatural urges" he had felt after traveling the White Road, and not for the first time she wondered if the slaying behavior of Taretel had been what he meant.

"Then why did you take the bones? I mean, why did *it* take the bones?"

"To reknit Everien. To make bridges. My bones can connect what the timeserpent has put apart. They are refulgent with timeness. They will bring the world back to itself."

His eyes turned toward the sky. "I am going now," he said. The skyfalcon was a mote; then it was gone.

"Taretel?" Istar queried. She jumped up and down before him, seeking his attention; but he turned away. When he turned back,

187

his eyes were alien. She shrank away from him. This was the aspect that could kill for no earthly reason. This was the part that had been taken for a Sekk.

"Be careful, Istar," she whispered to herself. Taretel took off, almost as if he, too, feared to stay by her. She wondered whether he had a conscience, or whether that, too, resided in the bird that had flown away with one of the bones of Eteltar.

SHE FOLLOWED HIM closer at hand now, and he continued moving parallel to the road beneath; why he didn't simply walk on the road, she didn't know, since in all this time they had seen not one single soul trafficking it. That night, she built a fire and roasted potatoes again. She still had cheese, but she disciplined herself not to eat it, in case it was the cheese that had made her sick. She burned her mouth on the potatoes that she wolfed down.

Almost immediately she was sick. The next morning she could not look at food without feeling nauseous. She knelt weakly by the embers of the fire and packed up the remains of what she had so that she could eat it later, and while she was doing this, something made her look up. He was standing over her.

Istar, cold and dizzy and distressed by her own weakness, could only kneel there blinking at the giant. He did not speak, and she saw from his expression that the skyfalcon must be far away. With his empty eyes, Taretel extended his hand to her. She took it. He drew her to her feet.

This is dangerous, she thought. *I must not trust him. Think of Ranatar. Think of the Hawk Girls.*

But she felt unwell, and tired, so when Taretel made to walk beside her, she lacked the will to resist the overture of friendship. But there was no speech, and his presence unnerved her. Istar managed to eat later that day. She was relieved, for she'd never subsisted on pure protein for so long, and she'd been afraid something was wrong with her. She ate potatoes and cheese and kept it down.

But the next day she was sick again. Snow began to fall, quickly quenching the springtime. On the following day, the skies were spectacular in their cloud displays. Istar sensed that Taretel was uneasy; when they found tracks in the mud beside the road—clawed feet the size of dinner tables, and the slither-marks of long, furless tails—she knew they must be close to another timeserpent barrier.

Taretel looked at these markings for a long time but did not speak. He also stared at the sky even when there was nothing to see. Every time a bird of prey came into view, Taretel stopped and stared at it. He seemed to lean in the direction of these birds, straining as if to leap into the sky himself. She felt sorry for him.

"Flying is hard, eh?" she said, remembering how Eteltar had taunted her because she could not fly. There were times she could have wrung his neck for showing off and mocking her. What she wouldn't give now to have him with her instead of this inscrutable one! Even so, to her surprise a strange, silent affection was building between them. Istar knew it as the comradeship that develops among people who travel together, but she did not think she was flattering herself to imagine that Taretel was also protecting her.

For the first time in her life, this was all right with her. Having the most notorious murderer in Seahawk for a guardian might not be altogether a bad thing, judging by the tracks left by the monsters of the Liminal. Besides, she was not feeling up to standard, and she needed all the support she could get. She continued to have trouble keeping her food down. She had been tired and persistently queasy as she dogged Taretel through mud and across swollen brooks. Now the river was patchily running beneath its ice below, and even the new-fallen snow was soft, a playful spring snow. As they drew closer to Everien, she thought of spring, and home in Jai Khalar, and she felt an almost-desperate need to see her mother again. Somehow, she thought, Mhani's madness didn't matter anymore. Istar would not mind the disjointed talk and the empty gaze if she could just hold her mother's hand and touch her gray hair.

She would find Mhani, she vowed. She had to know if her mother was alive or dead; and if she was alive, Istar would bring her back to Seahawk, and to hell with the opinions of the Clan.

Suddenly Taretel stopped and hid himself in the rocks, and Istar had to quickly dodge into a brake of fern and huddle there while Taretel turned to face upcountry again, gazing back along the valley toward Snake Country. After a few minutes she saw what she was waiting for. In the distance, a Pharician rider on a shaggy chestnut came trotting along the disused track by the riverside, snow flying away from his hooves. A minute later more men appeared, proceeding slowly along the riverside, all mounted, including a standard-bearer with Tash's flag. The red-cloaked black man that Istar assumed must be Tash himself followed with a number of other sword-bearing men and a couple of archers. Tash rode with his head up, scanning the countryside. The others looked weary and bored. Behind Tash some footmen carried a makeshift litter cobbled together from a stretcher and a tent.

Behind the litter came a group of infantry, some of them driving Clan prisoners before them. It burned Istar that Tash had captured Clansmen. She now wished she had been more forceful in Tyger Pass.

Then came some spare horses and the supply wagons. Dangling from the struts of the wagons were pheasants and hares, and a yearling doe lay across the back of one wagon.

"Well, well," said Istar. "Go on, then, Taretel. Take care of these Pharicians for me, and I will let you go free forever. All possible grudges will be forgotten."

She watched Taretel with great interest. She was considering Pentar's theory that Tash had only fled from their army in Tyger Pass because of Taretel. She looked at the lines of men on their horses, the wagons and arms-bearers, and thought that Taretel would have to be a greater warrior than Chyko to take on such a band single-handedly.

Still, even if they couldn't be conquered, they might be robbed. They had food. They had medicine. Istar looked covetously on the wagons. She felt weak and wished that everything she ate would not make her sick. Maybe she needed fresh food. Without it she would not be able to keep her strength up.

Taretel was behaving as if Istar weren't there, and she let him outpace her, trailing along behind him using rocks for cover, with an eye always on the Pharicians. When they camped that night, Taretel took off for parts unknown. Istar observed the Pharicians carefully. There was only one woman among them, but she dressed as a man. She was feeding the prisoners and performing chores at a ferocious rate. She never went near the litter or its mysterious occupant. Instead, a senior officer visited that tent from time to time, poking his head in to deliver things or take them away, but never staying. Istar wondered who was inside. She could scarcely imagine that Tash would have brought a woman into combat—there had been no litter in Tyger Pass—so the person inside must be either a high-ranking Scholar or an invalid. Whoever it was, they never seemed to emerge.

She watched Tash's men build fires, pulling her own cloak close and tugging the hood over her head. She was hungry. She gnawed on the jerky she had in her pack, managing to swallow some without feeling sick. Soon she could smell meat on the Pharician cookfires. She began thinking resentful and acquisitive thoughts. After all, her troop had beaten Tash; yet here she was, starving in the wilderness, while Tash hunted the game of her own country and built fires with Everien trees. She began to engineer different forms of sabotage she might perpetrate on this happy little parade. Long after the Pharicians had eaten and put out their fires and settled their animals for the night, Istar sat there, sticking her cold fingers under her armpits and plotting.

Then she saw Taretel rise from his hiding place a quarter mile away from Istar. His white cloak blended with the snow, and he didn't make a sound as he slid toward the camp under the moonlight.

He was gone for a long time. The camp was silent.

If he was killing, he was being stealthy about it. Unable to contain her curiosity, Istar rose and began to creep down the hillside. She hadn't gotten very far when she saw Taretel's white cloak flash against the darker fabric of the tent that was carried as a litter, by day. She inhaled with a hiss, for the sight stabbed her with the realization that there was more going on down there than she knew about. Then Taretel's white shape resolved out of the darkness and snow. He was very nearly on top of her and moving at a full run. He barreled into her, knocking her aside. She nearly fell into the mud, but he grabbed her cloak and tugged her after him up the hillside. Just then, a shout went up in the camp, followed by a general stirring of recumbent men.

Dragging her like a hurricane, Taretel mounted an old stone wall that divided two sheep pastures and ran along the top, where the snow had been blown away and they would leave no tracks. Istar glanced up and saw that the moon was still occluded but would soon break free of the clouds. She accelerated, doing her best to keep up with the long-legged giant. He was carrying an awkwardly shaped bundle, and every few strides he paused to get a better grip on it. When finally they reached the relative safety of the pine stand and Taretel stopped, Istar collapsed, totally winded.

On her hands and knees, she turned and looked back down at the Pharician camp.

No one had followed past the first section of stone wall. The Pharicians were stumbling about in the snow, making a lot of noise but not accomplishing much. Taretel had led her to the very top of the valley, ascending half a mile in a matter of frantic minutes; no wonder her heart was galloping like a trip-hammer. She gasped and spat, trying to recover her wind. The furs felt hot and she threw her cloak off. Taretel was standing and watching her. She knew she was too tired to fight him, and she also knew she couldn't win in a fair fight against Taretel. So she simply ignored him, concentrating on recovering her strength instead. She was so tired. She couldn't understand it: she felt like a little old lady, not Istar the climber-of-cliffs.

Taretel's booted feet appeared in her line of vision. He was sweeping the pine needles in their wake, making sure they could not be followed. When he passed close to her, he dropped the bundle he had been carrying, and she forgot about his visit to the litter and her lingering distrust of him.

For a joint of meat spilled out, still warm from the fire. Beneath it were flatbread, roasted nuts, and a length of white bandage. Istar put her hand to her head and felt that the old wrapping had slipped off and the cut had opened again.

"You think of everything!" she said to Taretel gratefully. But he melted into the darkness, and she didn't see him again that night.

TARETEL PROVED A better thief than his size ought to have permitted. After the first incident, it was several days before Tash's men let down their guard enough for him to slip among the horses at night and pilfer supplies for Istar. But when he did, he came back without upsetting the Pharician camp. He had discreetly taken an assortment of useful items. Tash was well outfitted despite having been on the road for a number of weeks, and Istar was thrilled when she saw the frozen fruitcakes and cheese that Taretel had obtained. But she still found it hard to keep food down, and she was tired all the time.

They were coming down from the snows, and sometimes in the distance Istar glimpsed a patch of sky so blue over Everien that she knew it must be summer somewhere. The sun never rose so high in winter.

"Taretel," Istar said once. "There are enough Clan prisoners in that wagon train down there to defeat Tash and his men, if they were to be given some help."

But Taretel's answering silence had an unusual quality; it was not the silence of opinions held at bay, or even of mere speechlessness, nor of stupidity. It was the silence of *difference*. He might bring her food, but he did not understand or care about her higher motives. She wished the skyfalcon would return, for if only she could speak with Taretel, maybe she could convince him to help her sabotage Tash and rescue her kinsmen. But there was no sign of the bird, and they were nearing the bottom of Snake Pass. The central river valley of Everien was, literally, right around the corner: soon they would drop through a narrow, steep passage, make a hairpin turn, and the lowlands would appear spread out before them.

Istar gave some thought to the topography of the area. Because the final section of the pass was narrow, steep, and treeless, there was no way that she and Taretel could hope to continue running a parallel line to Tash's men. Neither of them could fly, at least not in this incarnation. They would either have to slip ahead of the Pharicians, or fall in behind them, and either way they would be in danger of discovery.

Her thoughts repeatedly turned to the ambition of staging a coup and overturning Tash's command. The prisoners, many of whom appeared to be Seahawk, were being well cared for. They were uninjured and they were being fed. None of them were sick. Istar had observed the activities of the troop and she had narrowed down the location of the captives' weapons to one of two wagons, both of which were at the very end of the train. If she could get those weapons to the men, they might be able to break out.

It was a long shot, of course. And there was the problem of Taretel—would he aid her or thwart her? And how would Clansmen react to his presence? Her own men had wanted no part of Taretel.

Istar wrestled with different plans in her mind. She was tired of taking such a passive role, and she wished she could throw off the lethargy and vague illness that had plagued her lately. It seemed that she had done nothing for miles upon miles but follow

Taretel—at first out of obstinacy, then out of fascination, and now because he had spoken to her with Eteltar's voice, and she loved Eteltar.

Not that she understood Taretel. He seemed to be tracking Tash, but she was not privy to his purposes—or should she say rather, the skyfalcon's purposes? And the fact that they were drawing near to Jai Khalar intensified Istar's sense of urgency. She had the sense that something was about to break, and whatever it was, she wanted to be ready when it happened.

THE MAGICIAN

Tash's train moved on through the mountain pass, with me in a slow fever. Tash was more excited than ever, but I dreaded the next wall I would be expected to cross. What if the skyfalcon didn't come?

Days passed, and we encountered no barrier. Dario haunted me, and I got used to being surveilled. One night, the wind woke me. The curtain of my litter was open, and someone was looking in. I started to sit up, thinking it was Dario with more of her malicious intentions, but instead of the Wasp woman I saw white hair in braids. A whiff of a half-familiar smell came to my nostrils, evoking the playing card that had summoned the skyfalcon, so long ago.

The Magician.

The white-braided man watched me without making a sound, so that I wondered if my imagination were conjuring him.

"Are you the Magician?" I whispered. "Please, can you help me?"

He was gone as suddenly as he had come. But he had not been the product of my imagination. A few minutes later, the whole camp was aroar as one of the watchmen cried intruder. The Pharicians searched but found nothing, not even a footprint. I was not surprised. If he was the being I thought he was, he could fly, anyway.

THE MAGICIAN DID not help me. No one did. I had to come to grips with my situation with only my own very limited resources. I was riding on a litter in Tash's army. He mistrusted me but hoped to use me. I felt ill much of the time. I ate, but the food didn't seem to nourish me. My arm grew lines. I felt nothing in my right hand. Dario cast hateful glances upon me whenever she chanced to pass. I rode on the litter, speaking to no one, pretending to sleep, and I thought, Will I never be done with traveling? Will I never arrive at the place I am meant to be?

My old house seemed very far away now, and in my mind's eye I saw Mistel vanish in the trees, her life fled to vapor, or less, in that soulless between-place of the forest. Also there were gaps in my memory. I wasn't entirely sure whether I was myself or just a story someone had invented. And this outraged me, and made my blood surge, and I thought of Tarquin and wished I had not let go of him.

"I have to find Tarquin," I said aloud. Shiror, in the saddle beside the litter, gave a start, then turned to stare at me intently. I wasn't sure how long it had been since I had showed signs of life, but he was plainly surprised to hear me speak. His expression suggested that he didn't quite believe his ears. I cleared my throat in case he had not understood. "I have to find Tarquin," I repeated.

"They say Tarquin the Free is dead," Shiror said slowly. "He vanished at Jai Pendu."

I said, "I must find him. Please, take me to Jai Pendu."

Shiror did not answer. He looked at me a moment longer, then clucked his horse forward and rode away toward Tash, and I imagined he was going to tell Tash I was out of my mind: a reasonable conclusion to draw, I felt, under the circumstances.

But Tash came to me straightaway.

"It is time for you to tell me everything you know," he said.

We looked at each other. I'm sure he was expecting me to put up some resistance, to demur in some way. I did not. I answered without hesitation.

"I am evil," I said. "This is a proven fact. I have Enslaved men and driven them to their deaths. I would have driven them to worse if I had not been prevented. I have captured the spirit and essence of others without their permission. I have used living men to shore up my weaknesses, because I was not powerful and I wanted to be."

Tash shifted uncomfortably. This was not the conversation he wished to have, and he brushed my remarks aside. It was as though I had said nothing. Instead, he launched into his own concerns. "Tell me again how we will create energy if the Fire of Glass is truly destroyed."

"You, on the other hand, are a fool," I continued. "You are in over your head. Why do you try to hold and control something that is a tiger when you will never be more than a mouse? You should take your men and begone from Everien. Leave by the fastest route. You would have made a good terrorist and slayer among the men of the Pharician Empire, but in Everien you will never come to wisdom, only to pain."

He reached out and with a studied, thoughtful movement, slapped me across the face. I let the sting progress to a throb and felt my lip swell. I tasted blood. I liked it.

"Answer the questions you are asked," he said. "Your rhetoric vexes me."

"It's too late to try to discipline me. You can let Dario shoot me, but then you will never possess the Knowledge."

"How far have we to go?" Tash asked.

I decided to be honest. "There is one more time shift between here and the place that was Jai Khalar. I saw it when we crossed the bridge. It lies near the bottom of this pass."

"What else did you see?" he queried eagerly.

"Much chaos and ruin. And I saw an army, a very large one. It is coming toward the Fire Houses from the northwest, and its formations are Pharician."

Tash cackled with delight. "Good, Jaya, good! I've lost a castle but gained the Knowledge. Now, listen. You must take care of yourself and rest. You don't look well at all. As soon as we are back to civilization, I shall seek out the finest physicians to heal you."

I said nothing. How is it that men of action are invariably so naive?

YOU ARE AN
ANIMAL NOW

𝒯wo miles before the hairpin turn that would show them Everien, Istar observed Tash's men as they ran into another timeserpent seam. This time, the division was apparent to the eye. Clouds of insects seeped from ragged gaps in the timeserpent seam and drifted amongst the Pharicians. They were brightly colored, pink and purple like spring flowers—hardly as terrifying as the abominations Istar had witnessed when she crossed the seam before—but she was past judging things by their appearance. If the insects came from the Liminal, Istar did not imagine that their intentions were good.

Istar and Taretel had been going to some pains to secrete themselves from Tash's men. Even though Taretel had been successfully stealing supplies every few days, and had not come near to getting caught after that first night, he treated the Pharicians with extreme wariness. Now he watched Tash and his men with predatory intensity. Tash went to the litter and pulled aside the curtain. Istar strained to see inside, but she could not. She glanced at Taretel and saw that he was breathing fast through his nose, and the blood was up in his skin. Tash extended a hand and a slender forearm appeared from between the curtains, then the rest of the girl that was attached to it. A lithe young woman with a mane of red hair emerged from the litter and stood swaying on the ground, as if she had just stepped off the deck of a ship and was balancing herself upon waves that weren't there anymore.

They moved toward the seam and its clouds of insects. The girl seemed to drift rather than walk, and Istar noticed the solicitude with which the Pharician officers treated her. Even Tash seemed to adopt a different air when he was around her. Istar narrowed her eyes, taking in the girl's appearance.

"I have seen her before," she said to Taretel, struggling to pinpoint where and when, and *how* she had seen this oddly accoutred girl. Suddenly she snapped her fingers. "It was in Ristale! She was riding a black horse. I saw her in the Water of Glass!"

Istar shuddered as the shock of the realization hit her. Taretel was ignoring her, his gaze now fixing upon the sky, which was bare of everything, even cloud. Who was this girl? *What* was she, who had before been a vision in the Water of Glass—a vision that had once seemed to mask the true appearance of the Slave army and its leader, Night?

Closely attended by Tash, the girl walked up to the seams from which the insects came in drifts and puffs. She put her arms over her face and cowered for a second as the first wave of insects hit her; then, finding she had survived, she seemed to draw strength and move forward more confidently. Tash was saying something to her, and she was shaking her head in denial. She stopped and looked at the sky, just as Taretel was already doing.

Istar followed their gazes hopefully, but she could not see the skyfalcon, and Taretel showed no sign of returning humanity. Below, there were more words exchanged between Tash and the girl, and at last she was led back to her litter, where she disappeared behind the curtains. Judging from his body language, Tash was angry and dissatisfied.

"They can't get through," Istar breathed. "He expects her to find a way across, and she can't. That means . . . Taretel, that means it must have been she who got them into Snake Pass in the first place. I wondered how they had done it. It was she. And just now, I wonder if she was looking for the skyfalcon, too. You know this girl, don't you, Taretel? Taretel!"

He ignored her. In fact, he melted into the boulders and hurried away uphill, and she didn't try to follow. The Pharicians were now setting up the borders of their camp, which included several men posted as lookouts. Istar had to resist the urge to throw spiteful rocks down upon them.

BY NIGHTFALL, THE insects had landed on the Pharician camp like colored snow. They did not land on the ground, only on people and horses and certain pieces of equipment. The appearance of the camp was therefore very strange and disconcerting. Istar, secreted among a group of standing stones on the height, had escaped the creatures for now, but she was disgruntled at the idea that, if the insects did drift up this far and land on her, she would be immediately visible to the Pharicians.

The sight of the red-haired girl had rankled Istar. She had seen Taretel leaving the girl's tent, that first night when the Pharicians came. The Pharicians all deferred to her. In the Water of Glass, she had ridden a noble horse. What powers did she possess, and what was she doing in the wilds of Snake Country?

"I am going to find out," Istar said. Being so long in Taretel's presence, she had grown accustomed to talking to herself. "Besides, it's time I had words with the Clan prisoners. If Taretel can sneak into the camp, so can I."

BUT IT WAS not as easy as it looked. She had to wait for the dogs to be taken for their evening feed, a process that lasted only a matter of minutes. She slipped in among the wagons and located the cache of swords and bows that had been taken off the prisoners. Then she approached them from the back of the supply train. She bit her knuckle when she saw Pentar. He saw her, too; but before she could signal to him, the woman-dressed-as-a-man came sauntering over from the cookfire carrying a sack of flour, and Istar had to duck out of sight. She slipped behind an officers' tent and found herself in a narrow gap between tents that formed a sort of alley, with the silhouettes of two tall Pharicians walking toward her from the other end.

Reacting instinctively, Istar hurled herself into the nearest tent with her knife already drawn. She grabbed the sole occupant, steadying her knife against the throat.

"Don't make a sound," she commanded.

The person she held by the throat was the red-haired girl, and when the Pharicians walked past the tent without pausing, Istar realized with relief that they had not seen her. She kept her death hold on the girl anyway.

"I want to talk to you. What's your name?"

"Jaya," the girl whispered. Jaya was small and weak, Istar noted with satisfaction, and she looked almost deathly ill. But she suffered the pressure of Istar's knife against her jugular without flinching.

"How did you do it? How did you cross the barrier?"

"The bone," Jaya answered in a faint voice. "The skyfalcon gifted me it, and I made a bridge."

"Why don't you do it again? You failed out there today."

Jaya spoke as if reciting her words. "Tash will soon come and find you here. He kills without compunction, Istar."

"How do you know my name?" she snapped.

"I have the Knowledge of many things. And I have seen you. In Jai Pendu, with Tarquin. Tell me, have you any news of him?"

Jaya's speech was strangely formal, and her manner annoyed Istar as much as her words unnerved her. She grabbed the red-haired girl by the shoulders.

"Stop it," she hissed. "*You are an animal now*. Act like one."

She didn't know what possessed her to say it; she hadn't planned the words. Maybe she was jealous of Jaya and the airs the girl put on, her strange and medial behavior as if she could see through people and things to their elemental causes; yet it seemed to Istar that Jaya could scarcely lace her own boots without help. Everyone, Taretel included, raced in circles round this girl.

Jaya was not stupid, though. She could feel Istar's strong fingers digging into her collarbone; not to mention the fact that Istar was practically pawing the rug like a bull, head down, eyes fixed malevolently on the red-haired sorceress. She met Istar's gaze and swallowed her tears.

"Listen to me, Jaya," Istar said. "Where are the rest of the bones? Where have you hidden them?"

"I haven't got them!" Jaya protested. "There was only the one, and we used it. When I was on that bridge, I could see the shortest way to Jai Khalar; it is just across this divide. I could step through the barrier myself, but Tash will not permit it. And I cannot bring the others without a bone to make the bridge."

This was not what Istar wanted to hear. The skyfalcon had flown off with nearly a whole skeleton—what had become of it all? She was angry, and she didn't really care whether or not it was Jaya's fault.

"There will be trouble for you," she warned. "If Tash finds out that you cannot control the time membranes, he will drop you in an instant. How do you propose to get another bone?"

Jaya was trembling. "D-d-don't know," she stammered. "Things always just . . . happen to me."

"Well, that's not the way things really are in the world," Istar said, not caring whether she sounded harsh. "You want something, then you have to make it happen. Why don't you turn all your Knowledge toward figuring out how we can build that final bridge? How did you call the skyfalcon, anyway?"

"Call it?" said Jaya incredulously.

"It comes to you, doesn't it?" Istar's jealousy flared again, and she realized she had raised her voice. Her skin prickled as she heard someone walking toward the litter. Istar clapped a hand over Jaya's mouth to silence her, even though it had not been Jaya who had spoken loudly. They listened to the footsteps pass and recede into the distance. At last Istar released Jaya, who regarded her with a quiet, rather sad dignity. Istar was trying her best to be mean and heartless, but when she looked at Jaya's desolate eyes, she couldn't seem to maintain her hostility.

"Listen, I have to go. But don't give up."

"I never give up," Jaya answered in a low voice. Istar locked gazes with the red-haired girl, and found herself softening yet again. She gripped Jaya's hand.

"I may be able to help you, so think on what I have said, and be ready for anything. And call the skyfalcon again! But do not let Tash know we have spoken."

Jaya gave a frightened nod, and Istar seized a blanket and ducked out of the litter. She put the blanket over her hair where the insects had landed and used its cover to escape the camp. When she got onto the height she shook the brightly colored insects out until they had dispersed into the gorse.

Why had she been so nice to Jaya?

She really wanted to hit something.

DARIO'S BARGAIN

𝒫entar and his men had not been captive to Tash for long before Dario found an opportunity to visit the prisoners. She would not speak with them while Tash or Shiror were present, but the two of them were often preoccupied with Jaya, and the guards who had been stationed over the prisoners were low-ranking and, in Pentar's opinion, rather stupid. Dario allowed herself to be roped into cooking gruel and feeding it to the captive Clansmen, playing deliberately into the chauvinism of the Pharicians, Pentar realized; for Pharician men never performed drudgery of any kind when there was a woman to be employed, instead. It was this job of feeding the men that gave Dario a chance to communicate with the Clansmen.

"I can help you get away," Dario said in a hurried whisper. "But you will have to help me, as well. I must get rid of the last Sekk, Jaya. I failed the first time, and now Tash protects it."

Pentar slurped his gruel and said nothing.

"It's a fair deal," she persisted. "Your freedom, in exchange for Jaya's life."

"You are no longer a Clan sister to me, Dario," Pentar said. "You are with Tash now, and you did nothing to help Jakse."

"Jakse is a small concern compared to the red-haired Sekk. I cannot concern myself with particular allegiances. I can only concern myself with fighting the Sekk."

"You sound much like another Honorary I know," Pentar said. "But, as obsessive as she may have been, that Honorary knew what loyalty and trust were all about."

Dario said, "Tash is only using you to find his way back to Jai Khalar. Once we emerge from Snake Pass, you will have to escape, or bow to Tash and accept his rule. That is all he is doing by keeping you alive: serving himself, and testing you to see whether you can be made to comply. If you can't, he'll kill you."

"I know this," Pentar said angrily.

"Then why not get your freedom now? Kill the Sekk, and in return I will free you and you can return to your people. It is the best chance the rebellion has. You'd be a fool not to take it."

"Why don't you kill her yourself if you want her dead so badly?" Pentar asked.

"Tash likes her. If I kill her, Tash will kill me."

"And he won't kill you if he finds out you let us go?"

"No. Because I will go with you. I was never the traitor you think me, Pentar."

There was a long silence. "I don't believe you, Dario," he said.

She replied, "Do not judge too swiftly. Things are not always as they appear. Think about it, Pentar. That is all I ask."

Pentar thought about it, all right. But he was not sure he and his men would survive such an escapade. It would be down to timing, and to whether they could lay hold of their weapons before the Pharicians cut them down in their tracks. And he didn't trust Dario.

But she was persistent. She returned two days later, just after they had successfully crossed the bone bridge and were traversing Snake Pass. Pentar was preoccupied with the thought that Jaya had been able to lead the entire army across a boundary that none of his men, nor Jakse's, had been able to cross. It meant that she had the power to return to Jai Khalar and, presumably, take control. Tash treated Jaya with a weird combination of privilege and contempt; but it was Pentar's opinion that the girl was too weak and ill to take much notice of what Tash did.

By now, a variation on Dario's plan had occurred to him. He could take Dario up on her offer, use his freedom not to kill, but to kidnap Jaya, and then try to make an escape with her into the wilderness of Snake Pass, which he happened to be reasonably familiar with. Without Jaya, Tash would stand little chance of reaching central Everien. And, if Pentar could get Jaya on his side, he might yet recover from the debacle he had entered into the night he allowed Taretel and Istar to get away.

When Dario came back, he decided to feel her out for the details of her plan.

"Do you still want to go through with it?" he said.

"More than ever. What are you waiting for, Pentar? I have the drugs all ready. I can administer them at any time. The whole camp will sleep."

"Why do we have to kill her? Why don't we just drug her as well, and take her?" he asked, testing Dario to see how she would react.

"She is Sekk," Dario hissed. "She has great magic. I tell you, Pentar, you are a fool to throw away this opportunity. Tash will soon kill you. It is only a little way before we reach the border of Everien proper."

"There is no cover in this landscape," Pentar invented. "Give me a little more time to think, and maybe I can help you."

Again she went away. Then came the day when the bright insects poured out of nowhere, and Tash took Jaya toward what Jaya said was the final timeserpent barrier between them and Jai Khalar, and failed to open the seam as she had done before.

Word got about the camp. Jaya had said to Tash, "I can walk through this place. It will not hurt me. But I cannot lead you and your men."

Rumor had it that Tash had slapped and kicked the girl for her insubordination, but Pentar did not believe it. Tash thought Jaya was as good as the rain, and she was already very weak—Tash would not touch her. In fact, Pentar thought that time would do Dario's job for her. Jaya couldn't live long at the rate she was going.

He was sitting there in a stew about it when something moved among the supply wagons. He looked up and couldn't believe his eyes at first. There was Istar! She put a finger to her lips and suddenly ducked out of sight again. A moment later, Dario appeared, whistling jauntily.

"Let's do it!" Pentar said, thinking fast. "Let's do it *now*."

She looked at him in surprise. "But we have only been at this place for a few hours. Give it time—she will find a way across. Once she has helped us return to Everien, we will act."

Pentar had not been expecting Dario to propose this tactic. She was right: it was pointless to be stranded out here in Snake Pass when there was a chance Jaya could lead them into Everien. If Jaya were dead, they'd never get across the barrier.

"But we must act at once," Pentar said, his mind racing to think of a reason.

"At once? Why?" Her eyes narrowed suspiciously.

"It must be so," Pentar bluffed, stalling for time. "Why, for obvious reasons."

"Obvious reasons? What do you mean? You stall for weeks, and now you propose to act instantly?" She flicked a purple insect away from her eyes in annoyance, and Pentar had an inspiration.

"Ah, be careful with that!"

"What?" She glanced at her hand, at the insect that was now aloft.

"Do you not recognize these insects?"

She stared at him in confusion, and he knew he had her.

"They exude an odorless vapor that weakens the bones. I'm surprised you don't know about them, I thought you were an expert on insect poisons."

"I am a Wasp, of course," she answered defensively. "But I've never seen these creatures before."

"They are not dangerous in the short term," Pentar invented liberally. "But if we stay here another two days or even another day, their poisons will start to enter our bodies. There is no cure."

Her mouth made an *O* of surprise and concern.

"Very well," she said, and he watched her face as she calculated rapidly. "I have already served the meal, but I will make a supper cordial."

And she brushed more of the insects away as she left.

Pallo turned to his fellow prisoners and began whispering in Seahawk.

CONSEQUENCES

When Istar returned to the place among the standing stones where she'd camped, Taretel was waiting for her, and the skyfalcon sat on his shoulders. He looked like a king out of legend. Istar stomped up to him and threw the food she had acquired on the ground before him.

"Where are the rest of the bones?" she demanded, addressing her questions to the silvery bird.

Taretel shrugged and scuffed a toe at the cold meat. The skyfalcon took off and landed atop one of the standing stones. Awkwardly, as though it were heavy, the bird held a split stick in its beak, like a slingshot or tuning fork.

"Taretel! Answer me!"

"All of Everien must be knitted together again," he said softly. "It is not only one person or one quest or one union that must be satisfied. The length and breadth of Everien must be flown, and mended."

"And the part that we need to have mended before we can return to Jai Khalar? What about that?"

He shrugged again. "I cannot be sure."

Her tone was imperious. "Taretel! Stop hedging. What about that bone you've got right now?"

He rounded on her then. "It is not for me to say! Speaking to you at all is a difficult act and one that doesn't feel very good. Don't ask me questions I can't answer."

"Well, this is great," Istar muttered. She began rampaging around their camp, overturning things and making as much mess as she could. "We cannot get home; Tash has captured or killed all my men; you are widely known as a wanted murderer; Jaya is ill, possibly dying; you think she is as great as the blue sky—"

Taretel let out a strange noise, half grunt, half howl. He drew his sword in one smooth movement and topped a substantial fir tree with a devastating blow.

Istar shut up.

"Are you aware that you're carrying our child?" he said into the silence.

Her mind came to a standstill. She couldn't think, much less speak. She heard his words, but not their meaning. He continued to talk.

"When I say 'our,' I mean the child of our winged form, the sky-falcon and I, and yourself of course. You are very moody and hard to understand. Is it possible you don't know?"

"Don't know *what?*" Istar said stubbornly, unable to take in Taretel's words.

"Don't know the consequences of what we did. Don't know you're pregnant," he replied.

Her mouth fell open in outrage and she stood there. It began to add up. Her sickness, her tiredness, the softness of her belly. No blood these past two months. She had thought it was due to all the weight she lost on the cliffs, but . . .

"Impossible," she said.

He raised one eyebrow and looked at her. Then he began cleaning the edge of his blade, which was sticky with sap from the tree.

"Well," she amended, surprised by the matter-of-factness of her tone, "maybe not impossible, but highly unlikely."

Inside, she had already accepted that it could be true; but she was fighting it. Why couldn't she be having this conversation on the ledge with Eteltar? Why had she made such an issue with him of having to return to Everien? Why hadn't she just *stayed* and let everything happen as it was bound to?

"I mean, what is the point of my having an army, 'saving Everien,' being true to my people and all that, when I don't even have a people? My father is gone, my mother is insane, my sisters do as they please. I have no Clan, no king, no purpose, and now all Everien is a ruin. I should have stayed, and climbed the cliff, and been happy. I loved him, you know."

Taretel said, "I know I am not Eteltar, but—"

"No!" she agreed, half-sobbing. "You are not. He is lost to me, and you are a killer! Look at the position you have put me in!"

Taretel had begun to stretch his hand toward her as if to offer something; now he dropped it.

"I will honor my commitments," he said in a stilted tone. "I will shelter you while you carry this child. But we must get to a place of safety, and you must stop this wild emotional raving. It is not healthy."

She stared at him. "What do you know about what's healthy? And how are you going to help me if everything you do is devoted to *her*?"

Even as she said it, she knew she was being a bitch. Istar had been impressed by Jaya, entirely in spite of herself. There was something fragile and vulnerable about the girl. And innocent. Istar might be jealous of the attention Jaya commanded, but she had felt the same magnetism when she was with her.

"I hate this darkness," Taretel said irrelevantly. Then the sky-falcon launched itself into the air and flew off, still clutching the slingshot-thing.

Several minutes passed in silence. Taretel had retreated to his old pose: legs apart, hands clasped before him as though bound (they weren't), head down. Istar began to feel ashamed. She cleared her throat and said, "We still have to find the last bridge."

He didn't answer.

"Surely you know something about it, Taretel! If you are the voice of the skyfalcon . . ." She let her voice trail off with a wheedling tone, hoping he would take up her invitation, but he didn't speak. After a while she made up her bed and lay down, but she couldn't sleep. Her thoughts had begun to catch up with her.

Pregnant? Pregnant with *what*?

And she'd thought *herself* a half-breed.

She sank into strange, helpless dreams.

THE ESCAPE

$\mathcal{D}$ario's poison put the entire camp to sleep. The prisoners waited with bated breath while, little by little, silence fell over the Pharicians. The horses could be heard whuffling and blowing, occasionally shaking their heads and rattling their halters; but slowly the noise died out until nothing could be heard but the sound of wind encroaching on the camp. The moon came out. Pentar looked at it and wondered what other parts of Everien it shone on, if any. The reality of the timeserpent meant that this small part of the world, this canyon where he and his people walked, was like a boat on the sea, lost and unconnected. It was not even the same moon, he thought, that shone on his family in Seahawk. His children might be grown, or dead. His mate had probably found another.

Pentar shrugged into his gloom like a favorite garment. He watched Dario threading her way amongst the guards and prisoners, until she stood before him. She held the key to his shackles.

"It must be done quietly," she said. "They are asleep, but they will awaken if roused. I will take the men and wait for you over that rise."

She pointed to a gnarled hill that overlooked the river and the road, where a grouping of jagged stones stood on end, catching the moonlight. It looked as though two cloaked and sinister figures were standing there already, Pentar thought, and shivered.

"Why don't *you* do it?" he asked her impulsively. "Just give her the same poison, only more. She is ill enough already, is she not?"

Dario shook her head. "I failed once. She has spooked me, she has seen my soul. I dare not go near her."

"And I do?" Pentar whispered. "I was Enslaved once, by a

210

beautiful female Sekk no older than Jaya. Are you not afraid it will happen again?"

"She does not have her full powers," Dario hissed, and her eyes glinted in the moonlight. Pentar suddenly realized that Dario was not merely obsessed, she was actually touched. There was something entirely wrong with her thinking.

"Very well," he said, more determined than ever that Jaya should not be killed. "I will meet you there. But you must free the men and let them take their weapons. It's our only chance in the wilderness."

"Weapons and supplies," Dario said. "It is all arranged. Be quick, now. The average Pharician has a powerful metabolism, and Tash, especially, is a restless sleeper. Hurry!"

PENTAR HAD RECEIVED no further signal from Istar, and he was worried what she was up to. But to placate Dario he would have to hold up his end of the bargain, and he could not be seen to deviate from the plan. Dario would be watching. He stole alongside the red-haired girl's tent, shoved the curtain aside, and went in.

Jaya was awake, her food and drink untouched. Her arm lay useless on the furs beside her, its black scoring both ugly and frightening to see. He looked into the girl's pale, knowing eyes.

"Dario wants you dead," he said softly. "But I don't think that's wise."

He was a little unnerved when she simply stared back at him, failing to react to his dramatic phrasing.

"Come with me," he added, holding out his hand. "We will escape Tash. He will only use you for evil."

She didn't budge. "No," she said. "I am tired of being dragged from pillar to post. Escape yourself. I will say nothing to Tash."

Pentar sputtered with anger. "You don't know what you're dealing with," he said fervently. "Come with us! Tash will only harm you, I swear it."

She set her jaw and shook her head.

"Very well," Pentar said, and surprised himself by reaching back and hitting her hard across the side of the head with his shackled hand. She went limp, and his heart began to beat at an alarmed rate. He checked her pulse. She was alive.

He dragged the girl from the litter, taking care to pick up

enough of her furs to protect her from the cold, for he knew she had been unwell and it would not do to have her die of exposure. She was heavier than she looked, and he stumblingly dragged her away from the camp. A horse nickered at him, but no one else stirred. Dario had done her job well.

But Jaya was not so cooperative. After only a few strides she awakened and began screaming and struggling. Pentar clapped a hand across her mouth and tried to quiet her, but to no avail. She bit him, slammed an elbow into his eye, and caused him to fall down, dropping her in the mud.

"Tash!" she screamed. "Prince Tash! The prisoners escape! Tash!"

No one stirred. Pentar, humiliated, furious, and scared, in that order, grabbed her by one wrist and began dragging her toward the hill where Dario was to meet him with the rest of the men. She continued to shriek, and though he backpedaled through the mud and into the gorse that covered the hillside, he was beginning to think he would have no choice but to slit her throat. Then he backed into something solid, and stopped.

There was a great shadow there, with white braids, and a sword too large for an ordinary man to wield.

Taretel let loose a snarl.

KNOW HOW TO USE YOURSELF

Horses were whinnying and running around their tethers. The man's screams stopped suddenly and from my position prostrate on the ground, I saw the great cleaving blade dripping with blood, and furred boots, and black-clad legs of a proportion greater, even, than Tash's. I drew myself up to my hands and knees. The Seahawk warrior was lying beside me. There had been a lot of blood as he was dying, but none flowed now. The fight was over, and the loser's sword was clean. He had thrust me aside and I was uninjured but splashed with his blood. The victor had gone into my tent and returned with the bag containing the broken vessels from the cave: my comrades. I recognized him as the man I had mistaken for the Magician, some nights ago.

"I am Taretel the Free," he said, reaching down and grabbing my hand. "You don't know me, but I know you. Come quickly, before the whole camp awakens."

The skyfalcon was on his shoulders, but he had hooded it.

"I hate the darkness," he said, noticing the direction of my glance. "It makes me nervous; I should not be flying. But we cannot wait for daylight, so hurry!"

As he spoke he was dragging me toward the timeserpent seam. The insects were everywhere, visible even in the dark, painting the whole scene in surreal colors. They only landed on the living, and as I was dragged from the corpse of my would-be savior, I saw that they were rapidly deserting him, leaving only a grayness in the shape of what was once a man.

The slain man had been a Seahawk. I bit my lip, thinking of Tarquin.

As I was pulled along past quiet tents and nervous horses, I thought it strange that the whole camp was silent. Everyone seemed to be asleep. How could they have failed to hear the clash and cry of the fighting? The horses had calmed down a little, but I could see the whites of their eyes rolling as we passed them. They did not like our smell.

Even as I thought this, I heard a man's voice give a muted shout in Seahawk.

"Pentar?"

There was a rustling and the muffled clatter of a group of men approaching. Dario's voice could be heard.

"Is she dead? Is she dead?"

Meaning me, I thought. I picked up the pace. Taretel did not seem to be afraid of them, but I was. We raced over the broken ground, and I could see daylight beyond, through the wall made by the timeserpent. It was afternoon in the adjacent time frame. I glanced down at myself and saw I was covered in violet insects, so tiny they left no more sensation on my skin than dust. But my right arm with its black insignia was bare.

Dead, I thought. *Or never alive in the first place.*

"Ai, Pentar!" I heard a Seahawk cry in distress. I wished I could cover my ears. But Taretel pushed me forward, until the confusion and noise were behind me. Ahead, I could hear the singing.

Once again, I faced the discontinuity rent by the timeserpent.

Come, Jaya. Come back to your house, and let us put it right. We have Tarquin, you know.

"Go!" cried Taretel. "Hurry, before they wake. I will join you when I can."

I stood there hesitating. "Give me back the broken glass," I said. "It is not yours. You do not understand it."

He fixed me with a fierce gaze. "I am going to destroy these things," he said.

"You cannot!" I hissed.

"I must. They are broken, they are dangerous, and they must not fall into the wrong hands. I am going to melt them in the fire, and make them into one lump of glass, and then I shall cut it apart with my sword and scatter the pieces over Everien when I cross the next seam. It is the best undoing I can think of, and the safest."

I choked back a sob. I was not about to argue with him, thinking that he would probably kill me if I did. But to lose them *all,* every one of them. . . .

"They will live in you," he said softly. "You know the songs, now."

I gulped and stared at him. How did he know they had been singing to me?

Taretel said, "I have to go now, and the next time we meet, I may not have the power of speech. Jaya, do not be foolish. Do not allow the Pharicians to use you. Do not allow anyone to use you! You don't even know how to use yourself. Here!" He shoved a bag of food at me, then unbuckled his snow-lion cloak and threw it over my shoulders. "I will find you when I can! Now go!"

Taking my obedience for granted, he swung round and his sword came out in a moonlit arc. Overhead, I heard the eldritch cry of the skyfalcon as it took flight in the darkness. The Pharicians had begun to wake up and stagger groggily in search of the cause of the commotion. I didn't stay to find out what would happen to them.

I jumped across the Liminal.

WHERE IS PENTAR?

Ꝺꜱtar was awakened by screams. Swords clashing. The squeal of frightened horses.

She leaped up. In the camp below, horses were visible as luminous forms of violet and magenta. They were panicking, running into one another and neighing. She couldn't see what was upsetting them. It could be a mountain lion, or wolves, or practically anything, but there was no movement from the dark forms of tents, and the guards lay at their posts. She assumed they were not dead, but asleep, for the insects lay on them thick as snow.

Perhaps, Istar thought, these phantoms of the Liminal had enchanted the Pharicians somehow and put them to sleep. Hope surged in her. She strapped on her sword and stamped up and down to warm her feet. This could be her chance to meet with Pentar.

Before she could make her move, she saw with a thrill that a whole posse of armed men were racing up the hillside. She wanted to cheer as they came closer and passed into the shelter of the standing stones, their outlines luminous with the insects that had settled on their clothes and hair. They were armed but without armor, their clothes ragged, some of them barefoot. Some carried sacks or boxes, but most had only swords, and their braids flew behind them as they came. Behind them, in the camp below, Istar saw that at last torches had come out and people were moving to and fro.

"Seahawks!" Istar cried. "Seahawks, I greet you as kinsmen!"

But their leader was not Pentar, but the woman who must be Dario, and she had a bow on her back. Istar drew her sword. "Where is Pentar?" she called. "I am Istar Seahawk, and I seek Pentar, your leader."

The woman halted. The moon was not bright enough to reveal much detail, and Istar knew that Dario had not expected to see her. There was a fearful pause.

"I am not your enemy," Istar said. And again: "Where is Pentar?"

One of the Seahawks pushed past Dario, breathing hard from the climb. With a dull shock, Istar recognized him as one of the soldiers Grietar had entrusted to her command. The young man coughed out the answer to her question.

"He is dead, Istar. Your Sekk friend has killed him."

PHEASANTS FOR BOOTS

One benefit of the passage of the timeserpent was the premature arrival of spring in the valley of Everien—or in the part of it where Jai Khalar had once been, anyway. From her vantage high in the cliffs, Liaku observed the spectacle of a sky striped half in darkness, half in daylight, as one part of the valley lay in night, another in day. She sat tight on the sheer cliffs while on the lesser slopes nearby, avalanches roared down with the sudden undermelt of deep snow. Iceboats floundered and fields flooded. Herds wandered untended.

For one born to the regimented order of Jundun, the madness of Everien in the wake of a timeserpent was a dream at once delightful and awful. Liaku had the feeling of being at the end of time; of the dissolution of all rules. It was a free-for-all. Sailsnakes drifted in the second sunset. Before her eyes, a grain tower in the field below Jai Khalar spontaneously exploded. She saw a group of people walking on the riverside path vanish, only to reappear a hundred yards behind themselves, going the other way. Everything before her spoke of doom and tribulation; but to Liaku, it meant pure profit.

At first, she found so many trinkets and interesting objects to collect that she resembled a walking jewelry shop. Her acquisitive instinct, honed since birth, forced her to pick up everything she saw that might be of possible use: kitchen whisks as well as gold earrings; a snaffle bit and a lionlike jade bookend and a collection of silk scarves and a set of keys for who knew what doors and a pipe wrench and a set of salad bowls and a child's pull-toy painted like a spotted cow and a man's shirt that came down to her ankles when she put it on and a pot of cement and eleven kinds of bolts and a Pharician weed-pipe and . . . well, soon she was obliged to make nests in the white cliffs. Many nests. She had the impression that, on being swallowed by the timeserpent, Jai Khalar had managed to turn itself inside out and disgorge some of its contents, so that on the cliffs that it left behind were scattered a plethora of glittering objects, like tide-cast spoils of the sea.

Otherwise, considering that a paranormal, city-swallowing event had occurred, everything appeared eerily normal. Jai Khalar had never been visible in the first place, so this manifestation of some of its mundane trivia actually added to the landscape, where the devouring of the city in no way detracted from it. However, there was a marked lack of traffic to and from the entrance cavern: after a few Pharician messengers had entered and then immediately left, casting puzzled glances up at the cliff as they departed, Jai Khalar was deserted altogether. Either word had spread that the Citadel was gone, or people were too busy coping with their own local disasters to send traffic to Jai Khalar.

Liaku could not see as far as A-vi-Khalar. Where the Fire Houses had once been visible against the backdrop of mountains, there were now only shadows and smoke. She wondered what had become of Duor, and for many days she lingered in the cliffs, collecting loot and watching. She kept expecting Illyra or his men to come riding up to Jai Khalar, but they did not. In the first few days, there was a general haze of smoke from the river where A-vi-Khalar was built, but no other news. Liaku didn't start to put the story together until over a week had passed, and the birds began to come back.

Most of them were dumb messenger birds. They could tell her nothing directly, but as a rule they were sooty and some had been burned with oil or other chemicals. One had lost an eye. Only a few actually carried messages to Jai Khalar; the rest, apparently, were returning home because they had been let free. This did not bode well for the fate of A-vi-Khalar. Maybe the rumors of terrible weapons at the Fire Houses were true. Or maybe the timeserpent had gotten them. She thought of descending to the level of the valley, where there were survivors of the timeserpent attack: she knew this because she saw their iceboats and carts sometimes. She might have tried to find out more from them, but they did not approach Jai Khalar and Liaku wasn't willing to abandon the heights.

Until, that is, she ventured too close to the hole left by the Li'ah'vah.

It was the sound that attracted her. At first she had heard music coming from the gap, and then that had died away and for several days there had been silence punctuated by occasional bursts of bright birdsong. Then, one night, she was awakened to the sound of deep, slow breathing.

She lay still for a time, listening. Wrapped in her thick Everien furs, she was in no haste to move, and, anyway, the nights had been growing warmer and sometimes there was even a touch of rain. Tonight was cloudy, and mist lay on the white stones of the cliffs, so that it was almost impossible to see the contours of the land. The breathing was deep and hollow, and in her mind Liaku tried to imagine the giant that would produce such a sound. She had heard stories of the Everien monsters during her tenure in Jai Khalar, and she had even seen pictures of some of them depicted on gallery walls within the castle. If the breather was anything like the abominations in those pictures, she ought to get far away from it. Immediately.

She got up and began to grope among the rocks of her nest. She collected a crossbow that she was only just learning how to use, and some bolts, and she tossed food into a satchel. Then she began to climb away from the sound, which seemed to be coming from somewhere farther down the cliffs, possibly even the aperture where the Li'ah'vah had passed. Liaku had made a point of avoiding this place, although she checked its perimeter regularly because the hole itself sometimes spewed forth useful items, as if the timeserpent were spitting out the indigestible parts of the creatures and places it had devoured. In her mind she had already fixed the idea that the last place she wanted to go was down into that pit.

Still, it was very dark, and she was not familiar enough with her territory to find her way by feel easily. There was light shining piecemeal on the white rocks, and she assumed it came from the moon, which must be riding in some clearer part of the sky. She followed this light as best she could, until suddenly she came around a bend in the rock and, looking down, realized that this was not moonlight, for it shone straight up from below.

She was not where she had thought she was. She was directly over the Li'ah'vah tunnel. Light was coming out in misty tendrils, and within, something large and tar-colored was stirring.

Liaku watched as the thing came limping out, a shadow among shadows. It could be seen oozing across the white stones and then pooling down into the grass. She followed it from above, horrified and fascinated at once. While she watched, it slid noiselessly past the entrance cavern and toward a wooden hut that had been constructed alongside the river. The Pharicians had formerly been in the habit of stopping boats there to check their contents, and the hut was used mainly as a shelter for the guards and a storage point for the many tablets and scrolls they used to record information about goods transfer. Now it lay directly in the path of the crawling hole—for that was the best name Liaku could think of for this thing that wasn't a thing. The hole shambled toward the hut, lifted itself up like an oil-soaked rag, and flopped over the building. It stayed there a minute, shooting darts of light and sound from its interior. Then it retreated.

The hut was no longer there. The hole was the same size, as far as Liaku could tell. For several minutes it didn't move; for so long, in fact, that Liaku began to shiver and shift about in place to keep warm. Then, just as she was about to give up and go back to her nest, something shining flew from the hole and landed on the bank with a ringing sound. Another thing followed, and another, and by the look and sound of them Liaku would have had to guess they were coins.

Aha, she thought, perking up. She watched with great interest as approximately twenty coins, a dagger, a metal cup, and some miscellaneous iron fittings were spat from the black shape. The hole itself made no sound. When it was done, it carried on along the cliffside. She followed it until it vanished beneath an overhang and she couldn't see it anymore from above. Then, excited and afraid, she hastened down the cliff until she had reached the riverbank. She picked up every single coin. What she could spend them on in a ruined country such as Everien, she could scarcely imagine; but she was pleased to find them perfectly clean and unharmed. They were coins of Hezene's empire, the first she had ever possessed.

"The downfall of kingdoms is wonderful," she said aloud in byrd. "Ah, but Quiz, where you fly without me?"

IN THE DAYS that followed, Liaku made it her business to know where the hole was and what it was doing; as far as she was concerned, she had found an ideal source of income, and so long as she could outrun the thing and didn't accidentally get sucked up in her sleep, she had unlimited financial prospects. She tried to track the hole from the cliffs whenever she could, but this was not always possible, and she sometimes had to descend to the level of the valley floor. It was easier to find food down there, anyway, and although Liaku's requirements were small, she liked to hoard as much food as she could within her nests. She made her missions stealthy, though; for every so often a Pharician party would ride up to the cave entrance and check, just to be certain that the Citadel really was gone for good.

Surprisingly, for the most part Illyra and his men did not come near to Jai Khalar, but rode up and down the valley in orderly columns. There was no evidence to suggest that they were accomplishing anything other than terrorizing the Deer Clan, but they rode up and down faithfully all the same. The Deer Clan were soon set to tilling the fields alongside the river, guarded over by Illyra's horsemen. What the other Clans were doing, especially the rebels, was unknown. Liaku's view of the lowlands of Everien ought to have been unobstructed from her vantage on the cliffs, but in fact there were places in the valley that she simply couldn't see. It was as if her eyes refused to focus on certain regions, and if she tried too hard, she got a splitting headache. There were other unusual phenomena: mists that rose vertically; arrows of sunlight flickering from the north in the middle of the night; and shadows like the shadows of night shrouding those same regions during the day. Every day, Everien looked different.

Liaku was sitting in her main nest in the cliffs, looking down on the area where she'd last observed the Blackness eat something and spew out something else (in this case, a perfectly happy live pheasant and a single holey boot, respectively). She was thinking sad thoughts about the pheasant—wondering where he was now, whether he was alive somewhere or if he had actually been turned *into* a boot, which to Liaku seemed a disturbing fate—when she saw Quiz.

She leaped up and drew breath for a piercing shriek. Quiz was hanging in the sky, perfectly still, only the very tips of his wings vaning with tiny movements to hold his position.

Below him was the Blackness, opaque as a pool of oil.

Liaku held her breath. Quiz wasn't . . . *hunting* the Blackness. Was he?

Her eyes went back and forth from the pool of darkness to the bird. Quiz watched and waited. Ever so slowly, the Blackness began to crawl over the uneven ground. Like a living carpet, it took in an overturned oxcart, climbing over it and covering the lumpy shape, and then slowly flattening until the oxcart was gone.

It took in the bricks that paved a section of road leading to what had been Jai Khalar.

It took in some flowers.

Quiz followed it, focused and persistent.

"Quiz, please," Liaku whispered, crossing her fingers and arms and toes. "Please no mess with Blackness. Please come here. Come to Liaku. Quiz."

She didn't dare raise her voice. Across the valley, the air rippled and an indeterminate yellow mass shot out of nowhere, shaped itself like a spear, then dissolved into a flight of insects. They alighted on a hut, whose occupants rushed out and raced in circles, obviously being stung.

The Blackness went inexorably on its slow way. Quiz hung, silver and sharp against the soft gray clouds.

The hut was set on fire. The people fled. Liaku took no notice of the episode: it was just another outbreak of strangeness in Everien, a part of the general background, like the cows that could be heard bellowing by the river. Quiz hung. The tension in Liaku's body made her muscles ache. Her eyes stung from watching. But when it happened, it happened almost too fast to take in.

Like a shutter being drawn back from a lamp, the black pit sent out spears of searing light.

The skyfalcon dived.

Liaku screamed. She knew what would happen next.

She had watched the Black Thing enough times to know that it was not a living creature so much as a sort of irregular tide, mindless and unfeeling. It took things away and put other things in their places, like some kind of random mercantile exchange. Now it began to flash and sing out, and the skyfalcon was diving straight into its mouth. Liaku's throat closed. This couldn't be happening.

At the last instant, something fell from the skyfalcon's claws. Something white. And then Quiz pulled out of the dive, changing his direction even as the Blackness seemed to reach up its edges toward him, hungrily. The White Thing disappeared in a series of blinding flashes. Weird, high-pitched noises came drifting to Liaku on the breeze.

Quiz rose to his former height, still watching.

Liaku held her breath, waiting for the release of whatever items the hole was going to leave behind. She waited so long that she began to think she'd been mistaken about the idea of an exchange. Maybe it had taken the White Thing the skyfalcon dropped, end of story.

Then it moved a little, sliding back and then shimmying from side to side as if making itself more comfortable in the white stone. The hole released one more flash of brilliant light, and then faded to black. Now there was a body lying beside the inert hole. It was the crippled Scholar. He stirred a little, as though drunk or asleep.

Quiz circled once, then rose rapidly, and vanished from view.

Liaku sighed. "I prefer to have gold," she said.

INSTEAD OF
EATING WAKHE

$\mathcal{L}$iaku did not want to be burdened with Wakhe. For one thing, he was possibly the most disgusting human being she had ever seen. The very sight of him offended her. It was not that Liaku was being unkind in this assessment, it was just that in her world, in Byrdland, she had seen many byrdchildren and men and women die simply because they caught a fever, or sustained an injury in a fall that immobilized them, or developed a tooth problem that prevented them from eating. Liaku did not take her life for granted, and she was proud of her autonomy and her toughness. Someone like Wakhe would never have lived past his first weeks or months, had he been born in Byrdland. And yet here he was, revered as a great Scholar, served by others, privileged in every way. She had felt a little sorry for him during the time when Se had controlled him, but Se was gone, and though many people had died as a result of the timeserpent, here of all men was Wakhe still alive, still creeping around like a fool. It wasn't fair! She didn't even know if Duor had lived through the blast, and Duor had been young and fit and true. Yet here was Wakhe.

The whole idea gave her a creepy, unnatural feeling. Looking at Wakhe struggling alone on the ground while the shadow he could not see nosed past him like a crocodile too sated to bother with other prey—it was like looking at a worm writhing in a puddle, or a baby chick that has been injured by a cat and flops about, doomed but never giving up. It was horrific! Why didn't the old cripple just *die* as he had been meant to from the day he was born?

He began to wander in the direction of the cave that had formerly been the entrance cavern of Jai Khalar. She knew he could not see it, but she supposed perhaps he could feel the change in air currents, or could smell something that led him on.

Curious, Liaku went closer. She had food and shelter, and she had control over her piece of ground. She had no wish to help others—it was not compassion that drew her on. It was only that she was unduly fascinated by Wakhe, and she was pretty sure his infirmity would prevent him from noticing how close she was coming. If he didn't know she was there, he couldn't appeal to her for help, and then she wouldn't have to make a moral decision.

She watched him tap and stumble his way into the cave, where the rush of water obscured all sound of his movements. She trailed him, idly at first, but with more interest when he didn't emerge right away. The cave was almost totally swamped by the spring-swollen stream, and she could see nothing of what was within. She pulled her furs closer and padded across the slippery boulders. What in the Emperor's Nest was he doing in there?

In the darkness she saw eyes. Snarling and barking greeted her, and she stopped where she was. Some of the hunting dogs used this cave as an occasional lair, and she was wary of them. She cast about for a weapon, wondering as she did so why they had not attacked Wakhe yet. Surely he would scream, or at least have the sense to try to run away? Maybe they were stalking him, and he couldn't see or hear them. She shuddered.

The water of the stream was filthy, clogged with scraps of things that Liaku assumed had come from the vanished Jai Khalar. Most of them were waterlogged and useless: ruined lumps of animal fat turning to suds in the cold water, or torn and stained silks, or bundles of shit-stained straw. In a backwater near her feet floated the leg of a chair, its bottom carved to resemble a lion's paw. She picked it up and brandished it. It was slimy and cold.

The growls came closer. Liaku let out an aggressive byrd-shriek, one that had served her well when warning intruders off her Watch back home in Byrdland. Here, it only brought the dogs closer.

"Wakhe, you stupid shit! Come out now! Stupid!"

Liaku was unclear as to whether Wakhe could hear anything at all, but she yelled because it was the only thing she knew how to do. She couldn't even see him. Unless . . . She groped in her clothing. No. She had no Knowledge-light. She had left hers back in the nest. She bent and picked up a handful of gravel, throwing it as far as she could into the darkness.

"Come back, stupid! They eat you! Wakhe!"

She saw their eyes. In the filtered light that came from behind her, she saw their teeth gleam. Liaku was terrified of dogs, or she might have reasoned that these were not so long in the wild, that they had been raised and trained by humans and might be won over. But in Jundun, dogs were the killers used by the middle class, and they guarded the ground against any incursion by byrdfolk. She quickly began backing up, clutching the chair leg for all she was worth.

But now growls were sounding behind her as well.

She was surrounded.

Liaku scrambled for a higher position on the rocks. There were no struts to climb here, no chala, no Byrdland, not even a rock cliff to help her ascend to safety. The roof of the cave closed down on her. Panic tickled under her ribs.

Somewhere deeper in the cave, wet clicking noises echoed and swirled. Their tempo increased. Beats and counterbeats formed, like the desert dances that were sometimes performed in the marketplace of Jundun.

Slowly, deliberately, the dogs closed in. One of them, a huge brown-and-white mastiff with an iron collar and cuts on his muzzle where some victim had resisted, took a rush at her, snapping and snarling, only to retreat again as quickly as he had come. The others barked wildly and shifted their positions to close her in more effectively. Liaku swung the chair leg with poor timing and went off-balance. She recognized the draw tactic, but had no power to counter it.

"Quiz!" she whispered like a prayer. More fool she, that she had gone into the one place where Quiz could not help her, even if he could hear her pleading, which she doubted or he would have come before now.

The clicking went on. Then, from somewhere outside, came another sound, like singing, but not quite. Liaku screamed for help in all the languages she knew. The singing went on unaffected.

Another dog tried it out. This one was smaller but faster and more vicious. He came at her in a series of fast, snapping bites, catching her tunic and tearing it and then sinking his teeth into her leg. She clubbed him wildly with the chair leg gripped in both hands, but another had come behind her and jumped at her back from his hind legs, knocking her over the first dog and sending her tumbling on the wet rocks. They scurried after her in a pack, and when she got up they were on her again. She curled in a ball and rolled, thinking that drowning in the river would be preferable to being ripped limb from limb; but she was caught amongst the boulders and could not get to the water.

From the depths of the cave, clicking. From the mouth of the cave, singing. The dogs were biting her and rolling her around. One caught hold of her fur and shook it from side to side. Her head banged on the rocks and she was disoriented.

This is it, she thought suddenly. *Last chance.*

She found her courage and got her feet under her, charging headlong through the pack of dogs for the cave entrance. She drove them ahead of her as she went. There was a deep shadow between Liaku and the cave opening. She took it for a puddle, but when the first of the dogs backed into it and disappeared with a flash of light, she stopped cold and let the hounds do what they would.

But they didn't stay. They whined and howled at the singing that came from inside the Blackness. To Liaku's left, on the river-bank, Wakhe appeared, on his hands and knees, using his mouth to make clicking and whooping noises that swelled and echoed in the enclosure of the cavern.

"Oh Father Bird Who Brings Worms to the Loudest!" Liaku cried spontaneously. Two more dogs toppled into the Blackness; the rest slunk off with their tails down. She backed away from the Blackness. It slithered toward Wakhe, and Liaku found herself once again forced into the deepness of the cavern. She could no longer be quite sure where the edges of the Blackness were. She wondered if Wakhe was attracting it with his noises. The singing was still coming from inside the darkness.

"Wakhe!" she yelled. "Cut it out! You die! It going to eat you!"

But instead of eating Wakhe, the Blackness spat out a cylindrical object. It clattered hollowly and bounced off Wakhe, who grabbed it eagerly and began to beat on it.

"A drum?" Liaku said. "What going on? Can you *talk*? To this *monster*?" She was not sure which of them she was addressing. They were both awful. And yet . . .

Wakhe sat on the rocks and played his drum, and the Blackness sang back to him.

"What you say?" Liaku asked, scurrying over to be by Wakhe's side. "It understand you? Tell it not eat Liaku, and I bring you food,

clean water. No drink this river, Wakhe, understand? You big sick-
ies, you drink here."

He turned his face toward her, so she thought maybe he had
some use of his ears after all. He made nasty noises with his mouth
that Liaku thought sounded obscene. A timorous, beautiful
melody was emerging from the Blackness. The hairs on the back of
Liaku's neck shivered themselves erect.

"Make it move, Wakhe," she added, poking him for emphasis.
"Tell it move out way, Liaku go bring you food, yeah? And robes—
you cold without good fur, trust Liaku, I know. Make it move,
please."

At first nothing happened, but after a little while, the Blackness
began to ooze sideways, allowing a narrow pathway between itself
and the banks of the river. Liaku could not swim, but it was all she
could do to make herself edge along that pathway without giving
in to her fear and leaping for the relative safety of the water. As she
passed the Blackness, the singing seemed to infect her very bones.

Once outside the cave, she ran wildly, laughing. She kissed the
ground and threw her hands at the sky.

Then, soberly, she set about fulfilling her promise. Maybe
Wakhe was not asking for death just yet, after all. For if he could
call what he wanted out of the depths of the Blackness, then he
held command over a potential fortune, judging by all the wonders
of Jai Khalar that had been ingested by the Blackness.

She collected him good food, and wine to sway his senses, and
she removed her bed fur from her nest and gave it a good shake.
She studied the fur assessingly. Wakhe would need a proper cloak,
she thought.

GRIETAR'S PROPOSITION

$\mathcal{A}$s soon as he had finished speaking with the leaders of the Pharician army, Pallo sent for Grietar. Dheri had been privy to the first interviews, in which the king had learned that Hezene had risen smoothly to his bait and that the four thousand men who were to cross the H'ah'vah tunnel in the coming days were expecting to find Beule in charge—not Pallo. But the leaders had little of substance to say of Grietar, except that Hezene had sent him, and that there was something wrong with his eyes that occasionally rendered him an invalid. Eventually, Dheri was sent with two guards, to supervise Grietar's transfer from the castle prison.

The prison was an integral part of the castle and, as he led Grietar out of its depths, Dheri could not help but recall Pallo's words to him when they had been building the place.

"There may come a time," the king said, "when we have to confine a large number of men to guarded barracks. Men who may even outnumber us."

"You mean to capture another army, just as you captured mine," Dher said at once, catching on to Pallo's line of thinking.

"Possibly. It is not likely to happen soon by our reckoning, as messages will have to reach Hezene and then he will have to organize troops to send to us, and by the time they have come across from Ristale, many years will go by, here in the Oasis."

Dher had nodded, and for a moment, he thought, *Here is my opportunity to show loyalty to Hezene. If I betray Pallo and let Tiavel know that a large force will someday come here, he can plan to free them and take over.* Yet even as the sequence of thoughts flashed across his mind, he rejected the idea. Less, alas, because of principle than because of what Pallo said next, which Dher took as a great professional challenge.

"I need you to build a garrison for them that will not only house them, but contain them as prisoners in such a way that only a minimum of staff will be required to guard them. I don't care how you do it, as long as your method is effective. In time, when they have proved their loyalty, the captives can be integrated into our society, here, just as you are being integrated."

He looked piercingly at Dher, who realized that Pallo was not taking his trust for granted. This was to be Dher's test. Dher nodded, his mind already working busily.

"I need within this holding area to have three levels of security: one for those I trust not at all, one for those who have earned some privileges, and one for the men who are almost ready to join us."

"Three concentric rings, possibly," Dher suggested. "With the more loyal guarding the less so, and all of them surrounded by our present army."

"Think on it," said Pallo.

Dher went on to build Pallo a complex and ingenious prison, full of mazes, mirrors, traps, and hides, and he did it without conveying its purpose to the men who performed the labor. They did not know what to make of this structure, which was partially underground yet resembled no dungeon any of them had ever seen. It did not have cells, for one thing, nor any of the shackles, bars, or pits of conventional jails. Yet there was something sinister about the place, and after it was built and had lain empty for a while, mysterious and silent, people began to refer to it as the Waiting.

Now it was to be used for the first time, to hold four thousand Pharician fighters and one inscrutable Seahawk.

Grietar was very pale, his face ruddied by wind but his neck as white and soft as a girl's. He looked stiff, as if high on fear and unsure as to whether or not he liked the sensation. He wore a bandage across his eyes with slits cut in it that revealed just two flecks of blue and white. The guards explained to Dheri that he had screamed and fought when they tried to remove it, saying he suffered from an eye disease and could not tolerate light. When Dheri brought Grietar into Pallo's audience room and explained all this, Pallo immediately ordered the lamp extinguished and, by the red light of the banked fire, commanded Grietar to remove the bandages. Cornered, the man could not refuse.

231

They sat there in a strange silence, those two: Grietar with his head tilted back and his eyes half-shut beneath swollen lids, and Pallo with his hands steepled beneath his chin, watching. Despite the talk of his infirmity, Grietar seemed to be in fine health, his skin sun-darkened and speckled with thousands of freckles, his red hair shining. But he was mentally vacant, and Dheri found him strange.

Pallo, on the other hand, regarded the Seahawk with great curiosity. He looked at him this way and that way, leaping out of his chair to pace around behind the recumbent man, only to return and flop back to his former position. His brow knitted with puzzlement.

"There is something familiar about you," he said softly, not quite speaking directly to Grietar. The Seahawk stirred.

"Are we through?" he mumbled in Clan common. "Did we make it? My head . . ."

He brought a hand to his forehead; but Dheri was skeptical of the gesture. Dheri had experienced no headaches or confusion when he crossed into Everien, other than the obvious disorientation caused by time change. The prisoner had to be dissembling.

Dheri passed to Pallo the unusual book that had been confiscated from Grietar on his arrival. Pallo glanced at it once and then forgot about it. He was watching Grietar like a cat watching a mousehole.

"You are in the audience of King Pallo," Dheri said sternly. "Lord of the Oasis in the Ripping of Everien and master of all Pharicians who come here. Stand and account for yourself."

Grietar had jerked alert as soon as Dheri spoke. There was a sudden and total transformation in his carriage; he leaped to his feet and took a step toward Pallo. Dheri reached for his sword, but Grietar had lowered his head. Still his eyes could not be seen clearly.

"King Pallo," he said politely, bowing. He was perfectly self-possessed, as though he were not the one in the position of prisoner and supplicant, but in control of the interview. With any ruler but Pallo, such a posture would have spelled execution or at least punishment. But Pallo did not react as Grietar added, "It seems to me I know your name; were you not one of the heroes of the Floating Lands?"

"I was there, yes," said Pallo with the air that the flattery was irrelevant. He spoke to Grietar with the same openness he used with everyone. "Grietar, you are a Seahawk. Tell me, do you know what has become of Istar, my friend?"

"That depends on when you have last seen her," Grietar answered, a little nervously, Dheri thought.

"Oh, it's been *years*," said Pallo. "For me, anyway. I know she went to Seahawk to see her family, but there's been a timeserpent since then."

"Ah," Grietar said. "She went across Tyger Pass, I believe. But that was in winter, and it is a dangerous place."

"Tell me she is not dead!" Pallo cried, leaping forward and grabbing Grietar's arm emotionally.

"If she is dead, I do not know about it," Grietar answered gravely; but there was something in his manner that Dheri did not like. He vowed to watch his king and friend very carefully in this audience, for Pallo was not acting as circumspectly as he ought. This man Grietar had provided no explanation for his presence here, and his status with the Pharicians was unknown. They would only say that he was a Seer and that Hezene had sent him. Dheri smelled the Circle in this, but as yet there had been no time to explain about this to Pallo. There were too many other things to worry about, with hundreds of men already coming through from the H'ah'vah tunnel, and needing to be inducted into life in King Pallo's land. Indeed, Dheri wished Pallo would lock Grietar up with the others and concentrate on maintaining security against so large an army; but Pallo seemed unusually interested in the Seahawk.

"It is a fine army of men you have here," Grietar said deferentially. "And what is their allegiance—to you, or to Pharice?"

Dheri thought the question was impudent and had to suppress the urge to strike Grietar. He was hoping Pallo would be careful with this man. The king had never lost his habit of speaking guilelessly, yet Grietar was not the sort one would want to spill any secrets to. Dheri was already suspicious of Grietar's relationship with the Pharicians, and he had noticed the way the Seahawk looked on Pallo's resources. Covetously, Dheri thought. Also, his remarks seemed to come from an angle. Grietar was not simply curious. He wanted something. Dheri simply could not be sure what that was.

"Their allegiance is to me," Pallo said. "Pharice can break herself on the Ripping, but she will only get in a few men at a time. She cannot wield her might effectively against us. We eat everything she offers. These men have been made free."

"And has their Clan king no aspirations toward regaining the rest of Everien?"

Dheri did not like Grietar's tone, as if he were a magician at a bazaar trying to tease his audience into spending more money. Dheri was relieved when Pallo answered this question with one of his own.

"And how fares Seahawk, since the timeserpent?"

Grietar said, "When last I was there, the timeserpent had not come as far as my country. My people were hoping it would get stuck in Snake."

"And why would it 'get stuck,' as you put it?" queried Pallo. He threw himself into the most comfortable chair, inviting Grietar to sit on the couch opposite with a casual gesture. Dheri, watching, thought that Grietar was beginning to look just a little bothered by Pallo. It was understandable. The blond king looked no more than twenty-five, but he had all the sharpness and wariness of an older man. Perhaps Grietar would not find it so easy to play games with Pallo, after all.

"I am no expert on the theory of timeserpents," Grietar demurred with a nervous laugh. But Pallo pursued him.

"Indeed, I can see no reason to believe that the timeserpent should not go anywhere it pleases, anytime it pleases. As I am given to understand it, they are limitless creatures. But perhaps you know something that I do not."

Piercing blue eyes lit on Grietar's face and stayed. Grietar said, "You are in a terrifically good position here, tactically."

"Are you trying to talk me into invading Everien with these forces I have amassed?"

"I am not trying to talk you into doing anything. But you have built up a populous and powerful nation in a bleak and cold region of what could be a great country."

"We are powerful because we have to be to stand against the things that come from the Ripping," said Pallo staunchly. Dheri knew that Pallo would love to get hold of the rest of Everien, but the king seemed determined not to admit it to Grietar. It was as if the Seahawk was tempting him with something evil.

"I can get you across the Ripping," he said. "I have . . . powers."

"Powers?" queried Pallo in an innocent tone. "What do you mean? What kind of powers?"

"Never mind that," the Seahawk replied, his tone laden with implied secrets. "Know that it can be done. Why do you sit here waiting to be taken? You have a huge army of able men. The rest of Everien languishes in the grip of monsters. The Pharician hold has been broken there. If we swept through the Ripping, we could take everything."

"We?"

"Well. I intend to cross the Ripping and find my way to the Fire Houses. What has been started must be stopped."

Now he was talking Pallo's language, Dheri thought. The king had long ago privately admitted to Dheri the guilt he felt for his part in the conjuring of the timeserpent. Wittingly or not, Grietar had put his finger right on the softest and most vulnerable part of Pallo's will.

But Pallo was not as stupid as he seemed. Now he looked at Grietar with a fair impression of good-humored tolerance. "I am king here," he said quietly, and suddenly his face hardened. "You will ask my permission before going anywhere or doing anything, you will consult me before taking a shit, do you understand me, Grietar?"

"Of course, my lord." Grietar inclined his head slightly; it was as close to a bow as one could expect from a Seahawk, Dheri had been told. He wondered if all the men of that Clan were as obnoxious as this one, even Istar on whom Pallo lavished the highest of sentimental praise.

Pallo was saying, "All the people know me as their ruler, and many have done so all their lives. Look at me! I have not aged. They think I will not die—and what do I know? Maybe they are right. One thing is certain, and that is that you need me more than I need you."

"And what about the people from the Fire Houses? Surely you have seen the weapons they were building there. What happens when they come to your country with their weapons and their power?"

"Let them come," Pallo said complacently. "I am ready. I have a huge army. They are years, even decades, behind me, and in all likelihood they are still reeling from the effects of the timeserpent."

"So you believe," Grietar said. "But nobody has really been into

Everien since the Fire Houses exploded. No one really knows what is happening there."

Pallo shrugged. "Maybe we need never know. Maybe they will never come."

"Or maybe they have terrible powers of which you are totally unaware."

"In that case," said Pallo, "the last thing I want to do is go and invade *them*."

Dheri wanted to laugh, but he knew that Pallo's lighthearted manner belied more serious concerns that he would never show. And Grietar's next words could be seen to score points against the king.

"And what of your friends and compatriots whom you'll never see again if you don't go back? What of the loyalties you held—are they gone? Pallo, your name is known to us in Seahawk. You were Istar's sworn friend and ally."

"Not a day goes by that I don't think of her," Pallo said. There was a silence.

"The spirit of adventure and curiosity, it is said, is present in every Wasp born. Are you a Wasp, King Pallo; or has this exposure to the lifestyle of your Pharician father overcome whatever was Clan in you?"

"Your arguments are clumsy and obvious," Pallo said; but it was clear he was affected by Grietar's words. "Go away from me! Dheri, be sure he is watched. I do not trust this one."

He turned his back on Grietar to indicate that the audience was over. But Dheri saw Grietar smile secretively. He looked at the Seahawk's eyes and shivered inside. Pallo might be high on capturing himself another large Pharician force, but Dheri did not think Grietar would make a desirable captive. This man, thought the engineer as he escorted him to his cell, was going to be dangerous.

YES

"What do you think of this book?" Pallo asked, passing Grietar's confiscated volume to Dheri. It was evening and they had just finished a large meal. Pallo was slouched supine on a sheepskin couch, swilling a glass of brandy idly as he balanced it on his chest.

"I think it's a joke," the engineer replied promptly. "The pages are transparent. But this card is interesting. It looks like a fortune-teller's card. 'The Magician,' it says. Do you think Grietar is some kind of Seer?"

Pallo shrugged. "His eyes are weird enough to make him anything. But the card, Dheri, I am glad you mention it. The girl in the picture, she is my friend Istar, I would swear it."

Dheri scrutinized the picture. The girl knelt before the winged man with an attitude of supplication, almost as if she were pleading or even praying.

"*This* is Istar?" he said in surprise. "Your stories always make her out to be proud and strong."

"So she is," Pallo said. "As I'm sure her stories of me do not make me out a king! I keep thinking about her, Dheri. About what has become of her."

"You're going to do it, aren't you?" Dheri said.

"Do what?" asked Pallo mildly.

Dheri snorted. He slipped the card back into the book with stiff, old fingers. He passed the book back to the boy on the couch, who was looking at him with clever blue eyes between flushed cheeks.

"Invade Everien. Isn't that what everyone does, sooner or later?"

"Do you think I'm being brainwashed by that creepy Grietar?"

"I didn't say that."

"But you think it."

"Er . . . well, he is the type to brainwash, yes."

"To brainwash *me?*"

"Mmm, you are the type to be easily influenced, yes."

"So . . . to answer my question, 'Am I being brainwashed?', your answer would be . . . ?"

"Yes," Dheri said, and belched.

Pallo nodded. "Very well. You will side with Tiavel, then? You will rise against me?"

Dheri sighed.

"No," he said.

TWO HUNDRED MILES

𝒫allo's horse danced beneath him. After all these years, he was used to the nervous sidestepping of the typical Pharician warhorses from which all his stock were descended. He had been advised against crossing the fast and agile warmbloods with the smaller and sturdier beasts of Wolf Country, lest he spoil both breeds. In truth, the crosses his breeders had made had proved both tough and quick in battle, but they did not look impressive enough for the king to ride, and Pallo had appearances to maintain. He had learned to ride the warmbloods, and now their nervous ways didn't bother him. He sat easily atop the palomino stallion, applying his aids lightly and without really thinking as he guided the horse up and down the columns of assembled men.

He had been preparing this army for a long time, but he had not expected to ride out aggressively with them. He exchanged glances with Dheri, who rode by his side on a sleek black. Dheri's face was tense and flushed. His hair showed white at the temples. Pallo gave him a friendly nod. Dheri, too, had expected to use the fortifications they had so carefully designed and painstakingly built. Dheri's mind was full of ramparts and bridges, weights, surface tensions, optimal angles, secret tunnels, traps, and joinery. He was too old to think of charging into battle in an unknown land. Dheri had not been raw or impulsive even in his youth, and now Pallo knew he was worried about his sons and grandsons in the ranks of warriors. He was worried, as they all were, about the Ripping.

Grietar was nowhere to be seen. Perhaps Pallo had let him move too freely; but he had felt, lately, that he was held in the grip of forces too great to be controlled. On the morning when he had released Grietar from prison and brought him, at Grietar's request, to the Ripping Wall so that Grietar could show Pallo what the card was for, the event that had occurred was so breathtaking, Pallo still felt a shiver run up his spine when he recalled it.

Grietar had stood on the wall facing into the Ripping, holding the fortune-telling card in his left hand, and raised his hand high over his head. He had let out a piercing, complicated whistle of the sort that Pallo recognized as a Pharician birdcall.

Lightning had flashed in the sky. The Ripping had opened and purple insects had swarmed out and landed on everyone, making everything that was alive glow in a queer, spectacular way. And then, all in an instant, a great silver bird had fallen like a stone from the heavens, seized the card from out of Grietar's hand, and shot up again with an unearthly shriek. As it passed, it dropped a small white bone into Grietar's open palm.

Everyone who witnessed this event had been stunned and overcome with inchoate emotion. Grietar, for his part, had collapsed. He was clutching the bone so hard that his fingers could not be pried away from it even while he was unconscious; and when he woke and opened his hand, there were seared marks made by the bone.

Grietar had given Pallo a weak smile without opening his eyes.

"It is a strange country, Everien," he said. "Will you come with me now?"

After that, Pallo had had to reassess the silver-eyed man. An Everien skyfalcon would not fly out of the distant past and visit Grietar were Grietar not, essentially, worthy.

Right?

And Grietar, once he had recovered, claimed with full confidence that he could make a safe path through the Ripping.

"And Istar?" Pallo prodded.

Grietar shook his head. "We . . . that is, *I* don't know. I'm sorry."

This small honesty had impressed Pallo as a sign that Grietar was not as evil as Dheri believed. *He is only weak,* Pallo thought. *It is not a crime to be weak; I of all people can attest to that.*

But animals did not like Grietar. He was riding a placid and well-broken mare, not a war stallion, because none of those would let him come near without lashing out with hooves and teeth. Again, Pallo considered how little his army knew of warfare. The Pharicians had trained them in classical battle strategy on open terrain, adding variations to allow for Everien's difficult geography. They knew how to ride and shoot, but they did not shoot so well on horseback as from the walls, and they were more highly skilled in the hand-to-hand play Pallo had required them to study, expecting them to defend his castle from the walls and not horseback.

True, they had ridden small sorties to meet the monsters of the Ripping; but since the Ripping Wall had been built twenty years ago, they had never approached the Ripping itself.

Pallo noticed his captains in a conspiratorial huddle and rode toward them, only to observe that rather than talking, they were standing in a circle and urinating toward the center.

"What's this?" he laughed, and they looked up.

"Nerves," said Jerni seriously. "I've pissed about forty times this morning. When are we *going*?"

"Soon," Pallo said. "Now go and be an example to your men, and if you don't want to dribble all day, then stop drinking ale to fortify your nerves!"

Laughing, they saluted him. It no longer occurred to him—or them—that a young man with blond hair and a somewhat silly demeanor was commanding them. They listened to him, though he fell outside all of the stereotypes of a leader. Pallo had had little cause to doubt himself in recent years. His land had prospered, the ranks of his army had swelled, and he had enjoyed the respect and even adoration of his people. In the long term, the fondness his subjects felt toward him seemed to be a more effective deterrent to insurrection and plotting than any protective effort he might have undertaken in his own defense.

And yet, the fate of Lerien weighed on his mind, even after all these years. Everien's former king, too, had tried to rule by polity and gentle persuasion. He had failed dismally. Maybe, Pallo reflected as he looked on the excited faces of his troops, Lerien had forgotten that the whole thing was a game. For Pallo, it had to be. He was no king by nature! He was only playing. His whole rulership was based on this joke and it had worked out surprisingly well.

"Where is Grietar?" he called out to no one in particular. He did not want to keep the men waiting any longer than necessary, lest the whole army drown in a flood of its own urine. He reached the edge of the mass of soldiers and began to ride back along the army's flanks. The mass was subdivided into tactical groups; then behind came the pack animals, the women, and the spare horses.

Pallo had discouraged camp followers, which were a tradition in Pharice, where soldiers could be expected to be on the road of conquest for years at a time; but he could not prevent the soldiers from having cooks and healers in their midst, and if these women also happened to be young and good-looking, it couldn't be helped. Pallo only hoped the army wouldn't be so busy fighting over women that they forgot about their enemies. And there were other dangers. He checked to see that his rear guard was in place; he imagined the monsters of the Ripping claiming hold over the defenseless women and his flesh went cold.

Tovel came to meet him, swaggering along with his armor half-fastened and his shaggy Wolf mane falling about his face; his helmet was tucked under his arm.

"I hold you personally responsible for these deniax," Pallo told the commander of the rear guard, using the Pharician word for "helpless women" to emphasize his point. A Wolf woman overheard him and raised an ax over her head.

"We are not deniax!" she cried. "I am a healer, but bring me something fell to slay and I will show you who is a deniac and who is not."

Pallo took in her muscled arms and fixed gaze and had to agree. But the other women, busy with last-minute packing, were not armed except with knives, and he knew that the Pharician influence in his country had weakened their sex when it came to combat.

"Keep them out of the fighting, Tovel," he said in a lowered voice. "I am beginning to wish I had forbidden their presence altogether."

"We leave behind our children and homes, Pallo," said the Wolf woman boldly. "Lead us well. Not all of us are Pharician-bred, you know."

"I know," Pallo said. "Remember, we have been preparing for such a mission for many years. The rest of Everien needs us. We have advantages. We ride to rejoin the Wolves, and the other Clans."

"If there are any left," someone muttered darkly. Pallo turned but failed to locate the source of the comment.

"We need no conscripts," Pallo said. "If you are afraid, stay home and wait."

There were no other remarks.

"Where is Grietar?" he said again.

"He has gone to the Ripping." The voice came from behind Pallo; it was Dheri, and his horse was sidling nervously from left to right, reflecting his rider's agitation. "He's just standing there. Looking at it."

SINCE HE HAD gotten possession of the bone, Grietar felt different. There seemed to be less of him and more of Them—and the truth was, he liked Them better than he liked himself. He liked their power, their certainty. The way They removed the dirt and doubt from his life. Now that They had successfully summoned the skyfalcon and it had surrendered its bone, the worms within Grietar glowed and squirmed with anticipatory joy.

He walked toward the source of the Ripping with his sword in his right hand and the bone in his left. Like all Seahawks, he could use a sword; but he had never fought an Everien monster. He had heard that most of them couldn't be beaten with a sword, anyway—the blade was the armament of a man who fought other men. He carried the sword because it bolstered his confidence.

The Ripping itself was inaptly named, Grietar thought as he crossed the stone causeway over the river and climbed the stairs to the wall that was meant to protect Pallo's lands from the Ripping. The wall was fifty feet high and stained in places with what dark, monster secretions Grietar did not care to guess. Countless creatures had eaten at its bricks or slithered over its ramparts. Bones littered the far bank of the river. Grietar clutched the skyfalcon's bone like a talisman.

Within him, They whispered, *Yes. Yes. This is the Thing. We will pass Over.*

Resolutely he climbed. From the top of the wall he had a clear view of the Ripping. But it would have been better named the Frozen. Grietar put out his hand and rapped on what felt like a window. The view beyond was white and still. Snow was in the process of falling, each flake as slow as a star wheeling across the heavens. Birds hung in the sky, their wings moving so fractionally that it hurt Grietar's mind to look at them.

The rest of Everien was there, perfectly visible; but it had been wrenched away, leaving a great gulf, the name of which was Ripping. The Ripping itself could not be seen by men. Grietar's

243

eyes, human and unaided, could not see any gap at all. He could not perceive that something was alive and moving in the in-between. But the worms saw it. They shivered so hard in Grietar's eyes that flashes of light went off on his retinas and he heard a high-pitched buzzing from the back of his skull.

His gorge rose. Disgust might seem beyond the capacities of a man whose eyes were already teeming with malevolent silver worms, but the monsters of the Ripping were something else altogether. There was enough of the human left in Grietar to make him react in a primeval way.

Transparent creatures were writhing within the Ripping. Creatures such as Grietar had never imagined. They were fluid, exchanging parts and qualities with one another as easily as clouds. The pages of Jaya's transparent book flipped through his mind. He saw every being in that book manifested within the Ripping, but none of them possessed any integrity. None was whole. The monsters he saw presented the impression of life and purpose—they moved, they acted—yet they were formless in the long term. Again and again he felt himself shocked at what he saw. Then, rather quickly in fact, his mind shut down to interpretation. He saw shapes without meaning, colors and shadows without implications. A dumb, relieved smile broke across his face.

They were talking to him.

The bridge, commanded the worms. *The bridge, the bridge.*

With Their enhanced eyesight he looked down at the bone in his hand. It was made all of packed, swirling symbols in the unreadable Everien language.

The very source of the Ripping was a black pit in the earth. Grietar's body thrummed imagining the raw power of the timeserpent erupting from the earth, puncturing time and creating suction between this world and the next, all through the strange timefolding properties of its unreal skin and hollow, empty form. This dark vortex terrified all who looked into it, more than any monster or nightmare you could imagine. Grietar faced it now with his eyes full of Them, and he did not blink.

He thrust the bone into the Ripping and it vibrated in his hand like a struck tuning fork. Currents shot up his arm. His hair stood on end. His eye sockets rang. His toes curled.

He opened his eyes wide. The worms commanded him to. They had to see all of the possibilities: for when the skyfalcon's bone passed into the Ripping, the frozen waste beyond began to flicker and change.

A thousand scenes succeeded one another at a rate that made Grietar's lips numb. All the blood seemed to have rushed to his head as his worm-ridden eyes tried to process what they saw. Forests and fields of wildflowers. Roads and rivers. Things built in the sky, that did not fall. Pitted craters where everything was black and nothing moved but a buzzard, circling high and much too fast. A fern-laden forest where one gray wolf saw him, stopped in her tracks, and snarled. Spectral buildings. An empty hillside with dead trees and tall insects marching en masse along the ruined boles.

Then, the Light.

Red light. Blue light. Illumination of a sort unknown under the sun, shaking the night with weird intensity. Light that turned his white skin black and his black clothes white. And shaking in rhythm with the Light, the smell of animals and the mingled whimperings and wails of their cries. The whisper of their movement.

Grietar was past thinking or even reacting. He had become a receiver for pure sensation, and he was utterly passive. *They* controlled his actions, and now in the thrall of the Ripping and its contents, even They seemed paralyzed.

Grietar's eyes opened wider than wide. His head fell back and his tongue lolled out. Shock waves raced through the bone and up his arm, into his spine, and down through his feet. Pain irrigated his nervous system, cutting deep and cold trails through fibrous flesh and inert fluid. He let go the bone. He had to.

And then, like a bomb exploding, Grietar's brain lost contact with his body.

Emptiness.

PALLO RODE DIRECTLY to the gates in the Ripping Wall, where an elite guard watched the Ripping through slits in the wall itself, and from the walkway along its top. A group of them stood before the iron gates, awaiting orders to open the passage that would take the army into the Ripping.

"Where is Grietar?" he asked sharply as he rode up.

"We sent him away," their leader said. "He came by half an

hour ago and asked us to let him through. I told him the order to open the gates was yours to give, not his, and he went off in a huff."

Dheri, who had followed Pallo at a slower pace, now caught him up and pointed to a place on the wall a hundred yards to their left. At the top of the stairs, a lone figure could be seen, arms outstretched toward the Ripping.

PALLO SEIZED GRIETAR by the shoulders and forcibly turned him around. Grietar's body was stiff and his pale exposed skin felt slick with cold sweat. His eyes swam, their bright innards spinning like the workings of an imperial clock. He said, "There will be a bridge. Tonight, I think. The code must knit its way to the place of the Fire Houses, which are moving slower. Much slower. Then the bridge will be made."

Pallo touched the invisible seam between his world and the next. Frozen things hung in the sky. Trees bent with imperceptible slowness in a wind he could not feel. It was like looking at a very convincing, skillful painting.

"The Circle are at large," Grietar said in a triumphant voice. "We are free in the between-places. The Liminal is ours to reap. Do not fear the denizens of what you call the Ripping, King Pallo. You are with me. With us. They will bow to us and dog our heels. Soon we will come to the Fire Houses, then all this will be put right."

Pallo could think of nothing to say. For one thing, he had the feeling that Grietar was talking *at* him, not *to* him. And anyway, since when had anything been right with Everien? It would be like promising sunny weather all winter in Seahawk—a gross contradiction. In the old days, maybe, when he'd begged Istar to take him adventuring in the Floating Lands, Pallo had believed in quests and goals and making things better. But especially after the time-serpent came roaring through the Fire Houses and left him stranded in his temporal tide pool in Wolf Country, he had found that all his needs to appeal to a higher authority had gone unmet. Whoever had created the Knowledge had left no explanation of its workings. Whatever the Everiens had made or done, they were gone now and could answer for neither their crimes nor their miracles. All Pallo really had was a book of burned maps and his uncanny youth. By virtue of these, he of all people had become the higher authority to whom people now turned.

And if he had no answers to the questions and pleas of his subjects, how was he to expect the ancient Everiens to have answers to his?

"Dheri!" he called, never taking his eyes off Grietar. "Get Jerni and young Tiavel. Bring them here at once."

Grietar did not rouse from his stupor. He stood still like a dog patiently waiting for his master to return; Pallo felt nervous in his presence. On the ground below, in the gap between the Ripping and the wall built to protect his country from it, he could see something white, almost as if a section of the snow on the other side of the Ripping had slid through into Pallo's world. As he focused his eyes on the whiteness, he realized that it was mushrooming. It grew larger and larger, forming into a shape that was obscenely reminiscent of two testicles attached to a phallus, with the shaft thrust into the seam of the Ripping, where it vanished.

Pallo shuddered. Grietar was not watching this event; nor did he react when the two burly warriors Pallo had summoned appeared on the scene. There was a noticeable animosity between Dheri and the young Tiavel, son and namesake of Dheri's old commander, who plainly still regarded the engineer as his inferior, despite his status with the king. Pallo was determined that this mission should bring Tiavel firmly under his sway; he did not like the idea of a Pharician subcorps within his kingdom, and had done all he could to encourage integration between the Clans and their "invaders" so that the latter became subsumed within the Everien culture. However, with men like Commander Tiavel and his sons, this was not an easy task. Pallo was not a warlord, and he suspected that some of the Pharician-born gave him respect only on the surface.

"Tiavel!" he said heartily. "I want you to guard Grietar with great care. He is participating in some sort of transformation, and he may be dangerous to himself, or to us. It may be necessary to subdue him. Do not injure him, but keep him away from everyone else, and send someone to me at once as soon as he rouses and speaks."

Tiavel bowed, his face betraying no trace of his real feelings.

"Jerni, you are to instruct the troops to stand down until tonight. Keep a solid line of guards on the wall, and do not let any of the men stray too far from their weapons. I do not think we will be moving through until this evening, but I can't be sure. Where the Ripping is concerned, anything can happen."

"Yes, my King," said Jerni fervently, glancing at Tiavel to emphasize the reverence he felt Pallo was due. "We will remain watchful, but save our strength for tonight."

With that, Jerni was off. Pallo instructed Tiavel to take Grietar away from the wall and keep him separate from other men, and told him whom to recruit to assist him. Then he turned his attention back to the Ripping itself.

The white structure was growing larger, and its color was slowly darkening. As Pallo watched, it changed by degrees, until it had sunk into the ground and become totally black. The king stood there for hours, unaware of the impression his army was getting as their sovereign waited motionless on the walls, only his cloak stirring in the breeze. Men whispered amongst themselves but did not disturb him. At last, as the sun was going down, the object had become a negative of itself. Now it was the opening of a very dark tunnel, leading down into the earth.

PALLO STARED FOR a long time at this hole. In his mind, he was reading the pages of his long-memorized map book. Somehow, in the years since he had gotten this book off the Wasp woman in the Floating Lands, he had experienced the mounting feeling that his life must not end until he had discovered the purpose of these maps, and used them. They had served him in the Floating Lands, and again in A-vi-Khalar, but the itching recollection of the visions of cities and roadways and other, unknown, schemata, still plagued him. Before the book had been burned, he had seen *everything*, and then had forgotten it.

Which part of the book would have showed him this tunnel? Was he crazy to think he was living out some sort of fate, a fate sealed years ago in the Floating Lands, but one that would be true, forever?

Why was he still alive, unchanged?

Was it because he had been displaced by the Li'ah'vah?

Would he now age and die, if he returned to the place and time he had come from? Would the years catch him up?

As he watched, the hole grew larger and darker, retaining its tripartite shape with two bulbs and a protruding center. The snowscape beyond the Ripping was still bright and clean. Some of the birds had moved, and the snow was growing less. The light of that adjacent world shone on Pallo's face as his own world fell into true night. Behind him, on the safe side of the Ripping Wall, fires sprang up.

At last he turned away, just in time to see a messenger coming up the stairs two at a time.

"Grietar is awake," he gasped. "Tia has his hands full trying to keep him back from the gates."

Pallo took a deep breath. "Go to Dheri and Jerni, and tell them each that we are moving out. I want the men ready and assembled in marching form before the gates in a quarter hour."

Then he went to find Grietar.

TIAVEL WAS SINGULARLY unnerved. He had taken Grietar's sword away and bound the Seahawk's hands behind his back. This did not stop Grietar from rampaging around, speaking in another language, and spitting, kicking, or head-butting Tiavel when the latter tried to contain his movements.

"He's mad!" cried the young man, looking very much out of his depth. "What language is that? I can't understand a word he's saying."

Pallo watched Tiavel struggle with Grietar, and said calmly, "It is ancient Pharician. You would not know this tongue, but when I was educated in Jundun in my youth, I learned a little of it."

Tiavel's look acknowledged a little more respect than usual. "What shall I do with him, my lord? You said not to harm him, but he is not behaving reasonably."

By then, the section commanders had arrived, bringing more to help Tiavel, but Pallo would not allow them to gag Grietar or slap him into silence. He himself understood little of Grietar's chatter.

"Just bring him along," Pallo said. "Dheri, let us open the gates."

THEY BROUGHT TORCHES, and the army wended its way through the Ripping Gates like a giant, fiery snake. The tunnel, a hundred yards northeast of the gates, was wide enough for four to ride abreast. It dipped steeply underground. It was smooth inside, an almost-perfect cylinder with flexible walls behind which could be felt a humming pressure. The tunnel dived under the Ripping, twisted a few times, then descended yet again. Pallo looked ahead. He could see bright light, but nothing else. It was as if the hole went straight into the sky; but Pallo wasn't stupid. He was walking *down*, after all, not up.

"Jai Khalar," he muttered. "It's just like Jai Khalar, it's crazy, it's backward."

Pallo led the way, staggering: he felt slower and heavier with each step. The others did not seem so much affected; if they moved slowly, it was out of awe and apprehension, not physical duress. But Pallo was becoming light-headed. He was aware that he had not stepped out onto the snow-clad hillside visible from the other side of the Ripping, but onto a green hillside. Suddenly his perspective shifted, and he realized that he was indeed pointing down, but that somehow he'd been transposed to a great height.

He turned and looked back. He could see the dark tunnel behind him, coming down like a pipe from the clouds. There was nothing supporting it. He was walking down out of the sky itself!

Pallo stepped out onto green grass. He was too exhausted to walk far. He turned to see Dheri coming through the mouth of the tunnel with the vanguard, and made a gesture that said, "Wait for me."

Then his legs went out from under him. With a suddenness that was like an animal's pounce, sleep overcame the king.

When he awakened, he found that he had been laid on a pile of furs. Dheri stood guard nearby, and the rest of the army could be heard behind and around him, ranged along this side of the Ripping; but they had made sure that their king was the first to step forward into this new country. And it was a very different place from the one they had left behind. In the distance Pallo could see the familiar outflung arm of the Everien range that once had housed Jai Khalar. The peaks seemed to be floating, their roots buried in mist. The snow ended abruptly only a few miles away from Pallo. The land between that point and the mountains was iridescent green, scored in places with regular lines as if a giant had taken a huge rake to the earth.

A quarter mile away, nestled in some trees beside a cultivated field, was a traditional Deer Clan dwelling, smoke drifting from its roof.

No wonder Pallo was tired. He had walked two hundred miles in one night.

He let out a whoop of triumph, then burst into happy tears.

YOU FELT LIKE
A RODENT

Hezene's throne room was long and low-ceilinged, its walls subtly bowed so that subjects were drawn forward as they entered, and the room seemed to widen and spread as you moved forward. It was always kept somewhat dark. The tiles were arranged in a rainbow mosaic, with the red cutting a path down the center of the room, leading toward the throne. About twenty feet before the throne, the ceiling took a sudden lurch upward, so that the dais and the circular area immediately around it were surrounded by a circular vertical shaft. Light poured down from this shaft, glinting on the feet of the throne. The chair itself was raised above the level of the ceiling of the rest of the room. Subjects had to stand at the base of this monumental chair and crane their heads upward, into the light, in order to look on Hezene.

You felt like a rodent, Lor thought, bringing himself along with the aid of his walking stick, as you crawled your way through the subterranean darkness seeking the emperor. Not that many people ever entered this room, or saw His Illustriousness the Lord of Time and Master of the Seven Sands at such close range. Lor had had the privilege only once before, when he had been much younger, and much thinner. He had been brought in in a sack that was held suspended from the ground by two palace slaves, lest the byrdman touch the ground on an unsanctified day. Lor was allowed to look up at the emperor in His radiant glory only through slits in the cloth. The emperor had been younger then, too. Lor remembered being attracted to the throne, wanting to climb it—it was thirty feet high and ornately carved—wanting to eat it, wanting to piss his mark on it. Held in containment in his sack, he had trembled with excitement. The emperor had thanked him for the gifts of

Byrd and Chee, and then He had made Lor a freeman of the city. Lor's life had changed that day.

Today, much fatter, rather more cynical and world-weary, and more than a little afraid, Lor suspected his life was about to change once again. This time, he had no inkling why he was being summoned. If some information or favor was needed, Byrd usually came to Lor directly; but Byrd had not been seen in Lor's area for a fortnight at least. Was something wrong with Byrd? If so, why not send for the most skilled physicians? The most gifted Scholars? Why send for fat old Lor? He could not understand it.

But he could understand the psychology of the architects of Hezene's throne room, a psychology calculated to subjugate any human who entered. That understanding did nothing to prevent him from feeling cowed the moment he stepped inside, nor to stop him being awed when he came into that circle of light and looked up at the feet of the emperor, presiding from a height. Lor blinked and tried to steady his eyes. He could see the gold- and gem-encrusted seat. He could see the feathers that adorned it. He could even see the emperor, barefaced, unmasked. But the gilded perch built to hold the emperor's Speaker, Lor's friend, was empty.

Byrd was not there.

Lor shrank back, glanced around in fear. There were no attendants. There were no other birds. It was just he, fat old Lor the once-byrdman, and the emperor of the Pharician Empire.

The emperor made an impatient sound. Lor steadied himself and looked up again. He prostrated himself, energetically and in great fear. As he went down, through the dazzling light that poured through the skylight above the emperor, he glimpsed Hezene's head turning assessingly from side to side, tilting like a woodpecker's seeking termites, watery and thin-necked in the strong illumination.

"Lor," said Hezene in his own naked voice, which was weak and harsh at the same time. Lor shrank from it. Hezene never spoke to his subjects. Lor could not hear the emperor and hope to live, and with every word, he quaked himself into a deeper panic. "Your emperor has a mission of preeminent importance. It is a mission requiring the utmost in loyalty and discretion, and it could be yours. Do you accept your duty to your emperor without question or reserve?"

Lor's face was plastered to the cool mosaic. Without raising it, he made the ritual sign of grateful assent with his left hand. The emperor warned, "This mission may bring your death in the service of the emperor."

Lor swallowed and made other enthusiastic signs. Tears had formed in his eyes, but there was nothing he could do. If Hezene wanted his life, Lor's life was Hezene's. Even for pig fodder. Even as a joke, which he was beginning to suspect this whole interview was: some kind of sick joke for the emperor's amusement.

Hezene said, "Or it may mean worse than death. It may mean Enslavement and the slow ruin of all that you are. Do you understand this?"

Yes, yes, yes, signed Lor. Of course he did not. But no one refused the emperor. If he told you to eat shit, you devoured it and asked for more. If he told you to cut off your wife's breasts, you did that, too. If he told you to gut your own baby . . . well, Lor had no children of his own, but he was willing to bet there were some who had done just that, in the pleasure chambers of the emperor in Hezene's younger years, when every sickness of mind and soul had been explored by Hezene and catered to by his servants—of whom Lor was one, he was uncomfortably aware. This was going to be something bad. Lor could just feel it.

Even so, he was caught off guard by the emperor's next words. "Lor, you must go among the byrdmen again. You must find me a new Speaker."

With that, a gong sounded from somewhere behind Hezene, and a shade fell across the light. For a long time, Lor did not dare move from his prostrate position. He opened one eye and found himself in total darkness. The audience was over.

He turned on his hands and knees, which were aching from bearing his weight against the unyielding stone. Lor experienced a moment of real panic, then, thinking that he might never find his way out of this endless burrow of a room, lightless, featureless, and pregnant with doom. Then he noticed that the red tiles of the mosaic emitted a very faint glow. They were dimmer than fireflies, these lights, but they led him a path across the great floor. He crawled and crawled, demoted from rodent to worm, and when he got to the doors he slithered against them and cried and scratched, until finally a servant on the other side opened one door a crack, and Lor went toppling through. He was undone.

"I feel like a slug!" he gasped, wiping cold sweat from his face and neck. "I must lose some weight. This is terrible!"

LOR KNEW THAT the emperor's injunction was to become effective immediately. He did not have to be told how he must interpret Hezene's command: its meaning was as obvious as it was terrible. He must forsake his life as a freeman of Jundun and take to the chala immediately, and there he must hope and pray for the miracle of another Speaker that might attach itself to him.

Which would never happen. Lor had been grounded for too long, and finding Byrd had been sheer luck.

Taking this mission was suicide; or murder, if you considered that he was going to be acting against his own free will, in the name of the emperor. But this couldn't be helped. Hezene had spoken. What He gave, He could take. Lor muttered these things to himself as he shambled home from the palace, taking the streets like a freeman out of habit, though he should have climbed to the chala immediately to begin his mission. The news simply had not sunk in, no matter how many times he tried to repeat it to himself, to absorb the dull, awful shock of it. He returned home and called for Baqile to draw his bath.

He had been sitting in the bath for twenty minutes when the bell rang, and suddenly he was aware of his guilt. What if the imperial police had followed him? *Ah*, he thought recklessly. *Let them do what they will. I am dead already. I will not be deprived of a few last hours in my own, sweet house.* He could hear Baqile turning away the arrivals, who ignored the servant and came sweeping into Lor's private apartments with all the flair of the aristocracy. Lor's guest was a woman, accompanied by two eunuchs, one of whom was blind, the other deaf-mute. The woman's face was veiled and the shape of her body was hidden by her rich robes, although Lor would have said she was slender enough to be a byrdwoman, if she wished. Better suited for it than he, Lor thought glumly. He snapped his fingers for his robe so that he might climb from the bath. Baqile was wringing his hands and looking distraught; he dropped half the robe into the water while passing it to Lor. He was looking at the newcomer with . . . almost . . . *terror*.

"My lady . . . ?" Lor began, flustered.

"Zene," she provided. "We have not met but I know well who you are. The emperor saw you today."

"Y-yes," he stammered, clutching the now-soaking robe to his chest and remaining seated in the marble tub. Above, jays were squabbling and scratching on the chala. The woman's voice was very subtle, her tones as trained as a singer's, as calculated as a whore's.

She said, "You lied about the skyfalcon."

"Skyfalcon?" Lor was not up to pace on this subject. What skyfalcon? Who—?

"The skyfalcon that killed the bird that was sent to me, from Everien. It carried a message, which it was bringing to me, over there." She pointed in the direction of the palace; there was a court nearby where a number of the wealthier citizens lived in luxurious seclusion at the heart of Jundun. "But my bird was intercepted, and the message was stolen, and the bird got away. And you lied, Lor."

"I can't really remember," Lor dissembled with practiced ease. "It was quite a long time ago that I got the bird the skyfalcon had killed. From . . . Ral, was it?"

"From Liaku," said Zene. "Who is now in Everien, and in a position of great power—ah, you did not know that, did you, Lor? Perhaps she has forgotten her old friends. Or perhaps you are a stupid twit and not half the byrdman the emperor believes you to be."

"The message was addressed to Ysse, as I recall," Lor said.

"Was it? But the bird was mine. You know the law."

"Would you like a drink?" Lor said. "Some fruit, perhaps? If you will wait outside, my servant will attend to you. . . ."

"No." It was a clipped response, succinct and unfriendly.

Lor looked at her. He could not see her eyes. He stopped dodging. He was tired, and scared.

"What do you want, Zene?"

"Tell me what the emperor wanted of you today."

Lor felt his face go soft and malleable with the trauma of that event. He seemed to be choking. Finally, he said, "You know I cannot speak of that. The emperor's will is secret."

"Do not cross me, Lor!" she said shrilly, and a smell came wafting from her, a smell of burning and honey and desert spice and metal, all at once. Lor recoiled, afraid.

"You cannot stay here," he said. "Baqile! Call a carriage for the lady. I must retire now. I must retire."

He gathered the sodden robe about himself and climbed awkwardly from the bath. Baqile didn't seem to know which way to turn, and stood paralyzed with indecision, his eyes on Zene, one hand on his half-open mouth.

"Baqile!" Lor commanded again. "Escort the lady *out*."

Zene began to walk toward him.

"Did the emperor ask you to call Liaku?" she said softly, untwining the cord that held her hooded veil in place. Lor watched the air catch the cloth as she moved, revealing not her face, but a curved triangular shadow where the hood parted. Then it slid down, and he could just glimpse the contours of her features beneath the diaphanous veil. But her face was striped, like a tiger's. The hairs on his spine stood up.

"No," he answered in a whisper. "He did not. Baqile!"

"Did Byrd give you no special message? When he Spoke the emperor's Words, were there no words from Byrd to Lor?" These two sentences were uttered with caressing softness as she moved closer, and the veil stirred and began to slide away from her black, sleek hair. Then, in a savage tone, she added, "Speak, fat man!"

"He wasn't there!" Lor blurted. "Byrd wasn't there. Please go. Baqile!"

Whether Baqile was the victim of some enchantment, or whether he was merely stunned into inaction by the indecorous, even scandalous, behavior of the uninvited woman, Lor could not have said. He only knew that Zene was advancing on him. The veil never left her face, although he could discern the shape of her lips and her large eyes through its translucence. But now she parted her gown, smoothly revealing the décolletage between two round, ungirded breasts. Her skin was the color of wet river sand. It was decorated in a most disconcerting and unladylike fashion. And there was a dark space, too. . . . He fixed his eyes on it, curiously.

"We will soon see if you are to be of use to the Circle," she said.

Lor spluttered and fussed. "Ah, you should not speak that word openly. . . . I will pretend I did not hear it. . . . You must know that many among your, er, *group*, many are my good friends. . . . I beg you, Zene, do not be hasty!"

He had seen the hole in her breastbone. He did not know what it was, what it meant; but he was overwrought. "Listen, Zene!" he cried, warding her off with his hands and backing away. "I will tell you what the emperor said, for it is to be my doom anyway, I am sure. He has banished me to Byrdland again. I . . . I . . . I-I," and here he broke into hot tears. "I don't know what I've done wrong. I'm too old, I'm too fat, and now I've lost everything. Zene, listen to me. Let's make a deal. Take my house, my possessions, my servant!" Baqile's jaw dropped. "Just get me out of Jundun! I can't return to Byrdland. I'll be dead inside a week."

"Byrdland? Why?" she snapped, stopping in her tracks. Her eyes became vacant, as though she were looking at something over Lor's shoulder; but there was nothing there beyond a fruit tree.

He shook his head, thinking the reason for Hezene's strange order to be unimportant: now he was hell-bent on finding a way out of this mess. "Zene, if you ask any of your associates, they will tell you what a good friend I have been to your . . . cause. I am discreet. I know everyone. If you had been a man, you and I would have done business many times by now. But it doesn't matter that you are not a man. I will not scorn you—"

"Scorn me?" she shrieked. "You don't know who I am, little slug, so I shall grant you forgiveness one time. Speak to me in this way again, and you won't live long enough to draw another breath."

"Sorry, sorry, sorry!" Again he was backing away, crossing his hands in front of him in a canceling motion, as though rubbing out his own words. "Let's talk; let's do a deal; let's be friends! But I don't have much time. If the Imperial Air Police come and find me with my feet on the ground, I will be killed! Let me only send some messages, and you can talk to the others, who will vouch for me, yes?"

"Never mind the others," she said coldly. "I don't have time for this, either. Let's find out whether you are really useful to me. If you are, you will soon have no need to fear the imperial police, for you will be under my protection. And if you are not going to be useful, well . . ." She smiled. "You will see some wonderful things while you are dying."

"I'll be useful!" he piped. "I guarantee my usefulness! Highly useful, I shall—"

"Shut up."

Lor shut up. Zene unrolled a very delicate scroll with diagrams inked on tissue-thin paper. She showed it to Lor.

"The byrdgirl," Zene said. "The brat offends me. Word has it she possesses Artifacts—she and that drooling blind man. Now tell me what she is doing with these things."

Lor's eyes focused on the diagrams. There were symbols, pictures, lines, and schemata, none of which meant anything to him.

"I have had no message from Liaku," Lor said. "She does not belong to me, nor I to her. I know nothing about it, I swear to you."

"Puh!" she spat, and put the papers away. "For *years* we have been researching the Bridges and the Making Tools and other Artifacts of legend, and now we find that this . . . this . . . this dung-fluff actually *has* them! Are you aware how angry that makes us?"

"Er, I can make inquiries, you know. Can I see that scroll again?"

"No!" Zene shoved the document into the folds of her garments. Lor licked his lips furtively. His fingers danced. But Zene's attention was now turned inward.

She had placed a finger on the hole in her breast, and a golden worm began to emerge. It grew longer and longer, writhing like a living piece of string. Her eyes went back in their sockets and fluttered. She extended the worm toward him. He found he was frozen in place.

With a suddenness he could neither see nor understand, the worm shot into his right eye. Colors exploded. Sounds filled his teeth and head. He became erect and his body hair stood on end.

"You see," Zene said, "my worms are the stuff of Time. They know all times, past and future. They will know if you can help me. And if you can, that will be great good fortune for you, Lor. For in that case, they will take over your mind. They will become your commanders. You will no longer need to worry about anything but what they want you to do."

He couldn't answer her. He couldn't form words in his mind. He was flooded with pictures. Amazing pictures.

"Or," she suggested, moving closer so that her forehead almost touched his—sweat broke out across Lor's face. "You will die. But even there, I envy you. For you, Lor, while dying, will see all that the worms can see. And the worms remember times that haven't happened yet. They know a thousand truths. You will know them, too. And then you will die."

He wanted to be useful. He wanted to be useful. He wanted to be useful.

"Liaku, the byrdgirl!" Zene pressed. "Where is she? What is she up to? What powers has she got?"

He wanted to be useful. He wanted to be useful.

But from every single future that the worms built, Lor was absent.

He did not exist.

He looked at the moving pictures of the futures that might exist, could exist, would exist . . . and into the conspicuous absence of himself, he fell forever.

The worms did not need much time to make a decision. Zene stepped away from Lor's body as he collapsed. The worm shot back to her, cold and weary; it nuzzled for succor deep within her body, where her lungs made its nest, her heart its clock. Zene spat on Lor's body.

"A waste of time," she said softly. "Baqile! Yes, you, boy. Remove this piece of meat at once. And then attend to me in the courtyard. I will have new duties for you."

LOYALTY

Tol sat on his master's dead hip. The soft belly of Lor had ceased to rise and fall. Wind stirred the small hairs on Lor's forearms and chest. His smell had changed.

Distressed, the bird hopped from one protuberance to another, hoping that somehow Lor would return. Tol had been his helper for many years, and the two had had a strong bond. Tol would be lost without his friend.

In the house of Lor, activity hummed and buzzed. Zene was gone; she had wasted no time in sweeping out into the street and going her own way. But her people were now arriving to take over Lor's possessions and affairs. Baqile was scurrying about in a state of terrific agitation.

Mournfully, Tol passed his beak through Lor's clothes. Lor's hand was clasped to his chest, tucked inside his robes, as though he had been clutching his heart when he died.

But it was not quite so.

In Lor's hand was the very fine scroll Zene had showed him. Tol took it in his beak and dragged it from the corpse, secreting himself and the scroll in the shadow of a flowerpot. Tol was deeply pleased with his master, and now he desired to carry out Lor's last wishes to honor Lor's memory. For, even in the extremity of Lor's last moments, even in his fear—and even after all these years of the soft life—Lor had had the presence of mind to engage in a sly piece of pickpocketing.

THE CARNIVOROUS WISHING WELL

The initial products of the Blackness were so irrelevant and useless that Liaku almost despaired of her theory that Wakhe could talk to it. In the first two days following the incident in the cave, Liaku pitched in a chicken carcass, the pottery statue of an elephant, two blunt daggers, a cart wheel, and an incredibly ugly vase shaped like a fish. All the while, Wakhe drummed, and the hair-raising singing issued from the Blackness as though in answer. In turn, the Blackness pitched forth, respectively: a jar of foul-smelling ointment, a metal rod with a glass bulb at one end and some Everien writing on it; a pair of boots three sizes too large for Liaku but perfect for Wakhe; a strange contraption made of what looked like flexible glass carved in loops and holding a black liquid with silver flecks in suspension within its twists; and a large playing card.

If it had not been for the boots, Liaku would have ended the experiment then and there; but when she witnessed the glee with which Wakhe pulled the boots on, she knew that he did have some control over the trade with the Blackness. Liaku considered the relative value of what she had been throwing *in* to the Blackness, and decided that the only way to get things of real value *out* would be to improve the quality of her offerings.

So, on the fourth day she offered a bar of gold, a large pair of fur mittens, and a silk tapestry that had once hung beside the sail-snake fountain in Jai Khalar. To her great disappointment, in return she received a wooden crate filled with steel bars pointed on one end, reeking of oil and phosphor; a lightweight folded frame that sang like a violin and occasionally released harmless bursts of light but that had no demonstrable purpose; and a sealed glass flask of clear liquid that remained warm to the touch even after she submerged it in the icy river.

"None of these things help us!" she wailed at Wakhe as she cooked them a thin soup. She had managed to preserve a store of root vegetables and a found sack of Pharician oats that had been displaced from the stables to a high ledge, but other foodstuffs were in short supply. Any meat or fish she found or caught or shot with her sling had to be cooked and eaten on the spot, or the dogs would get it. And as no people other than Xiriel, Kassien, or Wakhe had approached Jai Khalar, she could not trade with anyone. Nor did she dare leave Wakhe and the Blackness alone long enough to seek out other people. Besides, what would she say if she found them? Her speech was foreign. The Clans hated the Pharicians, and they could not be expected to understand how she had been at least as oppressed as they by the Pharicians.

So she made soup with a few potatoes and a leek, and complained to Wakhe.

"We not in Jundun Bazaar!" she vented. "What I do with junk like this? At least gold bar I could maybe trade one day. Now I give away good things and get stupid garbage."

Wakhe was sitting cross-legged across the fire, rocking back and forth like a prophet and making spluttering trills with his tongue and cheeks. The constant rhythmizing turned Liaku purple.

"You get boots!" she raged on, shoving a wooden spoon into the metal horse bucket she was using as a pot and stirring the contents angrily. "What happen when we run out food? What happen when somebody attack us? You smell that smoke?" She pointed downriver with the spoon. "That fire come from fight between Clan and monster. What if monster come here?"

She went on like this at elaborate but repetitive length, not knowing whether Wakhe understood her or not. She didn't believe he was deaf. She had seen him startle at a sudden noise and she was certain he could hear the "singing" of the Blackness. But he gave her no gesture of reassurance, no complicity that she could ever see. She burned her mouth when tasting the soup.

"OK," she said at last. "You win. No more trades. Liaku keep what she find. Wakhe make own soup. I go to bed."

And she mounted the rocks to her nest nimbly, pretending—wishing—she were in Byrdland.

*

SHE DIDN'T DESCEND for three days, during which time she observed Wakhe and the Blackness through her spyglass. She also watched the valley.

The Clans were stubbornly battling with monsters that seeped from the seams of the timeserpent trail. Liaku watched through her spyglass. At first she thought that the monsters had devoured all the population of the central valley. She knew that Everien was a wild and thinly developed place, and there didn't seem to be many people living here to begin with by comparison to the plateau of Jundun. After the monsters had had their go at the people, it was Liaku's calculation that humans in Everien ought to be very nearly extinct. Yet more kept appearing. They fled from the monsters and hid; or they fought; or they wandered aimlessly and stupidly until the Blackness took them. On some of these occasions, the Blackness would slide right out away from the cliffs for a quick gorge on humans; but at other times, the people actually approached. Liaku would have liked to trade with them, but she never got the chance. She did notice that most of these people were not dressed like Clansmen. They must have come from far away. Their clothes looked painted on. Many of them were obese. Others were preternaturally thin. Some wore muscles like clothes: dumb muscles that they didn't know how to use, so that they might as well have been sculptures.

They didn't carry swords or bows.

They didn't seem to carry weapons at all.

They flashed lights at one another and called in a language she didn't know.

She wondered if they were Sekk; but they seemed too frightened and disorderly to be Sekk, from all that she had heard. And word about Everien was that the Sekk were ruined at last.

Yet these people kept coming, and being eaten, and coming some more.

Where were they coming from?

Liaku's curiosity ate at her day after day, until she was so tempted to descend to the valley and try to get to one of them before the Blackness could. If she had seen a person carrying something worth trading for, or stealing, or extorting from, she surely would have done just that. But before anything like that could happen, and while she was still snubbing Wakhe and hoping he would give her some kind of sign that he wanted to cooperate with her, Liaku's spyglass picked up a new threat. A train of horses was approaching from the south. She watched them for an hour but could see no banner. Their formation was too regular to be Clan.

Could Hezene have sent help already?

Impossible.

Then who were they?

She decided it was time to end the standoff with Wakhe, and hastened to find him. He was languishing near to the Blackness, drumming and listening. There had been no more physical exchanges. Wakhe had neither eaten nor moved, except to crawl to and fro as he shadowed the amoebic migrations of the Blackness.

"Dumb chick," she scolded Wakhe. "You start eating! We keep trying, yes? Now, quick. Ask for big cannon to defend us. Men are coming."

She scurried from place to place, collecting the strange items that the Blackness had offered her. She set up the singing-light scaffolding, thinking that it reminded her a little of Byrdland without the chala. The frame was designed to snap together without tools or bindings, and when she had unfolded all of it and placed it on the ground, it stood to form an equilateral triangle of about fifty feet in area. When it was standing there, glowing and humming, it looked very impressive. She placed the other objects around it: the box of pointed bars, the lit metal ball, the tangle of glass with its black fluid inside.

"Come on, Wakhe!" she cried, grabbing a sack and racing off to find things to throw into the Blackness. "We make many stuff today. Scare damn soldiers. Come *on!*"

Their yield for that day included, not a cannon, but a firethrower of the sort Duor had described to her as being made for Tash in the Fire Houses. There were also several containers of fluids that Liaku hoped fervently were poisons, for when she sniffed them, they smelled vile. She pocketed and tied these vials around herself, for use in case of emergency. She had not forgotten how nicely Ixo's poison had knocked out that horrible man, Se.

The Blackness had been wandering around aimlessly, but by the time Liaku ascended to her best vantage point to watch the riders draw near, it had slithered so close to Wakhe, she began to fear it might take him, after all. The Blackness changed its shape to form a broad, long line, which it proceeded to curl around the sitting Scholar until he was surrounded on all sides by what looked like a moat made of pitch. It widened and sprawled, and Liaku put her hand to her mouth, thinking that the Blackness was going to swallow Wakhe right up.

Then she realized it was protecting him.

"Hmm," she said, eyeing her collection of worthless booty. How was she going to convince the Pharicians that she was in command of the Blackness, and not the other way around?

Well, Wakhe could not move, and if the Blackness wanted to protect him, then it could not run away from her, either—could it?

Liaku was shaking all over as she built her plan. She was a flight creature, and the idea of walking straight up to something as powerful as the Blackness and trying to trap it went against all her instincts. Nevertheless, she was not prepared to be recruited as a byrdgirl again, or worse. Not after all she had been through.

There had been a rendezvous between the newcomers and Illyra and his men, about a mile away down the gate stream. The two groups re-formed to become one, and now the Pharicians were riding up the river, slowly, stopping to examine the refuse and ruin that they found along the way. Liaku hurriedly fetched the light-scaffold, disassembling it, dragging it across the uneven ground, and placing the loose parts in a triangle around the Blackness.

Wakhe threw his head back and drummed wildly. The Blackness flashed.

"Ah, crowshit bombs, I no wish to die!" Liaku cried, reassembling the framework with frantic fingers. The frame itself began to sing like Chee, only with deeper resonances shooting along the support beams. The Blackness fell into harmony with it: not a pleasant harmony, Liaku thought, shivering. She ran and fetched her other plunder and arranged it again. By this time, the framework was flashing and shrieking, and the ground nearby hummed and rumbled. Wakhe was bent over his drum, tirelessly communicating with the thing that surrounded him. The riders, seeing this commotion near the head of the river where Jai Khalar had once been, turned their steeds toward Wakhe and Liaku and began to advance. The sun was going down.

Liaku studied her handiwork. The Triangle sat on the blackness like a transparent pyramid, and inside it all sat Wakhe, oblivious to the effect. Liaku rubbed her hands together. Anybody who wasn't scared and impressed must be an idiot, she thought.

She dragged the box of metal cylinders so that it rested at her feet. She hefted one of them in her hand. She curled her lip and snarled at Illyra as he rode up.

"Ah," said Illyra. "I have heard about you. The Witch of the Pit, they call you. What are all these contraptions? And who is that weird old man over there?" He pointed to where Wakhe sat, surrounded by Blackness.

"I capture timeserpent!" she cried, pointing to the triangular scaffold that was throwing off sparks and making an uneasy music with the Blackness itself. "That Wakhe, who call timeserpent. He guard it now. It eat Jai Khalar, go down hole."

Illyra dismounted and began to walk toward her.

"It's the byrdgirl," he said in a humored tone. Turning, he called over his shoulder to someone farther back in the columns of riders. "Duor, you were a friend to her. Go and find out what in the name of the emperor she's talking about."

At the sound of Duor's name, Liaku's heart jumped. So Duor was alive! But would he be on her side, or theirs? She watched him guide his horse out of the formation and come forward, dismounting by Illyra's side and giving his horse to the leader.

"Give me a few minutes with her," she heard him say softly. "She is an unusual creature, but not evil. She may know much about what has happened here."

When Duor came up to her, smiling awkwardly, she noticed that he was taller by at least two inches. He was also broader, and he was working on a weak but perceptible beard. How had he grown so fast?

"You come from Fire Houses?" she asked suspiciously. He nodded. "How long your journey last?"

"Half a year, I'll wager," he said.

"Nonsense!" Liaku scoffed. "No half a year even since we leave Jundun."

"Time is different now," said Duor. "We had to come all the way around past the gates to the sea plateau, and we got bogged down in a time distortion that only let us travel half a mile a day. I thought we'd never get here. But, Liaku"—and he seized her forearm in a tight grip—"how did Wakhe get here? Everyone said he disappeared when the timeserpent came."

Duor was staring at the cripple with a fixed expression.

"Blackness spits him out." She mimed the act of vomiting.

Duor was shaking. "It took us six months," he said incredulously. "And you say Wakhe just *appeared*?"

Liaku nodded.

"Why didn't you tell someone? Illyra's going to have kittens!"

"Illyra never come here," Liaku said. "And why I tell? Who want go to Fire Houses, anyway?"

"Oh, Liaku," Duor said, "sometimes you can be a simpleton. Wait here. I will tell Illyra as gently as I can."

THINGS DID NOT turn out as Liaku would have planned. Illyra was not afraid of her scaffolding or the weird things she had collected, because he could see no evidence of their destructive power and he lacked the imagination to foresee it. However, within a very short time two things became obvious. One, that Wakhe could communicate with the Blackness; and two, that the Blackness was no longer free to move about like a roving mouth, devouring everything in its path.

There was a third result of the creation of Liaku's Triangle, but either nobody else but Liaku noticed it, or nobody thought it remarkable.

The strangely dressed people who had been getting gobbled up right and left were nowhere to be seen.

Neither were a fair percentage of the monsters.

"We are getting this area under control," Illyra would tell his men, as if the accomplishment were all his own doing.

To Liaku's relief, it was not long before Illyra took his men and rode farther up the valley, seeking rumored grain stores in the series of mill towns that lined the river. Duor and four men were left behind to keep an eye on Liaku and to try to find out what had become of the Citadel. Illyra was particularly troubled by the loss of Ukili, and he seemed to feel that unless he could produce her upon Tash's return, Tash would kill him. Liaku rather agreed with this prediction.

Liaku watched the Pharicians search the cliffs, scrambling and falling and slithering on the unforgiving rocks. She tried to keep her activities with the Blackness quiet, which was not always so easy to do given that Wakhe liked to drum back and forth with the pit. Fortunately, none of the men seemed to understand the significance of what Wakhe was doing. They all remembered him as a crippled fool, best left for dead. Duor knew what Wakhe had done, but he didn't say anything to the other men. He told Liaku that all would be reckoned for when Tash returned. He didn't speak of his father, but Liaku knew the boy was petrified that something had happened to Shiror. She tried to cheer him up by introducing him to various birds. She encouraged him to keep watch for Quiz.

"He returning soon, I sure," she said over and over.

But Quiz did not come. The only surprise visitor she had was a small, exhausted gray bird from Pharice. Liaku almost didn't recognize the visitor, he was so dull-feathered and weary.

"Tol?" she shrieked, lifting her hand to welcome the bird. He was carrying something. "Tol, where you fly from? Is Lor here? Come, Tol, I give you grain."

Tol was very sad, Liaku thought, and tried to comfort him and cheer him up. By the time she had a chance to look at the thin scroll he'd carried so many miles, Duor had joined her.

"I no believe Lor travel far," Liaku said. "But I no believe he sent Tol from Jundun to Everien. Journey too far for little Tol!"

The scroll was not a letter from Lor. It gave no indication of where he was or what he wanted to say to her. It was simply a single sheet of very thin, translucent paper, with fine ink drawings on it and a lot of Everien writing. There were notations in Pharician, too, but Liaku couldn't read them.

Duor took it away from her and puzzled over it. "They're machines," he said. "War machines, according to this, and . . . and . . . 'transport devices' . . . hmm. Tash was always bragging about the weapons he could make in the Fire Houses, but these don't look like those."

Liaku shrugged. She didn't care about the paper, she cared about Tol. In truth she had no wish to see Lor again, unless it were to show off to him all that she had become. But she felt sorry for Tol, who seemed genuinely miserable. She had a bad feeling about Lor's circumstances if he had been forced to send Tol all this distance with no proper message.

"I feed you many lovely things," she said to Tol. "And you sleep Liaku bed, yes?"

Tol began to cheer up slightly. *All birds like me*, Liaku thought smugly.

TWO NIGHTS PASSED. Duor was unnaturally obsessed with the diagrams. Liaku was busy tending to Tol and keeping Wakhe from alerting the four Pharicians to the fact that he could summon goats, giant lizard bones, and diamonds from the Blackness. She began to formulate plans for moving to a different part of the valley. . . . If only she could figure out how to get the Blackness to follow them. She was pretty sure it would follow Wakhe, but she also had the suspicion that it was attached in some way to the place where Jai Khalar had been.

In the middle of the third night since Tol's arrival, Duor woke her in the small hours.

"Look!" he said, pointing to the glass-light apparatus that had come from the Blackness, whose purpose she had never remotely guessed. Duor had arranged it to resemble a portion of one of the diagrams on the paper. It was no longer a strange monstrosity of design. Now it seemed almost . . . alive. It was humming and sparking like a firework about to go off. Liaku trembled and backed away.

"What you do? What you do, silly boy? Stop at once!"

He grabbed her shoulders.

"Liaku, listen to me. Those things you got from the Blackness? They're ancient Everien Artifacts. They are worth more than every city in the Annexed Countries and every pearl in the ocean and the platinum-bound body of the emperor's dead wife all added together. Liaku. Shh, do not struggle!" For she had begun to writhe in his grip. "Liaku. Lor has made you a very great gift. This paper tells you what these things are and how to use them."

THE COLOR OF ICE

𝔍nstinct like a paintbrush had colored Ice black and white. He was a creature of extreme contradiction, a flight animal who killed to live. He was three hundred humans who were no longer human, more than the sum of their parts, all bound together by the wild but true instincts of a creature who skated on time—a thing who was more than one thing. Ice's shadow, Midnight Blue, had borne Jaya through her dark journey. Ice would kill his shadow if he could, just as it would kill him: it was this incessant rivalrous battle of inherent opposites that gave the stallion his restless power.

Ice knew without thinking; sensed without knowing; and reacted faster than time itself. In an involuted, backward universe, he had to.

Tarquin he had taken up effortlessly—it had been time, high time, for that, for Ice was no servant of man but rather it was the other way round—and now it was Tarquin's need that drove him, even though Tarquin did not know where they were going or why. Ice was a being of the present: life was *now* and *here*. He had no concept of why he was taking Tarquin to the particularly dead and desiccated branch of the endless Liminal that was his destination, for "why" did not enter into the equation. Ice did what needed to be done. Whatever was necessary, as the blind old doctor with diamonds for eyes would have put it, to make things smell right.

Ice had to trust his own genetic continuity to provide a path through time and space. His Road was true. By contrast, he experienced the Liminal as the broken crystal it was. Once it had been a thing that grew according to its own fractal geometry, self-referential, beautiful, and slightly maddening to be inside. Now shattered and scattered, it lay like broken glass on a rough sea.

Between the jagged pieces of glass oozed particularly virulent forms of chaos: monsters, possibility-whorls, and timeserpent trails that sucked in code and never released it. The pieces of glass themselves Ice experienced like stepping-stones on the sea, only less simple. For these stepping-stones were in the habit of rearranging themselves indiscriminately and without warning, and the white-black horse had learned to take these tiles at speed, never touching down long enough to get stuck in one realm or another.

Yet, recently, someone or something had begun to impose a structure on the Liminal. A few sections of the broken crystal were now bound together with a white, sinewy substance. From a distance, this stuff smelled of skyfalcon. But up close, it smelled of man. If flexed with time, but it was stable, too. It joined some of the pieces of Everien's broken Liminal like the Everien bridges joined the Floating Lands. It brought peace to warring times. Ice was fascinated by it, and he found he had to walk on it. This was a new path, and it was his path now that Tarquin was a part of him.

Walking on this particular code was like walking on a great, curving bone. Ice liked it. The surface felt complex and real. It made running effortless. It let him slip past so many years and possibilities and places in a single stride. He could look down on the muck of chance that pooled like the blood of an injured Liminal—blood composed of too many mistakes, too many failures of meaning all mixed together—without being tainted by it.

And soon, Ice found that he was not alone on this bridge between times. From the other end of the bone a group of men on horses approached. The horses were timid Slaves that Ice didn't condescend to favor with a second glance. The men were numerous and well armed. At their vanguard was a red-haired Seahawk; behind him followed banners and tall horses and a blond man who styled himself king.

Ice stopped and stood there, uncertain.

In the face of the Seahawk, he had seen a terrible portent.

The man's eyes shone silver. Within his brain there were silver worms. Ice wasn't sure what this could mean, but he knew he didn't like it.

Ice began to back up, trembling. Instinct screamed at him to run; but he was not an ordinary horse, not a coward. He pawed the bone, snorting aggressively and quaking with fear at the same time.

272

Tarquin was carrying something that tugged at the worms with an invisible force. The red-haired man could sense this somehow, for he clapped his heels to the ribs of his mount and galloped toward Ice.

The horse was an unremarkable palomino, overweight and full of aimless hostility. It did not like the Seahawk, Ice noticed peripherally, and it bore his weight grudgingly.

Ice felt inside for the thing of Tarquin's that was attracting the Seahawk and his strange eyes, and identified it as the empty ampule he had picked up in Or.

The red-haired man's eyes looked at Ice in an ugly and acquisitive way. He pointed at Ice and Ice shivered all over. He could not run; his muscles had gone stiff and for a moment he was paralyzed. The red-haired man came on. Now he was smiling.

Ice leaned into the humans who lived inside him, desperate for help; but no one answered him. No one understood what was happening, least of all Tarquin himself, who should have been nearest the surface. Something was wrong. Something was desperately wrong, but the horse could not reason it through or come up with a plan. Under the man's silver gaze, he couldn't even move. The red-haired man came so close that Ice could smell molasses and chaff on his horse's breath, and a jasmine-scented Pharician soap on the man himself. Ice sweated and trembled. The man reached out to touch Ice and at last, with all the effort he could muster, the gray horse lashed out and drove the man back with a warning snap of his powerful jaws. The other horse shied and skittered away, and Ice could feel some of his paralysis lifting as soon as the threat of the touch was gone. But instantly the Seahawk leaped from his mount and came toward Ice on foot, and again, Ice was powerless to move.

Inside him, Tarquin was beating to get out; but Ice had never been so frightened as this. He did not understand what was happening. He had never encountered such a creature as this man. The Seahawk extended his left hand palm up in a peaceful gesture with one finger pointing as though to touch Ice gently; his right hand went to the hilt of his sword. Again, Ice managed to snap at the hand; but this time, the Seahawk was drawing his blade. There was nothing peaceful about the sword that came whistling up, flashing past Ice's terrified right eye in a blur of pain and blood. Suddenly, the timewalking horse found himself with no choice other than to leap off the bridge into the Liminal, disgorging Tarquin in the process.

Ice would do anything to escape those terrible silver eyes.

THE GRAVEYARD
OF EVERIEN

There was a weird buzzing around Tarquin's head, especially the right side. It stopped and started. It moved closer and farther away, growing more complex as more tones were added. Vaguely he realized he was lying on his left side. Something was tickling his right ear and the side of his head. He brushed feebly at his ear and the noise stopped. He sighed and began to sink back to much-needed sleep. The buzzing resumed, now louder, now softer. Something light bounced off his face—once, twice—then it stuck there. More buzzing from several different points around his head. Soon he was too irritated to find sleep again. He reached up to stop the tickling and his fingers came away sticky. The buzzing grew louder.

Annoyed, Tarquin started to sit up, but for some reason he couldn't lift his head. He experienced a moment of panic then, as he reached up and groped around his own skull a little frantically. He soon discovered that he couldn't move his head because it was stuck to his cloak, and his cloak was trapped beneath his own shoulders. As he came to full consciousness, he realized that his head was sticking to his cloak because it was bleeding. Moreover, flies had gathered on the wound. It was their noise that had woken him. Some were whizzing around his head, but many more were trapped in the sticky blood and tangled hair, and they buzzed as they struggled to free themselves.

He moaned. He remembered the sword cutting Ice, but he had thought himself only an observer in that incident, not a partici-pant. Even now, he had a strange, disassociated feeling when he remembered it.

Small wonder, he thought. He vividly remembered how Ice had devoured him; but the memories of being Ice were weirdly mixed-up and indirect, as though he had not really been there, other than perhaps in the way a child attends a party while he is still in his mother's womb.

His head hurt, but the blade had only grazed his scalp. His hair was plastered in a painful tangle that contained several trapped flies. He plucked one of them out and saw that its dead body sticking to his hand was not black as a fly's should be, but instead a jewel-bright red. At about the same time, he noticed a foul smell in the air, like rotten eggs. The desert sun was beginning to come up.

As the light grew clearer, he realized he had been mistaken about still being in the desert of Or. There were no Animal Guardians around him. The sand was dull gray and the sky roiled with muddy clouds. Puce shadows began to lift from the landscape like cobwebbed skirts, revealing wind-sculpted rock, dead grass, and sand. In the distance were bare mountains, so remote as to appear painted on the sky. Closer to hand, irregular rock formations towered over him. One of them was shaped like the corpse of a gigantic creature; and then, moving toward it, he realized that it was not *like* a giant body, it *was* a giant body. This thing had been a lizard the size of a two-masted ship, now petrified with everything intact but its empty eye sockets staring black and vacant. The corpse blended with the gray sand dune that had gathered around it, and it was large enough to be mistaken for a mountainous ridge of land. He walked up its foreleg, curious and amazed. He came to a place where the tough hide had been ripped open. He stopped. There was nothing wet or lifelike remaining within; but there were several glinting lines of metal wire, like silver nerves deep within this strange creature.

He backed away quickly.

"How could a creature grow wires inside it?" he asked. The wind wheezed in answer, spattering him with dry sand and bringing a foul smell. This place gave him an evil feeling. Everywhere he looked he saw colors that depressed the spirits. There were no birds in the sky. In the sand, he saw translucent insects like clumps of hardened mucus with legs and antennae. They moved sluggishly, but he avoided them. He didn't like to think what they were feeding on.

He tore a strip from the lining of his uncle's cloak and tied it around his head to keep the flies off the cut. They followed him anyway, crowding around his head as he looked for an exit to this place. There was no water, and although the sky grew brighter, the clouds didn't lift. His eyes began to sting with the effects of whatever was in the air that smelled so bad. He began to feel he was having a nightmare, for again and again the land formations he had taken for stone turned out to be the hulks of ruined monsters: furred humps, half-buried in sand; the pinioned wings of fliers that looked like a cross between a sailsnake and a spider, listing like beached ships; skulls without flesh, skins without bones. After a while he came to a flat area littered with body parts, dusty and desiccated but not rotted. There were more red flies here, flitting from one torn limb or claw to another. Everything was too large. Scattered in the sand amongst the cast-off dead parts were glittering prisms of varying sizes, some as large as Tarquin's hand, others so small as to fit in the nib of a pen. He picked up one of the larger ones and when the light shone through it, finely etched symbols were cast upon the dead sand. The wind hummed tunefully among the racks of ribs and in the spaces of spines.

This made him nervous. He had a sudden vision of the hulking creatures coming to life and lumbering across the sand to the call of the prisms. He dropped the glass as if it were on fire. Then he saw the ghost.

She was sitting under a dark brown cowl, her feet drawn up beneath her haunches, her arms wrapped around her knees, so that she might have been a bird on a perch. She was very thin and her clothes were in poor shape, though they had been well made to begin with. A gray braid came from the opening of the cowl and trailed down her front. He assumed she was a ghost because he could see through her. When she saw him, she blinked repeatedly, then spat on her fingers and rubbed her eyes.

"Tarquin," she said. "What has become of your horse?"

"I don't know," he answered carefully. "Have you seen him?"

She didn't answer his question. "I sit here in the graveyard of Everien, waiting for my daughter to come. Everything here is dead or banished or worse. It is a fit place for me and my injured mind. Only I can see the sorrow and ruin of the world. Everyone else is distracted."

"Not everyone," Tarquin responded grimly. "I am here, and little surprised about it. Is *this* death, then?"

"I wish the mouse would come," said the ghostly woman. "But I do not think it will. It was the mice that defeated them,

277

you know. The mice who multiplied. The mice, you see, are weak but multiple. And when the mouse patterns were stored, he used them, he did. The sorcerer Eteltar used them to test his timeserpent River"—and Tarquin's ears pricked up, for like Kere, Mhani had said "river" like "diver"—"and it worked! The mice were everywhere! Everywhere, I tell you, and everywhen. He was trying to make the timeserpent reproduce, and he thought the mice patterns would help because, after all, mice reproduce better than anything. But he never got to use it on the timeserpent. Only the mice benefited. Ah, they will chew holes in the very nature of the world and make a nest out of it, better than a sock, better than bird furze, I tell you. I wish my daughter would come."

"Who is your daughter?" Tarquin asked, thinking with sudden hope of Jaya; but he did not expect her to say,

"Istar. Alas, Istar."

Tarquin stared. The woman was a translucent image, her edges blurring and slipping like a thing made of smoke; but even so, he ought to have recognized her. He studied the cavernous eyes, the features thinned and weighted with the experience of more years than Mhani could have possessed: she was younger than Tarquin. No, he would not have recognized her.

"Mhani, is it you? What has become of you? Of Jai Khalar?"

The woman's head quested back and forth, and he noticed that the edges of her cowl were torn and stained. She answered in a high, disassociated voice.

"She will not know how to find me here; Istar is hopeless with the Knowledge, I'm afraid. And the rest of me is hidden away in somebody's hut below A-vel-Jasse, waiting for the Wolves to stop feeding me out of pity, or a round of plague to come and finish me off. It doesn't matter. No one can walk more than a few miles in Everien, these days, anyway. Istar would never find me, even if she was looking."

"This 'river' of Eteltar's, what did it do?"

"It divided things, just like it divided Eteltar. Just like you're divided right now—and a lucky thing, too, for Ice was born smarter than you could ever be. I'm only a spying old Seer without the Water of Glass to guide me, mad in the real world and nobody to talk to in this one, until you. And I don't even think I've got that. Something tells me you won't be staying. The seventh symbol is pulling you."

"Mhani," Tarquin said with emotion, "you helped me before. Is there nothing you can say to me now?"

"I've said it. Find the mouse patterns, and you will find Eteltar's test. Find his test, and you will find his formula. He has written it down somewhere, I am sure."

Tarquin groaned. "On a cliff in Or, so high that no one could read it . . . oh, Mhani, I am always lost."

Mhani smiled faintly. "It is not as bad as it looks," she offered philosophically. "Besides, you have very little to lose, now."

"But how do I get out of here?"

"You should know," she said tartly. "*You* broke the crystal and scrambled all the worlds. Now you will just have to find some way back to the Rose. You should hurry: Grietar will soon be in Jai Khalar, and the mice will not like it."

She faded like a snowflake melting, and then the hoofbeats came.

ICE BROUGHT STARLIGHT and a rush of cold wind, and the smell and feel of life. He charged straight at Tarquin, who had to relive the sensation of being devoured as Ice assimilated him. Then they were together; the graveyard was a shuddering blur as Ice accelerated. He was unwilling to let his hooves touch the ground for one step more than was absolutely necessary, for in an instant there was whiteness all round, and the sound of the sea.

Ice/Tarquin was near the edges of himself, but he did not slow down.

"The places you want to go are almost unreachable. We cannot help you there."

Tarquin recalled Kere's words clearly. He never would have believed anywhere was unreachable by the magical Ice—until now. Now he could feel how close they were to the fraying edges of things.

Faster and faster went Ice on the White Road; visions formed and disintegrated without defining themselves as past or future, as true or only fancied. The red-haired Seahawk was standing in the Fire House, touching Jaya's face as she stood looking up at him in fear; the timeserpents were dying, hacked apart by ancient Pharicians; Jaya was handling pieces of red glass, holding them against each other like puzzle pieces; the tide was peeling back from

279

the roots of Jai Pendu; Night was peering out from the trees of Jaya's forest; Night was riding Midnight Blue. Ice shied away in fear. *The trees leave, the trees leave,* Jaya was sighing. Tarquin's urgent need to find Jaya was powerful within him; but his nemesis waited in the forest, too. Ice felt Midnight Blue like iron feels a magnet. He began to pull away, and just as Ice was about to choose another path, a rush of wind beat about his head accompanied by a nerve-shredding feral scream. A skyfalcon was plummeting from above. It launched itself at Ice's head and Ice braked, going into a spin so violent that his insides flew out under the centrifugal force. In his extreme fear, he employed his final defense mechanism, the one that had saved him a thousand times before. He shed his topmost human: Tarquin.

Even as Ice changed direction, Tarquin was torn from the body of the horse. But he didn't land in Night's forest. Instead, he came down in fire. Inhaling fumes that seemed to bring the flames straight into his lungs, he hit the ground hard with a series of snapping noises as he crushed flakes of shale beneath him. There was so much spin on his body from Ice's successive changes in direction that he kept rolling, through the fire and over the burning stones, and then into black mud and, at last, wet snow. He thrust his face into the snow, wishing he could breathe its clean whiteness instead of the terrible air where the fire was.

He couldn't. He came up, spluttering and choking.

His first words were, "Fucking Ice. Fat, ugly pony, wait until I get my hands on him."

This time, even in only the briefest flash of his senses, Tarquin knew immediately where he was. The juxtaposition of lava and ice, smoke and the unliving shrieks of machinery all added up neatly to tell him he was in the place where he had met Chyko in the Liminal, while the red crystal was still intact. That episode seemed lifetimes ago. Now Chyko was not here to greet him, and it was dark, so that only the burning lava illuminated the scene. Patches of snow were sensed as gray areas within a larger blackness. Floating in the air at some unknown distance were points of light too large and rectangular to be stars, leaking small amounts of color into the night.

He rolled over onto his back in the snow. His face was burned, but he didn't think he was in worse shape than usual. *Why did Ice leave me here?* he wondered. He would have thought that he'd have more insight into Ice's behavior, now that he was a part of Ice; but when he felt around for an answer to the question, he got the feeling that either Ice did not know why he had come here, or, more ominously, that he had not had a choice.

What would happen to Ice if he couldn't get away from the sky-falcon? Would Tarquin be trapped here? This was a horrible place. He remembered it with loathing.

Chyko had been inside the red crystal. In Jai Pendu, the spiral road had climbed through the crystal, intersecting it in a complex geometry; but when the crystal that blocked the road was broken, a world had been revealed within each facet. And Chyko had been in one of those worlds, until Tarquin had broken him out when he broke the crystal in Jai Pendu. *This is that world,* Tarquin thought. Once, this place of ice and fire had been connected to the Way of the Rose.

Mhani had advised him to get back to the Rose.

Mhani was insane.

Good, Tarquin thought. *I sympathize with insanity.*

He picked himself up and began to walk. It was some time before he could get his bearings in the dark, and he went stumbling sideways across a snowy slope out of fear of passing too close to the lava again.

There were lights in the distance, not small friendly ones, but large, vague, moving lights, as if entire buildings were pursuing him. They issued sounds that were as unnerving as the cries of jungle creatures you couldn't see, and the ground trembled when they moved.

Then, all at once, there were metal things coming at his head; not missiles, but animate beings that hissed and clawed at him, their heavy bodies smashing around his head and shoulders. He knocked them back with his sword instinctively. It was like fighting a whole flock of armored bats. His sword whistled, hit, clanked, and shrieked as their claws scraped across it. The slow beat of large things moving out of the darkness grew deeper, and nearer.

Tarquin abandoned the fight and began to race away from the machines, with the lava on one side, the hill on the other, and the moving lights with their screams and whistles coming behind him. It was a random pursuit, until in the luminosity of the fiery lava he spotted what looked like a cart track—although by the size of the carts that had been using it, everything in this world was as

281

oversize as in the last. The track ended up leading him parallel to the worst of the lava and up a terraced hillside, until it passed between two high embankments, each fortified by metallic walls with bars of solid light lining their upper edges. It was not a welcoming entrance.

He looked back over his shoulder. The light-machines were coming closer. Rectangular apertures opened in their sides, and even more of the sharp, birdlike shapes emerged. Their winged shadows cut the sky apart and blew gray drafts of loose snow across his vision. His sword had a distinct notch in it where the blade had met the creature of metal. Beams of green-and-blue light laced the area between sky and ground like a cat's cradle of light, each beam a taut thread that moved across the snow and carved shapes in it. The armored wings made another pass at him. He shot into the passageway, ducking his head between his shoulders and cursing.

The passageway felt like a trap, a chute into which he was being driven; but at least there were no enemies coming from that direction. It was blocked by a gate whose bars were made of light. The light changed from yellow to red as Tarquin approached, and he halted a few paces away from it. If Everien gates were anything like Everien doors, he didn't trust this one.

He was breathing fast with indecision and whipping his head back and forth between what he felt sure were the frying pan and the fire, respectively; and then, to his utter surprise, there was a soft giggle, and Jaya's voice spoke out of the gate.

"This is the way to a maze, the symbol country. Here a deck of cards equals the deck of a ship equals a house of cards equals a deal. I have been sold and I have sailed. The ones who rose have not yet risen. The tree leaves. Enter only if you have been riven; but it is never the same river. Twice."

Silence.

"Jaya?"

She didn't answer.

"Where is Kere when I need him?" Tarquin asked crustily, rolling his eyes.

The shining fliers were coming in for another attack; there was no more time to choose. Turning his back on the danger, he pushed open the gate.

It was too easy. When he touched the red bars, they turned

282

green and admitted him at a stumbling run. Three fliers came after him; but when he turned to engage them, they had dissolved into collections of symbols that shot up into the sky as if they had exploded in a thousand pieces.

The gate shut behind him. Now it was yellow. He could see the moving shapes of the larger machines on the other side. There was no way he could go back through. He was starting to get the feeling of fate ganging up on him; of being a pawn. *I am going to stir up some shit here,* he resolved inwardly; but he didn't know how.

It was indeed a maze. The road turned and turned again; sometimes openings appeared to either side, and sometimes he ran into a dead end and had to turn around. Unlike the Snake maze, this puzzle offered no faces to guide him. The lights on the wall told him nothing: they changed to red as he drew alongside, but turned back to yellow again after he'd passed, so that he didn't even have a record of where he had been. He kept expecting something to come hurtling out of the darkness above to attack him, but the only thing that happened was that the walls themselves seemed to shiver ever so slightly, passing a sonorous, deep drone along their length in a wave that matched his stride, just as the light did.

"I am nervous," Tarquin said through clenched teeth. Walking unprotected into such a scenario went against both instincts and judgment; yet, as Mhani had so pithily pointed out, he was running out of things to lose. It is hard to have strategy when you lack assets and advocates. As for assets, he didn't even have the food or blankets that might have bought him time to study the situation; and his best advocate, Ice, had literally dumped him here.

Ice, he called to his insides, knowing that somehow the horse was there. He could feel Ice like a promise within him. *Ice.*

But Ice never came, and neither did dawn. Tarquin walked. Strangely, he was not tired, nor hungry, nor cold; not since passing the red gate. And some internal electricity kept driving him on.

It took all this while for Tarquin to catch up with himself, so that on reflection he realized that he felt different, now. Ice had torn him apart. He remembered it clearly; but there was no memory of pain. In fact, for the first time *ever,* maybe, he seemed to be seeing straight.

Everien. It dawned on him slowly. First in the way the word seemed to rock and pitch in his consciousness. *Everien. Everien.*

He had traveled enough in Pharice and even beyond to know

that Everien was not a world, but only one country, however unusual. And yet, paradoxically, while you were there, Everien made you think it was larger than all the other countries, seas, and wildernesses combined. Larger than the sky. Larger than *itself*.

Tarquin stopped in his tracks on realizing that one. The thought reminded him of Kere. He would never see Kere again. But maybe, now, he could come to understand the oddities of life that Kere had taken for granted, had never been able adequately to explain.

He walked on, shaking his head. He didn't feel as dismayed as he once had in thinking of Everien, its Knowledge, its Liminal . . . its ghosts. As he roamed his way from unknown to unknown, he began to perceive Everien with less fear.

It was changing all around him. Was it alive? Could it . . . think for itself?

For Tarquin's experiences of Everien had been mainly ones of landscapes. Open spaces, buildings, architectures of unknown purpose. Mountains no one had ever scaled.

There were never any Everien people.

Who had the Everiens been? What had become of them?

He halted again. It wasn't what *had* become of them, for according to Ice's chronology, they had never existed.

What *would* become of them.

He tried that out and couldn't make it work in his mind.

Timeserpent, he thought. *Anything could be true, couldn't it?*

That, he supposed, was the upsetting part. You could, after all, just surrender and abandon yourself to the idea that anything could be true—but why then didn't the world bend to your own thoughts? Why were some things true sometimes, and not others? Why, for example, was there ground beneath his feet in this moment—but perhaps it would disappear, later?

A small yearning came over him then for his Clan, their fires, their hunts, and their feasts and their fights. But here, in this endlessly folded creation, the reality of the Clans and their Animal Magic felt cozy and tiny and very, very remote from him.

Yours is the Way of the Rose.

Jaya had given him the flower, and he remembered looking at it. The petals of the rose lay curled and inviting, their scent intoxicating, their sexual suggestion alluring. The rose played on his mind by association—just like Jaya herself. But unfold the rose and see its beauty fail to yield to order. The rose, built by sunlight, shaped by the eyes and other sense organs of animals to take a form that would attract them, the rose had no self. It had no center; there was nothing inside it. A series of sensations built by observer and observed; a pyramid of possibilities fired by more possibilities, but arriving at nothing.

Once, Tarquin's senses had been all he had.

I smell it, he would think. *I see it. It is there. It is.*

Now he was not so sure. If this was the symbol country, then what would happen if he reached out and put his hand right through this wall that he was so laboriously walking alongside?

What would be on the other side of it?

What if there was *nothing* on the other side?

What if everything simply *vanished,* like the baby Kere into Ice's mouth? Like Tarquin into Ice? Like Jai Pendu into the boundless sea?

He drew back his hand, afraid now to touch the wall.

"I only want to find Jaya," he said. "I do not need to see the nature of Everien. I do not want to."

Nothing changed. The walls were still there, the lights, the lowering sky.

Who is making this? he thought suddenly. He had been having visions, impressions, since first he tangled with Night at Jai Pendu. Those had coalesced into Jaya with the most recent passage of Jai Pendu. And since he had revisited the floating city, he did not seem to belong to any one time at all.

Something must have happened, that second time at Jai Pendu. The first time, he had taken the Water and, all unknowing, had caused Night to steal his Company as compensation. But the second time he had not taken anything. He had only freed his men.

And broken the crystal. The structure that bound the worlds together.

So who is making this? Who is controlling where I go, when I go?

It was like being in someone else's dream. But he had glimpsed Jaya in the Liminal, handling the pieces of the crystal. Trying to put it back together.

He stopped again and cupped his hands to his mouth.

"JAYA!" he screamed. "Wake up! JAYA!!"

His voice echoed and reechoed. The sound built, grew louder until the walls hummed and popped with its resonance. Overtones jangled in the bones of his skull. His feet itched. Symbols appeared from out of the stone and glowed inside his eyeballs like invading insects.

From directly ahead of him, down the passageway between the two bulwarks of glistening stone, there was a rumbling, and then the light began to go.

"Godshit," said Tarquin, drawing his sword. Stupid, ancestral weapon: it could do him no good there. But it was all he had.

He was irrelevantly aware that his mouth had tilted into a lop-sided grin. Tarquin always smiled when things got really bad. He found himself licking his broken front teeth and then gnashing them together.

"Come on," he whispered. "Come on, then, come and get me."

The passageway ahead was moving. All the light in the walls had gone out, and he stood now in darkness. A little illumination from the growling sky above let him see the outlines of the passageway as it buckled and shifted. The screaming returned, the same screaming he had heard with Chyko when they had smoked in the snow above the lava. It was a wrenching, awful noise, and as the sound went away it gave a backlash that made his hairs stand on end, as if some inaudible frequency were eating into him like an acid, speaking directly to the older parts of him, the parts he did not know.

The passage began to change. Deep in the noise, an unkind melody took the lead. The ground under him thumped up and down. Stone deliquesced, then solidified again, with patterns of change swiftly rushing up and down in lines: branching, swelling, twisting. Limbs formed. Claws formed. Eyes formed; wings formed and then were corrupted and folded back inside the moving mass. Heat came off the thing. It rolled toward Tarquin, now one entity, now many. Parts dislodged and went scurrying off in one direction after another. Some of these grew legs and turned into bipedal opponents. Others skulked on the ground, turning jewel-like and sprouting crystalline branches.

Odors exploded all around as the tumult advanced. It was only on catching a noisome smell coming from somewhere *behind* him that Tarquin thought to turn.

There was no passageway behind him. It was as if he were standing in the middle of a ship, and the stern had been chomped by some sea monster and pulled under. He could see ragged edges of the stone walls, and beyond that, utter void.

There was nowhere to run.

Ice was conspicuously absent.

He drew his sword and hacked at the thing indiscriminately, but it only came on bigger and stronger. Like a mounting wave, a great mass of flesh poised above him replete with spines, arms, teeth, nostrils, poison jets, and susurrating gills. Human forms could be seen twisting and struggling within, then being reassimilated before breaking free of the skin. Whips with eyes that winked and shot acid lashed the air. Feelers groped toward him. The sound was filling him from his feet to his eyeballs. His teeth chattered.

"Stop it," he said. "Jaya. Stop this at once. Jaya."

The noise did not quieten.

Bitch, he thought. *Chyko was right.*

His sword drew blood that turned into bats and flew at him. The void shrieked at his back. All he had to do was kick off and away and these tentacles and claws and stenches and sounds would all be gone.

A clawed tentacle shot toward him and he grabbed it before it could cut him. He was taken off his feet and hung upside down while it plastered octopus suckers across his body, curling him within its grip. The claw curved and pointed at his throat. He kicked. He spat at it.

"*Ice!*" he screamed. "*Ice! Ice!*"

There were no hoofbeats. He strained backward, away from the claw that was now only inches from his jugular vein. His eyes squeezed shut with the effort.

A small, cool hand seized on to his own.

"Jaya?" He opened his eyes.

But it was Night. He saw its pale, sexless face, its eyeless expanse of forehead, its dry and expressionless mouth. He had forgotten how small Night was. He had forgotten its strength, as if its limbs were made of metal, not bone. Its hair shone obsidian.

Then the mouth moved and he heard his own voice.

"Don't let go."

Tarquin froze, then began to gag.

There was nothing in his belly to vomit.

Insect legs probed him. Something cold had clamped around his ribs and was squeezing, simultaneously driving small barbs into his flesh. He tasted copper, then shit.

"Don't let go. Whatever you do, don't let go."

It was his own voice, calling to Jaya.

Night was tugging him. Its eyeless face hovered white before him. He saw with disgust that it had no legs now. It was conjoined at the hips with the Beast.

"Don't let go!"

He gripped Night's hand. Night's black robes fanned wide, blocking his view of the Beast. In Night's robes stars appeared. He could hear their chiming above the roar of the basso profundo Beast.

Night tugged him into itself.

THE IMPOSSIBLE
QUESTION

When Istar found Taretel, he was surrounded by dead
Pharicians. One of them had been beheaded and Taretel was lazi-
ly kicking his head from one point to another, his huge sword still
drawn. Istar halted, bent over, vomited, and straightened.
Shaking, she wiped her mouth.

"You killed Pentar."

Her voice sounded inert. She felt as though she had a stone in
her soul.

Taretel gave no response. He didn't seem to notice her there,
and for a moment she thought of attacking him. But the skyfalcon
was nowhere to be seen. She knew Taretel would not answer her.
She drew a long, shuddering breath, and this time her voice came
out in a banshee shriek.

"Do you have any idea what you've done, you monster?" She
stormed toward him now. "You killed Pentar. *You killed Pentar*. My
friend. My ally. And you killed him—*why*? Because he dared touch
that . . . that . . . that piece of red-haired garbage?" A surge of violent jealously brought a rush of blood to her extremities. "He was-
n't going to harm her, you fucking maniac. He was trying to save
her from Tash, I'm sure of it. Oh, you're . . . you're . . ." As she
made her way among the ruins of the Pharician camp, dodging a
hysterical horse and stepping over bodies, the full enormity of
what Taretel had done began to strike her. It was not only Pentar
who was dead. It was not only the Pharicians who had been
guarding the captives. It was almost everyone in the camp. Istar
supposed that some must have escaped, because she'd heard horses galloping off while she'd descended from the standing stones
where Dario and the rest were hiding.

Taretel kicked the head toward her and she recognized Tash's face. She retched and spat bile.

"You're worse than the Sekk," she whispered. She thought of the food she'd accepted from him. The bandage for her cut head. She thought of the way she had let him escape; so this was how he repaid her?

He stooped and began to clean his sword on Tash's cloak. Istar noticed that his own cloak was missing. She wondered who had put up enough of a fight to take the cloak off the Seahawk, and this made her think of Pentar. She found his body in a gap between the tents, not far from the one that doubled as a litter for Jaya by day. She looked inside this, but there was no sign of Jaya.

"Where is she?" She raised her voice to be sure Taretel could hear her, but when she climbed out of the tent and returned to the place where he had been bending over Tash, he was gone. "Taretel! Show yourself!"

She looked everywhere, but she didn't find him. What she found was the end of another massive bone, penetrating the time-serpent barrier. A trickle of luminescent pink insects flowed across its surface and dispersed on the ground.

Istar was clearheaded for once. She moved through the camp collecting medicines and food, and she saddled one of the hobbled Pharician horses. She let the others go free, although she hadn't much hope for their survival in this rugged country, with mountain lions and worse waiting hungrily. Already vultures and foxes were making dashes at the carnage. Istar dragged Pentar's body away from the rest and poured oil on it, then set it alight. She knelt just on the edge of the burning, where the heat was scorching just on the edge of bearability, and clasped her hands before her. No tears would come. She tried to speak but no sound emerged, so she mouthed the words: "*I'm sorry. I'm sorry.*"

Then, with a sudden, decisive movement, she turned her back on the wreckage and strode quickly to where she'd tethered her horse. She mounted and let the animal run away from the flames, gradually soothing him with her voice and bringing him down to a walk. The timeserpent barrier loomed ahead, and the bridge of bone. Before the horse had time to think, Istar reached back and slapped his rump with a cry, squeezing him forward and lifting the reins to bring him up on the bone.

Together they burst into daylight and the horse's hooves thundered against the alabaster bone, which dipped sharply down like a ramp. There were no purple insects at all—and to Istar's delight, there was no monster waiting to finish her off. Instead, everything was blue sky and sunshine with a razor's edge. Below the bone, Istar saw clouds like a carpet; and through holes in the clouds, she saw gray geometrical shapes, like the repeating patterns the Pharicians were so fond of in their tile art.

The bone ended in cloud.

"You are a good horse," Istar said to her frightened mount, and his ears flicked back at the sound of her voice. She didn't think it would be fair to expect the horse to go first, so she dismounted and led him into the cloud.

Wind hit her face hard, and the horse danced sideways, nearly dragging his bridle out of the grip of her hand. The shadow of the skyfalcon passed over their heads; then the bird let himself fall gliding past Istar's line of vision, banking across her path and then flying away. Istar did not focus her eyes on him. Through wind-tears, she could see the green fields of her destination, far below. They were no longer on the borders of Snake Country. Instead, they stood on a twisting, difficult path that plunged from the foothills to the river valley, less than fifty miles from Jai Khalar.

The trail descended in abbreviated switchbacks. Four turns below Istar, the black form of Taretel was starkly offset against the white stone. He was not on the trail, but perched on a ledge that seemed much too small for his large body. As she watched, the sky-falcon swooped past him, then climbed again.

"Hey!" Istar shouted. "Taretel! Hey!"

She didn't really expect him to react—he hardly ever did. But he turned, looked up, saw her, and flung himself off the ledge. She gasped as he twisted in midair, landed on his feet on the trail with startling grace, and began to race back up the path to meet her. She stood there and let him come, astonished by his eagerness to meet her when he had only just deserted her, back there amongst the wreckage of Tash's camp.

He was breathing hard when he reached her. He was still running when he began talking, so that she had trouble understanding what he was saying. His chest was heaving up and down as he breathed, and she could see sweat coming through his dark tunic. He did not look so gigantic, she noticed, without the snow-lion cloak.

". . . for your friend. It had to. Be done. They were going to. Kill her. Istar. I couldn't let. It happen." He paused, gasping for air, and she reached out and touched his gloved hand with her gloved hand. He fell silent at the gesture, his eyes focused on her with an intense question in them. It was an impossible and unanswerable question, coming from a man divided in three and split across time, who had just murdered a person Istar cared about.

Well, Istar thought, maybe Taretel's tacit question was not unanswerable. Her answer should have been a resounding *No!*

But it wasn't.

"Does this mean you're talking to me?" Istar tried to quip, but she choked and finished on a gulping sob, spoiling the effect.

Taretel took his thumb and wiped tears away from the corners of her eyes.

"Come down from here," he said. "This wind is too much work."

Behind his head, she could see the skyfalcon twisting and rising and falling, struggling to stay in position against the eddies and gusts. To her own surprise, she smiled.

Then she punched Taretel in the gut. While he was bent over, coughing, she handed him the reins and started down the precipitous slope ahead of him.

THANK YOU

"*Taretel*, was it the Liminal we crossed? Do the bone bridges go through the Liminal?"

He nodded. He was still leading the horse, but now Istar was riding it. Once the slope of the trail had lessened, he insisted that she mount. "You are tired," he had informed her in a manner that Istar thought would have been better suited to a little old lady. "And look at the condition of your boots! No, don't make faces. You will ride."

Looking at the valley that was almost unrecognizable from the Everien Istar had last seen sparked thoughts of Mhani.

"The Liminal drove my mother insane," Istar said. "Why?"

"The Liminal was created by the Everiens," Taretel said. "At first it was only part of an experiment to encode Knowledge. It began with the storage of the mouse patterns in the form of sound, but it grew and grew. Thought begets thought. The thoughtverse grows and changes, for by analogy we can build. We can weave webs between ideas and realities. And we might chance on something. An abstraction hiding beyond our senses, buried in the concrete where we are blind, but an animal is not. Or a concrete thing arising from the juice of abstraction, like a lion with a man's head. Or a man with the wings of a skyfalcon."

Istar looked at him sharply. He went on. "Monsters. Possibilities. The Everiens had the animal patterns, which they believed to be essentially records of the interaction of variables across time. They saw the animal as the writing that could only be read by an invisible eye, an eye that crossed time. Animals are only histories. They are deep, they are survival, they are death and death and death. That is their sadness and their hope. An animal was a history, and a guess at the future—and, in time, the interactions of the animals and their world played out as a drama. The Everiens thought this was a pretty good game, so they stored all these animal patterns, codified as sound, and they played their own theoretical games with them, in an imaginary time. This was the Liminal, a place that had no substance but thought and sound: it was shaped time. Here in the Liminal they played with time as if it were something you could touch. And in the world of their games, time indeed *became* something you could touch. It wove and wound its way through the patterns of living creatures."

Istar heard herself gasp. "Do you mean the Everiens created the timeserpent?"

"The timeserpent created itself. It was latent in the animals. It was how the old patterns called to the new ones. It was a mathematical possibility; something abstract, an idea, a potential. Yet, within the patterns of the Liminal, it became expressed in sound, just as the animal patterns were."

"So it wasn't born?"

"The timeserpent was not bred, or created. It was self-engendered. The abstraction of animal forms had reached a point where the timeserpent came into being as a theoretical possibility. And when it was sung, it sewed holes in the very fabric that made it."

"Taretel, I'm not following you. We already know the timeserpent is amoral and maybe even immortal. But what kind of creature was never born or hatched or grown? If it could bend time to create itself, wouldn't that make it unstoppable?" She let out a spasm of laughter. "No. I can't believe it. What kind of creature is that?"

Taretel did not echo her laughter. "The kind of creature we are dealing with. The timeserpent."

"But even the Pharician gods haven't such power," she protested in an offended tone.

"When the Pharicians find out about the timeserpent, they will throw over their gods and make offerings only to Time."

Istar shuddered. Everien was cast out before her, ragged, torn. An army could be seen marching from the north toward Jai Khalar. Smoke lingered over A-vi-Khalar. Over Wolf Country, the clouds jerked like marionettes.

"I don't like any of this. How can we do anything but surrender?"

Now it was Taretel's turn to laugh, but there was no mirth in his voice. "It's not like that. Even if we did surrender, it wouldn't matter. The timeserpent isn't interested in you or me. There will be no mercy from it."

"I think you are a fine one to talk about mercy," Istar said suddenly. "Who have never awarded it."

"I have never received it, either," he retorted, his eyes flaring briefly as he looked up at her. Then he placed a conciliatory palm on her knee. Even through the glove, his hand was warm. "Except from you," he amended. "I am in peril, Istar. The worms are driven, and I cannot stop them. If only you knew the loneliness of timeserpents. They crave offspring; but they are doomed, for if they reproduce, they negate their own existence. They are not one species existing in many individuals across time; they are one individual, existing forever, immune to time. Unstoppable. Unchangeable. Eating causality."

"The Li'ah'vah, it is not a species, then? It is one specimen only?"

"Exactly, yes. In the scheme of causality, the Li'ah'vah came before the timeserpent. One Li'ah'vah, which the Everiens discovered and tried to use in the Liminal to send the abominations of the Fire Houses backward into a theoretical past in which they could not harm anyone. To send them to a paradoxical time and place from which they could never escape, so they could never be created. But the Everiens didn't realize that the Li'ah'vah's codes that were sent back could be drawn from the Liminal and into the world, and from the world they could be used in the Fire Houses, to make the Li'ah'vah become flesh—just as the monsters whom the Everiens feared but tried to hide within the confines of the Liminal, theoretical space. And what I did not know, when I journeyed to Everien, was that one day the Li'ah'vah would pass through the Jaya patterns that had been placed in the Liminal to guard the monsters and to trap the Li'ah'vah with conscience. I did not know that the Li'ah'vah would merge with Jaya's humanlike consciousness and transform into the timeserpent, with the desires of a human and the timeslipping ability of its paradoxical nature. Once it had made that transformation, it wanted offspring. It still does. And that has been my problem, in this time and in others."

Istar took this all in. She was silent for a while. Then she said, "But if having offspring will negate the timeserpent's existence, isn't that good?"

"Wanting offspring only meant that it would do anything, contribute to any cause, in order to change its code to an animal code. And that meant that it offered its venom and its bodily fluids, containing its codes, to the Circle."

"Do you understand these codes?" Istar asked eagerly.

"Everything I knew, all I was, it lives in the skyfalcon. There is no other way. The knowledge of things such as timeserpents is too great to live in a man. It breaks him by its very nature."

"As you were broken," Istar implied in a low voice.

He looked at her then. "It is not quite the same. I am no longer a man. I have trivided, and now I am pursued by the worms, you see."

"The worms?"

"They will have me in the end; this is the one thing I know for certain. It would take a miracle to save me, and I don't believe in those."

She remembered Eteltar saying something about the worms, up on his ledge, in the dry heat—it seemed so very far away, now, yet she could still smell the dusty air as it came off his wings when he landed, if only she closed her eyes and thought about it.

"The worms have everyone in the end," Istar said in what she hoped was a soothing tone, thinking that this conversation was turning madder by the minute. "Unless you burn to death, of course, and leave no remains."

He almost smiled then; she wondered how he could smile at such macabre talk.

"The worms are the echoes of the timeserpent. They are its death, too, and its means of being born, since the Circle have been using the venom all this time, to make themselves into shadow-beings, half monsters, and to prize the Knowledge from the future to gain control. The worms call me at all times. I fight them all I can, but sometimes to fight them is to join them, for the violence comes over me. Istar, it is all so twisted I scarcely know what to do anymore."

He walked in silence, and didn't look at her when he said, "All I know is that Jaya is the future, and we must be sure nothing evil befalls her."

Istar stared at the back of his head. Jaya again. She was finding it difficult to muster much enthusiasm for saving Jaya. But she swallowed her jealousy.

"Where do we find her, then? Let's not be all day about it."

"She has been picked up by that army." Taretel nodded toward the green, treeless land alongside the river. The cavalry section of the army was rapidly advancing from the north. "She is safe for the present, but we must get to Jai Khalar before they do. I sent her through the barrier for her own protection from Dario and the other escapees, but by the time I could make the bridge and follow, she had a long head start on me. From on high, I saw them pick her up. I should have gone with her, but that would have meant you were stranded on the other side of the barrier."

Istar's brow furrowed. "How so? You went ahead of me anyway."

"Jaya does not need a bone to cross the timeserpent barrier. She can step across it like a brook. So can I."

"Then why the bones?" Istar said with an air of disbelief.

"The first bone was for you. The second bone was for Tash—not for Jaya, for Tash, because I needed the Pharicians to keep her alive in the cold until I could reach her myself. And the third bone was for you also. How else could I bring you?"

"But you left me in Snake Pass without a word!"

"That is because I had an errand that would not wait. Jaya had Artifacts with her that had to be destroyed. And then I had to make the bridge. It can take time, you know, to match the two adjacent lands."

"You weren't gone very long to have done all that," Istar said.

"Not on that side of the bridge," he replied, unfazed by her skepticism. "But I lost a lot of time on this side."

"You could have come back for me."

"It had to be your choice, Istar. I could not force you to come with me. Fortunately, you came on your own."

"Where else was I supposed to go?" Istar said stiffly. "Snake Pass is no place for a pregnant woman."

"Exactly," Taretel said. "It is better that we are together, for now all the bridges are made, and I don't have to be flying about making stitches in the world, so we can talk."

Istar digested this a little. "Well," she said finally, "what now? There's a big army down there, and this place is a mess. I haven't the faintest idea what's become of Kassien or anybody else. Thank you for killing Tash, by the way."

Taretel laughed.

"You're welcome," he said.

WISHBONE

"*Whose army are* they, anyway?" Istar asked that night by the campfire. They had been moving to intercept the force all day long, but she still didn't understand what it was that Taretel intended to do. At dusk the skyfalcon had brought them two hares, which Istar had spitted and cooked over the fire. To her shock, Taretel was eating ravenously. She had never seen him eat before.

"I have been forced to bring them over from the north. They are led by a king who is not a king, a man who is old but looks like a boy. He has been tricked by the worms, and he shelters one of my enemies. One of your enemies, too, I believe."

She raised her eyebrows. "Oh?"

"Grietar."

"*Oh.*" Then: "What do you mean, you 'have been forced'? When has anybody ever forced you to do anything?"

He wiped his lips with the back of his hand. "You should try to eat, Istar. You've hardly touched anything all day."

She picked up a piece of meat in her fingers and put it in her mouth. It was too hot.

"You didn't anffer my queffion."

He rubbed his forehead. "It is not easy to explain."

She shrugged. "Never mind."

He looked surprised and a little disappointed that she had backed off so easily, so she decided to pursue the question.

"Does Grietar have some power over you?" she asked. "Something to do with finding the skeleton?"

He shook his head. "He has power, but not because of that. He has been given an Artifact, it comes from the same place Jaya comes from, and it can be used to bring me. Because he held this thing, he could have kept me with him, but I needed to be free.

298

The only way to deal with it was to bring him a bone and let him into Everien. That way he would forget about me and I could carry on with what I was doing."

"What about the other bones?" Istar said. "Do you still have them?"

"No! I put them in the Liminal and brought them one at a time to the places where they were needed."

"So you're not still carrying them around."

"I could not carry my own bones!" Taretel said indignantly.

"Of course not. How silly of me."

The irony was lost on him. He went on. "Not all of them at the same time, anyway. Nor could I trust anyone else with the task . . . although I did trust you, for a while." He smiled at her but she didn't smile back. This had become too strange. Taretel said, "All of the bones are in place to pull Everien back together, and soon their work will be done. But there is one problem."

"Only one?" said Istar sarcastically.

"See this bone?" He held up the forked bone she had noticed the skyfalcon carrying before. He passed it to her and she handled it with a shiver. It was a clavicle, but not a human clavicle; rather, a very large and hollow avian clavicle, fused where the wings would meet. "Please, take it. You keep it. It belongs with you."

"A wishbone," she said.

"Yes. A wishbone. It is the last bridge, and it has three ends. In order to complete it, I must divide."

"I thought you were divided already."

"I mean, forever. No more crossing back and forth. No more communication. No more memories of each other. One part of me will go back, and one part will go forward, and a third will . . . stay."

Istar didn't like the sound of that and started to say so, but he forestalled her with a look. "When that happens, the bird part of me will no longer have a voice, and the man part of me will no longer have a conscience. I would ask you, if we are still together and you go the same way as this man part of me, I would ask you to make certain I do no harm."

The eyes looking at her now were very much Eteltar's eyes.

"Why do you have to be a killer?" she said. "Why can't you just . . . stop?"

He sighed. "Because of the worms, Istar. They want to consume

299

me. I will not let them. I will not even set one foot on the road that will lead to my consumption by them."

"Everyone has to die," Istar said with a sigh, thinking that he was a little obsessed with this topic.

"I am not afraid to die!" Taretel laughed. "The worms, they are the opposite of death."

"You're right," she said at length. "I don't understand."

"Istar." He touched her cheek with his fingertips. "Please. Just do as I say. If the time comes . . . when the time comes . . . do not let me come to evil. You are a slayer of the Sekk, are you not?"

"Yes."

"Then, for your own Honor, do not let me come to evil."

She nodded slowly.

"Do you promise?" he said.

She took a deep breath.

"I promise."

Some kind of open door swung shut in his eyes then, and an answering draft of sadness brushed against her.

"Good!" said Taretel briskly. He leaped up, and for just a moment she was reminded of the spritely and fey Eteltar. "Come on, come on, no time to waste! Let's go!"

The skyfalcon fanned his wings and gave a shriek in her direction. She put the bone away and tried to smile.

THE WARCHILD AND
HER CONTRAPTIONS

𝒟uor enlisted the help of one of the Pharicians, a man called Thuun who had had a Scholarly background and understood the most advanced of the Pharician machinery as well as a smattering of Everien Artifactual lore. Together, the two pored over the scroll and began to experiment with the "gifts" tossed up by the Blackness.

Thuun made earnest efforts to talk to Liaku. He kept trying to convince her that she wasn't the important one, Wakhe was.

"The inside of Wakhe's mind isn't like ours. Wakhe has empty spaces where we have vision and speech and skeletal motion. Wakhe has extra strength and toughness and tenacity—if he didn't, he'd never have lived. He might seem stupid because he can't master the languages we have, but he can calculate a hundred times as fast as the quickest Scholar, he can solve puzzles easily, and he has a spooky ability to pick out details. How he reads and translates these patterns, I don't know. But it's possible that Wakhe can think in ways we can't think. That, to him, we are the blind cripples. That, to him, we are the ones lacking."

Liaku listened to several speeches of this kind, thinking that Thuun would surely recognize that his enthusiasm was irritating at the least; but he did not. So she took to throwing mud pies at him whenever he approached her, and after that only Duor ever talked to her. Liaku liked it better that way. Thuun had his uses, but she didn't want him getting any ideas about taking Wakhe away from her.

Duor, on the other hand, knew how to flatter Liaku when she needed it.

"Your instinct to put up this triangle around the Blackness was . . . well, almost psychic, I would have said," Duor told her. "You see, that triangle is a kind of model of the theory of the Eye, the Sun, and the Rose. It's like a miniature Jai Pendu. And when the Blackness is surrounded by it, as you can see, it gets trapped. It can't slink around eating things anymore, have you noticed?"

"No kidding," Liaku said. "Why you think Illyra never come here before? Before I put up the Triangle, people getting eaten all the time. Strange people, too, Duor."

She tried to explain to him about the people with their weird costumes and their pointless behavior, but he brushed her stories aside.

"Never mind all that. Listen, Thuun and I have a theory. We think that the Blackness is a kind of timeserpent passage, and that everything that used to be in Jai Khalar is down there. And maybe—considering that Wakhe was supposed to be in the Fire Houses, and considering that the timeserpent came from the Fire Houses through Jai Khalar and into the hills before it disappeared—maybe everything that was in the Fire Houses is in there, too. Which would explain these sophisticated Everien weapons."

He was very excited, Liaku thought. Duor had already professed his ambitions toward being awarded a dukedom by Tash when Tash discovered all the great weapons that he, Duor, had discovered. But he had forgotten one thing.

"Duor," she said innocently. "If timeserpent go down hole and disappear, how you know where timeserpent is?"

"Oh," he said airily, waving his hand. "It was last seen way out in Snake Country, by Fivesisters Lake. There have been no sightings since then."

"But . . . excuse Liaku be stupid, but, Duor?"

"What, Liaku?"

"If he timeserpent, can't he come anytime he want? Anyplace he want?"

Duor patted her on the head.

"Don't worry, Liaku. We'll protect you."

NOT THAT DUOR was entirely stupid, Liaku realized. For he and Thuun had done something to her Triangle to make it light up. Now she found that in the planes between the bars that formed the triangular scaffold around the Blackness, there were three views: one of the remains of the Fire Houses, one of the cliffs that had housed Jai Khalar, and one of the sea. The views and perspectives kept changing as the Blackness shifted and heaved within the confines of the scaffold, but all three were always present at greater or lesser distance.

"It's because of the Water of Glass," Thuun tried to explain to her. "It's still down there somewhere, in the Blackness." Then he ducked a mud pie.

By now, Liaku was reasonably convinced that, between the two of them, Thuun and Duor would like to take over her Triangle. But she vowed that that wasn't going to happen. They couldn't speak Clan common half so well as Liaku, for one thing, so they weren't able to trade with the Clansmen who began to come in greater and greater numbers once Illyra had moved his troops away. And they couldn't get near Wakhe. He was afraid of everyone but Liaku, and she liked it that way.

He was the key to it all. Wakhe tapped his rhythms, and somewhere in the Blackness, someone was singing back to him. Some one . . . or some *thing*. For the singing that curled from the Blackness was only occasionally reminiscent of a human voice. The song had an evanescent quality that made it almost impossible to identify the components of its timbre from moment to moment. Sometimes, having drunk too much plundered ale, Liaku lay back and watched the sky and listened, and she thought she could very nearly *see* the things the music was made of. But like clouds moving on a blue background, the moments didn't stay. Unlike the artistically created music of human beings, the music of the Blackness never posed, never embellished itself, never declared itself as such. It simply *was*.

When she wasn't drunk, the music made far less sense. All the same, Liaku's mind being as curious and flexible as it was, she found herself hearing patterns. She heard rhythms built and then violated; she heard elements of the music interact with one another like voices in a dialogue or trialogue, and then decay. She heard the slither and rearrangement of bones and blood, breathing, heartbeat. She heard things hard on the outside and soft within; and she heard surfaces that were porous and yielding that congealed over tough, static innards. She heard numbers pile on each other, subdivide, skip like mad rabbits or, severed from their dependents, limp. Colors and smell were intimated. The buildup of hate, fear, passion, ownership sometimes lay in her mind like a glaze over a sound that seemed opaque and impenetrable, but wasn't. Other times she thought she heard a tune, thought she knew where it was going, and was led into a blind alley of sound where everything that she thought was true went sour and turned into something else. Rules were made, broken, modified, inverted, remade, abandoned.

Liaku conducted her trade and listened. She was afraid Wakhe would exhaust himself and put her out of business. Even when he slept, his fingers twitched, and the earth beside the Blackness hummed softly. Discrete lights flared from the nothing. It was as if the Blackness and Wakhe were both possessed with a primal urgency. The sense of it reminded Liaku of migrating birds: an inexorable process driven by an energy out of all proportion to how things should be.

"Wakhe," she said to the ruined face of the cripple, wondering whether he heard and understood her. "Wakhe, you remind me of ant. Carry buildings on your back. Never stop. Never sleep."

She fed him well. She could afford to: the eager Clansmen brought her everything she could need that the Blackness did not provide. She disciplined herself in her dealings with them. There was a part of her that wanted to be generous, to make friends, to find a home here in this wild, twisted place called Everien. But another, cannier part of her said to be careful. What she had, others would want. It was only a matter of time before she was attacked, just as a Watch in Jundun would be attacked if it were not well defended by its inhabitant's favorite birds. So she made her preparations.

One rule was that she never gave away any weapon or defense that she had not tested herself. She found that once you had a couple of reliable war machines, you could defend the area around the Blackness and make it impossible for anybody else to get close enough to steal from you. And the Blackness was a reasonably good source of weapons, although Liaku often had to warn her customers that it was up to them to work out the full uses and potentials of each thing they had bartered for. Liaku only used a weapon enough to figure out its basic function, and to show off and discourage the Clanspeople from attacking her. Then she traded, and sent the people on their way. Still, the effects of her policy were sometimes spectacular.

Two days' ride west-northwest of Jai Khalar there was a particularly virulent seam sewn by the timeserpent. The discontinuity consisted of eight "punctures" where the Li'ah'vah had surfaced for a look around, each of which was now occupied by a different set of unfriendly and dangerous monsters. The monsters did not seem to be able to leave their areas and attack people in the countryside, but they did have the ability to cause displacement of people and animals within a radius of two or three miles of the timeserpent's breakages of the fabric of Everien, so that people could be unwittingly drawn right into the discontinuities and summarily dispatched.

It was only a matter of time before the Deer and Wasps who were dealing with this situation were forced to approach Liaku for help. Now, Liaku had no idea how to help them. She didn't understand half of the apparatuses that Wakhe called up, and Duor and Thuun were working off one sheet of diagrams, most of which were written in Everien. So Liaku had to . . . improvise.

Her main job was to impress the Clansmen. They were impressed with feats that reminded them of the Knowledge. Strength and courage were of no interest to the cynical Clans, for these qualities had let the people down too many times in the past. No: they wanted tricks. They wanted good tricks.

To set the stage, Liaku had set up two vertical panels that, when positioned facing one another, caused a field of static electricity between them within which could be smelled something sharp and tangy. Fortunately Liaku had never passed between the two activated panels, although she easily could have done it while she was figuring out what they were, for anything that was caught within this area summarily had its bones melted. There was no damage to other structures, so insects and other boneless things were entirely immune, and a full suit of metal armor could repel the charge that attacked the bones. But there were few, if any, suits of full plate armor in Everien, and Liaku's defense zone quickly came to be respected by all. She had to teach her birds to fly in and out over the top of it.

She staged a demonstration of these panels for the Deer leader who came to trade. She demanded one of the sheep that the Deer had brought in trade, drove it through the contraption, and gestured with a flourish at the sad result.

One of the Deer was spontaneously sick. The rest looked at her in fear.

"That was cruel," said the leader.

"*That*," Liaku corrected him, "Liaku's way of saying, 'No you steal from Liaku,' yes?"

Then she gave them a case of flamethrowers and took what she could use from their offerings.

Duor was horrified, but Liaku stuck out her tongue at him and carried on anyway. She had to look after herself, didn't she? And no one else had ever helped her, except maybe Quiz—and where was he?

The truth was, every time the Blackness gave up some precious commodity or removed something undesirable, Liaku felt a thrill that was surely as great as flying. Yet the experience left an aftertaste of unease and even fear. She was becoming like Lor: not fat, maybe, but compromised. She had sold herself to something. For the power of the Blackness was not hers to wield, no matter how clever her pretenses to the contrary might appear.

But she liked it.

With the help of Duor, she started answering Hezene's bird messages, which had been coming in thick and furious for weeks now.

"Ukili is well and pregnant with twins," Duor wrote on her instructions. "The name of the emperor is held high amongst the Clans. Signed, your faithful son, Tash."

Unfortunately, Hezene did not seem impressed. He kept wanting to know about the rumors of the timeserpent. Why could his men not get past the sea plateau? Why were the Floating Lands appearing and disappearing like Jai Pendu itself? Where were the trains of Everien tithe Tash had promised?

"Do not send soldiers to sea plateau," Duor wrote on her instructions. "Too dangerous. Monsters abound."

When Hezene responded that he had sent men through the H'ah'vah tunnel under Beule's command and they should be in Everien by now, Liaku shrugged. Nobody had had contact with that part of Wolf Country since the Li'ah'vah attack.

In time, Hezene sent back a long and eloquent scroll addressed "To the Warchild and her Contraptions." It included commentary from the imperial fliers, who had told Byrd that Tash was not anywhere to be found in central Everien, that the valley was in chaos, and that the economic hub was now in control of a "renegade byrdgirl and a crippled Scholar" whom no one dared cross because of the foul weapons they presided over. Hezene issued elaborate threats and veiled promises. He called Liaku an "illiterate nobody," accused her of murdering Ukili and making Jai Khalar disappear, and promised her a complex death. Then he told her he knew full well that she was operating outside the jurisdiction of the Circle and that they would soon close in on her.

Liaku snorted.

"I wonder what Byrd think of fool-shit like this," she said. "Come, Duor, we write back. To Hezene, Prince of Fleas. From Liaku, Queen of the World . . ."

Duor told her to put her head up Wakhe's backside, and Liaku tried to kick him. They scuffled. Duor put Liaku in a headlock and she begged off. In the end, they kept the imperial flier and sent back no answer at all. Liaku bribed the bird with fattening foods until, in time, it became hers. Even Duor had to admit this was one thing that the "illiterate nobody" could do better than the emperor.

I HAVE NO MORE
SERENITY

Byrd was in the reception room leaving a message for Zene in the Object Language when Delyl, his sixteenth daughter, came flitting in to find him.

"The emperor wants you," she sang, and the clarity of her voice reminded him of her mother. She saw his sadness and paused on the mantel. She attempted to groom him, a gesture that touched Byrd but also sent one of his tailfeathers falling to the hearth, where it could easily be misinterpreted as code for a rendezvous with Lor to obtain byrd intelligence. He swooped to pick it up, and Delyl promptly began nibbling on a corner of a day lily that was also in a critical position.

Byrd realized he'd better get rid of her. He said, "My darling, this room is soon to be sealed until the arrival of the guests tonight. I must ask you to fly away now."

"But why is it sealed, Papa? None of the other rooms are so fussed over as this one."

Byrd had had to answer this question before, as his fastidiousness about the condition of the red reception room was legendary and each generation of butlers and footmen had to be educated as to what they were allowed to touch and what must stay. Byrd recited his practiced explanation. "This is the room where the emperor had his first vision of the Grain Tithes Recording System, many, many years ago. I have given him my word as Speaker that the room will be kept perfect in tribute to that event. But we do not speak of it; the emperor believes it is bad luck." The emperor believed nothing of the sort, nor had the Grain Tithes Recording System come to him in a vision, but Byrd and the emperor were the only ones who knew that, and the emperor did not give audiences without Byrd since Byrd Spoke the very Thoughts he projected.

"Oh," said Delyl. If only she had been as thick as Chee, she would have flirted with herself in the gilt mirror and left; instead, she said, "But Papa, the room is always different. Once I came in here and there was ash all over the carpet. Surely guests at the reception should not be subjected to a mess like that!"

"These matters," replied Byrd, "are very deep. To answer your question briefly, the reason for the subtle changes has to do with the need to constantly mask chaos with order, to tame it. Do you understand?"

"Not really," admitted his sixteenth daughter.

"Well, then," Byrd said complacently. "You will when you are as old as me. Now, where am I to find the emperor?"

"Under the lemon tree," Delyl said, and Byrd made sure she exited the room before him. He watched the attendant lock it and pocket the key. Good. Tonight he had left a summons for all members of the Circle who were within Jundun to meet in the secret underground chamber for an emergency unscheduled convocation. It was not Down Day, of course, and this sort of thing was unprecedented. He was very nervous.

When he reached the emperor's side, Hezene was reading a message from the Ristale garrison, confirming that his army had passed into the H'ah'vah tunnel and that word would be sent as soon as they had reached Everien proper.

"I am disturbed, Byrd," the emperor told him. "There has been nothing from Beule all this time, and the bird that brought his first message asking for more men has died of old age; but you told me he was our best and strongest flier when we first sent him out. I remember him distinctly."

"Yes," Byrd agreed. "He was a cousin of mine, very swift. But the time disturbances in Everien may have affected him."

"I only hope they have not affected Beule!" Hezene said testily. "If I wanted an old man to wage war, I would have gone myself."

He lapsed into a brooding silence. Hezene had been more and more subdued lately. Ever since the news of the timeserpent had reached him, Byrd had observed the emperor sinking into depression. That, Byrd recalled, had been a terrible day for everyone.

Byrd had had to read the terrible message to the emperor seven times. Halfway through his eighth recital of Illyra's terse missive, Hezene reached up and crushed the message in his thin, dry fist.

"My daughter," he had sobbed, gulping but not shedding tears.

"Gone, Ukili, my favorite child. And my son Tash lost in the wilderness. Byrd!"

"Yes, O Poetry of the World That Is My Emperor?"

"We will have Everien, even if it is only a grave! I will not be ruined in this way. Hurry, send for the generals; we will need to discuss possibilities for invasion."

"It will be done, He Who Flies Without Wings."

"And launch an investigation. This business of a timeserpent in the Fire Houses—it reeks of the Circle. I want all known agents shadowed, and full reports to be given on a weekly basis. Instruct the Bird Police to stop all long-distance fliers seeking entrance to the city. Further"—and here he had reached up to idly stroke the side of Byrd's folded wing—"we will declare a month of mourning, for Ukili, for our men who sacrificed themselves, and for Chee."

Byrd let out a sad cry.

"For Chee," he echoed, and flew off to do his master's bidding.

MAYBE IT HAD been then that Byrd had lost his nerve for doing the work of the Circle. Chee had never harmed anyone, had never even had a harmful thought in her uncomplicated hybrid brain. And her voice . . . Byrd's eyes closed in sorrow and his head sagged on his neck. He would have no other mate. His life would be lived in solitude now, and even the singing of his daughters would not comfort him, for Chee's talent had been that which comes only once in a thousand years, if at all.

His role as a double agent had never been more difficult. He had to set imperial spies upon the members of the Circle, then ensure that their reports were not seen, or that they came to bad ends, or that they were attached to the wrong people in the first place. He wrote reports himself with the aid of young scribes who had to be bought off later, or murdered, or sent on apprenticeships to Min. He passed off the reports as genuine to the emperor, who seemed too distracted and upset to supervise him properly anyway; but Byrd was beginning to fray. He had heard rumors of what Zene was up to, and she was beginning to scare him.

A part of him had decided that the game was up. Even Lor was dead now, and affairs in Jundun grew nastier and more difficult to regulate. Losing Everien had been a more injurious blow than it appeared on the surface, for although the northerly country had

never provided much by way of trade, Hezene had always perceived it as a jewel and so did his subjects. His brief possession of
the territory had brought terror to remote parts of the empire,
who feared the weapons and knowledge of Everien even though
they had never seen them. And his announcement of an heir had
changed the power balance in Pharice, too. Hezene was, after all,
only one of a long line of emperors, and now people had begun to
look at the succession; but Tash was nowhere to be found. Rebel
factions gathered force. Territorial disputes flourished and distant
colonies languished without their due attention from Jundun. The
empire was under threat.

Besides which, Byrd was filled with a personal sense of doom.
He must contrive to leave Jundun and take up a life somewhere
else, away from all this, if only he could find such a place in a world
of men.

"Ah, Byrd," said Hezene now, tossing aside the note from
Ristale. "I wish you to accompany me to the red reception room. I
have to see something there."

Byrd froze. The emperor *never* went to the Red Room. *Never.*
Was he onto Byrd's schemes? Did he intend to arrest someone, one
of the Circle agents whose job it was to pose as an ordinary aristo-
crat and leave messages for Byrd in the Object Language?

All Byrd's worst fears came tumbling into his mind; but he
showed no sign of agitation. He merely flew ahead of the emperor
as his servants carried him through the palace to the perfect room.

"Wait here," the emperor said, stalling Byrd at the door so that
he was obliged to perch on a section of geometrically patterned
lattice in the hall. "I won't be long. Delyl?"

Byrd looked on in horror as his sixteenth daughter was invited
in with the emperor, and the door was shut.

He's going to murder my offspring, Byrd thought in a panic. *What
shall I do? My supply of Fortitude is gone. I have no more Serenity. I'm
done for!*

After only a few minutes, the emperor and Delyl emerged
together, Delyl looking composed and perfectly unharmed.

"Come with me, Byrd," Hezene said before Byrd could peek into
the door. "We have audiences for the rest of the evening. Some
trade matters from those annoying shipping magnates, the Tulu
brothers."

Byrd saw the attendant lock the door again behind them. He

was busy in Hezene's throne room until three in the morning—Hezene loved having appointments with people he disliked at inconvenient times, especially since he seldom slept himself and didn't care about being awake in the small hours. When Byrd was finally dismissed, he flew directly to the Red Room. The party had broken up and the room was a mess. He looked carefully for any sign of a message, but there was no rhyme or reason to the displacement of objects.

Then he saw it, a gesture so blatant it made him shiver with shock: on the mirror scribed in red rouge, the words *yes here*.

YES HERE? THOUGHT Byrd for the rest of that morning and most of the following day. Here, the reception room? But with whom? And why the open words on the mirror?

This was dangerous.

He had left a message calling for an emergency meeting, in order to warn those agents in most danger of apprehension to protect themselves; and also to ask Zene to cool things off for a while. After that meeting, it was Byrd's full intention to leave Jundun by any means necessary, even if it meant simply flying out the window and never coming back. But now Hezene had been in the room. Had he ruined Byrd's message deliberately? But if so, why the reply *yes here*?

He spent all day changing his mind about whether or not to go to the basement chamber. It could be a trap. It probably was a trap. And yet . . . how could Hezene know? All these years, he had never suspected. No one but Byrd knew the Object Language. He had tried to teach it to Chee when they were both very young, but she had been too dim-witted to understand, bless her.

It rankled Byrd all day and into the evening. Should he go to the secret chamber and hope that the message had gotten through to all the Circle? He couldn't leave the Circle hanging about in the tunnels; that, too, was dangerous. But how would he warn them? The Red Room was his only chance. Maybe, just maybe, the regular check made by the other birds who were allowed entrance would allow them to get a message to Zene in time to stop tonight's meeting, at least until he could find out what was wrong. He would have to go back to the Red Room and try to leave a message.

Hezene made it almost too easy.

"You are released from your duties for this evening, Byrd," he said kindly. "You are looking tired, you know. Get some rest, why don't you?"

Byrd started to go into the subbasement to see if anyone had arrived, and then at the last minute decided to alter the Red Room, just in case something had changed. Since the early morning, the room had been restored to perfect condition. Strangely, there was food and drink laid out as if for another party. No party had been planned for tonight. At least, not one that had been organized by Byrd.

Byrd gazed longingly at the open window. There was the chala; there was the sky. Inside him, something said, *Go! Go now! Quick, before it's too late!*

He stayed. The entrance bells were ringing; someone of note was coming.

Zene, you are truly crazed, Byrd thought to himself. He would tell Zene that it was over, leave her to do as she would with the Circle—and then he would fly out that window and be free. He took a deep breath and let it out. Then he flew out of the Red Room and landed on the grille in the hall, where it was difficult to see him because his markings blended with the patterning. He would see who was arriving, then proceed immediately to the cellars to tell any members of the Circle who turned up to leave at once.

A whole troupe of other guests were filing in, dressed outrageously. They wore masks and fancy dress as if for an Autumn Festival party. Aristocracy; scholars; entertainers. Animal handlers.

Byrd went cold. The animal handlers were familiar to him. Ras the monkey was there, and Jess the snake. Their humans were Speakers for them; but no one outside the Circle could know that. What were the Circle doing here? *Byrd had summoned them to the secret room.* No member of the Circle would be stupid enough to get that wrong. Besides, no one ever violated the rule that the Circle met only in the secret place. Certainly, one or another aristocratic member of the Circle would be seen in the palace openly; Se had been a regular attendant of the Red Room parties, and even Zene had turned up here a time or two with her husband, when it was her turn to ferry messages to the rest. But to see all of them here at once was inconceivable. Byrd felt as though the world were ending. His blood dropped to his feet, making him feel dizzy and weak.

Byrd doubted that these guests would recognize each other in costume; but the sight of the animals must have tipped off some of them, because he saw nervous glances being cast over shoulders. But it was too late. Byrd observed with a sinking feeling that imperial guards were closing in behind the retinue, making it impossible for the trapped personages of the Circle to change their minds and beat a hasty retreat. Soon they were all in the Red Room. The guards made to shut the doors, and Byrd hastily shot in before he could be locked out.

There was another Speaker already in the room. His own daughter Delyl sat on the mantel, and when the doors were closed, she began singing the welcome song. As she did so, she flew about the room altering objects in an intelligent pattern.

The message: *Hezene Welcomes the Circle. Death Comes.*

Suddenly the room was full of perfumes and musks. Fans were snapped and waved; eyes were averted behind masks; lumpy cloaks that hid deformities were rearranged. They were caught.

A small, cloaked man dropped his hood, and as one, the occupants of the room fell on their faces. Too late, Byrd recognized the emperor of Pharice, Lord of the Wings, Winds, and Wands of Power, Master of the Clock and Sands, and Keeper of the Perfect Feather.

"Good evening," said Hezene.

THE STOPPING OF THE CLOCKS

Byrd trembled uncontrollably. Hezene had found him out. Byrd would be murdered; he and all the key players of the Circle. How had the emperor discovered the secret of the Object Language?

He was given no time to speculate. The emperor wished to Speak, and even in circumstances as bizarre as these, it was Byrd's duty to form his words for him. Byrd snuggled up to the emperor's mind with a feeling of growing horror.

"I am delighted to see you all," Spoke Byrd for Hezene. "Thank you for taking time from your busy schedules to come here."

No one spoke or looked up. They ranged across the floors in degrees of prostration that varied according to size, flexibility, and rank. All of them, Byrd observed with some relief, appeared at least superficially human. Perhaps it would not come to a body search. Perhaps not all his secrets would be spilt.

"It is clear," Byrd Spoke for the emperor, "that a certain faction, which shall not be given the grace of a name, has taken its privileges for granted. I am delighted to see you all here, because now I know who you are." Byrd recited their names one by one, with the emperor studying their reactions intently. He finished in a purring drawl, ". . . and Zene, wife of my minister of transport— does Olaz know what you have been up to in your spare time, Zene?"

Byrd was stunned that the emperor even knew who Zene was. She had been, at most, a minor if vocal member of the Circle during the forty-three years of Byrd's Speakerhood; it was only in these most recent months since the timeserpent's invasion of Everien that she had risen to prominence. He considered her prophetic mind and her spooky ability to stay ahead of every situation, and wondered how she could have been stupid enough to be led here, now.

Maybe the powers of the worms were limited, after all. He could not say he would be sorry to see the last of Zene. She had been a thorn in his side, and after the episode with Grietar he had come to think of her as a real threat to his position in the Circle. For, although the very nature of the Circle was meant to be nonhierarchical, all members being equal, it was more the case that the Circle was formed by the constant stretching of its boundaries by various members opposing one another, pulling in different directions. Zene had begun to pull harder than anybody else, and Byrd didn't like that.

Now she regarded Hezene from her knees, her face shielded by the omnipresent hood, her hands clasped thin and tense before her bosom. Byrd looked at her subjugation with pleasure.

"What am I going to do with you, Zene?" Byrd said, giving sound to Hezene's words. "I have given it much thought, but I cannot decide. I could ask you to betray the identity of your informant, here within these walls."

Hezene's eyes stayed fixed on Byrd as Byrd Spoke these last words. Byrd revealed nothing. He had been practicing for this moment for many years; in a way, it was a wonder he had carried off his charade as long as he had. Strangely, though he had never laughed in his life and wouldn't know how, he felt the urge to laugh now. His comb stiffened slightly.

"But there would be no point in that," Hezene continued through Byrd, who was amazed as he uttered the rest of the sentence. "As I already know who has betrayed me."

Byrd experienced the difficult-to-suppress urge to take off and fly out the open window. There were plenty of other Speakers in the palace. Byrd had sons, daughters, grandsons, great-granddaughters . . . any of them could serve the emperor's needs.

Yet Byrd stayed. He could not break the habit of remaining by Hezene's side. Even now, with his own doom before him. He stayed.

"I could have you all interrogated. But that takes such a long time, and I am in such a very bad mood about all of this. I think it would be more prudent to make an example of you all. Thrace?"

One of the guards who had been standing by the door stepped forward. Thrace was the head of the palace police, a Pharician-born cross between a lion tamer and a warrior princess captured

316

from Min. He resembled a small but hostile elephant. He carried his chosen weapon, a half-man-high trident, as though it were nothing more formidable than a dessert fork.

"Thrace," said Byrd in the imperial Voice, "take off their heads. Never mind the blood. It matches the room anyway."

Thrace handed his trident to one of his underlings, who was even bigger, and received in turn a double-bladed ax, which he handled lightly and with total ease. Byrd knew these men well; they would kill anyone as easily as swatting a fly, and return to their dice games. To them, killing was like scratching an itch.

"Which one first?" he asked calmly. Zene was staring fixedly at Hezene, saying nothing; but the other Circle members had begun to collapse or run away in panic. Thrace's security forces soon restrained them and dragged them together into an unsightly heap in the center of the room. Overhead, the chandelier spun, scattering scented blossoms on the room's occupants.

Thrace descended on the mound of prisoners. In a grisly scene that Byrd, long inured to palace atrocities, would never forget, the guards pulled one prisoner from the tangle at a time. Limbs and tails were chopped off, deformities and enhancements revealed as, one by one, the Circle were murdered. Finally, the only one left was Zene, waiting to one side like a bystander, not a participant. When Thrace came to her, she pushed toward the emperor. Byrd saw her eyes swell out of her head as she stared at Hezene.

Hezene looked at Byrd, and Byrd at his emperor, so that neither of them saw the slice of the ax. But blood flew over both of them. Blood . . . and other things.

The emperor Hezene let out an anguished cry and fell back, clawing at his eyes. Byrd took flight, aiming for the window; but one of the security guards was pulling it closed. Byrd circled the chandelier and came to rest on the mantelpiece.

"The worms!" he screamed, as the emperor screamed the same thing. For those brief moments, they both Spoke with the same voice, and though the worms were not invading Byrd physically, his telepathic connection with the emperor meant that he could hear them burrowing deep, deep, into the mind of the Protector of the World and Harbinger of Plenty and Chief of Every Star, Hezene.

"Leave us!" screamed Byrd. "Leave us! Go at once and violate not our Sacred Silence!"

He whistled the complicated sequence that was to summon the emperor's bodily attendants. He flew about the heads of the guards until they fled and closed the door, swearing acknowledgments of their orders: empty the palace except for the most intimate attendants and one physician. Shut down the gates. Freeze the time of the empire and let nothing be done until the emperor's word is given.

No such order had ever been given in Pharice. The stopping of the clocks was unheard-of. Even an emperor so great as Hezene had never tested his control to such a degree, that everything should stop on his command.

Byrd didn't care about that. He gave the order, and promptly forgot it. He himself was hardly still. He shot from one side of the room to the other, sympathetic needles of agony going through his body.

Hezene roared and cried, and dark fluids poured from his nose and eyes and ears, but there was nothing Byrd could do. Nothing. When the attendants came, he bade them convey the emperor to his private apartments; by then, the entire palace had been rapidly emptied. There was a mass of people standing outside, looking up at the walls and windows. Byrd went to the window of the emperor's private chamber and looked out. Even the chala was still. The byrdfolk were still. The trading-bells of the marketplace were silent. No one moved in the streets. A wave of silence passed from the palace outward, until all of Jundun was frozen, and there was no movement at all, not even a ripple.

A couple of wild pigeons flew by, unaware of the insult they gave.

A small, starved part of Byrd's heart went with them.

The night was well advanced before the physician would speak to Byrd.

"I have never seen a case like this. There are jungle parasites in Tynes that can invade the humors, but not like this. His Ineffableness appears to have survived the infestation initially, but whether He will have the use of His faculties, whether He will even wake, is uncertain."

Byrd thanked him, dismissed him, and summoned Thrace.

"Let him speak to no one. We wish him to be dead before he leaves the palace," he said. "Then come back and stand outside Our Door."

After the sedatives had taken effect, Byrd ceased to hear Hezene's thoughts, which was a great blessing. It was also an ominous sign. Byrd kept a vigil over the emperor and made plans for what he would do if Hezene died. Deny the death, he decided. In fact, the sooner things got back to normal, the better. He decided to unfreeze the city at dawn.

Business went on, with speculation fluttering around the palace as thick as the dove's wings of the many curious messenger birds that had been sent from far and wide to inquire as to what extraordinary event had transpired. Byrd had general notices put out. He even arranged for a public apology to be read from him, Byrd, to the empire at large, expressing regret for his small, involuntary part in some intrigues of the Circle, "who are, fortunately, disbanded and dismembered, literally. If the emperor in His Wisdom can Forgive his humble Byrd, then the emperor's Speaker Now and Forever would only ask that the people of the empire do the same."

Whether or not they forgave Byrd, he was not to know; but as he had sole control over the emperor's comings and goings, people were forced to deal with him. Besides, things had a way of returning to the status quo given half a chance. Jundun functioned according to deeply ingrained habits. Byrd merely exploited those, and kept true knowledge of the emperor's condition a secret.

After a week, Hezene woke up, looked at Byrd through terrible eyes like an infinite honeycomb, and spoke. With his true voice, he spoke one sentence, and died.

"To fly to Everien is my desire."

BYRD FLEW PELL-MELL through the labyrinth of the palace, out across the chala, and finally to the Scholars Hall. Doryn and his cohorts worked on the upper level toward the back, where they were engaged in a project to domesticate the Island Sailsnake. Tethered sailsnakes blew in the breeze like giant kites; Byrd had always felt sorry for them, the elusive and friendly creatures, and now he felt especially sad. They were never meant, Byrd thought, to be beasts of burden. Then again, he was never "meant" to have a large brain and to Speak . . . was he?

Byrd wasted no time on pleasantries.

"Doryn, I require your best trained sailsnakes and suitable flying accommodation!" cried Byrd, shedding nervous feathers.

"Flying accommodation? You mean, for people?"

"Yes, of course."

"That is not our usual—"

"Shut up and see that it is done. The best gear you have to fly a sailsnake, and the fastest animals you can find."

"Er . . . in order to take size and weight into account, may I ask, the best gear for whom, Your Seven-Windedness?" answered the Scholar.

"For Me!" Byrd shrieked in the imperial Tone. "For Your Emperor, nitwit!"

Doryn began to shake and stutter.

"Ah, this is a m-most precip-pitous t-test, Your Scintillation! I c-c-cannot be sure they are ready to c-carry such p-precious c-c-c-c-cargo."

"Never mind that. Just get on with it."

"Er . . . wh-where to, Your Prominence?"

"Everien," answered Byrd. "And hurry."

UNDER DIFFERENT CIRCUMSTANCES, Byrd would have put out a message to Lor, to find an agent to dispose of the emperor's body in some creative way. But there was no more Circle, and Lor was dead, and Byrd's own children had fled the palace and were doubtlessly spreading slanders about Byrd everywhere they went. Fortunately, they only suspected a small segment of the truth. They had no idea what had happened to Hezene.

Still, Byrd was not totally alone. He knew every intrigue that went on in the palace and beyond, every angle, every opportunity. He could find helpers; and this time, they would not be half-animal helpers, like the Circle. They would be dumb humans, and Byrd would rule them. And it did not matter one whit to Byrd whether anybody ever knew his secret.

He would know. He would know that the Pharician Empire was his, all his. And he would do as he liked with it. It would be his toy.

The body was still warm and soft. It was not difficult, with the aid of Hezene's personal servants, to mount him on the flexible sailsnake and present the appearance that he was alive. Doryn might have been suspicious, but he was too protective of his funding to look very closely at Hezene, on whom one was not supposed to cast eyes directly, anyway, except during special ceremonies. The manner in which the emperor was to be strapped in was conducive, too, to the situation: for a sailsnake's rider lay across its back, distributing weight more evenly and creating a streamlined silhouette to best move through the air.

"You are going to fly very fast, my emperor," Byrd said to the dead man. He accompanied the sailsnake to the top of the highest tower in Jundun, and made the public announcement from there: the emperor was going on a vision quest, and until he returned, all his powers were passed to his Speaker, who could Speak His Will even when he himself was at a great distance.

Byrd knew it wouldn't work for long—but so what? It would be an interesting game.

He went to his gold-grilled window and watched the colorful sailsnakes carry away the emperor of Pharice. His game had been ruined and he was lucky to be alive. His emperor had died. The Circle was destroyed, and all his reason for being in power among the Circle was flying away on an easterly breeze. Inside his fragile, hollow-boned body, he steeled himself, for it was time to destroy his own sandcastle, to kick it apart with as much violence as he could muster.

The empire must not be allowed to run along under its own steam. The underlings of the empire must not discover he had lost control.

He would have to keep up the pretense that Hezene was still alive, and use Hezene's authority to make a ruin of the empire as swiftly as possible.

Yes, that was what he would do.

He, Byrd, would administer Pharice. How hard could it be?

The first rule would be to establish Force. Force; Control; Dominate. The small bird jumped up and down on his perch in an effort to convince himself he was capable of such direct action.

He had bribed Doryn generously. He had ritually murdered the emperor's no-longer-needed attendants. There was only one more thing to do, and it was a small one. With an effort, he mustered his imperial Voice. He placed his beak into the bell end of the summoning horn and Spoke the emperor's Words.

"Bring Thrace and his junior security officers to the throne room. See that they are blindfolded. I will Speak to them in one hour on the Aranokian clock."

He would let Thrace kill the juniors. Then he would blow a poisoned dart into Thrace's throat. He had one that he had been keeping for just such an occasion as this.

TAKE YOUR DIAMOND TIARA AND
YOUR BIRD AND GO!

"Duor!" Liaku cried, throwing stones down from her Watch on the cliffs to alert him. "Duor, we got big trouble from north!"

She put down the spyglass for a minute, looking around her land with a practiced eye. There were the storehouses that men had built for her treasures. There were the outer fortifications, slender fences made of a glowing Everien wire that electrocuted anyone who touched them. There were the barges on the river, guarded by zealous Pharicians she had stolen from Illyra, for she could feed them on cheese and wine from the cellars of lost Jai Khalar, but Illyra could offer only game and oats. There were the scorch marks on the earth where she had fired missiles at enemies, and there were the many roads leading to the Triangle that the Clans had carved in their efforts to get assistance in combating the monsters that plagued them from the timeserpent seams.

Liaku's little domain was a country of prosperity, activity, excitement. A place where fortunes were made and broken. And Liaku presided over it all.

Only now, as it came from the north, she was about to meet her doom.

It was not that Liaku was pessimistic or hysterical. It was not that she underestimated her resources. It was not that she lacked courage. It was only that the evidence of her senses was very frightening indeed. For, just a few miles to the north where the timeserpent seam passed nearest to the site of former Jai Khalar, there was a great host of men coming. Liaku knew that they could not enter this section of Everien by natural means; no one had been through that timeserpent boundary, and though there had been monsters leaking through the punctures, the host of riders and foot soldiers she saw now were not monsters. They were armed like Wolves and arrayed like Pharicians, their number was very large indeed, and, most alarming of all, they seemed to be riding down from out of the sky itself.

"Duor!" Liaku screamed this time, and finally he responded. "Duor, we got to run! He finally come! Must be Hezene . . . or . . . or . . . or something, I don't know. Duor, get Tol and pack my diamond tiara and some meat. We go *now!*"

Duor, being slightly more cool-headed than his young byrdgirl associate, was duly alarmed but did not show it so openly.

"Shh!" he admonished her when she began to shriek and jump up and down. "People will see you. We must be calm, and they will keep their confidence in us. Otherwise, we don't stand a chance."

"But, Duor," Liaku wailed, moderating her voice as best she could. "They gonna *slay* us. They feed the birds with our guts, I know it. . . ."

"Wait," Duor said. "I agree there are a lot of them. But we have a lot of weaponry, and Illyra is more or less on our side."

"Less," Liaku said.

"We can withstand a siege for a long time. I know something about this. I was in a siege once, when I was just a kid."

"You kid *now*," she interrupted.

"Liaku, you want to go? Take your diamond tiara and your bird and *go*. I'll stay and fight them. Me and Thuun are the only ones who understand the weapons configuration, anyway."

Liaku hesitated. She was unwilling to give up her power. Duor did not seem as afraid as he should be.

"What you gonna do without me?"

He shrugged. "We'll manage. We have Wakhe."

"Wakhe only alive because of *me*," Liaku said. She poked him in the ribs, hard. "What you gonna do? You not scared at all. What you up to, Duor?"

"Didn't you ever think," he said with a gleam in his eye, "that even a great army such as that one might like to engage in a little *trade?*"

I MIGHT AS WELL HAVE A
HANDLE IN MY BACK

After the Magician left me, I slid through the seam effort-lessly. Without the bone to hamper me and suspend me in the Liminal, I moved easily into this new time. I emerged on the same road, only the mud had dried and the riverside track was caked and cracking. The river itself was lower, and there were algae in the backwashes. The mountains were golden green and full of but-terflies. The sun was strong and the air had a quality about it at once hard and sweet, like rock candy. I shouldered the bag that Taretel had given me and broke into a run. I knew that the Pharicians would not be able to follow me immediately—and if Taretel was speaking truly, the skyfalcon was siding with me and would not give its bone to Tash, anyway—but I did not feel secure, all the same, and my blood was full of nervous fire.

I jogged downhill, quickly breaking into a sweat. My hair was always in the way, and soon I stopped to tie it back and pull it off my neck. When I began to run again, it toppled back to where it had been.

My arm was no longer hurting, but I had needle-sharp pains behind my eyes that came and went every few hours. I had to force myself to eat. I was quite hopeless, on my own. Jihan would have laughed himself sick to see me struggle. But I didn't care. Soon I had passed through the bottleneck in the mountains and was looking out across Everien.

Taretel's injunction filled my mind. I didn't want to stop and rest, or even to think beyond what was necessary to keep going. I was so full of fear of what Tash would do to me if he came through the barrier and found me that I simply acted in the only way I knew how. The going was all downhill, and the track was surpris-ingly good. As I hurried along, I took in the details of the valley that was now spread out along my right-hand side, with the white cliffs mounting to my left.

The fields in the vicinity of Jai Khalar were mud-black, the ground so thoroughly trampled and ruined that nothing could grow there. I saw the tiny specks of white that must be sails on the river, but over toward the Fire Houses there was nothing but a haze of black smoke. I looked up, but I could see no sign of the skyfalcon. I could see many burned patches in the earth; places where the divisions between fields had been dismantled and their stones moved to make cairns and primitive forts. There were the shells of houses and barns; but there were also tents and herds, so it was not the case that civilization had been wiped out in Everien. I saw the tracks of enormous creatures crossing the earth, and once I glimpsed a fish the size of a whale turning over in the river, flashing silver as its pointed snout punctured the air like a needle; then it was gone.

But the object on which my eye was compelled to fix was something completely incongruous in this chaotic environment: a large mass of armed men, moving in disciplined rows and led by cavalry. They were still some distance away, coming down the river from the direction of Wolf Country. These were the ones I had seen from the Liminal, but I had not told Tash about them. I wondered whether he would have considered them friends or foes; probably foes, I thought. Something told me that these men were new to Everien. They could not possibly maintain such formations for long, in a country divided by timeserpent and rampaged by monsters.

Better to avoid them until I knew more, I thought. But if I actively hid from them by taking shelter in a forest or a ruin, then the skyfalcon might not be able to spot me. And it seemed to me that I had to throw in my lot with the Magician. He was a violent one, but I'd liked his words to me. *Don't let anyone use you.*

Everyone uses me, I thought. *I might as well have a handle sticking out of my back.*

I would put my trust in the Magician, and stay in the open country. But I decided to go down by the river, where I might have a better chance of running into some Clansmen or even travelers on the road. I set off across the fields, trudging wearily most of the time, dizzy and faint. I ate and drank, and I was able to push myself onward with the promise of sitting with my feet in the water when

I reached the river; for it had turned warm, and the heavy cloak set me to sweating beneath its fur. By the time I reached the water, I was exhausted. As the sun dropped into a crack between the peaks, I sat slumped on a rotting log, dangling my lower legs into the river and feeling too tired to care very much if the worst possible mutant octopus should suddenly reach out and drag me in.

"Damn this poison," I muttered, and inside my head the time-serpent song sang back at me. "And damn that song. Damn you all to the rotting muck of the darkest forest."

I shuddered as I said that, for I had reminded myself of those blind times riding Midnight Blue, and the creatures that had leered at us from the darkness. Whatever unpleasantness might be happening to me, I was surely better off here than there. I sighed and closed my eyes as the liquid sun poured mellow rays over the river, the insects, the mud, and me.

I startled awake to the rumble of hoofbeats. The army was approaching! I scrambled off the log and into the shelter of the embankment, peering over tall grass and reeds to try to see how far away they were. There were scrub trees growing here and there along the bank, and I knew I would have plenty of hiding places, if I wanted. I didn't expect them to have much interest in me, apparently a lone peasant presenting no threat; but Chyko had taught me caution. I was wary of rape, and I secreted myself within the confines of a small weeping willow, from which I could look out and see the riders without being seen.

I was quite happy in my position until I noticed the dogs. They ran alongside the horses, which were only moving at a slow trot. They sniffed and doubled back and occasionally chased birds or hares, and they often darted off into the brush to check out some scent they'd picked up. I picked up my skirts and climbed the tree. It wasn't large enough to permit me to get very high, but at least I was off the ground. I saw a large short-haired hound with brown-and-white patches pick up my trail, bounding through the grass where I'd descended to the water, and then doubling back to the willow tree. He began barking furiously and the other dogs came to join him. They gathered round the foot of the willow.

"Go away!" I hissed. "I'm not bothering you! Leave me alone!"

They put their paws on the trunk of the tree and barked. They raced in circles. They would not shut up.

Someone from the first group of riders turned aside and began to ride toward me. He was calling the dogs!

"Thank you," I whispered, leaning my face against the smooth bark.

The man was young and dark-skinned, speaking Clan common with a thick Pharician accent; very strange, I thought. It was like no speech I'd heard. The dogs came away, and the man said, "Is that a person? We mean no harm. Come out."

I lowered myself and parted the branches of the willow, looking out hesitantly. The cavalry was going past, and this man seemed to be a sort of outrider or scout. Amongst the main group of horses I could see a banner showing . . . of all things . . . the Eye, the Sun, and the Rose.

I felt a bit bolder.

"Don't mind me," I said in the same language, showing myself a bit more, and the man raised a hand and turned his horse away, beginning to ride back to the others with the dogs making a small brown-and-black sea around him.

"Hoy!" cried a new voice. I saw that a rider who had been beside the banner was now cantering toward us on a horse that was not acting very happy to be ridden; in fact, her eyes rolled and she frothed, and the red-haired man who was riding her seemed to be having trouble controlling her.

"Stop her, Tia," said the red-haired man. He turned and called over his shoulder, waving. "King Pallo! Wait! There's someone I know here!"

I began to back away.

"No, no," I demurred, waving my hands negatively. "I was just resting by the river. I don't want any trouble, please, just let me go my way. . . ."

But the whole train was now coming to a halt. The king was now coming over, to judge by his horse and the fact that a banner-bearer came with him. He was young, and he didn't seem the least bit put out that his progress had been halted for such a trivial reason.

"What is it, Grietar?" he asked, glancing from me to the red-haired man.

"I have been sensing her all day," Grietar said. "The Golden Ones know her, King Pallo, and I am certain that our paths have crossed for a reason."

I continued to back away, but other riders had come around

behind me and I was cut off from the river. I stood wringing my hands.

"There's some mistake, I'm sure," I said. How had they gotten my signs for their banner? And how had the red-haired man picked me out? He dismounted and came over to me.

"I have certain instincts, you see," he said for the king's benefit. "I am sure I know this girl."

He walked right up to me; I tried to get away, but I tripped over a tussock and fell. I was completely out of sorts.

"She is hurt!" Grietar added. "Poison. We must see if we can do something for her."

"That's funny," said the young king in a puzzled tone, taking off his helmet and rubbing his blond hair. "I swear I've seen her before, too. I'm trying to remember where and when."

The red-haired man ignored him.

"It is all right, Jaya," he said softly, bending over me and helping me to my feet. "You won't be harmed. I know who you are."

That was the second time in as many days that someone had claimed to know who I am. All in all, it made one of us. I stood, trying not to shake.

"I'm Grietar," he added, clasping my hands warmly. I looked in his eyes, expecting them to be blue like Jihan's, but they were like quicksilver. They seemed to swirl and move within themselves. I looked away, fearful of being hypnotized.

"Is she Pharician?" the king called out, dismounting and throwing his reins to a graybeard who rode beside him. I saw the graybeard catch the reins absently, without removing his probing gaze from me. He was Pharician: I could see it both from his features and the way he looked at me. It was the way all Pharicians looked at women, both acquisitively and dismissively at the same time. I hesitated, wondering whether I should continue to speak Common as they did. Grietar was still bending over me on the pretense of helping me. He whispered, "Don't worry! I'll protect you."

Then he turned to the king, and said, "She is not Pharician, King Pallo. She is Everien."

Pallo stopped in his tracks, narrowed his eyes, and looked at me.

"What Clan?" he said sharply, and I saw his hand go to his belt. "Be careful, Grietar, she could be Sekk."

"She is not Sekk," Grietar said with an impatient snort. "King

Pallo, you are much luckier than that. This girl is *Everien* Everien."

Pallo blinked and continued to fire a hostile gaze at me.

"What do you mean, Grietar? Don't riddle me."

"She's Everien. The last of her people. The sole survivor. King Pallo, may I present Jaya Paradox."

I WAS IMPRESSED. Up until now, only the timeserpent had used my proper name.

The whole army was called to a halt and I was allowed to sit and rest for the better part of an hour, although it could not entirely be called rest as I was expected to account for myself to the king. Two deniax were summoned to chaperone me, and I was fed and questioned simultaneously. His questions ranged from the innocent ("Doesn't Tash know what problems he's already caused with his Fire Weapons?") to the irrelevant ("But why didn't Dario use a longer-acting sleeping draught?") to the almost-clairvoyant ("That's a snow-lion cloak, isn't it? Have you seen Istar?"). I did not always answer truthfully. I had not yet made up my mind whether I wanted to go with these people, although my weakened condition gave me little choice. It was not merely the debilitating effects of the poison that hampered my progress. By now, my feet were a ruin of blisters.

"Give her a horse," King Pallo said. "I will be eager to see what they can make of her when we get to Jai Khalar. And it lightens my heart to know that Tash is no longer in power."

There was a subtle inflection in his last sentence that caught in my ear. It wasn't anything I could put my finger on, but in that moment I flashed the realization that somehow Pallo had guessed that I'd offered to help Tash. He did not trust me.

I looked at him to see if I was right, and he held my gaze. No, he did not trust me.

I liked him for that. I did not trust me, either.

RETRIBUTION
IS AT HAND

𝒲e did not travel much farther that night, which came as a relief to me because in truth I was in no condition to be traveling at all. A very tough-looking, scar-faced Wolf woman called Brevel came to look at my arm, and she asked me about my symptoms.

"How long since the arrow struck you?" she asked, setting down her battle-ax and rummaging in her medicine bag.

"I have not counted the days," I said, "but it cannot have been more than a month."

"A month?" She stared at me in shock.

"What is it?" I said.

"You should have been dead in a matter of hours. This arm . . ." She trailed off, biting her lip, and said nothing after that. I had the sense that she was sparing me the truth.

"I will do what I can for you," she said. "But I am not a Wasp, and I have not the proper antidote. I don't even know if it can be obtained at this time of year, and we are not in Wasp Country now, but Deer Country, and the Deer are useless at medicine."

She looked into my eyes, peeling back the lids and humming to herself assessingly. I remembered poignantly my encounter with Mistel, and plucking up my courage, I said to this Wolf, "Forgive me, but I have a question about the Wolf people. It seems an intrusive question, but I promise you I am asking it respectfully and because I genuinely need to know."

She snorted through her nose and sat back on her heels, looking at me.

"Ask," she grunted.

"When a person of the Wolf Clan dies, do they have to be buried a certain way?"

"Why do you want to know this? Have you killed someone?"

Her eyes pierced me.

"I met a Wolf Grandmother," I said. "She told me she would exchange lives with me, but she said she needed to be buried under an open sky. And I wanted to know what that meant."

"Exchange lives with you, eh? Is that how you explain surviving the poison?"

I shook my head. "No! If anything, it has gotten worse since this happened."

"Huh." It was an indeterminate grunt. I waited. "Well, I don't know about exchanging lives. I don't think even a Grandmother has that power, although I guess the whole point of being a Grandmother is that people don't know what powers you have, they aren't obvious. But as for our burial practices, they are secret."

"I thought so," I said glumly. "I only wondered if there was anything I could have done."

The Wolf's manner softened. "I know you are afraid, child," she said. "No one can speak of what comes after, for no one really knows." She took a deep breath and then, rather in a rush, she said, "Her body must be dispersed in the forest, and shared by all creatures, either directly or indirectly. And the wind must blow over it for seven days, to free her spirit. That much I will tell you. We do not put people in the ground."

She must have seen the light of hope in my eyes, because she patted my hand before standing up.

"Exchange of lives or not, you had better rest," she said. "If it comforts you to believe it, then believe it."

As she walked away, I realized it was not so much what she had said, but what she hadn't said, that scared me. She hadn't told me I was going to die; but she had acted as if I were already dead. And she had spoken to me, a total stranger, of her Clan's death practices. She must believe I was not long for the world.

I WAS LEFT strictly alone the next day, allowed to ride on a quiet pony that had formerly carried only baggage, and attended occasionally by Brevel. But that night, the red-haired man summoned me to his fire, where he sat alone. There was a tension about Grietar, visible in the sinews of his neck and wrists, and in the swiftness of his disturbing silver eyes. He stood when I approached, then returned to his seat across the campfire.

"It's all right, Jaya," he said softly. "We can See you."

I started to move away, but his hand shot out and touched my wrist, and for a moment I was caught in that moving, silvery gaze.

"Don't be afraid. The monsters frighten you because of your human instincts; but they are not your enemies. Listen well, for you are a living part of a great story, and where it goes next depends on your actions."

His accent was no longer Seahawk, I noticed. It was High Pharician. Grietar's facial expressions and gestures had changed, also. In fact, I had the sense that another person entirely was speaking.

"Your makers are the same Everiens who played with Fire. Ah, do not look at me sidelong; in a world of symbols, a word may make all the difference, and my use of the expression is more than a play on words. Fire is the creative element, and though in Everien we see it symbolized in the Fire of Glass, it stands for its abstract cousin. Perhaps you have seen *that* spilling out of the Liminal."

"I have crossed the fires of the Liminal," I said shortly. I did not like his tone of assumed superiority.

"The Everiens used their Knowledge of patterns to capture the essences of animals, to mix and remix them. They made, as you would say, monsters."

"Why?" I said. "What did they make them for?"

"Curiosity. The burning desire for Knowledge. Because they could."

He made those qualities sound damning. I remembered my own "experiments" and thought, defensively, that there was nothing wrong with curiosity!

"And then," Grietar continued, "they made you. To guard the monsters and keep them from escaping the Liminal and attacking people."

"Aha! So they didn't like the monsters."

"By definition, no, they didn't like the monsters. They used the codes to create many wondrous things, and many terrible things. They needed you to keep the terrible things they built from devouring them. You and the monsters were buried deep in a theoretical time and place, and there you were to stay."

"You keep saying 'were,' " I said. "What about *now?*"

"It is only 'were' because you and the monsters were banished to the past, to Everien's past. Everien has not yet come to pass. None of the events that will result in your creation have occurred yet."

"Then how can I be here?" I laughed. "And how do you know this story?"

"I see the past and the future," Grietar said. "I have worms in my eyes that have their origin in the timeserpent. I can transcend time. And I know that in the far future of Everien, monsters will wreak havoc. There will be machines built to control the monsters, and there will be a great war. But in the course of this war, humanity will be wiped out. Except for you. By keeping you out of the way in a backwater of time, the Everiens hoped to protect something of their own world by seeding their past with the Knowledge. The Knowledge was encapsulated, Guarded, within the Sekk. The Sekk were never to have been human. They were abstract, rational beings. They had no human drives, no human or animal feelings, which is why they trigger the irrational in those they attempt to instruct, or sing to. They were too pure to be tolerated by living humans, but they were to have instructed you, when the time came. For you could understand their song."

"Me? What's it got to do with me?"

I asked the question with an air of innocent confusion. I didn't want to be drawn into this story. I wanted no part of it, no complicity, yet I sensed something of what he was about to say.

"The Everiens created you out of Knowledge. They made you to be a Guardian. *But you didn't guard the monsters, Jaya.* You set them free."

He paused and leaned back a little. Shadows stretched and knelt in the planes of his face. He said, "Now we must ask ourselves why you did that."

I sat there stony-faced. Whose tale was this, anyway? Everyone had a different version. Each person I met gave me a different accounting for myself, for the state of affairs in which I was embroiled. What if none of them were true? What if they were all true? *Where was the truth?*

I could almost hear the sibilant laughter of the timeserpent. I blocked the thought.

"I did not 'set them free,' " I answered defensively, thinking of my moonlit experiments. "They invaded my place and drove me away."

"The Company of Quintar invaded your place," Grietar corrected. "Virtually at your invitation, I might add; but it was not your fault. For you should ask yourself this: who started the chain of events that would lead to abstractions such as the Fire and the Water entering Everien's past at all?"

"I don't know," I answered.

"Eteltar, of course. Eteltar with his timeserpent codes. He was tricked by the timeserpent into changing its codes."

"Tricked? How?"

"The timeserpent absorbed *your* codes, Jaya. It used them to become more humanlike, to think like a human—which is ironic considering that you were anything but human, in those days. It used your codes and your humanness to communicate with the Snake Clan, and they in turn gave the timeserpent codes to the Circle to decipher. And we have done wonders with them. Although they are not fully understood by our Scholars, from them we have gotten the worms that you see in my eyes, and other powers of penetrative thought. We permeate every part of Pharician culture. We control everything, even the emperor."

"Then you should be in good temper toward Eteltar," I said. "And moreover, you ought not to need me."

"Eteltar is a curious figure in all of this. He opened the White Road that enabled Ysse and Tarquin to raid your home and steal from you. And he made it possible for you to slip into Everien, as Night. And, of course, he has cured the timeserpent, at least in theory. For it only remains for the timeserpent to consume its own cure, and it will be free to reproduce."

"Why would you want multiple timeserpents?" I asked, alarmed. "Isn't one of them bad enough?"

"*We* wouldn't want multiple timeserpents," Grietar said gently. "But once we hold the cure, we will have power over the creature. We can direct it. We can travel through it. We can wield it, like any weapon or tool."

I was paralyzed for a moment. I was only now beginning to grasp the scope of the Circle's ambition.

"Tarquin, of course," said Grietar casually, "has been something of an innocent victim in all of this. You will admit that you preyed on him, won't you, Jaya?"

"I did not free the monsters."

"But you did! You worked Knowledge that you did not understand. A book, a cloak, a lamp! What were these things to you? You knew nothing of the songs they were made of, the codes that comprised them . . . or the consequences of using them, even in a ritual way. But . . ." Here his tone softened. "I am not here to accuse. As it happens, the monsters were cruelly wronged by the Everiens. They were accidents, mistakes, and acts of deliberate grotesquerie. They were imagination gone wild, and the Everiens tried to hide them away, just as they tried to banish the timeserpent and trap it in the past by giving it your conscience to hold it there. But it is never wise to ignore the darker side, is it, Jaya?"

"No," I said in a small voice. I knew he was speaking of Night, my own shadow. The thought of Night gave me strength. I was powerful. There was more of me than was obvious to the eye. I didn't have to take this lying down.

Grietar was saying, "It was good of you to set the abominations free. For now the Circle can close, and the monsters that were banished can assume control. Retribution is at hand."

"I intend to revoke the timeserpent," I announced. "If you think I'm going to help you with your retribution, you are sadly mistaken."

"Jaya, Jaya . . ." Grietar was shaking his head slowly as if marveling at my naïveté. "Even if you had the Knowledge to revoke a timeserpent, you would not do it."

"Yes, I would," I said stubbornly. "And I will!"

"Are you so self-sacrificing as that?"

"What do you mean, self-sacrificing?"

"Will you return to being just a code, a page in a book?"

"What do you mean?" I said again.

He pulled out my father's book from his clothing. "Read it and weep," he said, extending it toward me; but before I could catch hold of it, he pulled it back. "Or maybe not."

I was really afraid now.

"You like being real, don't you, Jaya? Don't want to spend the rest of eternity as a bodiless code, falling forever through the Liminal, getting mixed and matched with who-knows-what, do you?"

I didn't answer.

"You see, I'm your father, Jaya. I made you. I built you. And I can dismantle you." He opened the book, flipped through the pages, and tore one out as punctuation to each word. "Anytime . . . I . . . want."

Grietar flipped the pages to the outline of a human being. The codes had filled themselves in since I'd last seen the book. The human was almost complete.

I gulped. "Is that . . . me?"

"Indeed, my daughter, it is you. And if you want to live, you will assist me. I have use for your talents."

Grietar was scary, I don't deny it. But I had heard this line before, and it didn't impress me very much. I decided to play along, but in the meanwhile to watch Grietar very carefully, to try to discern how much, if any, of what he said could really be true.

I QUESTIONED BREVEL carefully about Grietar, King Pallo, and the army's mission in Everien. She was straightforward and blunt in her replies, and although she was not privy to all information, she occasionally slept with one of Pallo's senior officers, and their pillow talk was not all of love. I learned about the Ripping and the time differential, and how Pallo was much older than he looked. And I learned about the skyfalcon.

I saw the skyfalcon, too, and I hoped desperately that he saw me: I made a point of always wearing the snow-lion cloak, even when it was hot, so that the Magician would always know where to find me. The skyfalcon came down to Grietar, but it was not friendly to him. Brevel told me that the skyfalcon had brought Grietar the bone that had enabled him to make a passage across the Ripping, and that Grietar was able to summon the skyfalcon using an Artifact that appeared to be no more than a playing card, but was very powerful.

It was not long, before King Pallo had his first run-in with Illyra's men. Illyra had ridden to meet us from Jai Khalar—or what was left of it—and King Pallo spent a long time talking to the messenger that Illyra sent. Soon word came back that Pallo had offered Illyra an alliance, but that Illyra would have to make peace with the Clans. Illyra sent back another messenger to report his laughter at this: peace with the Clans was accepted as given, for the Clans were helpless without the assistance of Illyra and his magic powers. King Pallo might have a great army, but he would soon learn to respect Tash's rule.

Where was Tash? Pallo sent back, and got a reply inviting him to a parley. Pallo chuckled and winked at me. He knew that Tash had been left in a bad position in the mountains, although I had not revealed my suspicion that Taretel had killed Tash.

The two leaders met in the middle of a field. Even from my position well back in the lines, I could see that the two men had utterly different body language. Illyra moved like a dominant male. Every gesture pressed downward, or drove the other man back. He towered over the slender Pallo.

Pallo, on the other hand, slipped around Illyra and occasionally gesticulated wildly as he made his points. Once I saw him jumping up and down in place. Once he threw up his hands and sat on the ground. As this went on, Illyra's manner became less and less certain. By the end of the conversation, the warlord looked decidedly hesitant.

King Pallo came back. "We are going to work together," he announced triumphantly. "Illyra clearly sees that he needs help. I have promised to defer to Tash as soon as Tash returns."

Dheri responded darkly to this—at least, this is what Brevel told me he had told her, late that very night.

"Tash was a legend in his youth," he told Pallo. "He knows all there is to know about horse warfare, and when he came here he had a huge army from Hezene."

"And well I know it," Pallo said. "But Illyra has admitted, indirectly of course, that most of those men have either been killed or have deserted and gone to live with the Clans, who seem better able to cope with the monsters than Illyra's formations can. He still has a sizable force, but I don't think he has much stomach for a big fight. Our men are fresh."

"Still," Dheri warned, "Illyra is not a man to put at your back. He may seem thick, but he is vicious."

"We will go to Jai Khalar," Pallo said. "I am eager for news of my old friends, and to see what has become of the place since I left, so many years ago."

Meanwhile, as I learned from Dheri by way of Brevel, Pallo was terrified that his age was beginning to catch up with him. Reportedly, he looked at his face in a hand mirror every night, examining it for wrinkles.

LIAKU'S TRIANGLE

Grietar's repeated failures to get any more assistance from the skyfalcon had weakened his position with Pallo and his advisors. They were still in awe of Grietar for the feat he had performed in helping them to cross from their isolation, and the fact that the skyfalcon was such a terrifying creature inclined most of the men to admire Grietar for calling it and enduring its abuse of him when it came. But Grietar had acquired a desperate air.

"You can walk through to the Fire Houses," he said. "It is easy for you. But you will not go without me, and for that we need a bone."

Within a few days it had become general knowledge that the skyfalcon had also befriended Liaku, and that she had a bone whose significance she did not appreciate. I watched with interest as Grietar tried to get the bone from her without divulging what it was for. He threatened her and the skyfalcon made a screaming pass at him; Liaku laughed. She demanded something valuable in trade, but Grietar had nothing. He went to Pallo and begged. Pallo appeared amused by Grietar's groveling; but I had begun to shiver.

"Why do you want this bone so badly, Grietar? Surely our objective was to hold this valley, and we are well on our way to doing that."

"We do not hold the Fire Houses," Grietar replied. "Nor do we even know what transpires there. This bridge can take us there."

Dheri cleared his throat.

"What is it, old friend?" asked the king.

"It would not be wise to seek another territory before we have established ourselves firmly here, I think."

"I agree," said Pallo. "Besides which, I don't want to go to the Fire Houses. I've come from there, and it was not a pretty sight.

Moreover, for all I know I will return to my true age if I set foot in that time frame again. It's not worth the risk; not for me."

"It is worth the risk for me, my lord," Grietar said.

"Yes, but you forget I don't trust you. Ah, Grietar, what would you have me do?"

"Give the girl something so she will give you the bone. What is it you want, girl?"

"Blackness very fond of Everien Artifact," Liaku said brightly. "Give big weapon for that. What you got?"

"Big weapon," said Pallo. "Hmm. I don't know about Artifacts, but here: I'm curious."

He reached into his vest and pulled out a battered and burned leather book.

"What's that?" Grietar said, an acquisitive light in his eyes.

Pallo's answer was both casual and cryptic. "Oh, just some old maps, can't read most of 'em anyway, she burned 'em."

"Don't give those away," Grietar said. "You're the king, you shouldn't be bullied by this creature—"

But Liaku obviously did not trust Grietar and I could see from her reaction that she believed the maps must be valuable if Grietar was so protective of them. Shrilly she interjected, "Give it! King or not, you must give your precious book!" With a shrug to Grietar and a half smile to the girl, Pallo handed over the item.

Liaku gave the book to Wakhe and the drumming began. I heard myself singing from out of the void; it was a very curious sensation, not only hearing my own voice coming from across time, which made my hairs stand up, but also knowing what was being exchanged, and why.

Liaku said something about big weapons and the next thing we knew, a naked sword rolled out of the Blackness.

"Big weapons, indeed," Grietar muttered, looking aggrieved. Pallo handed Liaku the sword. I knew it. It was Tarquin's.

"Very nice," she said. "Who want buy it?"

"I want it," I blurted. "Give me it."

"What you got trade, Red?" Liaku asked, fixing black bird-eyes on me. I smiled.

"King Pallo, that sword should belong to you," Grietar said with an air of outrage. "You gave the book, not Liaku. Or Jaya."

"Let me see the sword," Pallo said. Liaku handed it to him, her eyes gleaming with acquisitive interest.

"Don't worry, larva-man, I give bone for it."

Pallo exclaimed, "This is the sword of Tarquin the Free!" He had gone very pale, and he brought his hand to his face in a gesture of despair. "Is he dead, then? These are bad tidings."

I was shaking all over. I had a giddy feeling of both fear and its release, as I walked over to Wakhe where he sat just outside the protective field of the three-sided structure that housed the Blackness. Grietar made a move to stop me, but Pallo said, "No, let her. She is a curious girl, and I want to see what she does."

I bent down and leaned my head into the protected space.

I could hear the timeserpent, whispering to me; but I shut out the words. Lights began to flash in the Blackness, an organized strobing. I could hear the music.

Sing! I could hear Jihan in my memory, and I opened my mouth and added my voice.

I had learned to sing as Jihan meant me to sing: the timeserpent seam had taught me its language through all those long, inactive days in Tash's train. It was easy now—I could turn code to melody and back again. I listened, listened . . . everything was coming together. I could *see* the symbolic form of the codes, and then one by one all the cards in the deck flashed before my inner eye. If only I had had such powers before, when I was growing up in my house. If only I had understood, maybe I could have controlled the strange nightly events that brought Sekk and monster alike to the walls of my garden, and then let them in to terrorize me. For now I was not guessing my actions. Now, each card had a story, a set of symbols, an emotional contour—a personality. And there, at last, *he* was.

Jihan!

It was all I could do not to cry out in human speech. He was still there, but not in human form.

I am your house. I am your walls and windows to Guard the abominations.

But he was no longer my house. Jai Khalar/Jihan was folded up in the black pit where the timeserpent had gone. Jihan was an equation that no longer balanced. He was a mess.

But he had what I wanted. I could feel and see and taste it indirectly, and if I gave him the codes, he would have to turn over the thing I asked for. Fervently I hoped it would be enough to make Liaku and her skyfalcon firmly committed to my own cause. I leaned in farther. I felt myself split and slip into the symbol country of the Liminal, and all in an instant I was racing through halls and tunnels to the tower, deep in the timeserpent that didn't understand what it had eaten. The Eye Tower was overlaid in a ghostly way with the Way of the Eye in Jai Pendu, and when I took the thing I could feel in memory the time it had first been taken from me, and I had been dragged into the world as Night.

And then, just as easy as thinking a thought, I saw Tarquin in the Liminal. He had no sword, but he was alive. He started to look in my direction, and I hesitated. Did I dare communicate?

"You gotta offer it something." Liaku was tugging the hem of my skirt, pestering me. "Be careful leaning in you head; otherwise, it take *you*."

I shook her off, but it was too late. She had broken my concentration, and I'd lost sight of Tarquin. I kept singing for the thing I wanted, and I ignored Liaku's shocked gasp when I stuck my hand into the Blackness. I felt the thing form within the curve of my fingers. It was heavy and smooth. I drew it out. It was dripping a warm, clear fluid.

"Here," I said to Liaku, and handed her the globe. "This is for you. It's called the Water of Glass."

"It look just like dark Carry Eye!" Liaku squealed. Her clever, heart-shaped face was alight with interest, and she stooped over the globe eagerly. From the Blackness, I heard someone whisper my name, but I did not dare look inside again. I was sure the time-serpent would seek retribution when it discovered what I had done, and the timeserpent always whispered. I shivered and moved away.

"Here, what's this?" Pallo called. "How'd you do that?"

"It's mine to give," I said. "Liaku, it will show you everything that is happening in Everien, if you can learn to link it to the other Eyes."

Grietar stood, arms stiff at his side, fists clenched in a silent fury. I knew I would pay for this later, but I didn't care.

"Get the bone from the byrdgirl," he said to me through clenched teeth. But Liaku had heard him. She smiled, showing all her teeth.

"What you got?" she said to him.

"We can take it by force, you know," Grietar said.

"You will do no such thing," Pallo said. "This bullying a small child does not become you."

Grietar was seething, but he could do nothing with all of Pallo's army around him. He brought his attention to bear on Liaku, who looked in his eyes and did not look away.

"You have book," she said. "I see you looking at. I see you show to Jaya."

"You're not getting it," Grietar said. Liaku shrugged. Grietar looked like he was about to throw a tantrum. He mastered himself, turned away, and I thought the little scene had come to an end; then, suddenly, he turned back.

"Here!" he said, producing a playing card. He held it before Liaku between his thumb and forefinger. "This is a magic card," he said.

Liaku took the card and examined it. "Bird-man," she said. "Hmm. How magic?"

"You can use it," Grietar said in a wheedling tone, "to call your very own skyfalcon."

He neglected to mention, I thought, that he had tried calling the skyfalcon himself several times since we came off the bone into Everien proper. The skyfalcon had come, but instead of giving Grietar gifts, it had dived at his head and beaten him about the shoulders with its wings. I stared at him. Undoubtedly he expected that the bird would do the same to Liaku, and this was his idea of a good joke.

"Liaku," I said softly. "I don't think you should—"

"Shut up!" Grietar snapped at me. Liaku cast him a canny look. She took the card, laughed, and then flipped it back into his face.

"I no need this junk," she said. She put her fingers to her lips and whistled. Down came Quiz, who glared malevolently at Grietar, and took off again.

"See?" Liaku said cheerfully. She passed me the bone with a wink.

"I THINK YOU know where we're going," Grietar said.

"To the Fire Houses," I answered flatly. "But it is a bad idea."

"I'll be the judge of that," he said.

We left the camp in the middle of the night and rode across the bottom of the valley, crossing the river without incident. A-vi-Khalar was on the other side; but we could not see it. A haze of smoke and general darkness obscured what was left of the city and the Fire Houses. Except for Duor and the other Pharicians, who had escaped months ago, there had been no reports from this place. We expected it to be gutted and ruined, and when I took one end of the bone and gave the other to Grietar, I fully expected to experience a bad passage across the Liminal. This, after all, was the source of all the monsters. If they were going to haunt the Liminal anywhere, they should be haunting this very seam.

But the bone formed easily, and I stepped out onto it in an ultra-violet emptiness. I could hear singing, distantly, but it did not over-power my mind or blur my concentration. There was a distinct sulfur smell that seemed to come in sudden bursts out of nowhere: it prickled my nostrils again and again, but I didn't know the source. I felt tense and poised. I wondered what was going to happen, and at the same time, I felt helpless before it.

There are two ways to look at the future. As an absolute truth, or as an expression of one component of a set of possibilities.

If you could know the future—not all of it, say, but if you could have a window into a particular moment in time without seeing how the present will cause it—then it might be that no matter what you do, that future is set. Predetermined, as immutable as your past (but is the past immutable?). Anything that you do, now, merely adds twists to the way by which that future will come to pass.

Or it might be that the future you "see" is only a flash of possibility, and that you can steer a course through a whole ocean of potential futures. Which would mean that Jai Pendu is like a ship, sailing the oceans of possibility.

Either way, it means you're not standing on solid ground. Because if you stop to think about the fact that you can get a window on the future, and interact with its contents, then this surely implies that the future can interact with *you*. Or with your past.

I feel very shaky about this. I have no reason to believe I can be made of flesh and blood, but if Mistel is right, then Dario's arrow *has made me real*. And somewhere in my relative past, we would find I had indeed been conceived somewhere by someone, and that I *do* have a father. Could that father be Grietar? He certainly has the hair for the job.

I don't know if I believe him. I don't know whether he understands the codes he carries in that book, for if he does, why does he need me?

344

But if he doesn't, then how is it he knows so much?

And if Everien has an acausal nature, what does it matter what I do? Like the timeserpent being driven to reproduce, my codes, my human inheritance, drive me to strive toward goals even when I suspect they may be futile.

Or, as Mistel might say: *Oh, shit*.

THE JOURNEY ACROSS the bone was not a long one. All too quickly, I found myself in the warm, still air of a dark hillside. I had emerged just outside an A-vi-Khalar whose walls were breached and rubbled, and whose Fire Houses resembled an exploded volcano.

"Halt!" said a harsh voice in Clan common. "Stop and show your hands."

I willingly did so, and Grietar was compelled to do the same. I smelled our captors before I saw them clearly. They were unwashed, hot, and afraid. They made us lie on our faces while they checked us for weapons. Torches were lit during this process. I looked across the dusty ground to Grietar, who smiled reassuringly. *Great*, I thought.

The men were Clan, a mixture of Wolf, Bear, Seahawk, and possibly one Wasp. The Wolves were predominant. One of them unbuckled my sword and looked at the scabbard by torchlight.

"Xiriel!" he cried excitedly. "Come and look at this! Tarquin's sword!"

IN A SYMBOL COUNTRY

𝒲ith a sense of fatalistic irony, Tarquin half expected to find himself in Jaya's arms. She had always been associated with Night before, after all—and only Jaya knew what he had said to her, there in the mouth of the Li'ah'vah. But he was very much alone. He could feel his own fragile, human presence, and deep within him he could feel Ice curled up like a sea horse, an unborn thing, mute and powerless in this place.

If it was a place.

There was no more earth, only a symmetry of buildings. Surfaces were level and smooth, or slanting and smooth, or curved and smooth; but none of them looked natural. The buildings were conjoined to form one building that went on as far as the eye could see, forming a long, deep cleft that lay in complex terraces. Windows, clouded like eyes on the verge of death, reflected an expressionless sky. There were no birds that he could see. This anglescape was prowled by exoskeletal creations of metal and smoothstone, creatures that moved but did not live, made sounds but did not breathe.

He had glimpsed shadows of these things before, during those times when Ice had rushed him through the Liminal, and once in the fog and snow of Chyko's ice world, where he had had the unsettling impression that beasts of metal and fire were doing war with one another, indifferent to man and animal alike. Now that he could look at them clearly, these machines frightened him, as did the fact that there was nothing green or growing anywhere to be seen. Even the sky was dead. Studded among the buildings were lights of the same kind he had seen in the passageway of the Beast, but they were empty lights, without feeling, so that he would have preferred darkness.

The machines showed no interest in him. Tarquin was sitting on an empty plinth in the middle of a group of these lifeless beings, as if he were some sort of art object. The metal creatures moved around and past him in almost-total silence. There was no grinding or scraping of metal on metal or metal on stone, and there was no heat coming off them as there would be off animals. The only sound Tarquin could detect was a very faint, eerie singing like the voices of Sekk. It seemed to be coming from the ground itself. When he looked more closely at the smoothstone beneath him, its opacity disintegrated into a mass of moving symbols. He blinked, fighting back nausea, and disciplined his gaze to an unfocused acceptance of the things he saw. They were not real, he knew that now. They were only figments of the Liminal, imaginary creations from somewhere beyond the concrete world; but it would be better for his sanity if he let himself perceive them as real.

He stood up, coughed, and spat, just to remind himself that he could. Then he pissed on a clean wall. Blue symbols came out and spilled on the stone.

He struggled to orient himself. The domain of straight lines and dead architecture seemed to go on forever. Was this still Everien? If it was, the rough parts of the mountain had been smoothed. There were no trees. Every bit of Everien had been constructed into a city with the straight logic and right angles of convenience, relieved occasionally by a soaring, perfect curve or arch.

Too perfect, Tarquin thought.

Down in the center of the pit that Everien had become was a glint of water. Finding his way to it was like negotiating yet another maze. He made his way down thousands of stairs and miles of ramps, but he never got tired. As he went lower, the sky got darker, but there was no sun. He came to the oval pool that he recognized from the times when Mhani had guided him in the Liminal. He could see the gate that once had led him to the garden: it had been wrenched off its hinges and there was nothing beyond it but a featureless gray wall. He turned his eyes from the painful image and he could see, looming off to his left, the rising forms of the Fire Houses, glowing faintly, recognizable even in this unfamiliar context.

The sky was dark blue, but there was plenty of light. He felt he was underground; or in an Everien house, maybe, like the ones in A-vi-Sirinn that the Deer Clan had altered to make them more natural.

He made his way among the pillars to the edge of the pool. Once, he had met Mhani here, projecting herself into the Liminal even as she worked beside the Water of Glass in the Eye Tower. And if the Fire Houses were to his left . . . why, then, he must be facing north and this *was* Everien, simply unrecognizable. Transformed. He glanced over his shoulder to where the sea gates should be and saw a cluster of towers with a sliver of light between them: the outside world peeping in on dark Everien.

He turned back to the elliptical pool and he could see something more, like a ghostly etching in the dim air. There were outlines of three doors, insubstantial and faint, but perfectly familiar to Tarquin. Everything in Jai Pendu had been unforgettable. It was the place of Three Doors.

From the triangle between these doors came soft sounds. When he went closer, he could hear a girl's voice. He listened eagerly, and his heart sank. She was not Jaya, but an even younger girl, and her Pharician accent was thick and rather grating on his Clan-trained ears.

"Give it! King or not, you must give your precious book."

Was she talking to him?

"I am not a king, and I have no book to give," Tarquin said. Even as he spoke, a soft singing seemed to swirl from the darkness.

"Ask it what it seek, Wakhe," said the girl, and with her voice there was a rat-tat-tat of high-pitched echoes, and then a series of echoing *booms* as a drummer went to work within some invisible depth.

Tarquin hesitated. There was a pool of shadow between the three doors, and after a moment it resolved in his senses to become a hole. He heard the clicking and hissing of the timeserpent, but he couldn't see anything but darkness. He cleared his throat and spoke.

"I seek the codes of Eteltar's River." The singing echoed him again; then the drumming resumed. Through the sound of it, the girl said, "Weapons. We require weapons, of the most deadly kind."

Tarquin unbelted his sword with a cavalier attitude.

"It means nothing to me," he said, and tossed it into the hole. He didn't expect anything of moment to happen, and he was surprised when, an instant later, a leather-bound book came spinning out as though floating on air.

Tarquin caught the book before it could drift away. He opened it, and in the dim light he saw page after page of meticulously drawn and labeled maps.

"*Ah,*" he said. "The Fire Houses."

And he began to flip pages until he found A-vi-Khalar.

TARQUIN HAD BEEN standing mesmerized by the book for several minutes before he was cognizant of the fact that voices and rhythms were continuing to issue from the place of Three Doors. His concentration was only broken when he heard Jaya singing.

He dropped the book. Straining his eyes, he tried to see into the ghostly place of Three Doors. The Way of the Eye opened, and Night glided through the door. It passed into Tarquin's reality like living oil. It glided across the water of the elliptical pool and reached in. Still Jaya sang.

Tarquin's heart was beating wildly. He couldn't move or speak as Night slipped its white hand into the water and pulled out a shining thing. The thing was a code. With all his might, Tarquin concentrated his effort on descrying what the code might symbolize, but he could make out nothing beyond a complex Everien symbol character before Night's cloak dropped over the thing and then Night itself slipped through the door once again.

Jaya stopped singing.

He heard her say, "Here. This is for you. It's called the Water of Glass."

Was she talking to him? Could she see him? But she was giving the Water of Glass to someone else . . .

"Jaya?" he whispered. He would have shouted it, but he was still afraid of Night. From the darkness, other voices drowned out his voice, and he backed away from the triangle, confused.

He felt unreal in this place. Now that he looked at things more closely, everything seemed to be breaking down into its composite symbols. It was as if all appearances were illusion. Everything was just a dance of code, and it was a code he couldn't begin to decipher. He held the book of maps, but what if the book turned out to be more real than his own hands that held it?

He was fairly sure he could find his way through A-vi-Khalar to Eteltar's lab with the aid of the book; but he had lost Ice when he'd let the machines drive him through the gates into the maze, and then Night had brought him here. Night was starting to seem like an ally, which was an unnerving proposition. Where was Ice? How could Ice find him? How could he leave this place and become real again, a man-horse of flesh and blood and hunger and sleep?

In a symbol country, there must be a symbol for a way out.

A door? He walked in a circle around the place of Three Doors, but it was unreal, untouchable. He bent and touched the water, but it was still.

At length, he circled around the pool to the ruined gate. He tried to pass his hand through the wall of grayness that blocked the entrance to the garden, but his hand turned into code when it passed inside and he jerked it away, unnerved.

However, crawling through the wrenched bars of the gate was a single tendril of some kind of plant, at the end of which was a green and living leaf, three-lobed like the leaf of a tree, but in a rather strange shape.

The tree leaves.

He stared at it. The shape of the leaf reminded him of a bird with its wings spread. He took it between his fingers and bent his head to look at it more closely, and he saw that it was deep.

Very deep.

It was as deep as the mile-high skyfalcon, and when he looked inside he saw a forest, and two horses running as one; and one of those horses was his home.

His awareness shot into the leaf, and he was gone.

ONLY A SHADOW

𝒥ce 𝔀as 𝓻unning from the skyfalcon. No other predator could keep pace with him—except, perhaps, the timeserpent itself—and Ice was not accustomed to being driven in this way. Every step he had ever taken had been a step of free will. Now he was no better than any other herd animal, being hemmed in and controlled by a bird that had its own command of the White Road.

He ran between shards of crystal and under bones. Beside him ran his shadow; and then his shadow drew closer. It was the stallion Midnight Blue, that he had fought with, in the garden. Ice had not come out of their first fight well, for the bow of the Wasp had threatened him and he had been forced to change to Kere rather than risk being poisoned. The two stallions hated and feared each other; but now Midnight Blue, too, was fleeing the skyfalcon. Both horses tried to avoid each other; but the skyfalcon was there to force them together, beating its great wings, threatening with its talons. The forest loomed, and the shadow-horse ran among the trees. The skyfalcon pushed Ice among them, too, so that Ice had to dodge and swerve to avoid their boles. Still the bird pursued the two stallions, streaking through the air with its wings folded, powered by sheer force of will. Terrified, Ice crashed sidelong into Midnight Blue.

Black became white and white became black as the two horses were suddenly one. There was an enormous surge of power and now Ice and his shadow were flashing, pulsating from black to white, an explosion waiting to happen. Ice reared and pawed the air where the skyfalcon had been; but the bird was gone. It had ripped a hole in the Liminal in the shape of its wings, and now symbols poured out. Abstract figures whirled in the air like a swarm of bees. They stung Ice like a thousand needles, clinging to him in a net. The codes bit into him and penetrated his skin, his muscles, his nerves, his bones.

The codes were Tarquin.

Help, cried Tarquin as Ice absorbed him.

Shut up, answered all the other parts of Ice. The horse accelerated, trying to put as much time and distance between himself and the skyfalcon as possible. Midnight Blue drew a little apart, so that the two horses were running in tandem, just as they had always been meant to. And now Ice couldn't remember what he'd been so afraid of.

The black horse was only a shadow, after all.

FIND THE MOUSE
PATTERNS

𝔍ce knew where and when he had to go. The book of maps that Tarquin held was now as much a part of Ice as Tarquin himself. The place in question was A-vi-Khalar, and the time was the period between the departure of Eteltar on his forked flight path into the past and the later banishing of the timeserpent by the Everiens, which was to be so catastrophic as to raise the cliffs of Everien and displace certain Artifacts and buildings in time so that they appeared thousands of years before they could have been built. The pure timeserpent venom with six symbols must be included within this displacement if the young Eteltar was to find it buried beneath A-vi-Khalar. Tarquin's mission—Ice's mission—was to make sure that Eteltar did.

The logic of this ought to mean that Ice could do as he liked, and fate would place the venom where it needed to be; after all, Eteltar was known not only to have used the six-symboled venom, but to have derived from it a seven-symbol cousin, the empty vial of which Tarquin carried even now. Ice ought to be able to relax, secure in the knowledge that all was well.

But the seams of time had been ripped apart, the world was fraying, and fate had never been a thing to be trusted. Causality was not what it seemed. Tarquin had the six-symbol venom, and until it was placed in the correct time and location for Eteltar to find, deep in the past, then the seven-symbol River would not be definable.

And Ice needed all his wits about him to pinpoint the time to which Tarquin needed to go. Especially because this particular period of possible-history was not amenable to the activities of horses of any kind, let alone Horses of Or. Ice was going to have to be very careful. He would have to get Tarquin to the undercity so that he could find the lab, accomplish his task, and get out into the open again, where he could change to Ice and leave that time . . . leave it forever, Ice hoped. For he was about to venture into a time in Everien when animals were being captured right and left, their patterns recorded and altered, their histories ruined, their integrity destroyed.

Until now, Ice had always outrun his enemies. But he had no Guardian (For he had even eluded Eteltar's effort to fix the animal patterns long ago in Or, when he had stolen some of Eteltar's time-serpent River in order to acquire his special carnivorous powers and run faster than time—though no one needed to know about that but Ice!) and if the Everiens caught him, there was no knowing what they would do to him, or to the world, by using the patterns that were within him just as they used every other pattern they could find.

No, it would not be easy. The Everiens, in their frenzy to come to terms with the Li'ah'vah that had crawled out of their Liminal, would be ultrasensitive to time disturbances or displacements of any kind. They would not know the difference between a Horse of Or and a timeserpent; not yet, anyway. Ice would be relying on blind luck to get him in and out safely. As for the part in between, he would be totally dependent on Tarquin's abilities.

For eating somebody was a two-way street, as Ice had good cause to realize.

THE WHITE ROAD and its black underside carried Ice and his shadow to an Everien that neither of them had known before. Ice came to a halt in the middle of a barley field outside A-vi-Khalar. The grain was tall and green, and it whispered against the horse's flanks where he stood trembling, resisting the deep inner urge to run all the way home to Or. He was so frightened that all the splinters of himself threatened to spill at once.

The Fire Houses were humming audibly. Work was being done. Ice shook himself from head to tail, snorting away his anxiety, and Tarquin fell out, sending Ice to sleep in the White Road.

Tarquin stamped on the earth. Bugs jumped. Sweat came up on the back of his neck where the strong summer sun beat down. This was not the symbol country: he could feel it in the way the bottoms of his lungs tightened as he took a deep breath. He could feel it in the itching scab on the side of his head, where the Seahawk's sword had grazed him on the bone bridge.

He reached for his sword and it was not there.

He had the maps. He had the ampule. He began to walk toward the Fire Houses.

The outlines of the mountains were ones he had known all his life: they had been the backdrop of years. He knew those mountains as well as anyone could claim to know them. He had walked and climbed their slopes, fought Sekk monsters in their caves, forded the rivers that flowed from them in summer, and watched their avalanches in winter. He had seen Jai Khalar emerge from its own rocky spine like a dream, flickering and wavering, and then vanish again. These were *his* mountains. This was his Everien.

But outside A-vi-Khalar, there were very old, thick, and twisted trees growing where there had been no trees Tarquin ever knew. The grass was clipped short as though well grazed, yet there were no animal droppings. The buildings that comprised A-vi-Khalar were simple in form, sometimes no more than glassy mounds rising from the grass, so that Tarquin was reminded of the structures he had seen on the Snake Island, where the Snake city seemed to poke up into the jungle like the bubbles of a pearl diver. It was the same thing here, except the domes were bigger and not at all overgrown. They were as smooth and lucent as eyes.

Also there were towers, and other buildings that Tarquin had never known in his own time. The Fire Houses presided over all. He could see figures moving among the buildings and walls, and along the riverbank, where smooth, sailless boats lay like leaves on the water. He crept from bole to bole until he was near to the arch that formed the city's gate. There was no door or barrier that he could see, just an empty arch.

Ridiculous, he thought. How could you defend a city with no gate?

Then he got a closer look at the people, and froze.

They were Sekk. All of them.

Everywhere, Tarquin marveled, even as a shudder of thrilling horror passed through his frame. Everywhere there were Sekk. They had skins of many colors, many of them outside the range of human tones that were known to Tarquin. Some were dark blue, some shaded toward lavender, some were gold, and some were mottled and striped like snakes. They made his hair stand on end; but he couldn't stop looking at them.

They were beautiful in a way that just bordered on human beauty, without being purely human. They seemed . . . better. Faster, more graceful, more uniformly excellent; yet the teacher of warriors in Tarquin noticed the absence of variety in these people. The variety that characterized the Clans had been the source of much range of ability and accomplishment during Tarquin's heyday, when Ysse had been intent on bringing together the different tribes as one nation. Among Tarquin's elite Company there had been heavy men and thin, short, tall, stocky, lithe men—a wide range of physical types, each complementing the other to make up the group. By Tarquin's standards, the Sekk were all slim, and many were actually slight. Their bodies were the sort designed for running long distances, or climbing impossible cliff faces like spiders; they would not be hewers of coal or sprinters. Or fighters, unless they used bows.

For that matter, none carried weapons that he could see.

No gates, no weapons, he thought. *They will try to Enslave me. But this time I am the invader.*

The question was, How was he going to get in there? He was obviously not Sekk. His maps showed him the undercity, but getting into the undercity would be another proposition entirely.

There was one puzzle that had been tickling his memory for a long time, but he didn't know how to decipher it. When, in Jaya's house, he had exposed the Magician card and found himself in the laboratory of young Eteltar as the wizard uncovered the timeserpent venom, Eteltar had spoken of an explosion. His face had been covered with black soot. He had said he could see the White Road behind Tarquin.

True, Eteltar had also admitted to having tasted the timeserpent venom, so maybe he had only experienced a vision; or maybe he had come to the Liminal to meet Tarquin halfway. But if there had been an explosion that had opened a tunnel, then how had that happened?

Or, more importantly, *when* had it happened?

Tarquin knew that there were holes in the earth around the perimeter of A-vi-Khalar. Common perception held them to be old H'ah'vah tunnels, or escape valves for steam from the mysterious underground power sources. Tarquin didn't know whether anyone had ever tried to use those tunnels to get into the undercity, but to judge by the map he held before him, such a tunnel might be his only hope of getting inside if the Sekk were prowling the city itself.

He used the trees as cover to go up the hillside behind the city, where some brush had been allowed to grow. He combed the ground for any sign of a tunnel or cave or fault line, uncomfortably aware as he did so that there were *things* sailing overhead. Not birds, not kites, but things of some other kind that he did not care to identify gliding through the air.

He found two holes. One was too small to admit even a child. The other was a vent for noxious fumes, and it released heat that had scorched the surrounding earth and killed the foliage. He pulled his cloak over his face and squatted at a safe distance from the vent, hoping he could not be seen by those aerial creatures. He was unarmed, doubly vulnerable.

He could see down into the city from where he stood. He couldn't understand what the Sekk were *doing*. There didn't seem to be any physical work going on at all. Sekk walked in and out of buildings in no particular hurry, not carrying anything, seldom even stopping to talk to each other. There were no livestock that Tarquin could see. The occasional noises that drifted up from the buildings made no sense.

He did not like it here. He carried on his cautious search for a tunnel opening. He was operating on a hunch, as if some previously unknown sense was guiding him along this hillside, looking for an opening. He expected to find one. As if he had seen it before, or could infer it had been there, or . . . He paused in his search and scratched his head. *I'm becoming like Kere,* he thought. *Weird, and irrational.*

Then he saw the hole. Roots had grown across it and grass obscured its edges as cleverly as any Wolf-designed pit trap; but this was not a trap. Tarquin lowered his head inside and found that he could see well in the dark. It was a smooth tunnel, sloping downhill toward the city. Its walls were like H'ah'vah tunnel walls.

He didn't know how he knew, but with all the experiences of Ice sewn up inside him, Tarquin *knew* that the timeserpent had made this channel. Or would make it, or might make it . . . *ah, bloody nonsense* . . . it existed—*how to explain?*—it existed *in the conditional.* It was a maybe; but for him, here, now, that was good enough, because he could see it and touch its edges, and when he lowered his legs inside, he could drop down into it.

THE TUNNEL LED him directly to Eteltar's lab. He recognized the place from his first visit; but now it was considerably less dusty, and Eteltar was not there. Lights glowed softly from the symboled tiles, reflecting off polished work surfaces that seemed to Tarquin as clean and perfect as jewels. This must be magic.

He remembered that Eteltar had been on the floor holding a brush and the timeserpent venom container, but he had to assume that the container had originally been stored somewhere. He moved cautiously about the room, looking for a likely rack or cabinet or shelf. He thought it was strange that a huge hole had been blown in the wall but there was no dirt. The tiles were immaculate, many of them bearing perfect likenesses of individual animals worked into their surfaces. Tarquin touched one with a forefinger and it released a musical series of chimes and the tile sprang open like the compartment of a secret box. Inside, several tubes were arrayed together with thin glasslike cards and a spongy ball that looked like a marble but felt soft. There was a circular bracket holding an ampule identical to the one Tarquin carried, but this one was half-full of something pale amber. As the tile came open, there was a whisper of audible music—Sekk-like music, Tarquin thought, and recoiled. He quickly pressed the tile back in place and it went quiet.

"I feel like an elephant at a tea party," he said to no one in particular. The tiles were numerous, none of them had a picture of a timeserpent on it. For that matter, not all of them had pictures. How was he to find the right place?

Then his gaze alighted on the mouse tile.

Find the mouse patterns.

"Of course!" Tarquin laughed. He pressed the mouse tile in the same manner. It opened with a somber, deep melody, and he saw the empty fitting for an ampule.

He stood there for several seconds while the sad music played, trying to work out what had caused which, and how. The fitting would not hold the vial of timeserpent venom; it was too small. He could pour the timeserpent venom into the seven-symbol ampule that he carried and leave it in the mouse tile, but then what would become of the six-symbol vial that he had witnessed Eteltar find? *That Eteltar had tasted, that had caused the explosion that enabled him to be here, that . . . ah, gods, Kere, where are you when I need you?*

He must not switch the contents of the vials, he was sure of this. Things were complicated enough already. Instead, he put the empty ampule with its seven symbols into the mouse bracket and closed the tile. The music ceased.

He still had the original venom. What to do with it? How could he be sure Eteltar would find it? He couldn't just leave it lying about; it might roll on the floor and break.

Tarquin was becoming increasingly agitated. He could feel nervous energy rising inside him like a forest fire threatening to burst out of control. Was this what Kere had always felt like, when he was twitching and jerking? Tarquin found himself making unnecessary movements and thinking too much, repetitively, for no reason. He must be panicking. He tried to steady his breathing, which was short and sharp. His heart fluttered.

"Stop it!" Tarquin hissed at himself. This was no time to curl up in a ball and start frothing. He held the six-symbol vial up to the light, struggling to match its calligraphy with any of the panels on the wall. He was breathing much too fast, and his brain wasn't cooperating. Tarquin had never been able to read beyond the most fundamental pictographs used in Clan warfare, and the Everien symbols were a total mystery to him. Nevertheless, all he had to do was compare. He gritted his teeth and kept looking, but stars swam in front of his eyes. His hand was shaking. In a moment he would drop the vial.

Then his eyes fell on a tile with a picture of a person. The person was only an outline, a collection of plotted points. She was female. Her symbols were not the six symbols, or the seven symbols, but a quite different collection of pictographs. There was no reason for him to focus on this of all tiles.

But the hair, alas, was a giveaway. The rest of the body had not been filled in, but the hair was most emphatically colored red. He held his breath and touched the tile.

There was a whole collection of vials and tubes, and the music that came out was lengthy, complex, and full of whispers that made his hairs stand on end. There was one empty bracket. He slipped the vial into it; it fitted perfectly. He closed the tile.

"This is just blind luck," he said.

Suddenly, a splitting pain hit him between the eyes, and his knees went weak. For a moment he thought he would pass out, and he sagged against the tiled counter. Then, little by little, the episode ended, leaving him spent and shaken, but otherwise all right except for a slow ache in the back of his neck.

He straightened slowly and looked around. Now he was empty-handed. This would not do. He opened the mouse panel, and there was nothing there. No empty ampule. Nothing.

He let out a cry of frustration and confronted the wall of tiles.

"Where did you go?" he seethed. "*When* did you go?"

He began opening tiles at random, so that soon the room was full of weird music and disembodied voices.

"I hate magic!" Tarquin cried. "I hate the Knowledge. Damn this!"

The noise grew so much that he was forced to shut the tiles again. He stood there, hands on his knees, bracing himself stiff-armed with his neck stuck out and his head poking forward, addressing the tiles. He felt sure that in a moment he would charge headlong into the wall and knock himself out if he didn't think of a way through this.

"One more time, Tarquin," he said encouragingly to himself. "*Don't give up.* Sometimes you need deduction, and sometimes you need to be like a headless chicken. Just try something stupid."

There was a Seahawk tile. Superstition, and perhaps memory of the torn Seahawk in the desert, made him reach out and touch it.

A deep roar stunned him, and even as the tile swung open, he turned to see what was happening across the room to make a sound like an enraged ocean booming in an enclosed space.

The passage was gone. There was only a smooth wall where the hole had been.

He looked in the Seahawk cubbyhole. The ampule was there with its seven symbols.

He danced a jig. Then he lifted the ampule out, and opened it. Empty.

Before he had time to react, something white shot out of his peripheral vision, ran down his arm, across his body, and launched itself into the air. He jumped out of his skin, nearly dropping the ampule as he realized the white thing was a mouse. And it wasn't alone. There were white mice running around on the floor. First only a few, but then dozens . . . maybe hundreds! They seemed to be appearing and multiplying before his eyes.

"I have to get out of here," he told himself aloud, trying to step over the mice and leave the room without squashing them. Their squeaks filled the air. The passage he had used to get in was blocked now. "Aaugh," Tarquin moaned, scratching his head. He slid the ampule into an inner pocket of his tunic, and drew out the book of maps. "Looks like we have to do this the hard way."

It took him ten minutes to figure out how to open the door to the room, by which time the mice were knee high; when he did, he found himself on a metal gangway above a pit of unbelievable depth. Fire was visible, far below.

The mice did not follow him. He shut the door, then in a last-minute thought of mercy, left it open a crack so they would not die in there. He checked the map, guessing wildly.

He gulped and turned right. The map showed this area as corridors passing through many levels, but he saw now that it was just a latticework of flimsy iron walkways that crisscrossed above and beneath him. In places there were walls, but in more places, there was only emptiness. The only illumination came from the fire beneath.

Taking his best approximation, Tarquin went for the nearest flight of stairs and began to climb. He had a flash of recognition, as if he had seen this place somewhere before. . . . *Jaya, silhouetted, and everything burning.* . . . The stairs had been like these stairs, he thought. Skeleton stairs, with no stone. He felt nervous and dizzy trying to climb them even though he could look down into the pit below. It was hard to believe these scaffolds could support his weight, they appeared so thin.

His footsteps rang out and echoed. The air stung his nostrils. At the top of the stairs he consulted his map again, then swung left around a corner and suddenly confronted a Sekk.

She was taller than Tarquin. *It,* he corrected himself inwardly. It was female, hairless, wearing no clothing at all but with striped pigmentation on the body that made the Sekk look like an exotic lizard. Like all the Sekk Tarquin had seen, this one had not a trace of extra fat, and the muscles were lean and spare. The Sekk's face was dark green, almost black, as were the palms of its hands. He recoiled instinctively. He turned to run.

From overhead came a flash of light, and simultaneously his skull was struck with a painful shock that sent him jumping back, grabbing for the handrail to prevent himself from falling off the walkway. He put his hand to his head, wincing.

"You cannot pass," the Sekk said to him. He didn't know what language it was speaking, only that he could understand it. Perhaps, like Kere, Tarquin could now speak any language. "You cannot pass. This area has been sealed. This is an event area."

"Well, I'm not bloody staying here," Tarquin retorted, making a show of rubbing his sore head so as to cover up the fact that he had secreted the ampule within his clothes. "Who's in charge here, anyway?"

"You will learn," the Sekk answered with a hint of a smile, and the light flashed again, much brighter this time. He tried to duck, but it was too late.

SEEKING THE RIVER

𝒯𝒽𝑒 𝓇𝑒𝒻𝓊𝑔𝑒𝑒 𝒸𝒶𝓂𝓅 of the Clan rebels was an unexpected cross section of classical Everien weapons, contemporary Pharician adaptations on them, and homemade Clan ingenuity in the form of wooden walls, spiked pits, and round ovens spewing flames from some hidden underground source. Everywhere were fragments of smoothstone; structures of wire that were, unlike Liaku's Triangle, disassembled and dead; and pieces of shattered crystal that still hummed with Knowledge resonances. There were also hides tanning, and wooden casks, and I even saw a spinning wheel propping up the side of a broken tent frame, its fine wood canted into the mud.

Grietar seemed to know a lot about Xiriel, and with cunning words he quickly got the rebel Seer to trust him.

"You are right," Xiriel said in response to one of Grietar's remarks. "I am a man of divided loyalties; but I have done my best. I consider myself fortunate to be alive. And we have had some luck."

"Is that so?" Grietar said with keen interest. He was looking for goodies from the Fire Houses, I thought; but Xiriel's answer was to disappoint him.

"The way the Li'ah'vah broke, we ended up with a fairly neat division of survivors. Most of the Pharicians were on the Jai Khalar side of the rent. Most of the Clan rebels were on the A-vi-Khalar side. After the thing had passed and we began to regroup, the Clans far outnumbered the Pharicians. They were given a choice. They could join us, or go their own way; but they were not allowed to take any of the big weapons with them. All chose to go, even young Duor. Now that we are clear of them, we still have our own problems. The Deer have fled into the hills and will have nothing to do with us, which is a problem because it happens to be the Deer who know the most about the undercity, not to mention the symbols, the Knowledge, and all the rest of it. The Wolves are dominant. We are now totally cut off from Lerien and the rest of the original rebellion that started this whole thing. Our leader used to be Kassien, but on the second day after the timeserpent, Kassien challenged Stavel to a duel. Sword versus ax. Everyone's always made fun of Stavel for sticking with his Clan weapon, but they're not making fun anymore. Now we obey Stavel. He hates the Knowledge, even more so for his guilt in precipitating this whole crisis. So we have retreated totally from the Fire Houses. We have a stockpile of weapons in case Tash comes, but most of our energy goes toward foraging for food and dealing with monsters. Fortunately, there are not many. The ones that crawl up out of the void usually wander around the city, see there is nothing for them, and crawl back in."

He stopped talking. His dark hair was matted and greasy, and there were scars all up and down his hands and forearms.

"I could have been a great Scholar," he said, looking down at his hands. He was picking apart a piece of kindling with dirty fingers. "I don't know where it all went wrong. I just keep hoping that soon someone will come. That the rest of Everien isn't destroyed. I can't tell you how good it is to see your faces, even if you don't bring help, even if you don't understand what's happened here or what we've been going through. It's been almost a fortnight since the disaster, and my nerves are wearing thin."

"A fortnight?" I said sharply, and although Grietar cast me a silencing look, I knew he, too, was surprised at the way time ran here. Suddenly I felt very nervous. What was happening without us, back at Liaku's Triangle, for example?

Grietar leaped up. "We must see the Fire Houses at once," he said. "Our mission is urgent."

Xiriel looked surprised. "But you only just got here. You haven't told us anything about what's happening in the rest of Everien, or Pharice. What about Tash? What about—"

"Now!" cried Grietar, his eyes flaring, and Xiriel leaped back, suddenly wary.

"Do as he says," I murmured. "Grietar can hurt you. He can make things much worse than you know. Just do as he says, please."

Xiriel stared at me. "You're very beautiful," he said. "And familiar. Do I know you?"

"*No,*" I said firmly.

THE FIRE HOUSES stood as wrecked husks, teetering on the edges of the black pit left by the timeserpent when it plunged into A-vi-Sirinn. There was still a perceptible red glow cast by the Fire of Glass; but now the light filtered through the broken walls and onto the streets of the old town, giving what was left of the city a look of danger and menace. Strange noises issued from the black pit, noises that would not have been unlike the singing of my own voice from Jihan's pit, except that they were fainter, and they had been slowed down. Deep and sonorous, the singing discouraged people from approaching what they perceived as the epicenter of the greatest disaster Everien had ever known.

Besides, sometimes monsters crawled out of the hole.

The walls of the Fire Houses were still intact, and when Grietar led me across the rubble to look at what was left, I could see the fire-writing clearly etched in the ropy skin of the house that had given rise to the timeserpent. He was right: there were many symbols and codes written here, no fewer than had been recorded in his book. I picked my way around the corner of a broken wall and, standing on a narrow ledge above the timeserpent's pit, placed my hand on the inner skin of the Fire House. It was dappled, bumpy: the codes must have been impregnated in the very surface of the wall. I knew that it was possible to imbue a substance with mathematical meaning in this way, because Jihan had tried to explain the method to me. The subject, I remembered, had bored me and I'd promptly forgotten most of what he made me learn.

"I expect you to perform wondrous feats," Grietar said. "But first: we must find Eteltar's old experiments, which are said to be hidden deep beneath the city in his laboratory."

I looked around at the condition of A-vi-Khalar and remarked that the undercity could hardly be safe. The ground had collapsed in several places, and there were a number of places where whole sheets of smoothstone were balanced precariously, slanted and threatening to fall.

"If that fool Pallo hadn't gambled away his maps for a sword, we'd know precisely where to go," Grietar said.

"What do you need maps for?" I asked under my breath. "I thought you knew everything."

I was wearing Tarquin's sword. It was too heavy for me; I'd been taught to fight with a rapier, not a longsword, but I wanted to wear it because it connected me somehow to him. I had been aware of him on the other side of the Blackness, trading for the very book of maps that Grietar now missed. I wondered if there was any way he could be aware of me. I wondered if he could be looking for the same experiments as Grietar was.

We must meet again, I thought fiercely. *We always do. Somehow.*

Grietar was pacing around the circumference of the hole.

"The sound equipment is gone," he said. "Disconnected and vanished. But the codes are still here. Jaya!"

I had not been paying attention; now I turned away from the wall and saw that he had a rope and a grappling hook.

"We have to go into the undercity," he said. "Eteltar's experiments are recorded there, and if the laboratory is intact, we can get a sample of what he has made, or at the very least, its code."

"It won't do you any good," I said. "For the codes inscribed on these walls are the old codes. The timeserpent that the crippled one called cannot reproduce."

"I know that. I didn't say I wanted Eteltar's work so that I could call the timeserpent."

"Then what are you going to do?" I asked nervously. "What's this all about?"

"You mean you haven't worked it out yet? And we thought you were so bright. I need those codes, Jaya. The codes for the timeserpent River."

I must have looked disgusted or angry, because he cocked his head and looked at me with pursed lips and a judgmental air. "The Circle are not your enemies, Jaya. I thought you would be higher-minded than to condemn us for our cruel fate. Can't you see that we are victims of Everien every bit as much as you—and maybe more? Can't you see that we, too, are only trying to survive, to find our place in a world that doesn't want us?"

"Find your place?" I asked suspiciously.

"Every other species fits into its world. We are the outcasts. How dare *you* accuse *us* of evil! Evil is what made us without thought for our situation. Evil is what banished and oppressed us."

I sighed. "Very well, I see your point of view. But the timeserpent is my responsibility, and those codes you seek, this River—it is a dangerous thing. It will only cause trouble."

"Better that *we* should find it, who have some capacity to understand it, than that the Clans should have it," Grietar answered.

I had to agree there. Between them, the Clans and the Pharicians were turning Everien into a hellhole with each new discovery.

"Better that we should have it than that the timeserpent itself should chance on it," Grietar continued. "Can you imagine *thousands* of timeserpents?"

"No," I said shortly. "I cannot."

"Anyway, Jaya," he added in a friendly tone, "if we find it, we can destroy it."

"Destroy it?"

"Sure. That way our biggest problem will be one timeserpent."

"I don't believe you," I said. "You won't destroy it. You made a deal with the timeserpent a long time ago. You'll do the same thing now. You give it the River, and it gives you . . . what? Control of the empire?"

"We already have that," Grietar said smugly.

"A passage somewhere? To some point in time where you can have your revenge on the Everiens, maybe?"

"Maybe," said Grietar casually, as if it were of no consequence. "But we might be willing to break our deal with the timeserpent and strike a different bargain, with you, Jaya Paradox."

"Might be willing?" I said.

"Well, it depends on what you decide to do. We still don't have the code, so the whole thing is hypothetical. Lead us to the River codes, and we will be in your debt."

I didn't want the Circle in my debt. But there was something to be said for finding the River, if there was such a thing. In fact, the very idea of such an unusual "antidote" to the timeserpent's own venom filled me with curiosity and a deep intellectual itch to comprehend it. To discover that such a thing might actually exist was a kind of revelation for me. I wanted to know more.

Curiosity has always been my worst vice.

"All you have to do," Grietar said, "is open the seals and help us decipher the symbols. It's really very easy, provided you can read and sing Everien."

"And if I refuse?"

He laced his fingers and stretched his arms out, cracking his joints with obvious pleasure. "The worms multiply in me every day. Soon I will reach saturation point, and they will seek to find new homes. Another warm host for the Golden Ones."

My skin crawled.

"It only takes a few seconds to a minute," he added in saccharine tones. "And as terrible as the pain is, you forget all about it after a while."

"Get away from me," I said.

"Just do as I say, then, Jaya. Now, let us go into the undercity."

THE UNDERCITY OF A-vi-Khalar proved to be much larger than the overcity. We had to climb down through the black pit that Xiriel had called the void, and I was disquieted at the prospect because I could hear singing down there, and I had suspected for some time that Liaku's Triangle was connected to this pit at least on one side, or how were the armaments coming through? What I had not seen among the ruins of the Fire Houses was the agent who had delivered the weapons to Liaku, and I was very much afraid that some unseen killer was going to wait until we were down there, then start working the connection to the hole that was Jai Khalar.

But there was absolutely nothing I could do about it. Grietar was not in the mood to consider alternative plans, and I did not feel strong enough to argue with him. It took all my strength to hang on to the rope as we climbed down in the middle of the night. The undercity lay in a series of levels that sank deeper and deeper into the bedrock. When we reached the level that Grietar decided was right, we began roaming the passageways, most of which were at least dimly lit from within the walls themselves. At one point, Grietar dug a Knowledge-light out of a wall with his knife and carried it with him like a wan torch.

Some sections were blocked by fallen rubble from the timeserpent's passage, some had collapsed centuries ago by the look of them, and some were sealed with doors that could only be opened by the Knowledge. At first I watched Grietar covertly to judge whether or not he could understand the Everien symbols that kept the doors sealed. It soon became apparent that he could not; but he made no secret of it. He turned to me, indicating that I should help him.

I shook my head in refusal. "Those passages were sealed for a reason."

"Oh?" His eyebrows shot up in mock surprise. "And what reason would that be, Jaya?"

I snorted. "As it happens, I don't know. But I wouldn't be stupid enough to go breaking the seals."

"I would," he said happily, and gestured for me to proceed. I shook my head in refusal. He reached out and grabbed me by the throat. I kicked at him and grabbed at his hands to free myself, but he had picked me up off the ground and all my thrashing was to no avail. He pressed me against a wall and kept pushing his hands into my windpipe. I heard myself making choking noises and felt my face go hot. My eyes sparked and luminous colored fish swam under my eyelids. For a while I thought he was going to let me pass out; but he stopped just short, flinging me on the floor where I scrabbled feebly in moss and very ancient dirt.

"Does that make your job a little more clear?" he asked, standing over me, his dagger drawn. "Perhaps, here in the real world, your flesh feels pain when it's bruised, eh, Jaya?"

I was gasping for air. Even Chyko had not hurt me deliberately. I thought about Tarquin's sword but I knew I'd have no chance. I lowered my eyes, both of my hands going to my throat while I gulped air painfully. I wanted to cry but was determined that I should not. Slowly I got to my feet, and with an effort I began to examine the sealing codes.

"I don't know why this was sealed," I said in a whisper. "You must realize that whatever lies beyond is best left undisturbed. It could be anything. Poison gas. A plague. It could be deadly."

"Just open it," he said.

I sang the code that released the seal. What had looked and felt like a rock-solid blockage softened, then melted totally away, liquefying and draining into holes in the floor. I had expected a rush of dead air and pulled Taretel's cloak around to cover my mouth and nose; but the air was clean and warm, and there was a strong current to suggest that something was making it circulate in the passages beyond. Grietar did not wait for me. He strode into the new area, his Knowledge-light held out in front of him.

He broke a lot of spiderwebs, which reassured me because it

meant that whatever had been concealed here, it was probably not a toxic gas or disease, or the spiders and their prey would have been long dead. I had read of the Pharician emperors who had protected their treasures with all kinds of perils, though; traps were by nature creative and tricky, and I was still wary.

Then we entered the room that had Eteltar's name on it. Someone had been there fairly recently; dust had been disturbed, and there were three sets of footprints on the floor. One wall of the room had been blasted out by the timeserpent. I could feel its resonances in the walls. The footprints led away through that hole.

On the walls were set tiles corresponding to every single page of Grietar's books. But the images in the tiles lit up, and moved, and sang. And the codes were laminated over the images, creating a three-dimensional, complex visual effect.

"So this is how he did it . . . ?" Grietar snarled, holding up his Knowledge-light to see some of the darker patterns. "All his notes, his theories, his tests. And the codes themselves, every last thread and fiber of the timeserpent. He was a genius, you know, Eteltar. The only man to see inside time."

He had begun to poke around excitedly, and it didn't take him long to figure out how to open the tiles. He opened the Snake tile and found several vials, but when he looked at the labels, none of them satisfied him. So he moved to the human tile—I flinched—but there was nothing inside it. Then he began opening the tiles one at a time, so that the whole wall was revealed as a storage area of many pigeonholes, each coded by a different creature.

"Hold the light, Jaya," he said irritably. "We are wasting precious time here."

I held the light. Grietar went into animal after animal, searching.

"But it must be here," he muttered, exasperated. "The antidote."

"Antidote?" My ears pricked up, because I was thinking of my own predicament with the Wasp poison.

"Ah, you know what I mean," Grietar answered impatiently. "Not *literally* the antidote, but the cure for the curse of the timeserpent. It must be here."

"What curse?" I said, playing dumb. "What cure?"

"The thing that will repair its code. Make it possible for the timeserpent to mate itself and produce the offspring it so desper-

370

ately craves. Here, he refers to the new code in his notes. Calls it 'the River.' "

River, eh? I thought. Maybe that was how Eteltar had divided himself; he said he'd taken timeserpent venom. But it would take more than timeserpent venom to turn you into another species and let you live three lives in three different realities. It would take much more than that.

"Aha!" cried Grietar, interrupting my thoughts. "Here it is, hidden cannily under 'Mouse' of all things. Good joke, Eteltar! Here is the thing I desire."

He held up a small, teardrop-shaped ampule. He pulled the stopper off and stuck his little finger inside. His face fell; if I hadn't been so frightened, I would have laughed.

"It's empty," he whispered. The muscles of his face trembled as he struggled to control his emotions. I saw a vein beating in his temple, and a tic beside his right eye started to fire off. "Empty."

He stood there breathing deeply, and I prepared for a physical explosion of some kind from him; but he was thinking rapidly. He held the bottle up to the light.

"It doesn't matter," he said at length. "The code is written on the bottle. And you can read the code. We don't need the sample, so long as we are within the Fire Houses."

He grabbed my hand and rushed me out of Eteltar's lab.

ONCE IN THE main body of the Fire House again, Grietar seemed very conscious of the passage of time. He kept looking up at the stars and muttering calculations under his breath. I wondered if he had figured out how to compare the different time frames, and could guess how much time was going by in the adjacent frame. He shoved the empty container at me, pointing to the handwritten label.

"Sing these symbols, Jaya. These seven symbols."

I had no intention of singing anything, but I decided not to let him see it. I said, "What are these symbols? Why should I sing them?"

"Don't be thick," he snapped. "They are the symbols to cure the timeserpent. The River that will repair its code. I don't have the River itself, but if you sing into the Fire Houses, it will come to you. I know you can do it, Jaya. I watched you sing the Water of Glass.

You can turn the code into a reality with your voice."

"But why?" I said. "It's too dangerous. We talked about this, Grietar. You said we could destroy the code."

"Hah! I said maybe, and then only after I have a hold over the timeserpent. Will you call it here? Go on, call it. Because once I have the River, I will hold the key to its existence. It's desperate to reproduce, and it cannot. I could send it where and when I will, with the power that I possess over it."

His megalomania left me breathless. Blood rose in my face. He came toward me, his silver eyes spinning, his head bent forward like a dog stalking a rabbit. "Why don't you sing, my daughter?" He opened the book, smoothing his palms over its transparent pages. "I hold you in my hands."

"But it won't work," I said. "The timeserpent was already called, by the Clans and their rhythm-Scholar. Now it hides in the Liminal. And I happen to know, *Father*, that it is hiding from *me*."

I thought I had him where I wanted him, but I was wrong. He smiled.

"What makes you think it's hiding from you, Jaya?"

"Because it only comes out when I go into the Liminal," I said. "So in that sense, I am already controlling it."

I was bluffing, mostly; but I had to do something. And I did not see what was to be accomplished by my calling a timeserpent that was, in essence, already there.

To be truthful, I didn't want to sing, and fail. My only real power lay in what others believed my power to be. If I was proved incapable, I would no longer have any sway over anyone, and I would soon be killed.

Then I thought of something. A smile spread across my face.

"What if I sing the codes of the cured–timeserpent? What if I sing Eteltar's codes? Then you will have many timeserpents, and no power over any of them!"

He looked nonplussed only for a moment; then he brushed my words aside.

"But you wouldn't do that, Jaya. Because you know that if you did, you would destroy all of Everien, all of its times, forever. The timeserpents would be everywhere. You think a house full of mice is bad? Imagine a house full of timeserpents!"

I felt faint, but I stood my ground. In fact, I went to the edge of the pit and stood out of his reach.

"I won't do it. Try to force me, and I'll jump."

He looked startled and I was pleased at the power I now held—not that I wasn't terrified, as well. I only had the courage to make such a threat because I knew that his next move to coerce me would involve threatening me with the worms in his eyes. He had told me how Zene had infected him, and made it clear that he could do the same to anyone he chose, at any time. It reinforced his power over me. So I knew that I had to make an end to myself before he could get to me with the Golden Ones, as he called them. I stood poised, trembling, hot with fear. Slowly, Grietar smiled. "You do have a suicidal look about you, Jaya. Well. Don't do anything drastic."

Suddenly he turned his back on me and strolled away across the rubble. He laughed again, and the echoes shot up the walls.

"I don't care whether you sing." He tossed his book in the air and spun to face me as he caught it. "Think you're such a treasure, don't you, Jaya? Men killing each other over you, houses folding up and vanishing . . . but no. It's not you I need, not anymore. You're just the bait."

I hadn't expected him to say this, and I was totally caught off guard.

"Bait? For what?"

"For Eteltar, of course," he said casually, in almost a singsong tone. "Or Tarquin. Whoever comes first."

OF MOUSE AND MAN

Tarquin found himself in a terrible place, surrounded by dimly glinting machines and faces that spoke from oval panes of glass.

"He is the wrong one," they said to each other.

He could see them looking at him. He thought he was lying down, but he couldn't be sure. As in a dream, his awareness flashed from one face to the other. Each was framed by a dark oval like a porthole. The faces were larger and flatter than real faces, and as if the features were made only of mist or gauze, under their skin he saw the flashing, luminous symbols of the Everien writing.

They watched him but never touched him. He couldn't feel his body and wondered whether Ice had eaten all of it, or only the soft viscera.

The faces murmured to each other and watched him. He never wondered how he could understand their language, because the words were not like spoken words. They were cold images that trailed in the wake of an uneven music, like voices coming from the vicinity of the faces though their mouths did not move. They were arranged in a semicircle above him, among shadowy mechanical forms, and he felt as dominated and vulnerable as a baby in a cradle. The faces were not human, nor of any animal. He was afraid of them. He did not think they had ever been alive. Night began to seem friendly and approachable by comparison to this lot. Like a family ghost.

A female voice said, "He must have come from uptime. Through the tunnel. Like the other one."

A deep voice said, "This is not the same one. The one who came before had white hair. It was also a male, but bigger, more dangerous."

"This one is dangerous enough," said a shaking voice. "These wanderers must be multiplying. We will not be able to contain them."

"Like a houseful of mice, are the wanderers from the Clans," the female remarked.

Tarquin thought: *All my civilization, a houseful of mice?*

He had a new empathy for mice.

"The mouse patterns are safe," said a man in a bass rumble. "There is no cause for panic."

They talked some more about patterns, and codes, and impressions. Tarquin did not understand what they were saying and could not see what any of it had to do with mice . . . or with him. Then, after a while, the female brought the discussion round to Tarquin again.

"But he is only half-here," she said. "Where is the rest of him?"

Bass answered her. "Something binds him to another time-trail."

"Just like the big one. The one who flew."

"This one is not so erudite as all that, Carmyn," the deep voice told the female in a gently condescending manner. Tarquin did not like the deep voice.

Someone else asked, "What will we do with it?"

"Do not hurt him!" said the female in a worried tone. "He is only an animal. I won't let him be harmed."

The bass voice sighed.

"I mean it, Reben," the woman persisted, her voice rising. "And I am afraid for the other one, the one that disappeared before we could take him up."

"That code is not my problem," Reben said defensively.

"*Our* problem . . ." one of the other voices asserted. "All codes are our problem."

"Watch this one," said the shaking voice. "See what it does, and we may be able to infer what the other is doing. Did anyone see how the split happened?"

"Let's check something," Reben muttered. "Let's get the patterns."

There was a noise of insects in Tarquin's ears, and a light flashed in and out of his eyes several times, vibrating so quickly he thought the world was crumbling to bits. Then silence. His eyes focused again and he saw them exchanging glances with each other from frame to frame.

Several of them spoke at once.

"The winged one."

"He has broken into the patterns."

"Now this one is divided, too."

Another silence.

"Take its patterns and make a copy," said the shaking voice in a bored tone. "We will observe how it interacts with its patterns, and then decide what to do with the original." Then they all disappeared, and the machinery went dark.

TARQUIN LAY FOR some time with only a nominal awareness of the periphery of his body. Drafts of warm, dry air passed across him from time to time. There was no smell of the outdoors, nor of living things, nor of stone. In the light created by their faces and symbols, he had been able to make out that he was lying in a shallow depression within a firm surface that yielded just enough to be comfortable beneath his bones. He knew he was in a cavernous space with regular, tapering walls rising from a base that was slightly elliptical. The room reminded him of something, but his mind was not terribly clear and it seemed too much effort to fish around in his memory and pull out what was familiar about this place. He felt weak, and the fact that it was so dark discouraged him from stirring.

At length, he bullied himself into sitting up. It was stupid to just lie here; sooner or later they would return, and he didn't think their intentions were good. The sounds that had drifted around while they were communicating reminded him too much of Sekk music for his comfort. What if he were in a Sekk lair, somewhere deep beneath the earth? If he surrendered his will to them, he could become as murderous as his own Company that Night had captured.

He slid out of the depression and his boots echoed when he clambered to his feet. His head was pounding as he began to move around. What little light there was was diffuse, without direction. Over his head he thought he could just make out a faint, rhythmic pulsing of a very weak redness. There was a sense of a large, vaulted space above, and the echoes confirmed it; but on his own level, Tarquin was hemmed in by oddly shaped structures carved in

Everien smoothstone, some glimmering with cold light, others dark and still. He did not know what any of it was for and did not want to imagine.

Then he remembered something. He reached into his tunic and felt for the ampule, but it was gone.

So was the book of maps.

He threw back his head and released an anguished cry. The walls cried back in a series of shivering, soulless echoes.

He stumbled around the enclosure until, stepping on a sensitized plate in the floor without knowing it, he inadvertently opened a panel in the wall. The floor hummed softly as the mechanism worked, then light poured in. Shading his eyes, Tarquin staggered out of what he now knew must be a Fire House, and into daylight. There were no buildings immediately around the Fire Houses, although the walls that Tarquin knew so well did encircle the whole of A-vi-Khalar. Instead of buildings, there was green grass, a peaceful, well-groomed hillside.

It suggested nothing of what lay within.

There was a Sekk approaching him. Tarquin was too dazed and disoriented to do anything but watch it approach. There was something familiar about this one.

The Sekk had silver hair and blue-violet eyes. Its skin was smooth and youthful, so fair it might have been bleached, and Tarquin did not believe any blood could flow beneath it. Yet the wide bones of its face were somehow familiar, even the set of its lips and the straightness of its nose. It was certainly male; but bloodless. The look it cast him was not a look of challenge, but of curiosity.

"I have seen you before," Tarquin said. "Twice. Once in a dream, and once in a Monitor Eye. You were talking to Eteltar."

The Sekk took this in. Its face reacted, but Tarquin did not know how to read its expression. After a moment it said, "I have only been created just now, here, from you. If I am going to speak to Eteltar, it hasn't happened yet. Not that anything would surprise me anymore."

The voice startled Tarquin. He had a cousin called Laertar, and the sound of the Sekk's voice reminded him of Laertar's voice, down to the inflection and accent.

"Do you mock me? Why do you speak Seahawk?"

"Because you do," answered the Sekk. Tarquin remembered

that people used to confuse Laertar for Tarquin based on their voices, though they didn't look alike.

"But what's Seahawk got to do with you? You're a Sekk!"

"I am you," said the Sekk in Laertar's voice.

"Get away from me!" Tarquin shouted, lunging at the creature and driving it back. His sudden movement should have startled the Sekk, but although it moved, the thing showed no real fear of Tarquin.

"I am you," said the Sekk again, "but the animal drives have been left out. Fortunately. Look at the state of you."

"I don't need to look," Tarquin snarled. "I can feel what kind of condition I'm in. What do you mean, you are me?"

"Not literally, of course," the Sekk answered. "I have been made from your patterns, though. I am not a human, I'm a projection. But to you I am quite real, and I can function here in Everien because the machines will listen to me. As far as the machines are concerned, I am as good as a substantial thing."

Tarquin suppressed a growl. "Faces in boxes, and now you tell me you are me but aren't me, just a projection—hey, why is your nose so straight?"

"Why is yours so crooked? You keep breaking it."

"Where are the humans, then, eh? Answer me that. I want to talk to a real person."

"There are no humans in Everien," said the Sekk. "Everien is kept in physical isolation from the rest of the world. The monsters are out of control. That is why you see so many mechanical creations. Humans cannot come here."

"If you're not human, what are you?"

"I am a Made creature, born in a Fire House of patterns implanted by my makers. My personality is based on a human stereotype, as are my processes. They made me as an exercise, so as to better understand you. The others here were designed for more specific purposes. Many of them are amalgams, like your Sekk."

"But what happened to the people?"

"They left. Most of them went as soon as the monsters started getting loose, and the rest, well, after the Liminal got too big and gave birth to the timeserpent, they fled. Everien was chosen because of its geographical remoteness. So they watch from a distance."

"You mean, through the Eyes?"

The Sekk did not answer. It tilted his head and regarded him curiously.

"Were those humans I saw, in the flat glasses? They didn't look human."

"Do I look human?" asked the Sekk.

"No," said Tarquin. "Not really."

"I am modeled after humanity precisely."

"Then why don't you look like me, if you're supposed to be me?"

"Because the contemporary form is more effective. You are old and worn, and you have various structural flaws and idiosyncrasies that mar you."

"Thanks!" said Tarquin.

"Besides," the Sekk went on, "there is a rift running down the middle of you, and we could not code for that. I am only an approximation."

"A rift?" Tarquin commented innocently, thinking with satisfaction of Ice and all his inhabitants. "I wonder what that could be."

For all that he was eager to change to Ice and get away from this place, he was intrigued by this Sekk he had seen in visions. And he was even more fixated on the need to get the River back and leave this time with the ampule in his hand.

"Maybe," Tarquin said slowly. "Maybe you can help me. When I was captured, underground, I had some things with me. They were taken away while I was knocked out. What's become of them?"

"They have been destroyed," said the Sekk. "Reduced to their codes, and the patterns stored. It makes for less . . . clutter."

"Clutter?" Tarquin slapped his forehead exasperatedly. "I've gone to a lot of trouble to get that *clutter!* I need my things back!"

The Sekk eyed him. "You will not need those things here."

"Look," Tarquin sneered, grabbing the Sekk physically and squeezing its shoulders between his hands. He was aware that it had been modeled to look very much like him, only younger and fitter . . . it was a strange and disturbing feeling, to touch it. "You aren't my judge. You aren't my ruler, or my parent. You're supposed to be *me*, aren't you?"

The Sekk stared back at him. Tarquin didn't know what it could feel, what anyone could feel, without the benefit of the animal patterns. But he sensed that this act of facing him was having some effect upon it.

"I need those things. You should be on my side. We are the same."

Suddenly, it said, "I cannot get your things back."

Tarquin dropped his eyes and let go. He was going to hit this Sekk in a minute.

"But I can replicate them. Wait here, Tarquin the Free. For I don't think any harm can come of this."

The Sekk went back into the Fire Houses. Tarquin waited, and waited, but soon he grew impatient. He stuck his head in through the open aperture, and he could see the silhouette of the Sekk highlighted against glowing equipment.

One of the bright boxes came to life. A face looked out. Tarquin began to draw back, but when he heard what it said, he stayed.

"You are aiding Tarquin the Free," said the face.

Tarquin's Sekk didn't move. A singing noise came from it.

"It is futile," the face said. "Purely academic at this stage. Tell us your rationale for these actions. Is it something inherent in your personality to disobey us, or do you have a reason?"

"Both," Tarquin said, stepping into the room. The other boxes came alive with faces, all staring at him in what he thought to be a highly grotesque fashion. "Why should I obey you? Why should this . . . set of patterns obey you?"

"We are wiser than you," said one of the faces. "Do not play with what you don't understand."

Tarquin spat. "That is what I think of Everien."

His Sekk turned to look at him.

"That's not true. You would give your life for Everien. Many times you have offered this. I know. I have experienced it. I am your patterns."

"Well, I've changed," Tarquin said. "And Everien is only a word. *This* is not Everien."

"What is it, then?" said the feminine voice in a tone of amused tolerance.

"It is all some kind of magic trick," Tarquin said. "Jaya is the only good thing about Everien! With her garden and her mind-castles, her innocent belief in her father, in the sanctity of his books and his magic. . . . It is *her* Knowledge that made us think Everien was a great and high civilization. But Jaya herself is a trick you

380

played on the timeserpent to make it behave."

"All true," said the dead voice. "She is an excellent trick. She even made the timeserpent believe in her so much that it tossed her into the concrete world."

"The consequences of that," put in the bass voice, "are disturbing. Now she is mortal. She cannot control the timeserpent anymore. If the Circle gets hold of it, we will have a return to the old madness. We will have monsters everywhere in the high country."

"We will have worse," said the dead voice. "We will have nothing, for in a flash the timeserpent can render us as we never were and never will be. It can leave Everien and eat our past, present, and future. It can consume all of our world. That is our fate."

"I don't care about your fate," Tarquin grumbled. "I care about my own."

"They are one and the same," the dead voice replied. "We are your future."

"Then I hope you are eaten," Tarquin said. "It sounds as if you deserve it."

"You shallow bundle of selfish emotions," the female voice accused.

Tarquin snorted. "I am not about to engage in a contest of insults with a glass box." He looked around for a stone to throw, to put out the lights. A strong urge came over him, to dismantle all this metal and sound and light and expose it to the wind and the rain. But he knew that would be impossible, and pointless besides. He climbed over some sort of desk and made for the door that the Sekk had left open.

"I'm leaving," he announced. "And if I see the timeserpent, I'm sending it here *first*."

He staggered across the lawn. The sky looked false. Sekk drifted past him without taking notice of him. *No wonder their lives look so pointless*, he thought. *They aren't alive.*

Then he caught up with himself. Fleet as a youth, the silver-haired Sekk with his patterns came running up behind him, and overtook him. It cradled his knife and his supplies against his body, and it had a red ampule in its too-pale, too-soft hand.

"Thank you," said Tarquin, taking the ampule with a slight bow of gratitude.

"But you cannot leave," the Sekk told him in his own voice. "This place is surrounded by high walls, machines, powers of energy that make being struck by lightning seem like a tickle. You may wander wherever you will; it doesn't matter. They will study you. But you cannot leave."

Tarquin thought about this a second. He opened the bottle, casually, and glanced inside. Liquid gleamed within, and the smell of roses drifted into the air of this remote and lost future. He closed it again, and smiled.

"You cannot leave," said the Sekk again in a warning tone, and he saw that already machines were moving to block him. He laughed.

"Watch me," said Tarquin. He didn't even close his eyes, or take a deep breath, or think. He simply exploded into Ice, and took off.

He was going straight to Jaya, this time, wherever she was. He wouldn't know his destination until he got there; but when he did, he wasn't surprised. He had been there before.

SOMEONE'S CALLING

𝓘star rode and Taretel walked toward Jai Khalar, and they did not make very fast progress, especially because the skyfalcon kept returning to warn them to hide in forests or behind walls or under bridges, as Pharicians swept by on their fast horses, intent on whatever missions Illyra had sent them on. The skyfalcon had also informed them that Jaya was with the new army. By now it had preceded them to Jai Khalar, and if Taretel had a strategy for how to get Jaya away from the people who seemed so fascinated with her, he did not share it with Istar.

He shared one or two other things, though, and they came as revelations to Istar.

"For every bone, there is a bridge. I have been busy flying up and down the land, in and out of time frames, knitting Everien together. For every move the timeserpent makes, I make a countermove, to put together again what it has torn asunder. But I am running out of myself, and the times are now smoothing together again, just little by little, so that one day all Everien will be as one again. But that cannot stop the coming of Jai Pendu."

"Jai Pendu? That's *years* away."

"Not anymore. It is coming soon, and we must get there before Grietar."

"Grietar? What has he got to do with this?"

"Grietar would have liked to have me, last winter," Taretel said. "He nearly did, but I eluded him, and then you came. If Grietar had gotten the bones from the beginning, they would now be in the hands of the Circle in Pharice, and I do not like to think what the art of the Circle might have made of them."

"Grietar is a fool!" Istar said. "He's not to be taken seriously, believe me."

"There you are wrong. Do not underestimate small men like Grietar, Istar. They are the most dangerous of all, for they have nothing within themselves, and so they will do anything in the belief that they can become someone. But there are no such short-cuts, in the Knowledge or in anything else, and such men can wreak havoc on their way to finding out they are nothing and never will be anything."

They were half a day's ride from Jai Khalar and beginning to run across signs of some intimidating armed defenses. The skyfalcon was constantly flying back and forth between the two travelers and Jai Khalar, and sometimes other places that she could not guess at, for he would fly so high, she couldn't even determine his direction. Istar made camp with an air of foreboding, expecting to be attacked at any time. But it was not an attack that disturbed their uneasy slumber. It was the departure of the skyfalcon, for the second time seen flying at night against all his instincts. He had been sleeping in an aspen tree; suddenly he went zooming up out of their camp in a lunatic spiral.

"Someone's calling," Taretel said. "I must go."

"Wait!" She grabbed his arm, tried to make him turn to face her; but the skyfalcon had already launched himself into the air and was flying toward Jai Khalar. "Taretel! Who's calling you? *Wait!*"

His eyes were blank. It was not the man, Taretel, who was leaving her; it was the skyfalcon.

"That's it," Istar said. "I've had enough of this divided-man stuff. Taretel, let's go!"

She used Taretel's momentary stillness to her advantage. She leaped over the fire, tore up the stake holding the horse tethered, seized her pack and her sword, and threw herself bareback on the brown stallion before the tall Seahawk had time to react. She saw Taretel turning toward her with that vacant look on his face.

"Come on!" she said. "Just because you can't talk doesn't mean you're stupid. Let's go! Let's follow him!"

She kicked the horse into a canter, leaving Taretel to run after her in the dark. After she had gotten a little distance from Taretel, she sat back and stopped giving the horse impulsion with her legs. Soon he slowed and she was able to bring him to a halt with her voice and her weight. She checked the sky. The skyfalcon was nowhere to be seen, but she had picked up his direction when he took off, and she was almost certain he was going to Jai Khalar. All roads seemed to lead there. She glanced back. Taretel was running after her, flat out.

"Good," she murmured. She leaned forward and looped the end of the horse's lead rope through the other side of his halter and across the top of his nose to form a hackamore so she could control him better. Then she urged him forward again, making for the road she knew would take her quickest to Jai Khalar.

There was no way Istar and Taretel could hope to catch up with the skyfalcon, for all that he was loath to fly at night; but she and the horse were both fresh and the pale chalk highway was clear before them. As for Taretel, he had always been stronger than any man Istar had ever met, even when his endurance was fueled by no sleep and little food.

By morning they had reached the turning at the gate stream, and Istar was struggling to come to grips with the sight of what had been prosperous, green farmland and was now a trampled mess. On the lawn outside the entrance cavern and along the bottom of the cliffs nearby, a large army was bivouacked. There were temporary wooden walls bristling with strange weapons. There were Pharician warhorses staked out on the grass, grazing with all their battle gear on.

Not far from the entrance cavern, a large group of men were gathered, apparently having a conference. She could not see the leader who presided, for there were too many heads blocking the way. There were also guards posted all around. To the right, not far along the cliffs, was a set of strange-looking fortifications, shining and angular like a cluster of gigantic, flat teeth made of metal. There was considerable activity over there, as well.

She drew her horse to a walk. As usual, Istar had realized the impetuousness of her ways rather too late. She couldn't see the skyfalcon, and she was only operating on a hunch that he was here. She had left her protector behind her. And this place was full of enemies.

At the last minute, she decided to turn around and regroup. Surely the skyfalcon would return, and then he would tell her what should be done. Or answer her questions. She must not make a suicidal rush now, when she didn't even know what was going on there.

But she had lingered too long, looking on her old home. Even as she began to turn her horse's head, a sentry spotted her, and the hue and cry went up. Before long, riders were galloping at her from three different directions.

"Right," Istar said to the horse. "I guess they made up our minds for us."

And she charged.

She made for the central huddle of men, whose backs were to her. She had inferred that whoever was the leader was there, and she had heroic ideas of taking him out before she was caught. Lately it seemed to Istar that she had stood back and watched others fight far too much; she had been passive and accepting for far too long. It felt good to ride headlong into . . . well, into disaster, admittedly, but it felt good.

She dodged around an assailant and ducked a volley of arrows. The group of men conferring had begun to break up and turn around in reaction to the sound of her approach. There were officers in a variety of uniforms, a strange mixture, she noticed parenthetically, of Clans and Pharician. They didn't act threatened right away, only surprised.

Istar charged into the middle of them with her sword drawn and her eyes blazing. If she could have seen herself, she would have shivered at her own resemblance to Chyko. As it was, the Pharician guards pointed their spears at her as one and closed in around her, so that she was totally surrounded.

"I am Istar," she said in the deepest voice she could muster. "I know that Tash is not here because I have seen him dead on the ground before me, so take me to whoever commands you."

The spears gave a collective shiver as though each man were exercising the greatest restraint to stop himself from skewering her. A throaty voice said in Pharician, "You lie. Tash is not dead."

"Who is your leader?" Istar repeated in Clan, tossing her head. The speaker came forward, a tall, gaunt man with complicated facial scars and a golden breastplate. At a nod from him, the others closed in, turning the butts of their spears on Istar to try to push her off her horse while footmen ran forward to grab her bridle. Istar instinctively seized one of the spears as it drove at her kidneys and was dragged off her mount and dumped in the mud. Men surrounded her and picked her up, but her sword was out and she was kicking and swinging it. Someone seized her under the arms from behind and she was considering whether it was worth her life to cut him as the others closed in on her, when there was another command in Pharician by the gaunt man. In the same instant, the man behind her applied pressure to her wrist on a nerve point that brought her such agony she had no choice but to let go of her weapon.

"Fuck!" she spat.

The crowd parted and the gaunt man stood over Istar, who was now being held down by three large soldiers.

"That is Tash's horse you ride," he said in a soft voice, now speaking in Clan common. "Is our prince dead by your hand?"

"Who are you?" Istar said. "Are you the famous Illyra?"

"Make way, you oafs!" said a new voice, and a much more heavyset Pharician with higher rank insignia appeared at the gaunt man's shoulder. "What riffraff have you got here, Vornu?"

The gaunt man said, "It is the Honorary, Istar."

"I am Illyra," said the new man, "and you are stupid. Why do you ride into our midst on Tash's horse?"

Istar was scanning the clouds for the skyfalcon, but there was no sign of him. She was beginning to regret leaving Taretel behind in such a rush.

"Who called the skyfalcon?" she said belligerently. "I wish to have words with him."

Illyra laughed. "It's not a him who calls the skyfalcon, it's a her. And you are in no position to be making demands. I have many torture methods that I have scarcely had time to practice, you know. Answer my question."

"Tash's horse was running free after he was beheaded in Snake Pass and his men were killed. It seemed a good animal, so I took it. I did not kill your prince, but I would have if I could."

Illyra screwed up his face into a mask of ugly contempt.

"You are a proud and arrogant little piece of work, aren't you? Clearly you have no idea what we can do to you, how we can make you suffer. Vornu!"

The gaunt man stiffened.

"Vornu, have her tied up properly. I have plans for her. And someone rub down the horse and feed him. I wouldn't have recognized him as Tash's. He looks like a furry goat."

But Istar had been picked up and carried less than fifty yards toward the base of the cliff, when there was a commotion off to the right and a new group of men broke onto the scene. They were not dressed as Clan, but they weren't Pharician, either. Instead, they wore simple uniforms decorated with fur and feathers.

"There was a Seahawk with a mighty blade making mincemeat of your guards," one of them said calmly to Vornu. He was a gray-beard painted as a Deer, but with Pharician features, in an officer's uniform. Vornu turned with a look of alarm on his face. "Do not worry," the graybeard added. "We have shot him with a Wasp tranquilizer and he is asleep. I have come to see you on another matter. King Pallo understands you have Istar."

Vornu's mouth worked.

"I am Istar!" Istar shrieked. "Who wants to know?"

The graybeard glanced once in her direction, but his expression did not change. He addressed Vornu with a composed air. "You will turn her over to us. King Pallo wishes to see her immediately."

"She is our prisoner," Vornu said heatedly.

"She is *our* ally," replied the graybeard. There was a moment of tense uncertainty; then, to Istar's surprise and great relief, Vornu signaled to his men, and she was summarily dropped on the damp ground. The graybeard gave her a hand up.

"We outnumber them, you see," he said with a smile. "They'd do anything not to fight us."

Istar brushed herself off. "Did you say 'King Pallo'?"

"THEY'RE ALREADY GONE, Istar," Pallo told her. "Grietar and Jaya left last night. I found out this morning. They went toward the Fire Houses, with one of the bones that crosses time. I have sent a guard to stand on our side of the bridge and prevent anyone from crossing. I do not wish to make contact with the Fire Houses until the rest of the valley is under control."

Istar could only blink at him.

"You sound very serious," she said. "Since when have you got such an authoritative attitude?"

"Since I have been stuck being king for forty-odd years."

He explained to her about his country, and she tried to listen, but it was hard to pay attention with so many more pressing matters on her mind. She told him about Taretel and the skyfalcon.

"The skyfalcon turned up just ahead of you. It stopped with Liaku only for a short while. Now it's flown off toward the Fire Houses. Grietar has a card that allows him to call it at will—but it hates him, Istar. All animals do."

"Call it?" she said sharply. "I don't like the sound of that."

Pallo nodded. "It is all more supernatural than I can take, and I thought I was used to such things. Liaku's Triangle has been acting weirder than weird, but I don't know what to make of any of it. I haven't even got my maps anymore, and more fool I."

Istar took in his words without understanding their meaning. "Grietar and Jaya? It's not a nice thought, Pallo. I don't like it. Why are they going to the Fire Houses, now of all times? And why is he taking Jaya there?"

"More like, why did *she* take *him*," Pallo corrected. "I observed them together. It was he who needed her, and not the other way around."

"If she turns out to be evil, I will kill her," Istar said. "Poor Taretel. If one feather of that skyfalcon . . ."

"Istar, you must calm down."

"I have no intention of calming down, and you know it!" she flared. Pallo suddenly erupted with laughter.

"I've missed you, Istar," he said, wiping his eyes. "All right, what do you want me to do?"

"Just give me a fast horse, and one for Taretel. You will have to be careful with him, and forgive him if he has killed anyone. He can't help it, and he can't speak. He's part skyfalcon."

"Ah," said Pallo, raising one eyebrow. "Naturally."

Istar was gripped with a sense of urgency that would not let go, even though Pallo kept encouraging her to relax and "let things develop." There was something about the way the skyfalcon had gone. It had not been natural. It had been . . . under compulsion. And to find that Grietar could summon the bird they called Quiz with the simple flashing of a magical card . . . was more than Istar could bear. She waited for Taretel to wake up for half a day. She went with Pallo to see the Black Triangle and marvel at it. She questioned Liaku about the skyfalcon but learned nothing new, except that he was called Quiz. A clock in Istar's head was ticking madly. Still Taretel did not rouse. She grew impatient.

"Damn you for shooting him," she said to Pallo, who took her reprimand mildly.

"I'm sorry, Istar, but he was slaughtering Illyra's men and in a touchy political situation, that sort of thing is such bad manners. He will wake up refreshed, I assure you."

"Well, I can't wait," Istar said. "I'm going."

"Please don't bring any monsters back with you," Pallo implored. "Or timeserpents."

"Yes, my lord King Pallo," Istar answered, bowing as she left his presence. "No timeserpents." He threw a peach pit at her.

Taretel was still groggy when she had Pallo's men mount him on a fast charger, the largest that could be found. The graybeard, Dheri, looked askance at her for taking a man riding in such a condition.

"If I were you, I would pray he wakes up soon," he said, reaching up to adjust the saddle pad on the horse's tall withers. "It's a long way to the ground."

"Believe me, he's comfortable at altitude," Istar answered, and, taking the charger's bridle, rode off toward the Fire Houses.

THE RECKONING

$\mathcal{G}$rietar held the transparent book in front of my face. "Sing," he said. "Sing me a monster."

"No."

The skyfalcon flew into the Fire House and out again.

Grietar began to laugh. He waved the card in the air, flaunting his ability to control the wild creature.

"You see?" he said to Jaya. "I knew he would come. The skyfalcon must come when I call, and the fact that I have you only makes it sweeter. But where is the man-part, I wonder? Skulking on the bridge? He is afraid of us, Jaya. More afraid than the worst fear you have ever felt, and it eats him from the inside out like a disease."

"You could be talking about yourself," I muttered under my breath. I felt sick, and I'm sure it wasn't just the poison. Grietar was feeding off the fact that he was forcing me to help him. I felt sure he wouldn't feel half so confident if he had been on his own. I wished I could think of a way to sabotage him immediately, right here and now, but I couldn't. He had me firmly under his control.

"Sing, Jaya," Grietar said again. "Sing it and drive them away, or else I will take Taretel and make him into something you don't ever want to see."

Outside, there was a sound of voices and booted feet. Grietar looked out through the broken wall, and said, "At last. The reckoning."

TARETEL MIGHT HAVE been groggy, but his horse jumped over the scruffy Clan guards who waited on the other side of the bridge, and he rode it up through the ruins while Istar, not so daring, left her horse with Pallo's guard on the Jai Khalar side of the bridge and went over on foot. She was immediately waylaid by Xiriel and his people.

Xiriel was overjoyed to see her, but she had no patience for him. She started to try to answer his questions, but too many of the things he was asking would take too long to explain, and she was afraid of what Grietar was doing in the Fire Houses. Xiriel didn't seem to care about that; didn't grasp the significance of it at all. She looked around at the ramshackle camp and thought that he of all people should take more care about letting people into the ruins. But he was not himself. Something in him had broken. He was not obviously mad or deranged, but he was no longer the Seer she had known. And he kept grabbing at her physically to keep her back, as though she could impart some life force to him that was missing.

"Xiriel, let me go!" Istar said at last, pulling herself away roughly. "There is no time for this! Go back to the bone and if Grietar tries to leave, stop him. Use any force you want."

Xiriel did not look happy with his instructions, but he didn't follow her, either. She ran through the rubble to the Fire Houses. Taretel was already there, as were Grietar, Jaya, and the skyfalcon. Jaya was the picture of abject misery, Istar noticed.

Grietar said, "All we want is the information that rightly belongs to us. We know you used it. You tested it on the mice."

"The Everiens tested everything they ever did on the mice first, if they could," Taretel said dismissively.

"Do not attempt to squirm out of it! You used it on the mice and they are everywhere."

"It has nothing to do with you," Taretel said.

"But it does. We are the Circle, temporal refugees from the slaughter system of Everien, and if the timeserpent belongs to anyone—"

"Which it does not," Taretel interrupted belligerently, and was ignored.

"—it belongs to us. Whatever codes you obtained were stolen by Tarquin the Free. We had an exclusive arrangement with the timeserpent. Its codes were to be ours, in return for our work on them."

"Work?" Eteltar scoffed. "You did nothing to help the timeserpent. All you did was make more freaks like yourselves."

From somewhere in the Fire House—Istar couldn't be sure where because of the echo—a voice was softly singing. She looked suspiciously at the girl and saw that she was huddled near the edge of the pit, her head bent over a book that she held open on her knees. Istar began to sidle toward her.

"We are now relatives of the timeserpent. We are its . . . representatives, shall we say? You are bound to share your work with us."

"I am bound to nothing," Taretel declared. "I paid the price for the River and the White Road and everything else I discovered. I owe you nothing. But"—he gave a short, ironic laugh—"I will say this. You would do well not to seek the River. For it is the River that has reduced you, once so great and high, to a parasite that depends on a human body for immortality."

Grietar snarled and the worms wriggled from his eyes, writhing in the air in a futile effort to get closer to Taretel. He was unperturbed.

"You are too cocky," Grietar hissed. "We are the Circle, and we will have you, and the codes that are in your mind. We can do it."

"You will no sooner have me than you will have the sun in the sky."

"Oh?" Grietar took a step toward Istar. "She is precious to you, is she not? We can have her now, or after you are dead. For you know you will die here. You choose."

He reached out to grab Istar, but he was too slow. The point of her sword pressed against the base of his throat, stopping him effectively.

"You are no match for me, Grietar," she spat. "I wish I had killed you in Seahawk when I first felt the urge."

But he only smiled. The next thing Istar knew, her sword had been knocked out of her hand by a tentacle as thick as a gatepost. It banged into her on the recoil and she fell to her knees, stunned. There was something *alive* in the pit of the Fire House.

"Ah, there you are, on your knees where you belong." Grietar produced a large playing card from his vest. He held it up so the picture was clearly visible. Istar recognized herself and Eteltar on his cliff.

"Where did you get that?" she gasped. "Who drew it?"

"Never mind," said Taretel. Istar looked at Jaya, who was whispering to herself, almost inaudibly. Out of the darkness of the pit,

Istar's eye began to construct an impression of the monster that had taken her sword. If anything, it was worse than the one that had attacked her on the first bridge. It certainly smelled worse than anything she had ever known. Grietar began to move toward her again, and she made an effort to rise to her feet so she could kick him if he got too close.

"Why don't you kill him, Taretel?" she hissed, looking at the Seahawk giant out of the corner of her eye. She needed to keep the monster and Grietar in the best part of her vision, so she could react quickly if one of them struck. Jaya was still singing. *Crazy bitch*, she thought. *Whose side is she on, the whore?*

"I cannot," Taretel whispered. "If I kill him, the worms will invade me."

"We won't let them!" Istar insisted, on the edge of panic herself because she had no sword. She couldn't understand how Taretel, who had wiped out an entire battalion of Pharicians, including Tash, single-handedly, would do nothing against this creepy Seahawk. Worms or no worms, he had to go. But Taretel seemed to be inordinately anxious. The skyfalcon glided overhead in long, looping circles, but it never came close enough to touch.

Grietar was holding the card aloft. "Fire," he said. "The creative element. The maker and the killer of us all. The Fire of Glass is all the power of the Way of the Sun."

The card burst into flame. He let it go, and it drifted to the floor in swaying zigzags. Istar gave a strangled cry and lunged for it; but it was gone. Taretel staggered sideways, the sword sagging in his hand. Grietar came forward, his eyes seething. Taretel put his hand over his own eyes, shuddering. Jaya abruptly stopped singing, and the lurking monster vanished.

"No!" she screamed, standing up. "Grietar, no!"

"The worms," he gasped. "Istar, the worms . . . they are only what will remain of the thwarted timeserpent, but they are as evil as anything can be."

Istar hesitated, not knowing whether to support him or go after Grietar.

"Get out of here!" Jaya screamed at Taretel, and then at Istar. Her voice broke. "Get out of here *now*!"

A look of irritation passed across Grietar's face, but he continued to focus on Taretel. "We will take you home now. You belong with us. Maybe you were not made like us, maybe you thought you chose the way yourself, but the Way of the Rose is never really chosen. It is a fate. You are locked in a spiral; you will fall into the Rose. You will be nothing in the end."

"You do not know the Way of the Rose," Taretel gasped. As Istar watched him it seemed to her that his physical power and strength were draining from him. He did not shrink or sag, yet some invisible change had come over him when the Winged Man's card burned to nothing. "Do not speak to me with a man's voice. You have never been a man, you don't know the meaning of it."

"We are better than man," said the worms in Grietar's voice. Grietar smiled, a friendly and cheerful expression passing into his features in a way that made the hairs on Istar's spine stand up. "Why have you not fallen? Why do you not go? You have no sky-falcon left in you. You are only human, not even human—for there is an emptiness in you waiting for the worms to fill it. You will be taken now, Taretel the Free. You gambled and you lost."

With that Grietar stretched his hands out toward Taretel, who swayed on his feet. He gripped the sword and looked at Istar.

"I know I asked you to do this, but now that we are come to it, I cannot put the burden on you. It is not too late for you. Use my body, and wish."

"Taretel—"

"I always said I would not break myself, no matter what, it would not be me that destroyed me. Istar: take a dead man's advice. Never make promises. They have a way of being unkeepable."

Taretel took his sword and drew it across his own throat. Istar, mouth open, couldn't move. Grietar gave a roar of rage. Worms burst from his eyes and mouth, writhed in the air between him and Taretel, and then slithered back to Grietar, defeated. All this while Taretel's lifeless body was going down. Warm blood slapped Istar's face. She fell on Taretel, her hands on his slippery hands, her face against his. His eyes were shut. She thanked the wings of her ancestors for that.

She gave the sword an almighty tug and it came free of Taretel's grip, sliding from beneath his weight. Both her hands on the sword and she could lift it, but it was the weapon of a giant, not a small woman bone-weary with grief. There was something absurdly ponderous about the way she had to move as she went after Grietar. She could barely keep the blade high enough to parry, let alone deliver a stroke in attack; and when she did move the sword, her muscles couldn't control its weight. Her wrists gave out. It was too much for her.

Grietar was laughing in a high, insane voice. Istar drew strength from his ridicule. She would make him regret his laughter no matter what was required.

Istar gritted her teeth, took short, quick breaths through her nose, snorting like a horse, and braced her body behind the blade. There would be no opportunity for her to practice her art here. She lined up her shoulders and back against the strong drive of her legs, and hoped. She would use the sword like a club and count on the sheer weight of it to penetrate Grietar's defenses.

It was not a strategy she would have chosen, for Istar's skill as a fighter depended on her speed. She had never been so slow as this. She raised the blade and brought it down, but Grietar stepped easily aside. He was animated now, his rage and disappointment at losing his chance to capture Taretel's spirit having crystallized into a manic intensity that brought every lineament of his face and body to a taut readiness. He was not going to be easy to predict. The worms were filling his body with drugs that would make him faster than she, stronger, more ruthless. Never had Istar felt so limited in her own humanity. Never had she felt so soft. She thought of the small thing living in her belly and let out an involuntary cry of protest at all the disadvantages that came with the obligation to harbor it; but the outburst brought no satisfaction. Her voice sounded weak.

She hacked at Grietar, catching him across the shoulder with the tip of Eteltar's blade. The sword might be heavy, but it had an incredible reach. As she stumbled into him, trying to follow the first cut with a second, deeper one, he pivoted on his right foot and spun around her like a dance partner to stay out of range, laughing all the while. He was too fast. He made her dizzy. Istar turned to face him and he knocked Eteltar's sword aside easily with his own, moving within the radius of her arms where she could not effectively use the long weapon. He was bleeding thick amber blood where she had cut him.

He staggered against her, and she found herself recoiling.

She had seen the worms in his eyes. Felt them look at her; look into her; look through her.

Oh, no, Istar, she said to herself. *All those Sekk, all those times resisting the Slaving. You will not fall now.*

But she couldn't seem to get away from them. She stepped back, but the worms seemed to spiral toward her out of Grietar's eyes, seeking her eyes like light itself.

Then: a small miracle.

The wings of the skyfalcon filled her vision. She blinked, and before her there was a man with two huge wings spreading from his shoulders. For an instant she flashed the memory of Eteltar spreading his wings against the red desert backdrop, and a shudder of relief passed through her. But the man surrounded by these silver wings was not Eteltar. He was not a being of mingled essences, a definition of Animal Magic. He was a ruined Seahawk with worms in his eyes, and now he was falling to his knees, his head ripped open by the beak and talons of the great bird that clung to his shoulders. Gilt worms spurted from his eyes. He was screaming melodically, singing a song that made her shiver.

Istar danced back from the worms that came from Grietar's rent head. Her gorge rose. She bent and began to drag Taretel's body away from the worms, terrified that they would somehow take him even after death. He had stopped bleeding, and he was very heavy. The skyfalcon finished with Grietar and took off, and Istar found herself on her knees near the end of the bone. She crawled away from Taretel's body and vomited until there was nothing left in her guts. She looked back at his body but could not take it in. She sat there for what seemed a long time, not crying, not thinking. The worms were crawling across the floor of the Fire House, drawing toward one another like iron filings, or like a gathering pool of liquid. She shuddered. She bent and kissed Taretel's bloody lips, his eyelids. She pressed her face against his. " 'Use my body, and wish'?" she quoted back to him. "I wish you were not dead."

She waited for a moment, some tiny childish part of her expecting the words to work like a charm, to make him sit up and be well. But it was not to be, and the worms were crawling closer. What if they could still catch him, even when he was dead? Her resolve stiffened.

Then she pushed him off the bone and into the pit.

The worms stopped at the edge and shrank back.

Istar realized that Jaya was nowhere to be seen. From outside, the skyfalcon screamed. The worms were coming closer. They seemed to be congealing, so that they formed a slender stream of silver that quested forward, almost like a living snake. She shuddered and, dragging the too-unwieldy sword, ran from the Fire House.

Quiz was there, and she could just see Jaya climbing onto the bone and vanishing. Xiriel was still there, looking after her in wonder; even as Istar watched, he mounted the bone.

"Xiriel, get back!" Istar shouted. Quiz arrowed down and knocked Xiriel aside; he rolled over in the mud and looked up at her as though she were crazy when she approached. "Don't cross!" she said breathlessly. "Someone will come to you, but don't cross now. Just stay here and *wait*."

She ran up onto the bone. The skyfalcon shadowed her, bursting out of the Liminal in the same moment that she did. Her horse was still there, as was Pallo's guard. He startled and challenged her; then, when he realized who she was, he offered to help.

"Where is Jaya?"

"The red-haired girl, she came before you and rode off on the same pony she came in on. She didn't look good, but I had no orders to stop her."

"How long ago?" Her words came out clipped and breathless, and he looked at her suspiciously.

"You are covered in blood, plainly distraught, lady," he said.

Istar looked at him with a foul expression. "You sound like a Pharician," she said, striding to her horse. "How long ago?"

"Yesterday morning."

"*What?*"

"Three days you've been in there, I make it. And she some time before that. She'll have reached Jai Khalar by now, even on that little pony. Are you—"

"I'm going back to Jai Khalar. I suggest you send word to Pallo that this bridge should be more heavily guarded. There are hostile rebels on the other side, and he will want to be careful to take them on under his own terms, not theirs."

She mounted her horse and started for Jai Khalar. It was easy, she thought, to give orders and ride and endure whatever had to be endured. It was easy. To think, that was hard. To feel—that was impossible.

She must remain focused.

*

BUT BY THE TIME she got to Jai Khalar, that focus had crossed the edge into manic obsession. She went straight to Liaku's Triangle, as it was clearly the center of the action here. She asked everyone she met the same question.

"Where is Jaya?" Istar asked. "Where is Jaya? Where is Jaya? Where is Jaya?" She asked it so repetitively, so obsessively, and with so little regard to any other information that was offered to her, that at length Pallo was brought away from what he was doing and tried to answer Istar to her satisfaction.

"Jaya is gone. She went into the Black Triangle. She was devoured, Istar."

"Bollox," Istar said. "I don't believe she was devoured. You told me yourself she reached right into the Blackness and pulled out the lost Water of Glass."

"She did, she did," Liaku chimed in. She was pacing back and forth before her precious Triangle, guarding it against all comers. Wakhe was asleep in a tent nearby, exhausted, apparently, from all his efforts. "Jaya reach in, take Eye, and Blackness not hurt her. But she can sing, Jaya. Her voice same as voice of Blackness."

Istar looked keenly on Liaku.

"Where do you think it goes, Liaku? Where does your Blackness take people?"

Liaku shrugged and stepped on her own feet, looking suddenly awkward.

"No know. But once I see Quiz give bone to Blackness. I not know it bone, then, but I pretty sure now. And Wakhe come."

"Wakhe would have come from the Fire Houses," Pallo said.

"Would he?" Istar said thoughtfully. "He was there when the timeserpent came, he even *called* it, and you were displaced all the way to A-vel-Jasse but he just sat in the Liminal for a few months and then showed up here?"

Pallo shrugged. "How should I know? What are you saying?"

Istar turned to the byrdgirl. "You saw him come here? Do *you* think he came from the Fire Houses? Do you think all of your treasures come from there?"

"Yes, some things come from Fire House, maybe," Liaku said. "Some things, like Water Glass, come from Jai Khalar."

"And the third side of the Triangle?" Istar prompted. Liaku looked at her blankly, but Pallo inhaled sharply.

"Istar . . ." he began in a tone of gentle admonition.

"Oh, come on, don't you see it, Pallo? Three cities, three ways, three doors. Nine years. Everything's in threes, and the only missing aspect is Jai Pendu."

"You don't want to go back there."

"No, you're right, I don't. But I am pledged to protect Jaya, and I'm sure that's where she's gone. If she is indeed related to Night, that's where she'll go. Where else can she go? If there's a problem in Everien, to be sure it has its source in Jai Pendu. We cannot deny that, can we, Pallo?"

"We also cannot deny that Jai Pendu only comes for one day every nine years. Does anyone here know what year it is? What day it is? What month? *Everien is a land of broken time.* How can Jai Pendu come?"

Istar bit her clenched fist, thinking. "I don't know," she said. "But Taretel seemed to think it would. And if Jaya can call time-serpents and sing Artifacts, she can get to Jai Pendu. The question is, how am I going to catch up with her?"

She looked at Liaku's Triangle.

"NO!" said Pallo in so stentorian a tone that for a moment he could have been mistaken for a proper king. "It is deadly, Istar. There must be a better way."

Liaku was shifting from side to side as though either holding her bladder or keeping a secret.

"What's with you?" Istar said abruptly.

"You can look in my Eye. If you want."

Before Istar could refuse, the child had gone running to bring the mysterious orb to Istar. Pallo studied her face anxiously.

"Are you afraid?" he asked.

"It drove my mother mad. Of course I'm afraid. I'd rather see you stick it in one of these cannons and fire it into a volcano than use it."

"Istar, you don't have to use it," Pallo said. With his usual instincts, he had homed in on the fact that Istar was not merely agitated or tired. She had said nothing of the battle, although she supposed the blood on her clothes must give something away. Still, Pallo had not known any of the story of Eteltar, or how she felt about him; yet he was scrutinizing her very carefully. He would soon twig on that she was anguished to the point of complete irrationality. The fact that she wasn't crying and screaming was not a good sign, considering what had just happened. Even Istar herself

400

knew this. She was right on the edge of going berserk, but she wasn't going to lose control. She had a job to do.

Pallo was talking to her in a soft voice. "You don't have to go anywhere. Jaya is not your responsibility, whatever Taretel or anybody else says. You don't have to go back to Jai Pendu. Just settle down and let's talk all this over."

Liaku returned with the Water of Glass and set it on the ground at Istar's feet. She looked up into Istar's troubled face, and said simply, "Quiz also love you. Liaku help you, Istar, you only ask me, yes?"

Istar blinked and said nothing. She picked up the Glass and walked away with it. She was amazed by how heavy it was.

"What am I going to see?" she said aloud. Her voice was almost gone. She had screamed and sobbed so much that there was nothing left. She closed her eyes. "Show me where Jaya is," she whispered at last.

It was just as she had suspected. Jaya was already climbing the streets of Jai Pendu. And the Floating Lands were there, their bridges spontaneously beginning to assemble themselves in preparation for the arrival of the Floating City. Far out to sea, Jai Pendu could be glimpsed, like a cloud that was as bright as the moon.

"Oh, Mhani," Istar sighed to herself, like a little prayer. Then, to her surprise, the figure of her mother appeared in the Glass. Mhani was sitting in a derelict hut, wrapped in furs, coughing. She looked up as if she could see Istar, and said, "I always knew you had the talent, if only you would have taken it up instead of playing with swords like a boy."

Istar choked on her own surprise.

"A-vel-Jasse, twelve miles north-northwest, in the pine forest beside a waterfall. I'm sure I'll be dead by the time you get here, but it's nice of you to try."

Istar covered her mouth as the image vanished. What else could she See in this thing? *Eteltar . . .*

Something heavy crashed into her from above and behind, and she fell over, dropping the Water of Glass onto the muddy ground. Quiz had barreled into her from above, and now he turned in the sky and came to land on her shoulders. He was very heavy. She staggered.

"All right," she conceded. "I won't look for Eteltar. But you've got to get me to the Floating Lands. You've got to get me there yesterday, Quiz. Jai Pendu is almost here."

"Let me come with you," Pallo said eagerly. "I can help, I know the way."

Istar realized that a crowd had gathered and were observing the drama at Liaku's Triangle.

"I don't need you to come, Pallo," she said as gently as she could. "Quiz will come with me. I think he knows the way."

JIHAN'S ADVICE

$\mathcal{I}$ $think$ $\mathcal{I}$ was in the Blackness for a long time. I know I didn't run straight for Jai Pendu. When I got into the Blackness, I could see all three places: Jai Khalar, the Fire Houses, and Jai Pendu. And as before, I could see Jihan's eyes looking out at me from within the intricacies of the house of cards.

I only needed a thought to move, here. I thought of Jihan, and there he was, surrounded by the imagination room I had never seen him enter, the room that had been forbidden to me. The skylight sent scintillating beams of sun into his bright red hair. I thought of Grietar and shivered.

"Tell me if I'm right, Jihan," I said. He folded his arms and cocked his head, as though waiting for me to recite the solutions to mathematical problems in some lesson. Waiting to judge me. I gathered myself.

"The Everiens had a fine solution for their timeserpent problem. When they had fed the Li'ah'vah the codes for me, they had forced it to create the maze that would become its own prison. For the timeserpent wanted only to live and make offspring; but for a timeserpent, these two acts are mutually contradictory, a paradox. For, among other things, a timeserpent that destroys the world that made it by changing the past, ultimately destroys itself.

"The Li'ah'vah knows this—or at least, it did know it in the days when first it consumed me, and that is why it lived in its sad prison, using its timefulness to pretend to be another timeserpent, to mate with itself, however futile this act would prove. The conscience of the timeserpent with its human face meant that the Everiens had escaped the worst ravages of their crime.

"But they had not escaped all ravages. For there were monsters and abominations who were displaced in time, too, and these creatures came to form the Circle. They sought news and information of Everien constantly, and when they got hold of the barren time-serpent's eggs and other fluids, they, too, were in a position to alter reality. The conscience of the Circle was not so pure as the time-serpent's. They were and are a mixed lot, with contradictory motivations and beliefs and habits. They are hard to understand.

"The Pharicians murdered the timeserpent deep beneath that volcano, hundreds of years ago. They murdered both ends of the timeserpent together, so that it could not escape: it was busy defending itself, for each end of the timeserpent had come to think of the other as a separate being. So they both died."

I paused and scrutinized his face to see whether I was right. His expression told me nothing conclusive. I plowed on.

"But by then, the code for making a Li'ah'vah was floating around the Liminal, waiting for someone who knew how to use it in the Fire Houses. The Li'ah'vah could be killed in flesh, but the idea of it, the potential, would remain forever in the theoretical space of the Liminal. So it was that Wakhe called up the Li'ah'vah again.

"This one that now hides from me knows that if it absorbs my essence, it, too, will develop the thought patterns of the hybrid timeserpent. That is why it is careful to keep itself apart from me. Rather than assimilate my patterns, it warped reality so that I could exist as flesh. It knew I would be weaker this way. It knew I would not be able to pursue it, to trap it as the Everiens had trapped it."

"Yes," said Jihan unexpectedly. "You have got that part precisely correct."

I shivered. The implications were beginning to come clear for me.

"So what are you saying, Jihan?" I asked.

"You are going to die, Jaya. You have been poisoned, and though the poison works on you very slowly, still it works. When you die, the Knowledge of the timeserpent vanishes. All the Everiens are dead, and even Eteltar, who had some Knowledge, is divided and half-dead already. You are the last one, Jaya."

"And when I die?"

"The Li'ah'vah will be free to devour all times. I will not confuse you with all the mathematical permutations of what may happen to the world—" ("No, please don't," I interjected. "I feel faint enough already.") "—but it is certain that consciousness as you know it, as humans know it, will be gone. Everything in the world will be a part of the Li'ah'vah in one way or another. Everything will be subject to the laws of its existence, which are antithetical to the laws of all other animal existence. If you had stayed under my protection, in the house, you might have survived even such a catastrophe. But you did not, and I cannot find fault with you for that. It is the hallmark of our species, this spirit of adventure."

"I have never heard you talking of such doomful things," I said sullenly. "I'm not dead yet, anyway. There must be something we can do."

He shook his head doubtfully. "It's all very uncertain, Jaya."

"Yes, yes, I know, but I've got to do something, and quickly, before I'm too weak to even move."

He paced. "Well, if the timeserpent could be persuaded to take you, as it took you from the house and deposited you in human form, that would be different."

"Take me? You mean, swallow me?"

"Yes. Although I don't see why it should. Better for the time-serpent if you should die."

"What if it takes me?" I said eagerly. "What then?"

"Why, then you would return to being its Guardian. For the Li'ah'vah would in all likelihood discover the error of its ways in ruining the human culture that must give rise to it. Equally, and probably more powerfully, it would acquire your . . . er . . . animal instincts."

"Animals instincts?"

"Those human characteristics which were taken out of the Sekk, but left in you since you were to be a specimen of humankind. The reproductive drive, in particular, seems to have gotten to the timeserpent last time. It was gripped with an agonizing desire for offspring that were antithetical—"

"—to its nature, yes, I see. So you're saying, if the Li'ah'vah eats me, it will absorb my patterns just like the other time, and retire quietly to a cave and dig itself a maze, and that will be the end of the trouble. Yes?"

"Except for the Circle."

"Who will never rest."

"Yes, Jaya. You have got it precisely."

There was a silence.

"It's not a very good solution," I said. "Will I still die?"

"You will return to your original, abstract form."

I didn't say anything. *All of this for nothing,* I thought. *And the Circle free to start it all over again, if they decide to come looking for me.*

I turned my attention to Jai Pendu. It was already sailing toward me, coming to greet me eagerly. I stepped across to meet it.

MOST OF THE Way of the Rose was an intact structure, a tall, spi-rallene red crystal with a hollow core. A road had run up the inside once, but that was gone. Now the chamber was empty, except for the broken pieces of crystal that lay on the floor. These were the shattered remains of the panels Tarquin had broken in order to fight his way up to the top of the spiral. They lay quite still and silent, shaped in complex curves and edges—the remains of a once-alive, growing thing that was now inert. I recalled what Jihan had said of my father's Knowledge.

Jigsaw pieces scattered in time.

I picked up each of the pieces and started to put them together.

As I worked, I examined the slices of crystal. I could switch between sense-modes. I could hear the patterns. I could see the worlds within, and their inhabitants. I could conjecture and imag-ine the implications of each of the theories within these pieces of broken crystal. I had thought that the armload of glass pieces from the lake, the remnants of the Sekk Guardians, contained a fabu-lous array of Knowledge. But this crystal, which was itself the size of a house, this one flooded my mind with recollections, stimulat-ed me in ways I'd never dreamed of. I came to understand more, in those brief hours I spent rearranging it, than I had ever learned in all of my life up until then.

Putting together a jigsaw without knowing what picture you're making is notoriously difficult. Putting together those shards was the same way: the jigsaw was three-dimensional, and I didn't know what shape I was supposed to end up with. In fact, I didn't even know if my intuition was right. Maybe these pieces had no relationship to each other. Maybe they didn't add up to anything, much less an object that could attract a vengeful Li'ah'vah.

But, as I observed to Istar although she didn't like it much, things have a way of happening to me. Fixing the crystal didn't take me very long at all. Once I realized it was an egg, putting it together was child's play.

Mind you, it was an egg the size of a bathtub. Moreover, the panels of crystal weren't completely smooth. When the light struck it a certain way, I could see that someone had inscribed something on the surface. Everien writing. Code.

The code was summarized, expressed in seven symbols, very similar to the six symbols needed to call a Li'ah'vah; but not the same. I didn't know the meaning of the seventh symbol.

I curled up inside the egg and, after something of an awkward struggle, pulled the last segment shut from the inside. I held the hilt of Tarquin's sword clasped tightly in my hands, with the blade lying flat against my forehead. It remained ice cold and my fingers grew numb.

I now hesitated as to what to do. The timeserpent would soon leave the Liminal and make itself free, for I was now captive within the red crystal. Perhaps it would wait for me to physically die, so as to be completely safe; but that did not suit my plans. I needed to convince the timeserpent to eat me alive. There was no other way I could envisage tricking it into its captivity. My conscience would force it to return to the maze of Paradox, and the world would be safe from its ravages. But only if I lived long enough to be eaten.

The song that was in my head now all the time, a soft and insistent mantra insinuating itself into my consciousness, day and night—that song began to crescendo. And as I sat huddled in my egg, I read off the code of the seven symbols and I saw that it corresponded perfectly to the Unknown Music.

"*Sing, Jaya!*"

Little by little, I had come to understand it. Singing is translating. You translate time and dimension into breath and pitch. You weave a web to the world, you unfold the hidden. I do not trust Jihan, but here at the end of everything, I find I have no other truth.

I began to sing the seven symbols.

SAILSNAKES AND
VERTEBRAE

Quiz led Istar to a series of bridges beginning in Everien proper, passing through the sea gates, and then jumping across the sea plateau like stepping-stones. Each one shifted time, but she didn't know whether it was shifting forward or backward, faster or slower. All she knew was that she had to trust the skyfalcon. And he was always overhead.

Halfway across the sea plateau and between bridges, Istar's horse reared and spooked. She fought to control the stallion: he was more horse than she was used to, for she had demanded speed. Then she saw what was upsetting him. Flopping in the grass ahead of them was an injured sailsnake. Istar dismounted and hobbled the horse so that he couldn't run far. Then she approached the sailsnake.

She had never seen anything so large or so beautiful. It seemed to be made of the flimsiest tissue, but she knew its wings could withstand incredible gales and searing cold, for it flew at altitudes no bird except maybe Quiz could endure. This one was struggling because there were leather straps tied to it, restraining it; it flopped in exhaustion. Istar went closer, trying to see if she could help it without getting attacked, because sailsnakes could be very dangerous when angered.

Then she saw the body, decomposing but still attached to the poor sailsnake's midline cartilage. She covered her mouth in disgust.

"What will the Pharicians think of next?" she wondered aloud.

It took her well over an hour to cut the sailsnake free, and she was buffeted by its wings and knocked off her feet several times. In the end it took off and hovered over the sea, apparently none the worse for its ordeal.

"Thankless creature," Istar said as it flew away. She didn't bury the body. It was some old man, with the eyes already rotted out of his head. She carried on with her journey, even more anxious for the time she'd lost.

Or thought she'd lost.

The bridges, she realized after she had crossed four of them, were vertebrae. And they continued all the way across the Floating Lands. Jai Pendu was coming, just as Taretel had predicted. He had even built a bridge to it. Istar let her horse go and ran across the top of the Floating Lands on foot as the Floating City came to land.

"This is much easier than last time," she said to Quiz, and then hoped she was not jinxing herself.

SINGING IT A LULLABY

𝔍n the place of Three Doors, standing guard outside the Rose Door with a wild and wary look on her face, Tarquin found his foster daughter Istar. There was something about her expression that made him suddenly feel very sorry. She did not deserve to be mixed up in this, and he had done little to ever stop her, or help her to live a better life in any way. Regret ached in him.

But she took in his arrival without rancor or even surprise. If anything, she looked relieved to receive reinforcements. When he approached on foot, she stepped deferentially away from the door.

"I'm glad you're here," she said, grasping his forearm in the greeting of equals. "He told me to protect her, but I don't think she wants to live. I think she's going to kill herself."

Tarquin looked at her face, which was shadowed and drawn with pain. He bent and put his cheek to hers.

"You should go now, Istar," he said. "You and I are overdue for a long talk, and I hope we will have it one day, but now you must go. This is a dangerous place, and something tells me it's just getting worse all the time."

She leaned into him for just a moment; then she drew herself up. "I will wait for you," she said. Rather than argue, Tarquin squeezed her hand, then raced off to the center of the huge, empty space. There was a red egg the size of a chariot, and Jaya's voice was pouring out of it like smoke from a thousand hairline cracks. Carved all over the egg were Eteltar's secret symbols.

"What in the name of the Great Squid of the Deep is this?" Tarquin cried. "Istar, give me your sword."

He turned and saw that she was holding up a two-handed blade of absurd proportions. "That's not yours," he snapped. "Yours was just like Chyko's, wasn't it?"

"It's Taretel's," she said. "This is all I have left."

"Ah, never mind," Tarquin said, and took out his knife. He banged on the surface of the egg. "Jaya! Stop singing at once! This is madness."

Jaya stopped. Inside, he could see her curled up, and between her knees her hands were clasped around the hilt of his own sword. He growled a little and shook his head, feeling the collection of selves jump and shuffle within him like the tiles of a Pharician board game. He focused on the egg. It had been separated into segments, then placed back together again. The joints were so smooth that he couldn't get a grip on any of them. He beat on the surface with his closed fist.

"Jaya! Push one of these pieces out! Come on, you can break out!"

He heard her voice clearly; if anything, it was amplified.

"Go away, Tarquin. I don't want to break out. Don't interfere."

He spat on the surface of the egg and rubbed it with his tunic, trying to see her better.

"Jaya, come out or I smash the egg with Taretel's sword."

Through the red crystal they confronted each other eye to eye.

"I mean it, Jaya!"

She grimaced and poked out a segment of the egg near her feet. It rolled onto the floor and he could look inside clearly. The crystal segments were thick, and there was not as much space inside as the egg seemed to take up from the outside. Her feet were braced against the sides.

"You must let me confess," Jaya cried. "I have done all the bad things you have ever survived. I was meant to be the ruler of the Sekk. I was Night, and I stole your Company. I drew you to me, and I let loose the thing that will destroy Everien and all its people. I called the Li'ah'vah, so that I could escape the monsters."

She was distraught, but Tarquin waved away her words. He put the empty section of shell on the ground. It thrummed menacingly in his hands, and he shook himself all over like a dog to be rid of the vibration.

"Tarquin, aren't you listening? I called the Li'ah'vah."

"Yes! But it has already eaten you, and you have passed into human form. It tore Everien up in pieces, but because it has assimilated *you* it is now not merely a mindless Li'ah'vah, but a timeserpent wearing a human face, possessed of human thoughts, desires

411

. . . and conscience. It has retreated to the maze of you, Jaya, where it waits in its own prison."

He beckoned to her to come out, but she shook her head.

"No," Jaya said. "That's what happened before. That's how it's *supposed* to be, but that isn't how it *is*. The timeserpent has broken out of the maze. It has used all of you. The Circle, the Clans, Ysse, Eteltar, *all of you have been used*. Even I have been used. The life force of the timeserpent is strong. It is not limited by our laws."

"Maybe so," Tarquin said, still gesturing at her to come out. "All the same, Jaya, you're not doing yourself any favors sitting in an egg singing it a lullaby."

"I'm trying to catch it," Jaya said. "It will come to me, and I will return to the Liminal, and it will be trapped because my will and desires are going to become a part of it. I will take it back to the maze. Now that I know what is happening, I will somehow manage to Guard it."

"Brave words," Tarquin said. "But you couldn't do it before, all alone. You can't do it now for tenfold the reasons."

"You don't know that," Jaya said.

It was turning into a children's snapping contest, and he shot back, "Give me my sword."

"What?"

"My sword. You've got it. I want it back. Give it to me."

She seemed puzzled and, hesitatingly, released the hilt. He reached in and took it, and at the same time seized hold of her arm, thinking to pull her out forcibly. But when his hand closed on her forearm, she let out a cry of pain so sharp that he dropped it at once, ashamed. He stepped back, swinging the sword in frustration.

"Jaya, look around you!" He gestured to the crystal walls, but he meant Jai Pendu as well. "If the timeserpent comes here, it eats all the Knowledge. Doesn't it?"

He had learned a thing or two since he'd last spoken to Jaya, and he could tell now that she was realizing it.

"Are you trying to commit suicide?" he prodded, sticking his head into the hole in the egg. "What is this idea of yours?"

"Get it out of the world," she said intensely. "That is my idea. Let it eat me and all the Knowledge. If you have seen the future, then you know what will come of it."

"That's no excuse." He backed out, took up his newfound

sword, and began cutting whistling eights in the air with it. She leaned toward the opening and yelled out after him.

"No? What should I do? I can't kill it. Nothing here is so simple. Remember, Tarquin, you saw two timeserpents? Male and female, barren. They were one serpent. They were two ends of the same thing. And they were reproduced in their venom. That is how they had been trapped. The Everiens had banished them to that cave, and they had used my mind to keep them there. So long as one of them never got out, they would never be able to carve time. But if one of them were called to a different location or time, then their powers would again be opened. They would get away from their prison. And they would be free to devour everything the Everiens had ever wrought, turning it all to paradox. When Wakhe called, the timeserpent escaped, and it took me with it. I had to go. That's why I let go of you. It's . . . it's like an instinct with me. The timeserpent is my charge and *I must answer for it.*"

"How could the Everiens use your mind? Is it something to do with the Jaya maze? The tunnels with your face on them?"

"It is to do with the nature of what I am. I was created in order to Guard the timeserpent. If the timeserpent is kept hidden, then none of the other monsters can get out, either. For the monsters were banished to the Liminal, and it is the Liminal that connects real and imagined time—or real and imagined location, depending on what view you want to take. As long as the timeserpent is in the Liminal, the worlds are safe."

"But the timeserpents were really *there*. The Snake Clan was really there. . . . Are you saying I was in the Liminal all that while? Even Kere witnessed it."

"The Snake Island was real. The Everiens chose an isolated and remote place that had no history. It was an unstable volcano. The timeserpents should never have met humans, should never have communicated with them. But they did. And the Pharician Scholars—ancestors of the Everiens who would start all these experiments—they got wind of the timeserpents, and took their venom, and connected to the Liminal, where they mixed with the monsters who were so desperate to escape. So the Circle was formed. The worms of the Circle went to Everien and dredged up the echoes of times that were not yet to come. The times when the patterns would be stored in the laboratories of Everien, far from Jundun, where they could do no harm; or so the Scholars believed.

413

And this aroused the Sekk, who tried to use the Clans that were living in Everien to be their servants."

"But the animal patterns had been removed from the Sekk," Tarquin put in, nodding, for he was starting to put a story together that he could understand. "And when the Sekk tasted the animal patterns of the Clans, they craved those primitive emotions. They drove the Clanspeople to acts of frenzied excess."

There was a shuffling of movement within the egg as Jaya turned around so her head was near the opening. She seemed excited by the fact that he finally understood her. "And the Clans retaliated by seeking more Knowledge, which was beginning to sprout backward in time thanks to the efforts of the timeserpent to be born. The more Knowledge the Clans found, the stronger the Sekk grew, and so the more Knowledge that was needed to keep them back, until finally Eteltar stumbled on the White Road."

Tarquin cleared his throat. He still was not sure he comprehended what his part in that had been. He muttered, "The Snakes told me their codes were flawed and that was why they were trapped."

Istar had wandered over from her post by the door and had been fidgeting and looking like she wanted to say something. To deflect attention from himself and his confusion about Eteltar's lab and the different bottles and the labels and Kere and the Sekk and . . . everything . . . Tarquin looked at her. She was obviously gathering herself for something, but she kept her eyes down—no longer the proud and bold young adventurer he had encountered in Jai Khalar, he thought regretfully.

"I'm just a stupid Honorary," she said in a hoarse voice. "I had everything to lose, and I lost it all. But there is one thing he told me." She glanced up at them and her eyes flashed as she said his name. "Taretel, I mean. He said animals are deep time. He said they are death and death and death, and that their patterns in the Liminal, their possibilities, created the timeserpent."

"Yes . . ." Jaya said encouragingly, leaning out of the egg to look at Istar with furrowed brows. "It's true that an animal species changes by dying in certain patterns. And by reproducing."

"But a timeserpent can't die," Istar said. "It can be contained, but it can't be destroyed."

"Or the Everiens would have done it," Tarquin muttered. "They destroyed everything else, from the look of it."

"Well," said Istar. "Animals don't need to slip time, because they have offspring to go into the future. So . . . if a timeserpent has no offspring, it's for a reason. Because it needs to slip time."

"You call that logic?" said Jaya, then caught herself because Istar had flushed bright red beneath her dark skin. She reached out and touched the girl's shoulder. "I'm sorry. It's a thought, but it's so . . . backward."

Tarquin guffawed. "It's a Kere thought," he said.

"Who's Kere?"

"It's a Jihan thought," Jaya added thoughtfully. Tarquin was thinking through the problem from all the angles that Ice's presence afforded him—and there were a lot of angles. He felt excitement pulling together and rising inside him, like a small invisible *majala* in his spine. His mind began to spin; but he found he liked it.

Istar said, "Seriously, now, you must listen. Please. He tried so hard. I will quote you what he said to me. Taretel. He said, *If only you knew the loneliness of timeserpents. They crave offspring; but they are doomed, for if they reproduce, they negate their own existence. They are not one species existing in many individuals across time; they are one individual, existing forever, immune to time.*"

Tarquin echoed her. "If they reproduce, they negate . . . yes, Jaya, she may be right! Here is the key to it all. The codes were flawed, yes. But what if it was the very flaw in the timeserpent's codes that enabled it to slip time? The very thing that stops the timeserpent from having offspring must be the thing that makes it immortal."

"*Must* is a strong word," Jaya said. Tarquin ignored her. Istar was staring intently at him, trying to pick up on what he was saying.

"So . . ." she prompted

"So if you repair the flaw, you destroy the timeslipping ability."

"Fix the venom, and get the timeserpent to drink it." For the first time ever, Tarquin saw Istar smile.

Tarquin brandished the ampule he had gone to such lengths to obtain. "Eteltar said he fixed it! He said it was fixed!"

Jaya looked very grave. "If you are right, then we are all saved. But if you are wrong, then we take a great risk letting the timeserpent come here. Because Jai Pendu holds the Knowledge. Give it to the timeserpent and you will wish you had dealt with the Circle instead. Evil can be comprehended. The timeserpent cannot. Tarquin, what if you are wrong?"

THE HATCHING

The red egg was shaking. Tarquin had not answered my question, and when I repeated it, he dragged me out of the egg.

"It's coming," I said. "What if you're wrong?"

"Stay out of the way, Jaya, for Time's sake. And keep quiet! No singing."

I turned to Istar. She looked so wan and sorrowful, and there were lines of tension in her face and neck that did not belong there. I took her a little away from the egg, to a place just beside the open door that led to the place of Three Doors.

"Go now, Istar. You must not stay here. It is too dangerous for you. Please."

"Taretel said to protect you."

She was staunch, even though her voice broke on Taretel's name.

"I have Tarquin," I said. "Taretel would not have wanted you to die for me. Truly! Now go, quickly, before the causeway is swamped. I hope you are right, Istar, about the River. You have done extraordinary things. But you must not stay here."

She looked across at me, eye to eye. I knew what she was thinking. *No weak little girl is going to tell Istar the Honorary what to do.*

"Yes, *go*, Istar," Tarquin barked from across the empty hall. His voice flew up the broken walls of the crystal.

"*Please*," I said again. Istar planted herself in front of the door, legs akimbo, hands on hips. Her eyes turned blank, like a guard on duty who refuses to be distracted. "Tarquin . . ." I implored.

He came storming over, charged into Istar, and picked her up across his back.

"You may be Chyko's daughter in your blood, but you're my daughter now. You are not going to die here."

416

He dumped her unceremoniously into the place of Three Doors. While she sprawled on her backside, irate, he pointed a warning finger at her as though she were a child.

"Get your backside off this crazy island and return to Everien. I may have no right to tell you what to do, but I do have a reason and it's a good one. You are going to live. As your father didn't, Istar, you are going to live your life. So go. Don't let me find you out here or I'll have your ears fried in seal fat for breakfast!"

He slammed the door.

"She can't open it," he muttered. "It's not her Way."

"Do you really think she's going to obey you?" I said.

"No. But I had to—" Suddenly he froze, put out a stiff hand to block me going any closer to the egg. It rocked and shook.

The egg swelled visibly, but it did not break. The red sections of crystal stretched and separated, and the dark body of the timeserpent became visible in the interstices. The red surface of the egg was becoming nothing more than a colored pattern on the timeserpent's black body, so that as it uncoiled, growing larger and larger, there were diamonds and swirls and triangles of red decorating its skin. There was a burst of discordant music as the timeserpent's end became visible. Its painted human face was crying out in its native language; the clicks and hisses came at me in a tangle of thoughts and ideas.

You called me, Jaya. You have the Knowledge I need to Become. I will swallow you, again and again, always, until we are one.

But Tarquin was between us. He couldn't understand the timeserpent's language, but that didn't stop him from interposing himself between the Li'ah'vah and me.

"Ah-hah!" he cried. "So we meet again. I have fulfilled my mission. Here is the solution you asked for. Come and taste your children."

The snake sent out a swift and subtle tongue toward Tarquin, tasting the air around him, and with a lightning movement, Tarquin tossed the ampule into the timeserpent's open mouth. The ampule disappeared, but the timeserpent showed no reaction. Tarquin began to back away quickly. The Li'ah'vah swung around and opened its jaws for me.

Come, Jaya, whispered the timeserpent. *Come and I will save you. You will die here. Don't make Everien be for nothing. Come to my Liminal. Live in me.*

417

Tarquin had a firm hold on my arm just above the elbow. For all of my brave stand inside the egg, my feverish shut-eyed waiting to be Eaten, now that I was faced with that inexorable mouth, I had no wish to throw myself into it. Not for a second time.

"She will only ruin your life," Tarquin said to the timeserpent. "You don't want her moral conscience. It will only get in your way."

I knew Tarquin could not hear its words to me, but he seemed to know what it wanted. He spoke directly to the timeserpent.

"I have for you a better gift. Take the River, and be free. You will make many timeserpents, and you will no longer limp through the universe failing to breed as all things are meant to do. No longer will you be flawed by your human makers. Eteltar has cured you."

Eteltar the Dead, the timeserpent gloated. *As Jaya will be the Dead, too. I have waited long for this day.*

It shot its head toward me and, as if his sword were an ax, Tarquin brought his blade down on the top of its snout. The time-serpent recoiled momentarily, but it was only startled. It was bleeding from a small cut. An instant later, it had reared back to strike Tarquin. I was rooted to the spot, my mouth dry, my throat empty, my heart racing. Tarquin turned and piled into me, shoving me ahead of him toward the door that led out of the Way of the Rose. I felt the rush of air as the timeserpent lashed out, striking to either side of the open door with each of its jaws just as we slipped out through the middle. The snake was too big to follow us.

I hesitated in the place of Three Doors. This in-between place was as dark and ill defined as always, a disorienting emptiness in which three doors were set in a triangle, but they had no solid walls between them, and they did not seem to be attached to any structure. I knew quite well that the Three Doors is an unstable triangle; in fact, on the other side of the Blackness that comprises it, I could see flickers of Liaku's Triangle, of Jai Pendu and Jai Khalar (from where, for an instant, I thought I glimpsed Jihan's unsettling blue eyes gazing at me, at one with the windows and doors) and the activity around Liaku's Queendom. All of the clocks were different; but ours was the fastest time of all.

"This day passes too quickly," I whispered hurriedly to Tarquin as the timeserpent hurled itself against the door to the Way of the Rose. "Jai Pendu will soon sail. You must leave, and quickly."

But the timeserpent was not about to be so easily defeated. For now there were lightning flashes in the air around the perimeter of the Rose Door. The timeserpent was beginning to break down the conceptual wall that held it within the Way of the Rose. Tarquin saw the cracks and leaped back with a shout, stumbling over his own feet and fetching up against the shadowy outline of the Way of the Eye. He thought the cracks were electricity.

"Lightning, Jaya!" he cried. "We have to get out of here."

My head reeled. Since the Li'ah'vah had showed itself, the infernal singing that had plagued my brain for weeks finally stopped, and in the welcome, numb silence I tried to think. I was turning over routes through the avenues of Jai Pendu in my mind, trying to figure out the fastest exit. So it was that I did not see Tarquin open the Way of the Eye—not until it was too late.

He was confronted with a wall of water. I heard the echoes of his curses rebound in unexpected ways off the invisible surfaces of the place of Three Doors; then, before I could react, the water reached out and pulled him *in*.

"No!" I screamed. "Tarquin!"

I seized him around the waist just as he was being drawn in, and though I set all my strength against it, the Way of the Eye pulled him deeper. His torso was immersed in the water and his feet were gradually coming off the ground, rising. . . . I tightened my grip and threw myself down and back, huffing and spitting wildly, twisting as I went. The water lay on the other side of the door like a column of living glass: transparent, powerful, and willful.

I could see stars on the other side of it.

I didn't know where it was taking him, but he wasn't going. Not if it was up to me.

But my vitality was at a very low ebb, and the water was impossibly strong. I gritted my teeth and held on. I thought my tendons would snap.

I must not lose him. Must have Tarquin. Do anything. ANYTHING.

The realization acted as a kind of trigger. Suddenly, I felt myself infused with an incredible strength, a power that had a seemingly endless supply as though I could tap right into the magnetic field of the earth itself. I pulled Tarquin free.

He came flying through the door and fell over me, soaking wet, coughing, spewing fluid. I kicked the door shut. I pulled him out of the way and sang the door shut before he could drown; then, ignoring the Way of the Sun, I used my newfound strength to drag the half-drowned Tarquin away from the Three Doors. Displaced from that place, we found ourselves in the white bowl at the bottom of Jai Pendu, and its three towers hovered above our heads, unsupported. Around and below us waited the long and complex descent to the causeway that connected Jai Pendu to land.

Tarquin was coughing and rubbing his eyes; the water that had poured out had been icy seawater, and he was not himself. He was still doubled over coughing and preoccupied with himself as I led him up the side of the bowl so that we could look down on the pile of white symmetrical orbs that was the final hill of Jai Pendu. The city was morphing before our eyes, as though Jihan were shuffling the deck at high speed.

For myself, I felt stronger than I had in a long time. Something had cured me. I felt invincible.

"Now you must leave," I said. "This day is disappearing before our eyes. Look at the causeway!"

Though I pointed to it, he was in no condition to look, and he paid no attention to me. But I was worried about him. Waves were rushing over the white stone. Tarquin would have to race through the city to get out in time. It didn't matter for me: now that the Li'ah'vah and I were here together, it would be a simple thing to get it to take me in. But I did not wish for Tarquin to be trapped here with us, the Paradox and the snake. And then, suddenly, I remembered something.

"Where's Istar?" I said, glancing around me in a sudden panic. We had both told her to go, but there was no sign of her in the city or on the nearest of the Floating Lands, which she should have reached by now. "I should have known she wouldn't heed you," I muttered, and pushed myself off the wall. "She has gone to the Way of the Sun." Even as I spoke, I looked up. Over our heads, the whole structure of the three towers was quaking and humming as the timeserpent sought its freedom. I felt my lips peel back from my teeth instinctively. The timeserpent was going to be trouble, soon. Very soon.

"Oh, shit. Istar." Tarquin finished blotting his eyes. "She hasn't left Jai Pendu, has she?" For the first time since I'd pulled him from the water, he actually looked at me. He looked at me, and then he leaped back.

"Night!" he cried. "Don't come any closer."

420

I stared at him. "What are you talking about?"

But before the words were even out of my mouth, I had glimpsed my own hand, raised in a defensive gesture. It was completely black, two-dimensionally black, like a paper cutout. Like a shadow on a wall.

I had become a shadow of myself.

"It's still me, Tarquin," I whispered. "Don't believe everything you see. It must be the light in Jai Pendu, or the time, or . . . or . . ."

But I hadn't the courage to go on defending myself. The way he looked at me stopped me short. And then, hazarding another glance upward, I saw the reflection of us in the mirror of the bottom of Jai Pendu. There was Tarquin, skinny, bruised, half-collapsed on the rim of the white bowl. And there was I. Wearing white robes, and everything else about me blacker than the deepest hole.

I had wanted to be strong. I had needed to be strong. And now I was.

"You're right," I conceded. "I am Night."

He shivered and coughed again, but his eyes never left me. They held fast to me, not with the intense affinity I'd come to expect, but with mistrust.

"I will not try to take you, Tarquin," I told him. "I will not follow you. You have nothing to fear from me. I swear it."

He did not look convinced. "How can you see?" he whispered, and shivered as he looked at the place where I had no eyes—at least, not that he could perceive. The question made me realize that I was neither wholly Night, nor wholly Jaya, and I could have tried to explain this to him in terms of himself and Ice, but there was no time for this.

"Tarquin, if you go your way, I swear to you, I will not pursue you or harm you. You go your way, and I'll go mine. Agreed?"

"No," he snapped. "What have you done with Jaya?"

"I am Jaya," I said. "I thought you knew that by now."

I must not waste time arguing with Tarquin. I looked back at the place of Three Doors. I couldn't let Istar stay in there. Not with the timeserpent abroad. "Tarquin, you must leave. *Now.* You have tried your best to split the timeserpent, and it has not worked, and now you must go. As you see, there will be no happy ending for us. But if you would honor anything that has passed between us, ever, then *you must leave now.* I do not wish to spend all of a theoretical eternity with the thought of your death here on my mind. Please. *Go!*"

I turned my back on him and plunged back into the place of Three Doors. The water had drained away and I faced the Way of the Sun in my shadow form, as the very opposite of the Sun. It was the last place I wanted to go.

If only Tarquin had not come, I thought. *I would have stayed in the egg, and the timeserpent would have come for me, and even now it would be devouring my mind and returning to its prison. And all of this would be a dream to me, but wouldn't that be better than the look in Tarquin's eyes? I wish I could sleep again.*

I opened the door.

HONOR

Istar climbed the steps of the Way of the Sun. She had been there before, but it didn't matter. This was different. She was fitter this time: leaner, tougher, more tenacious. She was not troubled by the climb. She was also light-headed, nauseous, weighed down by grief and disappointment. Here in the brazen sunlight that seemed to focus on her with unreal intensity, Istar felt herself finally being forged. Like a piece of metal, hammered and shaped and dipped in fire and then water and then hammered some more, in this final climb Istar was coming to a condition of polished and sharp perfection. The sun hit her hard because she was shining back at it like a mirror.

She didn't know it, of course. She thought she was done for. She thought she had lost.

She didn't know that the meaning of her life was never going to get more clear or certain than this strenuous but simple act of climbing steps that were too big for her. She only knew that she was trying desperately hard to undo a wrong, and there was nothing else in the world for her other than the thoughts of the Seahawk she had killed, the skyfalcon that had spoken to her through Taretel, and finally Eteltar, whom she'd left behind to die without her.

She climbed the steps.

At the top, the stairs were broken off as though something had taken a bite out of the structure that supported them. They ended in a crumbling edge, beyond which there was only sky.

But this sky contained a multiplicity of suns, all whirling and jumping from place to place. The ocean below was scrambled. It lay blue and black, white and gray, green and gold, in uneven patches that tilted and mixed with one another. If Istar had not known better, she would have thought she had inhaled too much of Utar's dreamweed. But even dreamweed could not play games like these.

In an utterly incongruous twist, the city below, the white city of Jai Pendu, was perfectly still. When she looked down on it, Jai Pendu was as ordered as a precision clock. It was simple, elegant, and motionless where all else was moving. There the Knowledge lay articulated in all its glory, content and maybe even smug in the midst of times gone mad.

Istar stood there. She could feel a humming coming through the soles of her boots, like the pulse of Jai Pendu. She looked across at the adjacent tower and saw that it was shaking.

Then, like a memory come to life, a shadow flashed across Istar from above. Whirling fearfully, she saw the wings first. Then she saw the man. She fell on her knees.

"Istar."

He landed lightly on the top step, balanced on the edge of the world without the slightest care. His wings shielded her from the sun.

"You cannot come here anymore, Istar. It is not for you." He bent and stroked her cheek, tried to raise her up, but she stayed where she was. She intended to beg.

"Take me back," she pleaded. "I'll never try to climb away. I'll never leave. Just take me back to the place we were."

"I can't."

"*Please*, Eteltar. I didn't understand, then. I didn't know what I was up against. I didn't know about the skyfalcon, and . . . and . . . and Taretel. In the end I loved him, too, and he—at the end—ah, it was awful. And the bones, they . . ."

He smiled down at her and tapped his collarbone. "See? They are in my body, so don't you worry about the bones."

Tears were streaming down her cheeks. "*Please*."

His face sagged so deeply, she wished she hadn't said it.

With the pad of his thumb he smoothed a tear away from the corner of her eye. "It is not a decision, it is a fact. I can't. It's not possible. Not now. Come, stand up for just a moment and look out on the world with me, Istar. Before we say farewell. Come, stand up."

He virtually dragged her to her feet. She didn't dare cry. Inside she knew that she would have the rest of her life to cry about it.

424

She wanted to be present for this moment. To make it last.

But there were so many suns in the sky, so many oceans, so many angles of the horizon, that she shut her eyes and clutched Eteltar's hands, inhaling the smell of his wings. With her eyes shut she could feel the humming beneath her feet more clearly. It was a beat, a pattern—and a strange one. She pressed her ear to Eteltar's chest and tried to listen to his heartbeat instead, but she could still feel the weird rhythm, growing stronger, pulsing through her entire body.

"You have to go now, Istar. Jai Pendu is breaking up." He put one palm on her belly. "Go quickly, and take good care of yourself. I will be with you whenever I can, in my own way."

She tried to avoid the inevitable by not looking up at him, burying her face in his chest instead. But he was turning her and gently pushing her down the stairs once again, his wings outstretched for balance; through his frame, she felt the air catch and almost lift him.

She was intent on prolonging this departure as long as she could. Then two things happened. First, in the blink of an eye, the adjacent tower deliquesced and began to flow away as water, flooding the city below. Second, there was a flash of silver as something serpentine moved from that tower to the Way of the Sun, and the hairs on the back of Istar's neck stood up as she recalled the time she had seen the H'ah'vah at close range beneath the mountains of Everien. She turned to look up at Eteltar and realized that he had frozen, his face petrified with searing, intense thought.

Below Istar, the stairs began to crumble and crack.

"It's in the structure," Eteltar said. "Hurry! Quickly, we must get down before it—"

An eyeless head poked out of the stone that supported the stairs. It quested around blindly, then returned to the inside of the staircase. The rhythmic vibrations were now so fierce, they made Istar's teeth jump in their sockets. The stone exploded before her eyes and she saw the body, silver with patches of black and red, as the Li'ah'vah emerged from the rock and kept coming. She was dimly aware that she was moving up and away, that as its head rose, so did she. Her feet were off the ground and she was dragged through the air, and then she was falling. Eteltar's arms were around her and together they plunged toward the base of the stairs. With a mighty effort of his wings, he steadied their progress and then let Istar go. She tumbled onto the steps and rolled upright. Eteltar landed just above her, crouched with arms reaching toward her protectively, as if both to guide her through the door and keep anything from getting near her.

Above, the timeserpent turned around ponderously and began slithering toward them.

"It wants me, Istar. If I go, it will leave you, I swear it. Do you understand?"

Istar was paralyzed with fear and could neither speak nor think. All she could see was Eteltar's lean form, his extended wings, and, behind him, the moving bulk of the Li'ah'vah that was turning its intentions toward them.

"Istar! Do you understand? I do not desert you! I will lead it away from here, and you must escape." He came down the steps and took her by the shoulders, just as Taretel had done on the bridge; the resemblances were uncanny. "Do not blame yourself for leaving me. Credit yourself for finding me at all. No one else has ever done it. Istar, whatever I said to you, you were a good climber."

"Y-y-you said I should fly."

"You will do more than merely fly. Have courage! You carry our child. *You must escape.* Do you hear me?"

"I must escape." She mouthed the words; it was the best she could do.

"Hey!" He gave her another shake. "Believe what I say! Believe it and nothing else. You are no longer an Honorary male. Forget all of that, for it is a false honor. You are Istar in your own right. Beyond that, you are my mate and if we will speak of honor, then you must honor our union. If you won't honor yourself, then honor me, honor *us*, by valuing your own life. Istar, do you hear me?"

He was physically shaking her. She saw the timeserpent rear up behind him. It was all she could do to whisper the words "I understand. I will honor you."

"*Us*," he corrected, and launched himself into the air. The timeserpent made a snatch for him, but he was up and away. He flew around the other side of the tower of the Way of the Rose and plummeted toward the sea. Istar held her breath as the timeserpent went after him. She saw the White Road curving across the sea—how it had gotten there, she didn't know. Tarquin must have brought it somehow. Eteltar flew over its path, and the timeserpent raced along the White Road. It seemed to be picking the road up behind itself as it went—or swallowing it, for after it had passed, there was no White Road. The timeserpent plunged effortlessly into the rock of the sea plateau. Istar strained her eyes after Eteltar.

The door behind her burst open.

"Come on, girl, this is no time to go on quests." Jaya's voice startled her. "Istar, come quickly."

But Istar could not take her eyes away from the sight. She resisted; but Jaya was much stronger than Istar would have given her credit for. She seized Istar's arm and pulled her through the door. The sun and the sky disappeared, and she was back in the Black Triangle. Suddenly she felt she couldn't go on. She turned toward Jaya for counsel and was faced with a small black creature with no eyes and sexless features, and white robes that seemed mainly to hide its nothingness. She let out a scream and leaped back, instinctively covering her belly. She could still feel Eteltar's hand there.

"How did you get here? Where is Jaya?"

"Don't ask," Night replied grimly. "We must leave. It's collapsing."

Even as it spoke, the place of Three Doors was wavering and flickering like a picture imagined in fire. There was an intricate noise of breaking glass, crumbling stone, and shrieking metal as the city started to come apart. Night seized hold of her again and displaced her out of the Triangle, just as it folded up to become a line, and then a point—and then nothing.

I SEW THE STARS WITH A
BRIGHT NEEDLE

We climbed to the edge of the bowl and looked out. We saw the timeserpent reach Everien and begin whipping from one end of the land to another. Each bridge that held Everien together rippled and swayed as the timeserpent systematically devoured them, leaving nothing behind. There was a peal of thunder and the sun disappeared. The world went black and cold. The wind howled and the sea tossed.

The timeserpent plunged beneath A-vi-Khalar and disappeared.

I held my breath. I could feel the tension in the land, and a ferocious, complicated humming that seemed to come from the very marrow of my bones.

Istar saw it first.

"The Floating Lands!" she gasped, pointing.

The bridges were swaying and breaking as the Floating Lands began to drift apart. A blackness rolled over Everien, so that the Floating Lands were silhouetted against an impenetrable void. Each island was trembling as though beaten like a drum, but from within. Flakes of rock sheared off and fell into the sea. Dirt whipped away in the wind, and little by little, the true shapes of the islands were revealed. We watched them pull away from each other and drift around us, and then past us, as they moved out to sea.

The ocean had long since covered the causeway. With all of Everien under darkness, I felt calmer. Stronger. My arm did not hurt so much. I could barely make out the outlines of Tarquin and Istar as they watched the world transforming itself before their eyes. Now waves were rising and crashing against the base of the island, licking at the mirrored underside of Jai Pendu. The last island began to sink. We were floating, untethered.

Then the water around us boiled. We were not alone.

The timeserpent swam circles beneath us. It spiraled out of the depths until its luminous face was directed straight at us like a terrible arrow.

It drew itself up into the city.

"The River didn't work," I whispered to Tarquin. His back was turned to me as he looked out over the sea. I was angry and wanted to beat him with my fists, but I knew that as Night I mustn't touch him, or he would let go his pent violence. "You should have let it take me in the egg—at least then, you would survive!"

To my surprise, Istar rounded on me. We could barely see each other in the dark. She hissed, "Shut up! The River is good. If Eteltar said it worked, then it works."

But the impossible serpent wended its way through the avenues of Jai Pendu, slithering toward us as though it had all the time in the world, because it did. The timeserpent had us cornered now. Jai Pendu was floating away from Everien.

I knew it was going to speak to me sooner or later. To taunt me, confuse me, lie to me, make me feel crazy. Gloat.

Now, as it closed in on us, the timeserpent spoke its final chant. I was the only one who heard it, but I'm sure the others felt it. The timeserpent's intentions twisted the very air.

I am the god you built. I have no place or purpose. I take you apart and put you together. My offspring are dead. I cut the void in pieces. I sew the stars with a bright needle. Fear me. You will not understand me. You will only die, and end. I am without end.

It was almost upon us now. Tarquin stood up to it. I didn't know what he intended to do, because there is no way to stop a timeserpent, but he did. He put himself between the Li'ah'vah and Istar and me. The two beings faced each other among the spires and lattices of the empty city: the man and the abstraction. The man's hands were empty, but the abstraction's stomach was full. Full of the cure to its own infertility.

And like a flower dropping its petals all at once, it fell apart.

Without any warning, the River had taken effect. The timeserpent silently disintegrated into thousands of worms, bright and quick—and these swirled around Tarquin like a tide so that for an awful, helpless moment I thought they would swarm over him. Istar must have thought the same thing, because she gave an inarticulate cry and clapped her hand over her mouth in horror.

But they didn't touch him. With one mission, they parted around Tarquin and raced into the heart of Jai Pendu, where stacks and stacks of empty white eggs had lain in a pile beneath the place of Three Doors. These eggs had lain there for an eternity, hollow.

Now the timeserpent crawled into its own eggs, and Unhatched.

It was over.

Tarquin came staggering toward us. I wanted to embrace him, but something made me hold back. Everien as one lay under a final, complete blackness; but Jai Pendu shone with its own light. Tarquin was looking at me, not with joy or relief or even the simplest comradeship. He was looking at me with fear. And loathing.

UNLESS

Tarquin's mouth worked. The sight of Night aroused such a terrible mix of emotions that he didn't trust his own judgment for a second. He looked to Istar for a cue and saw that she was calm enough in the presence of Night—a strange sight, he thought, considering that she had made her reputation as a Sekk hunter. Istar crowded around him, slapping his back and uttering Seahawk words of praise. But he had no time to gather his wits before the next problem set in.

"We must go back," Istar was saying. "Quickly, before it's too late."

"I can't return to your world," Night said. "My glass was broken by Dario. Everien is forbidden to me."

He knew her voice; knew it better than he'd known his own when he'd heard the Sekk speak with it. She was Jaya; but the vision before him was Night. Her voice came out of its mouth.

"You were there as Jaya," Istar said.

"As Jaya, I am dying. When I tried to drag you out of the water, I collapsed. Now I must revert to my old form. But there is no hope for me in a human body, you must see this."

Tarquin stirred and fixed his gaze on the creature he had so long considered an enemy. "I have not pursued you over worlds and times to watch you die. Night, let Jaya come back. You do not own her!"

"We are the same!" Night said in Jaya's voice. "If only you would accept that. And in the time I come from, there are no people."

"I know," Tarquin said. "There are only Sekk, and machines."

"Monsters and machines, warring. Nothing else. That is why when you came to Jai Pendu the first time, I called you. That is why

431

we haunted your people. But all the Sekk are gone now, except for me. I was meant to be immortal and abstract, but now I am human, and Dario's arrow is slowly killing me."

"What about Everien?" he said in a hoarse voice.

"Everien will be a ruined world, but you will not live to see it. The place of the machines is the future of your people, Tarquin. That is what will become of the Pharician Empire."

"Unless . . . ?" Tarquin prompted.

"Unless what?"

"There is always an 'unless.' There must be an alternative. The fabric of time is already altered, is changing as we speak in ways we can't imagine."

Night's eyeless forehead turned from side to side. Its mouth said, "You have changed much, Tarquin."

"You don't know the half of it," Tarquin answered. "I can do things now that I couldn't have even imagined, before Ice. So I know that this desolation of monsters and machines may come to pass, no matter what we do. But if we go to the future of the machine wars, skip over this catastrophe and enter the world after it is over—then we are in no danger. We can fight."

Night smiled. "That is all I ever wanted."

Now it was Tarquin's turn to shiver. He knew Night wanted him. When he had resisted before, Night had taken his men instead. *Better to go willingly,* he thought, remembering what Kere had said about becoming Ice. *Besides, I am a timerunning horse now. I am more than a man!*

"But I do not know how to fight those machines that live there. I don't think I could stand being surrounded by Sekk all the time— even a Sekk based on me. A man can change, but he can't change *that* much."

He was talking half to himself, pacing back and forth in and out of earshot of Night. Then he thought of something. It was a "Kere" thought, and he wanted to send it away, but it taunted him. He spun on his heel and addressed the black-clad figure.

"What if I race ahead, and the Everien I leave behind doesn't end up becoming the future that I have visited, and that I think I would be going to? What if the Pharician Empire falls? What if something else, something we have done here, catches up to us and the future we are about to send ourselves to doesn't come to be? Will we annihilate ourselves?"

432

"If we do," Night said, "it hardly matters, because your Everien, the Everien of the Clans, will have moved in another direction—one that does not lead to the timeserpent, and ultimate destruction. But maybe the two worlds will merely move apart, like two ships following different courses on the same ocean."

He didn't know how to answer this.

"I am the Guardian for humans," Night said. "I have seen myself in the book. I am the template for a person. Thanks to the timeserpent, I have stepped off the page. I am the last Everien. It is my responsibility to make sure the timeserpent doesn't kill the Everien that you worked so hard to save."

"I don't know what it means," Tarquin said uneasily. He looked around for Istar to gauge her reaction, but she was nowhere to be seen. He shivered. "I don't know what to do."

A LITTLE SYNCHRONICITY
GOES A LONG WAY

𝕿𝖍𝖊 𝖜𝖔𝖗𝖑𝖉 𝖑𝖆𝖞 in darkness and cold, an indeterminate state, and we were floating somewhere beyond it, trying to guess at possible outcomes. Nor could we agree. But we tried to work out a plan. Tarquin and I talked for a long time in the darkness and the cold. He was not easy to communicate with. He had seen too many contradictory things, and he was full of a horror of the Everiens he had passed through as Ice, on his way to this place and time with me. This place where we would make our decisions.

"Jai Pendu is already sailing away from Everien," I reminded him. "When the sun comes up in Everien, we will be far away. And for Jai Pendu, there will be no sunrise. That is why you must make the White Road and take Istar back. There is no future for either of you here."

"Then you must come, too."

"I cannot. Jaya is on the verge of death. And the eggs—"

"Fuck the eggs!"

"Ah, that's easy to say now, but if Jaya dies, my patterns will disintegrate, and then there is no Guardian for the eggs."

"Then I will take you to a time and place to prevent Jaya's injury, just as Ice did."

"Will you take me to the time and place of the birth of the timeserpent? For the two are the same. You would undo all you have done. Give it up, Tarquin. There is no reason for bitterness. I understand."

"But there must be another way! With all the doors, the crystal . . . we must be able to leave."

I shook my head. "I don't think so," I said. "The timeserpent has done a good job on this place."

"She's right."

434

Istar appeared, sweaty and disheveled. "I have been up and down this city. There's nothing here. It's all empty. There's nothing. The Triangle that lets you into the place of Three Doors has folded down to nothing. We are sitting in an empty castle, which itself lies under a pile of timeserpent eggs that lies under a floating pile of rubble, in the middle of the ocean. There's nowhere to go, and no way to get there."

"Don't be so gloomy," Tarquin said, standing up.

"Hah!" barked Istar. "That's rich, coming from you. You're the King of Doom, Tarquin the Free."

"Not anymore," he said. "I can see better possibilities, now."

"Oh?" Istar glanced from me to Tarquin and back. "Has this Sekk been singing to you? Oh, it's all right, Tarquin—I won't kill it. I've been in love with a Sekk myself, or the next best thing. I know you're not in your right mind. I won't bother you."

She turned and stalked off.

"Istar!" Tarquin called, starting after her. "What is the matter with you? You sound too much like Chyko."

Her shoulders sagged, and she stopped. She turned toward us.

"You're right," she said, looking Tarquin in the eye, without hostility for a change. "I've been told to live. I won't . . . I won't go that bad way."

Tarquin was watching her carefully. "You understood Eteltar pretty well, didn't you?"

She shrugged, but her expression brightened. "As well as anyone, I guess."

"And he told you to go home, didn't he? Did he say how?"

"How? Eteltar, no, he just said to go, to live, to honor . . ." She paused, her voice trembling, to collect herself. "But Taretel did say something strange. On the bridge, before he died. He said, 'Use my body, and wish.' Strange thing to say. But then again, he didn't know where I'd end up. He didn't know I'd be here."

"Maybe he did," I said. "Taretel and Eteltar were the same. A little synchronicity goes a long way."

Tarquin champed his teeth, thinking. " 'Use my body, and wish.' "

"But his body is back in the Liminal," Istar said. "Or in the timeserpent, if it devoured the bone bridges as it went."

"Which is itself a paradox," Tarquin muttered, pacing and thinking.

"I still have a bone," Istar said suddenly. "But it's no good, he told me so."

"Bone?"

"What bone, why didn't you say so?"

Istar opened her pack and drew out the fused clavicle. "Taretel said it was an impossible bone, because to make such a bridge you would need to divide three ways, as he had divided. And he couldn't do it, because it was after all his bone. One of him would have to be dead."

"It's a wishbone," said Tarquin. " 'Use my body, and wish.' "

"There are three of us," I said. "I can cross the Liminal, and Tarquin, you are Ice. As for you, Istar . . . we will have to think of another way, because I don't think an ordinary human can carry a bone bridge. You need a sense of when you are going in time, and people don't have that."

"I will stay here," Istar said stoutly. "And leave the bridgemaking to the two of you. Quiz will keep me company."

She nodded at the ruined remains of the three towers, where Quiz was now perched, watching us. He looked like a silver flame against the black sky.

"Quiz!" I gasped. "Of course. He can make the bridge for you, Istar. He will take you where and when you need to go."

Even Tarquin could not manage to find fault with this plan.

"I will stay behind," I said. "Jai Pendu is my place. If it sinks with me, I will not be sorry."

Istar nodded. "It's better, Tarquin," she said, for he was glowering at the idea of leaving me behind. "You cannot send Night into the unknown. At least Jaya is safe here, with Night."

"Safe?" Tarquin pointed down at the city, which was flooding even as it sailed out to sea. We were in total blackness. "If we are in the world or out of it, Jai Pendu is doomed. There is a deep sea-trench running from Seahawk to the north shore of Ristale. Already we are in a hundred feet of water. Soon it will be a thousand. Jai Pendu will sink without a trace."

"Then all the more reason for speed," Istar said. "Come on, we will do this from the highest point. Don't be afraid, either of you— look, there's Quiz!"

Liaku's name for the skyfalcon had stuck, however inappropriate such a lighthearted name might be to a raptor with Quiz's powers.

436

"They're his bones, Tarquin," I added. "He must know what he's doing. He won't let Istar die."

"He won't let you die, either," Istar said. She was already mounting the pile of eggs. "Come *on*, you two. Let's get to the highest point."

We climbed up the side of the pile of eggs and into the white bowl at the top. The bottom of the three towers still floated above the bowl, supported by some unknown force, and without the Black Triangle there was no way for us to displace ourselves into the place of Three Doors. However, the mirrored underside of the towers was broken into sections and it was possible, using a rope that Istar had brought for use in the Floating Lands, to climb up physically into the remains of the three Ways. I went first, trying to conceal my dismay at the ruin of all the Knowledge. Istar did not seem to mind in the slightest. She tossed sections of metal and glass around as though they were toys, then began climbing through the rubble, looking for the best place to stand and start the bridge. Quiz came down and landed on her shoulders.

"I'm hoping the skyfalcon can help me find the right time," Istar said. "I'm going to step off the edge and . . ." She paused and looked down. She gave a little laugh and shrugged. "Lucky I'm not afraid of heights!"

Tarquin went to the edge, too, and I was left standing knock-kneed and scared on a slab of broken smoothstone: all that was left of the three towers of Jai Pendu. Darkness whipped around us, starless and extreme. The waves hit the base of the city like a heartbeat.

"I will go first," Tarquin said. "Then Istar right after me." He turned and looked down at me. I could only see the outlines of his face in this light. "Jaya."

"Yes?"

"You hold your end and whatever you do, don't . . . let . . ."

"Go," I finished.

"I will come back for you," he said. "Until I do, don't try to cross, because the bridge might not be finished."

I held the bone firmly, planting my feet and breathing deeply. I was afraid.

Quiz took one branch of the bone in his claws, and Tarquin took the other in his left hand. Tarquin and the skyfalcon looked at each other; then there was an explosion of light and Ice was stand-

437

ing on his hind legs on the edge, his front hooves pawing the air in a stallion's battle rear. A huge feeling of current came through the bone and entered into me; but it was not painful. The bone swelled, and my teeth hummed. Ice came down, into free space, but he didn't fall. He was running on a patch of light, and the skyfalcon was flying alongside him. I had to hold the bone with both hands: it was as big as a tree now. In the space of instants it grew bigger and bigger, lengthening as Ice gathered momentum. Now it could be seen as a solid thing, a bridge reaching out into empty air. I could no longer hold it in my arms at all, but had to fling my whole weight down on it where it rested on the broken smoothstone. Istar gave a battle cry and ran after the white horse and the bird, whose paths could be seen diverging ahead.

I could see the thread of light from Quiz's talons, where he held one end of the growing wishbone against the tension. It stretched to make a bridge, one that would take Istar all the way to an Everien where the timeserpent was no more. She was turning away to follow the skyfalcon; and Ice was veering off into the unknown.

Then all of them winked out, as if a velvet curtain had been parted and quickly pulled shut again after them. I was left alone, in darkness.

I held fast to my part of the bone. I did not let go; but I was not so foolish as to believe Tarquin really could, or would, return for me. I am Night, after all, and he hates me. Anyway, that blackness was too impenetrable, too final, to be anything other than the end. I held the bone because I had promised I would, and Tarquin had finally made me see that promises are necessary. It would be a kind of lifeline, just for a moment; for it could not save me, but it could prolong my contact with Everien for just a little while. Knowing it was there comforted me. It was stretching across time and space to possibilities whose outcomes I would never know—yet I could still be a part of them, in my small and isolated way.

Yes, I am Night, and I always have been. It was my isolation that made me reach out, and my desperation. You cannot know what these things feel like, if you have never been beyond the world. But I have been beyond the world and in it and beyond it again. And standing there alone, holding the bone, I knew I must be Night, or die. If I reached inside of myself I could just feel the faint presence of Jaya's human life; but it would not last long now. Not long.

Jai Pendu was sailing and sailing. The city was underwater and only the white bowl with its eggs remained, like a coracle floating with no destination. The darkness gathered all round me like a familiar cloak, just like in the forest. But now there were no stars in the velvet mantle. I had no horse, and there were no trees; just broken fragments of dead Knowledge all around me, and a pile of unhatched timeserpent eggs that I would have to Guard. Forever.

HEALED

𝒥star stepped off the end of the bone and into a wood. Quiz could be seen high above her. She stopped in her tracks. She had no idea where she was. She whistled for Quiz and raised her arm, but he was no more domesticated than he had been before, and she had to be content to study him at a distance.

She stumbled around in the forest for a long time before she found a watercourse that she could follow. When she climbed it, she got a view of a mountain valley covered in trees. To the southeast, a river wound through lush grassland, and beyond that rose the mountains that sheltered Jai Khalar. But there were no roads that she could see; no disruptions in the cloud cover; no jumping suns; no fires covering acres, or pits left by monsters.

It was a wild land, yes. But not that wild.

Istar took a deep breath.

"Is it true, Quiz?" she asked, knowing that the skyfalcon was too high to hear her voice; but he could never be too high to know her thoughts, or so she liked to imagine. "Is Everien healed at last?"

She began to walk downcountry, making for the area where her vision of Mhani had placed her; for she had a feeling the bone had not terminated here by accident. Mhani, too, had been both a hero and a victim of events in Everien, and whatever Istar might feel about the injustice and tragedy she had suffered, she at least had her own wits about her. Which was something.

In time she came to a Wolf Clan village, where she was treated with suspicion at first, and then with more tolerance as the people there gradually came to realize that their land had been returned to them. "Healed" might be too strong a word for Everien's condition, Istar realized as time passed and she saw all the travails that

440

lay ahead of her and her people—for the Knowledge had vanished without a trace. She found her mother in very sorry condition, but well enough to travel, gently. It was time to go home to Seahawk and face what she had left behind there.

She did not believe that Everien was healed, or restored, but she did believe it was possible to live here, for people, and for animals. She simply didn't know how she was going to do that, after everything that had happened.

COMMITMENT

$\mathcal{D}$arkness, as $\mathcal{I}$ have remarked so many times I want to beat my head against it, were it only solid—darkness is infinite. Until something happens to interrupt it.

My darkness was interrupted by the arrival of a skinny boy on the right prong of the wishbone. He had white hair that stuck up at all angles, and he was very skittish. I recognized him, of course; and for his part, he approached me as though we were old friends.

"It was a bugger of a problem," he confessed, sinking smoothly into a sitting position and folding his limber legs around one another. "We had to make the bridge, and when we got there it was a mess, Jaya, much worse than we'd expected. Wars that actually tear up the earth and sky are too much for us, I fear. I don't know how we're going to get used to the idea of it."

"But you can't come back here," I said. "This is nowhere."

"Let me finish my story. We had to make the bridge and then we had to make sure it was secure and not about to get gobbled up by a passing horror show of an Everien Liminal abomination. Then I had to run back in time and find myself a knowledgeable Wasp. I didn't want to interfere with Everien in case it meant some kind of new time crossover and we don't want that! So I had to rummage around what's left of the Liminal, and finally I got hold of Chyko, of all people. I lied to him, I'm afraid—I hope you don't mind, is this upsetting you?—I told him the antidote was for his daughter Istar. I thought it would be the best way to get his help without starting up old quarrels."

"What are you talking about, Kere?"

He drew out what looked like a brandy flask.

"You have been poisoned for a long time, and I don't know whether this antidote is going to leave your body completely healed and undamaged, but the fact that you survived as long as you did suggests that the temporal makeup of your tissues is sophisticated enough to juggle the poison around and prevent you from taking a fatal dose all at once. Still, the particular poison Dario used is a bad one. You'll need to drink this up, and another dose tomorrow, and again the day after. By days I mean—"

"I understand," I said faintly. "Kere, where is Tarquin?"

"Er . . . well . . . he's . . ."

"He's not dead, is he?" I leaped up in alarm.

"No, no, no—well, yes, in a sense, but no, not dead, only Eaten . . . Jaya, I'm only the messenger, can you just please take this antidote and see if it works?"

He held out the flask. I took it and looked at it, considering.

"If there's anything worse than being an abstract pattern doomed to spend an eternity watching timeserpent eggs, it's got to be being a young woman alone on an island watching timeserpent eggs. I'm not sure I should take this, Kere."

"But you have to!" Now it was Kere's turn to leap up. "You have to, or Tarquin will . . . I don't know what he'll do . . . I'll . . ."

"Tarquin hasn't even come here himself," I said. "And it's for the best, I'm sure. It was just a romantic dream of his, that we should be together."

"He didn't come because I got the antidote off Chyko and I wanted to give it to you. And because, if he came, you might say no."

"I am saying no. You can tell him that I release him from all obligation, all bond between us, implied or otherwise—"

Kere had put his hands over his ears and began spinning in circles, humming loudly so as to not be able to hear what I was saying. It was highly childish behavior; but then again, he was a child. I watched him run around the empty white bowl, faster and faster, until he began to change. He was a white streak. He was Ice. He was a flash of light. He was Tarquin.

He stepped toward me.

"Take the antidote," he said in a low voice. He was very serious, too serious. He made me nervous. "Kere traveled a long way to get it for you, and you know what a problematic bastard Chyko can be. Take it, or so help you, I'll knock you down and pour it down your throat."

He was moving toward me in a threatening manner. I didn't back down. "And don't even think of trying to displace me again like you did in Ristale," he added. "I am as big as you are now, or bigger, and I won't be pushed around, Night."

He was standing at arm's length from me.

"Go on," he said. "I'm not leaving until you do."

I unstoppered the bottle, but some inner defiance made me tip it as if to pour it out on the ground. Quick as a snake he grabbed my hand and stopped me.

"What are you playing at, Jaya?" he said. His eyes bored into me. I knew he could only see my blank, abstract face as Night; but it was as if he was looking into my eyes, Jaya's eyes, the real Jaya. "When I pulled you out of that egg, I thought this suicidal martyr nonsense was over. Do you want to live or not? Do you want to be real, or just a code? This is your one chance. Now, you'd better take it, because if you don't, my heart will be broken."

I drank.

When he put it like that, it seemed pretty easy.

The antidote slid down my throat, and I slipped into Night. A cold shudder filled me, from the rims of my nostrils as Night's breath entered my body, to the razor-sharp edges of the Knowledge stamping itself deep within me, that I now possessed as if it were my very own. In this way, Night slid into me and vanished.

I felt old and afraid.

Tarquin was eyeing me sidelong.

"You look the same," he said in a suspicious tone. "You look like Jaya. Are you all right?"

"I don't feel the same," I whispered. I was suddenly grateful beyond all measure, because what he had made me do had been right, and I wouldn't have had the courage without him. Tears sprang up in my eyes, then drained away, because I was no longer in conflict. We looked at each other. It was that old power moving us, that animal magic from deep time.

"What now?" Tarquin said. "What do we do?"

Suddenly I was conscious that we were standing there, two people in a big white semisphere that glowed faintly, in an ocean of darkness. From above, in the ruins, the arc of the white bridge could be seen curving into the sky, splitting in two, and then disappearing into nowhere. There were decisions to be made.

"You have been to the future," I said. "Kere tells me it's bad."

"Everyone in Everien who knew how to run the experiments is dead. Even the Sekk patterns have been wiped. The descendants of

444

the Pharicians who hold sway over the continent from their power center in Jundun, they possess great Knowledge but they are terrified of the perils of Everien. That is why they never go there. That is why they invented the Eyes, so they could have physical isolation from the experiments and watch over Everien from a distance. It's hard to see what chance we have in such a future."

"I have many chances," I said. "I understand the symbol-language. I can speak to the monsters—well, sing to them, anyway. I can operate the equipment that the Everiens left behind."

"Where does that leave me? Just a backward Clansman, without even a sword!"

"You are already a creature of many times. Do you forget that you reside in Ice, and Ice in you?"

"I do not forget," grunted Tarquin uncomfortably.

"It's all right, Tarquin," I said. "I didn't mean you. Me. Not you. For it is not your burden to bear. The future Everien is my world, and I will go to it. You and Ice can be free to go where you will."

"Not without you, we won't. I love you, Jaya."

"No," I said. "Pfff! It's nonsense."

But he was looking at me and I wasn't sure. Strangely, you strive to be something that someone will admire, even if that "someone" is theoretical or imagined. You try to live up to invisible expectations. And then a true person worthy of your admiration comes along and gives you every affirmation you could want, and for some idiotic reason you go "pfff!" just like that.

"Tarquin," I said, "where I come from I'm not even real. I'm only a piece of code. Like a Sekk. You think you can touch me, but you can't really, because I'm not really here."

He reached across the dark air and touched my face. His fingertips were rough with calluses.

"Liar," he said. I started to protest, and he said, "Let's go to where you really are. Let's do what we can to change what we can."

"You don't know me—" I began, but he cut me off.

"You just can't begin to know how I feel. Everything you do, every part of you I can see, is beautiful to me. And the parts of you I don't know and can't see . . . like . . . Night—" He said the name with an effort. ". . . they draw me in like a mystery."

It must have been the darkness that made him speak this way. People don't say things like this in broad daylight.

"I'm not a mystery," I said. "It's not what you think. I'm not

445

wonderful or alluring, I'm just in trouble. I'm in a situation I can't see. That's not mystery, it's confusion."

"No," answered Tarquin. "*I* was confusion, before. I had no sense of direction. I knew what I was running from, but I wasn't running toward anything. Now I have you."

"Stop it, Tarquin," I moaned. "It is hard for me, harder than you know. But when you offer yourself to me it is harder still. Don't you see I can't believe in anybody but myself? I can't love or become attached. I can't trust or be trusted. I can't make a promise of any kind."

"You must," he answered promptly. "You must promise yourself to me. There is no other way I can act on your behalf."

"I cannot!" I cried. "You can't ask the ocean to promise! I don't know what I am. What I would be promising."

I heard my own breaths fast and ragged in my throat. I was aware of his silence, his listening, and suddenly I felt self-consciously frantic. I tried to be quiet, but I was overwrought. Tarquin did nothing. I gulped and swallowed tears.

"I have nothing to promise," I said. "I have nothing to give."

There was another long, intense silence.

"You won't have anything to give," Tarquin said to me, "until you promise it."

I listened to these backward words. I tried to understand. He said, "A quest makes a warrior of a boy. A promise gives strength where before there was none. Without commitment, to something or someone, you are nothing. My commitment is to you. Once it was to Everien, but that is too big a thing. I commit to you, because you are the shelter I never had, the resolution and the quiet out of all the noise. Because I saw you in the garden and I felt something. I can offer myself to that. I can give you the best of myself. What more do you need?"

"But that's *crazy*," I said.

He shrugged. "They have been saying that about me for years. So what?"

I reached out and we touched fingertips.

"Well?" Tarquin said, a lopsided smile beginning to open his face.

"We are the future," I said, feeling giddy and awful all at once. "You and I, no one else."

He laughed.

"Right, then. Let's go make a mess of it."

MAGIC

Quiz led Istar back to a very different world indeed. It was a world in which effects followed causes, and the sun followed a predictable path in the sky, and monsters were a thing of memory, or imagination. Istar would not have recognized it.

The Knowledge was gone from Everien, leaving scars and burned places where it had been; leaving families divided and political structures on the verge of collapse. The Pharicians were too embroiled in their own internal problems to look as far as Everien; their empire, after all, teetered on the brink of disintegration following the death of Hezene. And in Everien, King Pallo was rapidly disbanding his rulership, arguing for a return to the loose confederation of states that had existed before Ysse's rise to power.

"Yes, we will always fight," he acknowledged. "But we do not wish to emulate Pharice, and fight by the thousands. And I don't want this job anymore. I'm getting old."

And he was. Not drastically, not as rapidly as he should be; but the crossing out of the Oasis had changed Pallo, and his life no longer seemed charmed. He became obsessed with good works and civic duty, which made him less and less interesting as a king, especially to men who had been trained all their lives to expect and even thirst for battle.

Istar did not stay to see it all shake down. She traveled from Wolf Country with her mother, and then she went home, heavily pregnant, bitterly disappointed, and numb with her personal loss. She wanted to be happy for Everien; for Pallo; for Mhani; the Seahawks; the Hawk Girls; everyone who seemed to have cause to celebrate—which, in her mind, was synonymous for everyone but Istar. She wanted to feel a sense of accomplishment.

Everyone said she was a hero.

I've been here before, she thought, remembering the days and weeks that followed her killing of the Seahawk at Jai Pendu. *They all think I'm a hero and I feel like shit. What is the matter with me?*

With the funds she had inherited, and the lands she summarily took over from Grietar's family as compensation for the damage he had done, she was a wealthy woman, and in practice if not in name, she was considered preeminent in her Clan. She downplayed it. She got rid of her greedy relatives quietly, finding homes for them far enough away that she needn't listen to their advice about husband-finding or child-rearing. She made gifts to Pentar's widow and children. She was tired of death and battle and anger, and after Ostar left, she began digging up the back garden, which was far too tidy for her comfort. She found she couldn't even kill an earthworm or a beetle, which made her progress slow. But she found some surcease of her misery in the act of working with her hands. There was very little else she could do, restricted and oppressed as she was by the thing growing inside her.

Her sisters had made progress in their unlikely friendship with the Hawk Girls, and when Liaku joined the household the whole fjord began to resemble a bird fiesta. Quiz zoomed in and out of A-Tar-Ness at whim; he had no tenderness for anyone, and he killed a lot of sheep that Istar had to pay for and apologize for. She liked to watch him fly; it was the one thing that alleviated her sadness.

But most of the time, she was inconsolable. Her grief was not lessened by the inference that it had all been fated, that there could have been no other, better outcome. If anything, the idea that she was a participant in destiny only sharpened the point of her anguish. She felt like a pawn and she hated the hand that had been playing her. Her grievances and tangled emotions knit themselves in her mind, and unraveled, and knit themselves again, so that she could remember nothing else.

And her belly swelled, and she waddled about indoors, never daring to venture far from a chamberpot. And there was no one to fight with—except the Hawk Girls, who were learning Pharician, especially the insults, from Liaku. Istar was thoroughly unhappy, and she thought this would never change.

Then her daughter was born, tiny and helpless, with eyes the color of honey. And white hair.

And wet, awkward, uncontrollable wings.

Word went out that Istar had given birth to a monster.

Istar was delighted with the wings. She was still sad every day and every night, but not constantly; there were times when she forgot her troubles altogether, for a while. And, little by little, she began to fall in love with the tiny creature.

As for Istar and Eteltar's daughter Skytar, she was famous. But not always in a good way. People came to see her and bring gifts, but some went away looking unnerved, although they never said so to Istar's face.

One day the Clan Elders made the arduous journey to see Istar and her child. Istar, highly flattered, opened the door and let them in, offering her best food and drink. She had begun to perk up—having a small baby in the house made it hard to be sad all the time, and she was too busy to brood on her past. Her hair was freshly braided and her waist was slim again, and dressed in simple robes without sword or armor, she looked every bit the young Seahawk bride. Except she had no mate of any kind—unless you counted Quiz.

She smiled at them. She had been working on her manners—Pietar of all people was coaching her—and trying to act more feminine. But the first question that greeted her came from a chubby old fisherman with a red face.

"The skyfalcon who sits on your roof, is he vicious?"

"Yes," Istar said, her smile remaining fixed on her face as though painted there. "He is vicious and often strikes without provocation; but then again he does more good than evil, on balance. And I'm crazy about him."

"Aye, we've heard he's no good. May have to get rid of him."

Istar's nostrils flared but she kept her voice level. "He is the last of an ancient species. He is more deeply imbued with the Animal Magic than all the fish in the ocean, sir."

The old fisherman snorted. "Ah, Animal Magic—it's good for stories and tales by the fire, but it's for children, don't you know? And the Knowledge, that's even worse. Best to be rid of all magic, I say."

Two old women were nodding agreement. Only Hiltar seemed to be apart in her opinions.

"Yes, magic is such a nuisance, especially when it has avoided visiting your trousers for thirty years," she said drily. The old man pretended not to hear her.

"The Animal Magic is real," Lyntar began earnestly, but Istar silenced her with a gesture and she retreated to the shadows, where she and Pietar and Liaku were listening. *Women and animals,* Istar thought. *We have to stick together.*

An old woman who had traveled a hundred miles spoke up.

"We have heard much of the offspring of Istar Seahawk by the winged man Eteltar. And as we are a people plagued by monsters and evil abominations of every kind, we must be sure this child is safe to have in the Clan."

Lyntar and Pietar caught the scent of where this conversation was headed, and Pietar picked up the baby, Skytar, and cuddled her protectively, ready to dash out the back door. Skytar's wings were not visible in the swaddling.

But Istar's civility was extremely thin. She had not forgotten who she was. She promptly picked up a rolling pin and went on the assault.

She didn't remember the details, really. They were old people, frail and supposedly wise; she couldn't very well skewer them and leave them for the crows. But Lyntar told stories afterward about Istar chasing a whole pack of Elders all the way down to the harbor with her rolling pin, and Quiz flying overhead dropping skyfalcon shit on their heads. Skytar would hear the story a hundred times during her richly eventful youth among the bird-women of A-Tar-Ness.

But most importantly, for Istar everything changed after that. Because the magic was not gone from Everien, after all. It lived in her house, and one day it would fly.

EPILOGUE

𝒯arquin t𝒽e 𝒻ree had never been free, until now. And I had never been tied down, until now. I guess when you find yourself in a world without precedent, all bets are off.

And the things you thought were true are only thin panes of glass and light shines through them unresisted. And your energy is spent, but still you must go on.

And what you set out for does not exist.

But a thousand other undreamed-of things do exist.

And the truth is like water, clear, flowing, distorting that which enters into it, and always changing. And you will never go home.

But home is not the only place worth going.

There are bigger things to see. To feel.

To be swallowed by, says Ice on the far side of Tarquin.

THERE IS A place called Everien. It is buried deep in these mountains, some would say, but I would not be among them. The nature of Everien prevents it from being enclosed or located in the way that our minds would wish. I believe Everien is revealed according to the same mysterious power that operates when billions of flecks of blue algae permeate the sea and make the sky blue under sunshine. The blue sky is not the algae, nor the sun, nor the sea, but some interaction of them all that is so indirect as to qualify as magical from where we are standing, looking up. Like the blue sky, Everien is a place no less real than the good, fragrant mud of a farmer's springtime pasture; yet its truth is hidden inside itself. Everien is the key to its own lock, and it is the door, and it is the room beyond.

Anyone can play games with time, and most of those games

would be wrong either in theory or in practice. I have seen what happens when Time plays games with us.

I no longer worry about myself. The questions of my own existence, my nature, my purpose, that plagued me for so long do not seem to matter anymore. I simply go on, acting and reacting, running from one thing to the next.

It's not a bad life. Tarquin and I are together, which we both thought was impossible. Whether this means that I have gained flesh and substance, or that he has lost it, doesn't really matter. Either way, we find ourselves beset. We are the only people in this world after the end of the world. Someone or something smarter than we who cares nothing for us is calculating and rearranging the world we live in, making doors and breaking windows, wrecking our plans and turning us into opportunists at best, fugitives or victims at worst. Creatures have been set loose that would make meals of us. Yet we find magic, too.

Some people wish they could live their life over and do it differently. In the realm of Paradox, this is possible; but you won't catch me returning to change things. I will turn my face into time's wind.

I take none of it back.

ABOUT THE AUTHOR

VALERY LEITH is an American in England.